THE EXCESSIVE WATERS OF THE RÍO DE LA PLATA
AND OTHER NARRATIVES

Armando Lindner

LAS EXCESIVAS AGUAS DEL RÍO DE LA PLATA
Y OTROS RELATOS

ISBN: 978-17350932-1-5

The cover picture is of the author's father, Marcelo Lindner. It was taken by the author in Buenos Aires.

La portada es la foto del padre del autor, Marcelo Lindner. Fue tomada por el autor en Buenos Aires.

With a strong virtual hug, this book is dedicated to
Serge and Deborah, and especially to my inspiring,
and very musical, grandchildren Orly and Avi.
May they learn one day to write in cursive, and to
be as kind to their descendants as my grandpa was
to me.

Dedico este libro, con un fuerte abrazo virtual, a
Serge y Deborah y, especialmente, a mis *talentosos y
musicales nietos*, Orly y Avi. Ojalá que un día
puedan escribir en letra cursiva, y ser tan cariñosos
con sus descendientes como mi abuelo fue conmigo.

Table of Contents

Índice

Author's Foreword

One writes mostly about what one knows or has experienced. Each significant situation, if associated with a memorable emotion, can provide a basis for a short story. In fiction, our imagination may expand and distort the original idea, but the writer's art should maintain the germinal facts at the core of the narrative. The inspiration for these stories, which are meant to be intriguing and entertaining rather than philosophical or political, may have been an enduring contact with a person, a friend or a patient, leaving an indelible mark on my personal history. Now fiction allows me to transfer my recollections to the reader. Of necessity I had to change some of the names and locations to maintain confidentiality, or for purely literary purposes.

I grew up in Buenos Aires. I remember well the taste of Titas and Rhodesia, somewhat similar to Kit Kats here. No special memories attached. However, I must have been four or five, walking by the corner on Boedo street and Cochabamba, by the café where there used to be a kiosk selling candies and cigarettes. I was strolling hand in hand with Lito, my grandpa, and asked him to stop and lift me up to see the candy. By then, I was probably a declared "banana freak". The first thing that caught my eye was a brown and yellow banana-shaped treat, that my kind grandpa bought for me for the first time. This became a custom, and whenever we walked together and passed by that corner kiosk, he would buy me another banana treat without asking. I remember the taste and shape better than its name. This was only one of many examples of how great a grandpa he was. He died too young, on the same year I graduated from medical school. The corner kiosk itself was gone by the time they built a highway over that corner on Boedo street and my grandparents' house was demolished.

My retirement as a physician and medical educator allowed me the time and freedom to revisit, and sometimes re-write, these stories with a present-day perspective. I wrote the first draft of each narrative with a favorite fountain pen, using cursive, a handwriting style that my grandchildren find very hard to decipher since it's no longer taught in schools. Sheltering-In-place during a pandemic was the final push for achieving one of the goals of a well-lived life: saving or at least improving some lives as a physician; marrying a wonderful woman, fathering a son to be proud of and writing a book.

Armando Lindner, Seattle, June 05, 2020

Notas del autor

Uno escribe sobre lo que más conoce o sobre lo que ha vivido. Cuando una situación es significativa, si está conectada con una emoción memorable, pueden surgir las bases para un cuento. En ficción, la idea original puede ser magnificada o distorsionada, pero el arte del escritor consiste en mantener los hechos germinales como núcleo del relato. Estas historias, que intentan ser entretenidas o curiosas, más que filosóficas o políticas, han sido inspiradas por la memoria de un contacto con alguna persona, un amigo o un paciente, que dejara una marca indeleble en mí. Ahora la ficción me ayuda a transferirlas al lector. En ciertos casos, me vi obligado a cambiar nombres y sitios para mantener la confidencialidad, o por simples razones literarias.

Crecí en Buenos Aires. Aún recuerdo el gusto de las Tita y las Rhodesia, parecidas a los Kit Kat nuestros; la gran diferencia es que estos carecen de memorias asociadas. En cambio, cuando yo tenía unos cuatro o cinco años, me llevaban de paseo por la esquina de Boedo y Cochabamba, frente a un café con un kiosco de golosinas y de cigarrillos. Yo iba de la mano con mi abuelo Lito y le pedí que me levantara para ver los dulces. Para entonces, ya tenía reputación de ser "loco por las bananas". De modo que lo primero que me saltó a la vista fue un bombón de color amarillo y marrón con forma de banana y que mi abuelo me regaló por primera vez. Esto se hizo costumbre y siempre que pasábamos por el kiosco de esa esquina, él volvía a comprarme un bombón igual sin preguntarme. Recuerdo el gusto y la forma que tenía, pero no su nombre. Este ejemplo es uno de los muchos que revelan: ¡qué grande era mi abuelo! Él murió muy joven, el mismo año de mi graduación en la Facultad de Medicina. El kiosco de la esquina ya había desaparecido, pues construyeron una autopista que cruzaba la calle Boedo, y demolieron la casa de mis abuelos.

Mi jubilación como médico y docente en la Facultad de Medicina me ha dado tiempo libre para corregir y, a veces, para escribir de nuevo estos cuentos con una perspectiva actual. Siempre comienzo el primer borrador con mi lapicera de tinta favorita, en una letra manuscrita que a mis nietos les cuesta descifrar, porque ya nadie la enseña en las escuelas. Estar confinado en casa durante la pandemia me dio el empujón necesario para lograr uno de los objetivos de una vida bien vivida: salvar o, al menos, mejorar la salud de algunos pacientes; casarme con una mujer maravillosa; procrear un hijo que me enorgullece y escribir un libro.

Armando Lindner, 5 de junio de 2020

I- ENGLISH

Matsumoto-San and the White Silk Scarf

On a memorably luminous evening in the Pacific Northwest, Matsumoto-san, an accomplished tango dancer, absent-mindedly left behind a striking white scarf at our milonga. This small act of forgetfulness sent me on a quest to find out about the origins of her scarf. Moreover, to try and explain her uncanny ability to improve the weather.

The scarf was made of white silk of uncommon smoothness and sheen, with an elegant monochrome weaving pattern, and I assumed it had been made in Japan, Matsumoto-san's country of birth. Along with the beauty of the cloth, I noticed another, unusual detail. Woven into one corner of the fabric was a small inscription formed of irregular black characters in a language I could not identify.

I called to let her know that I had discovered the scarf. I judged from her voice that she was extremely concerned about having misplaced her precious garment, a family piece that had been entrusted to her. I proposed that we meet as soon as possible in the new Olympic Sculpture Park café by the Seattle waterfront. I speculated on a fact well known to Matsumoto-san's friends: there was an improbably high frequency of sunny days whenever we included her in an outdoor activity, like a hike or a kayaking trip.

The following Saturday we sat at the outdoor

café under a brilliantly blue sky, facing west towards the Pacific. From our vantage point on the hill we were astonished to see, emerging from the haze beyond the barges and ferryboats on Puget Sound, and framed in the background by the Olympic Mountains, another large body of water, with a fractured shoreline, a river running into it, and very tall skyscrapers on the opposite shore. Simultaneously, we both felt that this mirage reflected the distant structures of Tokyo Bay, a landscape quite familiar to Matsumoto-san, and an area that I had visited once.

After we were served a smoky oolong tea, unfortunately in plastic cups, I asked Matsumoto-san to tell me the story behind her exquisite scarf. She seemed eager to talk about it, and began with no further prompting:

"Well, Maurice, it was a gift from my mother at the time I left Japan for a job in the USA. On July 17th, 1999, we were in Kyoto for the Obon festival. Our family has a tradition of transferring the scarf from mother to eldest daughter on that occasion, and we have kept this custom alive for many generations. I imagine that the fabric's exquisite quality and the great care its owners have taken of it have contributed to its preservation."

"I'm puzzled by the inscription in the corner. Do you know what it means?"

"My mother and I have always been curious about this inscription and have wondered about its significance. Certainly, it is not a label or trademark and it's not written in Japanese. It's frustrating that I cannot identify these characters."

"I'd like to hear more about your mother and about your family traditions."

"My mother is an unusual person. She suffers a bit from a compulsive disorder, which I confess to have inherited to some extent. For instance, she has a passion for cleanliness, washes her hands frequently, and is unhappy when forced to touch the handles or railings in public transportation. She likes to 'purify' the kitchen and bathroom floors with salt and water, as others do at the entrances to funeral homes, or when Sumo wrestlers throw salt on the ring before their combat." She paused, a little embarrassed at describing her mother's behavior, but then continued in a more relaxed fashion:

"My mother followed another uncommon practice, which I have never seen in other Japanese homes. Every Friday eve at sundown she would cover her head with the white scarf and then light candles, while softly humming a melody she had learned as a child from my grandmother. Sometimes I've been tempted to continue this family practice, which I associate with a sense of calm and happiness after a week of hard work. I feel similarly when I've attended a Shinto religious ceremony. It may not surprise you, a keen dancer, that I feel equally satisfied after dancing a tango with an expert partner. I felt that sense of rhythm and connection strongly at the last milonga, which may explain my absent-mindedness in leaving behind my precious scarf ...”

We then examined the inexplicable characters woven into the scarf. The cursive script mixed curvilinear and straight branching segments, which looked unlike any I had seen before. My first impression was that they resembled Hebrew letters, but with my rudimentary knowledge of this language I was unable to decipher them. Faced with the unknown origin of the strange inscription, I let my imagination take over, and I speculated that it might be ancient and have some connection with the ritual practices in her mother's family. I proposed that we consult an expert in the field.

“That would be wonderful,” Matsumoto-san said. “I never had an opportunity to probe this mystery. But I'm concerned that you not take too much time away from your own activities. I know about your boundless curiosity, but I hope you won't neglect your own work on that paper you're writing on the therapeutic effects of tango on neurological symptoms.” (I was not surprised to hear Matsumoto-san voice her concern, because she is a psychiatrist and a skeptical researcher. I also admire her warm, sympathetic approach to extract intimate information from people who remain unaware that her questioning is precise and directed).

"Never mind that, Matsumoto-san. I need some diversion from my work, and a short break to investigate a family mystery would be welcome indeed."

I may have responded too quickly, since I later learned how much effort exploring this curious issue would involve. In any case, I have always admired those who can take on an intellectual challenge, and I, like Matsumoto-san, am primarily a researcher. This was my opportunity to engage in a different field without feeling guilty.

Taking advantage of my large network of acquaintances, we obtained an appointment with Rabbi Moshe Bensimon, a respected wise man and a retired leader of the local Sephardic community. He was now approaching one hundred years of age with surprising lucidity and an exceptional understanding of historical facts and Hebrew traditions. He was also a co-author of a heavily used Hebrew-English dictionary.

The rabbi's home, near Seward Park, was small and welcoming, with an imaginative garden carpeted in flowers and wild herbs, reminiscent of some in Haifa, and it was decorated with many family photographs, antique maps and engravings. An old woman draped in a black pashmina shawl opened the door, greeted us with a soft Middle-Eastern accent, and quietly receded to the kitchen to prepare an aromatic and very sweet Turkish coffee to serve to us while we waited for Rabbi Bensimon. When the rabbi appeared, he immediately got to the point of our visit. We described Matsumoto-san's family traditions and showed him the scarf. Bensimon felt its elegant, smooth texture with his gnarled arthritic fingers. Then he put on a pair of old-fashioned, high magnification reading glasses and examined the inscription. Moments later he exclaimed:

"My friends, you have come to the right place! What you bring me is very curious and excites me in my old age. First, I should tell you that this text was not written in modern Hebrew but in Aramaic. It is a language with a three-thousand-year history, which Jesus spoke! His disciples and the apostles used it to preach the Gospel. It was the dominant language for Jewish worship and everyday life for centuries. It is the original language of the Talmud before it was translated into Hebrew. I am disappointed that I cannot understand these words, so I cannot translate them, but I can try to pronounce them phonetically for you."

Mumbling aloud for a few moments, he managed to pronounce words that caused Matsumoto-san suddenly to stand up in a state of agitation I had not expected and begin to vocalize the rabbi's words using an intonation of her own: "Ama-te-ra-su-O-mi-ka-mi, 'Amaterasu-Omikami'! That's the name of the sun-goddess in Japanese mythology."

Matsumoto-san said these words over and

over in Japanese. She seemed to radiate an inner light as she did so.

"That is indeed remarkable!" said the rabbi, who was by now standing next to Matsumoto-san, learning to pronounce the words she had kept on repeating. "Please tell us what you know about your sun-goddess."

"Amaterasu is perhaps the most important Kami—a Shinto deity—and is considered the divine ancestor of the Imperial House of Japan. We celebrate her every July 17th (when I was given the scarf by my mother) with short processions, and also on December 21st, the winter solstice. I can still recall one version of the myth that I learned in my childhood.

"Amaterasu had a mischievous and insecure brother named Susanoo. Susanoo was a storm-deity, and one day he decided to prove his powers by whipping up a tempest. He made the world turn very dark and cold. Strong winds scattered the harvest in the field and blew away all Amaterasu's beloved flowers. In great despair, she hid herself away in a cave and refused to come out, which made the world remain depressingly frigid and sad. Finding the situation untenable, the Japanese people were joined by eight thousand Kamis, and together they danced and sang outside the cave begging for her to reappear.

"She was finally persuaded to come out when a Kami placed a mirror on a crack between the rocks outside her cave, allowing her to see and admire her own beautiful reflection. Ever since, we Japanese rejoice at her coming out of seclusion to bring sunlight back to the universe, and we worship her for her warmth and compassion."

Matsumoto-san stopped for a moment, reflecting on her story, and then provided an additional element: "Amazingly, there seems to be a connection with the fabric of my scarf, because Amaterasu is also credited for her use of silkworms, and for inspiring the art of weaving with a loom."

Her excitement lessened somewhat, as she seemed to consider the implications of this legend. "Rabbi, I believe maybe all of this is just coincidental. I cannot accept that there is a credible link between a Japanese Kami and old Hebrew traditions, and even less of a connection with my family."

Rabbi Bensimon seemed more awake and rejuvenated than he had been at the beginning of our visit, but except for his fingers, he seemed pretty spry and excited right from the start. He resumed the conversation with great energy:

"My friend, your story of this extraordinary myth and the customs in your family brightens my day and softens my old-age stiffness," he pronounced. "First, I believe the use of Aramaic to transliterate the name of Amaterasu-Omikami on your scarf has important implications. It seems logical to speculate that ancient Hebrews visited your country many centuries ago and left an indelible mark upon some of the early Japanese. I am also interested in the date on which you received the scarf—the 17th day of the seventh month. Are you aware that this date of the Obon festival coincides with Sukkoth, the celebration of the harvest in the Jewish tradition?"

Rabbi Bensimon was obviously enjoying himself, and he slowed down his discourse a bit, savoring every word while searching for old memories. Soon he re-started with increasing enthusiasm:

"I will tell you a story I heard from my most senior teachers when I was a young seminary student at the Istanbul yeshiva. By the time of King Solomon in the tenth century BCE, the twelve tribes of Israel were at the peak of their prosperity." He continued slowly, searching for the proper wording. "The two tribes in the south region of Judea eventually gave rise to the modern Jewish people. On the other hand, when the northern region named Samaria was conquered in the eighth century BCE by the Assyrian army, the remaining ten tribes of Israel went into exile and were lost to history, for all practical purposes. My teachers believed that these tribes migrated north across the Euphrates River, to where Iraq and Kurdistan now are. During that epic march, which may have taken centuries, they followed the Silk Road east toward the China Sea until they arrived at the ocean. Our ancestors were able mariners, and it would not be a surprise if they had managed the crossing to Korea and Japan."

He stopped to rest a moment, and Matsumoto-san, who until now had been restless but quiet, could no longer refrain from interrupting the rabbi. Her disbelief was palpable:

"Excuse me, Rabbi. Your narrative is fascinating, but I would need more concrete proof that the tribes actually passed through all these countries and interacted with their people. Everything seems unconvincing and far-fetched," she said (a little petulantly, I thought).

"Let me give you other compelling examples. You can verify that the Pathans of Afghanistan and Pakistan, who are Muslim, have many customs inherited from early Jews: they practice circumcision on the eight day after birth, keep similar dietary laws, and some wear the black box called tefillin or 'phylacteries' with God's precepts and inscriptions from the Torah on their foreheads. Incidentally, this same custom is followed in Japan by the Yamabushi, a sect of ascetic mountain hermits who practice Shugendo, a syncretic religion mixing Buddhist and Shinto elements."

"Now, that is quite interesting, Rabbi. I must confess that when you mentioned the Yamabushi it evoked a forgotten memory. Many years ago my mother took me on vacation to the sacred mountains of Kumano and Omine. I have a strong recollection of one of her relatives, a Yamabushi priest with the black box on his forehead, blowing a horagai, which is a conch-shell horn, in our honor during a ceremony."

"My dear, even though you may feel skeptical about my theory, this tradition is reminiscent of the blowing of a shofar—a ram's horn—during the Jewish High Holy Days. I realize you are very hard to convince, and I will keep an open mind in case there are other explanations for this coincidence. But let me tell you also about the Menashe tribe, who after their expulsion from Persia... in 361 BCE, by Alexander the Great, went to the border between India and Myanmar, changed their names to Shinlung, and converted to Islam or became idol worshippers. One to two million people who are conscious of their Hebrew ancestry remain there until today. Some of them had migrated to China, near the Tibetan border. These are the ancestors of the present day Chiang-Min, a small tribe in Szechuan province, who were the only monotheistic group in an area where the term 'God' was unknown until their arrival."

We were quite amazed by the rabbi's ability to remember all this history from his youth. He did look fatigued by the effort. So we paid our respects, thanked him effusively, and prepared to leave the house. Before dismissing us, however, Bensimon made yet another surprising comment, and one unexpected from someone who was almost a century old.

"Unlike the traditional or oral sources in my old yeshiva or any of the universities, today's cyberspace libraries are unimaginably vast and may be considered infinite. You may be aware that Borges—the Argentine writer—had prefigured this concept in 1941, in his short-story 'The Library of Babel.' For these reasons, I suspect that you may find more information on the Internet regarding the Aramaic inscription."

After the interview with the elderly sage, we walked by the shore of Lake Washington, reflecting on our new information. Matsumoto-san was quiet for a while, but eventually she opened up and began to think aloud.

"I am thrilled by the Rabbi's knowledge, and the possible connections with my family's traditions. But at the same time, I'm uncomfortable about these revelations since they could drastically change my understanding of my ancestry, and of my behavior and abilities."

As we walked, her gait became progressively more determined, until she was almost marching, which forced me to adjust my step to match hers. Suddenly, a band of unruly teenagers accosted us on the narrow trail, and aggressively demanded that we clear the way for them to pass. I was not surprised to see Matsumoto-san adopt a martial stance, an attitude I had noted in the past. She then stood sideways, first with her right leg forward, then the left one, always with her weight solidly planted on the ground, as she projected with remarkable speed several forceful and precise up and down and forward swings with both arms, rapidly splitting the group without actually hitting anyone, yet conveying the message: "Don't mess with me." This opened a clear path for us, while the gang retreated fearfully, with no argument and in disarray.

Moments later she looked a bit sheepish, as if she wanted to be excused for acting so aggressively. "I'm sorry if I have startled you with my reaction to the gang. Do you remember I once mentioned that the Matsumoto clan has a long history of belonging to the samurai caste? I was trained in aikido and kendo during my schooldays and cannot help but defend myself from aggression. This may be why I was so surprised when the rabbi mentioned the Yamabushi, who are also known as fierce warriors supposedly endowed with supernatural powers. Don't take me wrong! I make no such claims. I was just well trained when I was in secondary school and have continued practicing the martial arts until today."

Bensimon had predicted I would find my sources in the nearly infinite libraries on the Internet. He neglected to point out that historical facts alone would be insufficient to explain my friend's behavior or her effects on the weather. Nevertheless, given my own Jewish ancestry, I was intrigued by the possible passage of the ancient Israelites through Japan, and I followed the rabbi's suggestion and entered cyberspace with great curiosity.

I was highly rewarded when I came across a contact in Japan itself, a bible scholar by the unlikely name of 'Kubo,' offering evidence for the connection between the two races. Initially I was distracted by the sound of his name, and I imagined him as a small, geometrically shaped but studious character, sitting in a small, three-mat-sized room, under weak fluorescent lights. I suspected him of a possibly evangelistic intent and a less-than-scientific attitude, a man who was given to great flights of imagination and conjecture. But the further I delved into his writings, the more I saw that I was wrong. I realized that his knowledge was extensive and his inquisitive mind merited respect. I was eventually won over by his good manners and diplomatic response to my e-mailed inquiries. Always he concluded his e-mails with a respectful and captivating: "Shalom, from Tokyo."

Mr. Kubo directed me to an especially convincing book, which I was able to locate at the University of Washington. Entering the beautiful Gothic-Revival building that housed the Suzzallo Library, I headed for the Old Manuscripts room and was struck by the church-like light filtering through the stained-glass windows and coloring the bookcases. The religious atmosphere disconcerted me at first; I had intended my endeavor to be purely scientific.

I was soon admiring The Japanese and the Ten Lost Tribes of Israel, published in 1980, by Joseph Eidelberg, a Jew who visited Japan and remained for years in a Shinto shrine. He lists hundreds of Japanese words that have similar sounds and meaning in Hebrew. For instance, "Goy," a non-Hebrew or foreigner, resembles "Gaijin" in Japanese. "Daver," to speak, in Hebrew is like "Daberu," to chat, in Japanese. The similarity between the Hebrew word "shamar" (to guard), and the Japanese "samurai" (the guards who served the nobility) was highly persuasive.

Following other suggestions from my cyber-acquaintance, the all-knowing but obscure Mr. Kubo, I studied and found compelling an argument made in the molecular biology journals about the genetic origin of the Japanese. Their blood types and those of the Jews were apparently very similar, and the characteristics of about twenty-six percent of the Japanese DNA are unique to them and never seen among the Chinese or the Koreans. This made it easy to speculate that Jews coming by the Silk Road at the beginning of history may have left an indelible nucleic-acid mark among the population of the long-isolated island of Japan.

The light shifted on the books strewn across the table, breaking my concentration. I looked up at the window and saw an entrancing sight: a slow and steady flow of raindrops sliding down the glass, forced by gravity into a curious branching pattern, repeated interminably on their way to the sill. The shape of this fractal pattern (in which each drop cluster was identical to the one that preceded it) suggested the analogous image of Amaterasu's genes drifting down through subsequent generations. Accepting the unproven premise that Hebrew visitors might have interacted with the Japanese, the Imperial rulers and the hierarchy of the Shinto religion, one could imagine that this intimate contact allowed the genetic features to be passed down to the present Matsumoto family.

Sitting in the scholarly environment of Suzallo Library, I started to daydream and weave conjectural relationships between the migrant Hebrew tribes and the Japanese people, and especially with the remarkable talents of my friend Matsumoto-San. I recalled a quote by Borges, who had observed that "all collaboration is mysterious." He had cited examples of interactions across time and geographical divides, sometimes within a dream. For instance, a Mogul emperor in the thirteenth century dreamt of a fabulous palace and then built it for his wife. In turn, Coleridge dreamt, in 1797, about this same palace and immediately composed from his partial recollection of the dream the lyrical fragment "Kubla Khan." In an analogous collaboration, in 2007, a Japanese woman in

Seattle, possessed of an unexplained power to improve the weather, misplaces a mysterious white silk scarf. Her friend's investigative curiosity helps to uncover her possible ancestral relationship to the most revered Kami in Japanese mythology, and perhaps to one of the lost Hebrew tribes.

I was reawakened from my late-morning reveries by the sudden awareness of a rapidly darkening sky through the stained-glass windows. Soon a powerful wind began to blow, bending the treetops outside and destroying the flowerbeds of the Forestry School garden. A deluge flooded the brick pavements of Red Square. The extraordinary storm seemed to last for hours.

While waiting for the tempest to abate, I phoned Matsumoto-san to describe my findings and complain about the unseasonable and unexpected bad weather. When I reached her, she told me she was holed up in a cave-like cabin on Lopez Island, possibly ruminating on the implications of our recent meeting with Rabbi Bensimon. She said she was in a funk, still assessing her new understanding of her family history, and not wanting to come back to town for a while. Concerned by her isolation and inspired by the Amaterasu myth she had related to us, I persuaded Matsumoto-san to walk to her favorite pond in the woods behind the cabin to observe the colorful fish. Perhaps she would glance at, and be delighted by, her own reflection on the mirror-like surface. Finally, I asked her to return to town the following day for a meeting at our favorite espresso bar. I specifically requested that she bring her extraordinary white scarf. I hoped she would bring along a more receptive and understanding attitude toward the new possibilities that our visit with the rabbi had revealed.

The following morning, just before our meeting, an immensely blue sky opened up over the "Emerald City," and bright sunshine illuminated the old brick walls of the café in Pioneer Square. Amaterasu, —I mean, Matsumoto-san— arrived early and was waiting at an outdoor table, with a warm cappuccino and a much less skeptical expression on her face. Her white scarf was loosely wrapped over her shoulders, its edges floating lazily in the gentle morning breeze.

The Excessive Waters of the

Río de la Plata

Neeraj Prasad, a Hindu sailor, materialized in Buenos Aires one winter day in 1965 as a dialysis patient in the hospital where I was a medical resident. The arrival of an extremely thin, dark-skinned foreigner dressed only in white homespun cotton pants and a long shirt down to his knees was unprecedented and shocking in its exoticism. At the time, East Asian immigrants were a rarity in our country. Treating this man from India was an honor and an opportunity to interact with someone very different from the average in Argentina—an insular country at the tip of South America, which wrongly perceived itself as the geographic center of the universe. This encounter, which was to become a medical mystery, would expand my perspective in such disparate areas as the physiology of kidney and body fluids, the importance of water in Hinduism, the forecasting power of astrology, and the unpredictability of romance.

Supporting Neeraj's arm was a tall blond woman with blue eyes, radiating self-confidence and good health, draped in a black Karakul fur coat. (My Russian grandmother would have called them "Astrakhan.") The British owners of the Southern Cross—Neeraj's ship—had hired this multilingual

Danish nurse to assist him during his hospital stay. I sighed with relief (and admiration for her poise and elegance), when she told us she would help.

Neeraj seemed fearful of the strange surroundings, but Eva got him settled in a private room while I waited to obtain his medical history and examine him. He had arrived with few personal belongings inside a medium-sized burlap sack, from which he extracted a curious metal vessel, which he called a "kindi," something used in most Hindu homes, he said. It was small and round and had a long straight-necked spout angling out from its belly. He spoke to the nurse in English, which she could not understand.

"May I have some water, please?"

"Bring him a jug of water", I translated. "It's OK, fluids are allowed."

Having filled his kindi, he took a long sip directly from the spout, and then washed his hands and face with its contents, before asking a curious question:

"Doctor, can you tell me which way is the south?"

"The south is that way, towards the window, why do you ask?"

"A kindi should not be facing south, because it might invite death to someone dear."

He then carefully placed the kindi on the bedside table facing in the opposite direction.

He was soon bare-chested, very comfortably

sitting cross-legged on his bed, seemingly unaware that he offered a striking sight in the cool hospital room. I spoke to him in my broken English (his was better than mine) about his transfer to our hospital.

"Mr. Prasad, what happened when you got sick on board the ship?"

"Yes, Doctor Sahib. Please call me Neeraj. We were bringing freight from Bombay, as we rounded the tip of Africa towards Argentina. I felt sick by the time we entered a different-looking sea, with brown-colored, muddy water. I lifted some with my bucket, and it shocked me it was not salty. My fellow sailors said it was the 'River Plate,' which is not really an ocean. (Indeed, he was on the Río de la Plata, the shallow, wide estuary between Argentina and Uruguay, which a great writer has called the "Lion-colored river.")

"We were sailing over a dredged channel marked by closely spaced, anchored buoys, when I suddenly felt weak and vomited bright red blood on the shiny deck I had spent hours scrubbing."

"Was this your first-time bleeding from the stomach? Were you feeling sick before?"

"Yes, Doctor, I had bled a little in my stools, once. I was feeling sick and very sad for a while, because of our evil bos'n, who did not like me. He was a Brit who hated Indians and abused his deckhands. He forced me to scrub the wooden deck all day with 'holystone,' to paint bulkheads, to polish brass, and to grease the fittings and anchor chains. I was exhausted, tasting acid in my mouth, and feeling burning on my chest."

"Excuse me, sir," Eva interjected. "Neeraj fainted, and they brought him to the infirmary in shock. No blood was available to transfuse him. It took two days for the ship to reach the port, and to bring him to the hospital where I work. By then, he was making very little urine, as he had developed acute kidney failure. They transferred him to you for dialysis, explaining that this treatment has only recently been introduced in Argentina. I will provide nursing care during the night. I must leave now but I will come back at eight this evening." She put on her striking black coat, gave a friendly squeeze to Neeraj's shoulder and left us alone.

When I examined Neeraj I saw thick calluses on the dark chocolate-colored skin of his knees, from the forced deck scrubbing. I spent the rest of the day with my colleagues in a whirlwind of activity, preparing for his first dialysis.

Though we lacked experience with this new treatment, we excelled in enthusiasm. We would be using a dialyzer, recently invented in Europe. Thus, we inserted catheters in his arm vessels to circulate the blood. This blood tubing was surrounded by a water bath (the dialysate) containing salts and other substances, which would clear impurities and normalize the composition of Neeraj's blood.

Neeraj did well from a medical standpoint, although he felt no better. He disliked the repeated needle pricks we made to obtain blood samples, yet never complained loudly or expressed frustration. He remained calm and never lost his enigmatic smile. After dialysis he sipped small amounts of water three times from his kindi, repeating a name in a low voice (he would also do this after a bath or a meal). He said this prayer was called 'achamana,' to help him to remember God and to become pure."

"That's very interesting! While you are looking for spiritual purification, we are doing precisely the opposite, trying to purify your body with dialysis treatments."

Eva returned as promised at eight, this time in a more conventional dress, with a lab coat over it. She had brought Neeraj a vegetarian dinner, though his appetite was poor. That night I managed to join them for conversation, an opportunity to interact with both, my extraordinary patient and his Danish nurse. (I soon learned that I had competition for her attention. Gregarious, almost flirty, Eva was befriending Giovanni, a fair-skinned son of North Italian immigrants, who worked maintenance on the evening shift). She tended Neeraj smoothly and efficiently. Disguising my admiration of her fluid moves, I questioned Neeraj about his past history.

"I was born in Varanasi, Doctor, by the sacred River Ganga. I heard from my mother many times that when I was born my uncle sprinkled drops of Ganga water over my skin to purify me, so

I would become like him someday. My mother was very spiritual, so she called on an astrologer to calculate my horoscope. After doing so he turned very serious and told them that water would influence my life, from my birth to my last breath. My family took this forecast quite literally, because Hindus consider water the building block of life for all beings. Thus my parents named me 'Neeraj,' which in Hindi means 'born from water,' like a lotus flower or a pearl."

"Do you think this horoscope actually predicted things that happened to you? Has your life really been influenced by water?" (These were not traditional medical questions, but rather the product of my increasing curiosity about this unusual patient.)

"When I was a child, I used to run near the river, by the ghats, where bodies are cremated waterside. But I knew people on the shores of the Ganga, and a fisherman took me under his wing and I became his apprentice, selling our catch in the village markets. Each time we left the landing, I was asked to empty a clay bowl of water over the boat's prow to bring good luck to our fishing. I really loved the contact with the river, but the earnings were poor and I had to find a different job.

"I was then hired to help an old perfume maker on a small street in Varanasi. I had to mix oils and fragrances in the secret formulas he had perfected. We used oils like sandalwood, cardamom, jasmine sambac absolute, roses, sweet fennel, and frankincense—names that I still smell in my imagination. Then one day he gave me a sample of his greatest creation, 'Essence of Ganga,' which he told me to keep forever. In turn, one day I would be allowed to give it as a gift to the person I appreciated the most."

Neeraj then reached for his sack and pulled out a two-inch-long brown perfume flask, which he offered to Eva and me to smell. Its pungent odor reeked of river, moist earth and ashes, which to me suggested death. It had the opposite effect on Eva, who touched Neeraj's hand more tenderly than Florence Nightingale would have prescribed, I thought.

"A friend took me to Bombay, where they offered me a job as deckhand on a freighter. I have travelled to many lands, and have once been to Copenhagen, a city that I remember warmly. My only bad experience in years was with the bos'n on the Southern Cross. But you know, Doctor, I still feel restless about being a sailor. Old Brahmins talked of the ancient prohibition against Hindus crossing the ocean. Now I fear I am sick because I have transgressed this old prohibition."

"Don't say that, Neeraj!" Eva interjected.

"On the other hand, this rule benefited Muslims and Arabs who were not affected by it, and who could ship pepper and other spices out of India." Neeraj smiled shyly, as to minimize his previous comment

When leaving his room I realized that Neeraj looked amazingly like the regimental water-carrier Gunga Din, the hero in an old movie based on a Rudyard Kipling poem, with Douglas Fairbanks and Cary Grant.

* * *

Neeraj's second dialysis proceeded without complications, and lab tests showed that his blood composition was normalizing. He was more alert and talkative, relating well to Eva, who kept him company each evening. One night, when the ward was quiet and most patients were asleep, I found his room lights dimmed and a lighted candle at his bedside, (surely against safety regulations). He was telling Eva about his life in India while she reclined on the other empty bed in the room, lying on her side with her right hip and right arm extended, and with her feet tucked behind her knees. From our opposite vantage points, Neeraj and I watched her in awe, recognizing at once that we had experienced the same vision: "The Little Mermaid"! Eva's pose was strikingly similar to the statue in Copenhagen Harbor, which Neeraj had actually seen from the pier. Like many other sailors, he had literally fallen in love with her. For my part, I had only seen her in pictures, and I had read that in the old days, a sailor who looked at the statue was told to throw water on his head and chest and to cool his feet in the water, to ward off the mermaid's magic. Now I felt as if I had been to Copenhagen and fallen under the Mermaid's spell.

That night I dreamed that I was descending a dark staircase in the hospital, holding hands with a blond woman who resembled the Little Mermaid. We sought privacy in a deserted photography darkroom, where I turned the heat up on the water-rinsing bath, releasing steam. Soon we were locked in a tight embrace, and then we melted in a haze of red safety light and fog. That memory is so strong and persistent that I can't be sure it was only a dream.

* * *

The next day I asked Eva to join me for a drink after work at a typical milonga, where we sat next to the dance floor very close to the dancers, watching the couples pass by in a tight embrace, focused on the music.

"Did you notice how women close their eyes as they dance? They seem to enter a special inner space... I think this dance must help people relate to each other more intimately. That's what I like, personal relationships, knowing new people and having friends. What do you like most?"

"I love my profession, understanding the human body, to make people feel better and stay healthy. But I would have to study with good teachers. Neeraj's problem motivates me to go to the

USA to become a specialist. Besides, the political situation in this country is getting more difficult every minute, another reason to leave soon. I have good friends but not a steady girlfriend who would keep me here, only my family."

"Maybe I can find a good reason to keep you here!", she said, unexpectedly. "But now I have to rest. I start work much earlier than you do."

* * *

The next couple of dialysis sessions left Neeraj feeling worse, with severe headaches. He preferred to sit straight up on the bed with his legs crossed, and to follow the ancient yogic practice of lowering his head and pouring salt water from the kindi into each nostril alternately, then draining it on the opposite side, to clear his headaches and purify the sinuses. Our staff was alarmed and amazed by these practices but didn't prevent them.

He started to gain weight and his face and eyelids swelled a bit. He slept more and spoke very little. Eva swabbed his sweaty forehead and massaged his arms and legs with oil. Then we read an astonishing laboratory report: the sodium concentration of Neeraj's blood was falling, which meant that the water content of his body was excessive. This was reflected in a larger cell size, which explained his headaches, since brain cells have no place to expand in the rigid skull. Since dialysis was designed to remove the water, these results were mystifying.

Our senior nephrologist, at a loss to explain the water excess after dialysis, demanded a brainstorming session with the medical staff to discuss the mystery. After hearing our comments, he summarized the possible explanations. Neeraj had water intoxication, and he must have a source of water gain. In spite of our efforts, we could not determine the source. His intake was limited to only 500 ml each day, and the volume of water in the dialysis tank was always the same, as was the amount of added salts, which the chief technician had confirmed using a sensitive lab scale.

"Unless one of you has a better idea, the treatment of choice is surely intensive daily dialysis for two or three additional hours, starting now. Get going with it!" he ordered.

We did as we were told, hoping for improvement. Yet over the next three days our patient became more lethargic, his speech was sometimes incoherent, and he had two seizures, which left him confused for a few hours. The sodium concentration in his blood became even lower, even though we were trying hard to keep him from gaining more water. At one point, Neeraj looked around, as if hearing a voice or someone calling him, and pronounced several times the name "Saraswati." Finally, he called for Eva and me.

"Doctor Sahib, I hope you will cure me with

dialysis, but when my people believe the end of life is near, they say 'that my water and rice have arrived." Then, I wish you would follow the Hindu customs." He stopped, pulled the small flask of Essence of Ganga he had shown us earlier, and held it in his hand. "Before I pass away, please pour a few drops of sacred water in my mouth. Afterwards, I wish to offer Eva the remains of the sacred water as a gift."

He then replaced the small flask in his sack and began to meditate. Before long, his breathing slowed, grew deeper, and we could no longer be sure if he was still aware of our presence. Eva held his hand for a few moments, then withdrew it gently, and we left the room together.

"Eva, I feel terrible about this. I think we have done everything we can for Neeraj, but I worry that it all may be futile."

"Why are you so doubtful?"

"I am not superstitious, Eva. I do my job and concentrate on technical issues, but I now find myself obsessed with Neeraj's horoscope. It predicted his interactions with water—his birth by the sacred Ganges, his job as a sailor, his sickness while on the great Río de la Plata, and now this mysterious, intractable water intoxication. Is his destiny determined, regardless of our efforts?"

"I share your feelings about predestination. Like you, I am not thinking as a nurse, and my emotions are winning against my more rational thoughts. I am afraid that a dramatic outcome may not be far away. But Neeraj remains calm under the circumstances. Seen from his perspective, water is involved as much in the generation of life as in death."

"Yes, Neeraj is strangely calm, even though he knows his life end may be near. His religious beliefs may play a role in this acceptance of his fate. But I would like to understand how Hinduism explains the irony that water, 'the building block of life for all beings,' can also be excessive and literally make a person drown in his own fluids. He is getting worse, as if an unstoppable force were at work in him."

"Now you really sound superstitious. What force do you have in mind?"

"It's really strange, Eva. I checked the Encyclopedia Britannica and found out that Saraswati—the name Neeraj pronounced after waking up from the seizure, as if someone were calling him—was the River Goddess in the Rig Veda, the oldest Sanskrit text. I learned that the sacred river of the same name had dried up and its location is unknown today. Could it have resurfaced in the Río de la Plata?"

"I never thought of the Río de la Plata as sacred. It's a muddy, sometimes smelly river, aspiring to be an ocean. It's ugly enough to make you sick. I miss the Baltic Sea and its cleaner waters, the region where I grew up."

* * *

During Neeraj's next and final treatment, all of us continuously monitored the proceedings to ensure that nothing went wrong. The chief nephrologist paced in circles around the dialyzer, observing every detail.

But to our dismay, Neeraj became nauseous, experienced a severe headache and finally had a generalized seizure, forcing us to discontinue dialysis. I remembered Neeraj's wishes in case he neared death, and I darted to his room to recover his precious perfume flask. I ran like a madman back to his bedside, and with a trembling right hand I sprinkled a few drops of sacred Essence of Ganga in his mouth. Then I gave Eva the bottle to keep as Neeraj's gift. Tragically, Neeraj never woke up from his deep sleep and died peacefully a few hours later.

After this devastating outcome, I collapsed into a chair in my bedroom holding my head in both hands, searching for an explanation of Neeraj's death. My mind cycled between rational and supernatural causes. Were we guilty of our collective ignorance about dialysis, or was this his inescapable destiny? Neeraj's horoscope had predicted that water would influence his life until the bitter end. But how could water, "the substrate of all life," be the instrument of his demise? I had no answer to that. Nor would I begin to understand the spiritual aspects of this experience until many years hence.

Later that day, as Eva prepared to return to her usual job at the other hospital, Giovanni, the maintenance man, approached her and took her aside.

"Miss Eva, before you leave there is something I must tell you. I hope you can tell me what to do. I cannot decide if I should tell my supervisor about what I have done."

"What have you done, Giovanni? Is it something related to the patient's death?"

"I don't know, Miss Eva, but I may have made a mistake last week when I was working in the dialysis room. I am responsible for cleaning everything, including the water tank in the dialysis machine. It is made of stainless steel, and it gets crusted with the salt and impurities after each use. So I scrub it thoroughly with a wire brush. Six nights ago I was scrubbing as usual when a white tape fell off the inside of the tank. I didn't know its exact location in the tank, so I replaced it with a brand-new piece of tape at a place where I hoped it used to be. I was confused and afraid to tell anyone. I have a family and do not want to lose my job. What shall I do now?"

Eva realized something terrible had happened, even though she did not fully comprehend its significance. She came looking for me, drew me into a corner and told me what she had learned. With a sinking heart, we went to find the senior nephrologist to relate the grim new information. We all filed into the dialysis room to investigate at once.

We discovered, horrified, that the tape marking the water level was placed much higher than normal. The higher volume had forced water into the patient instead of removing it! It was our fault, and not Giovanni's. We should never have used the primitive tape system to indicate the water level. By the time we found out, it was too late to help Neeraj. We had been looking for a rational, scientific explanation for Neeraj's worsening. Ironically, his death was caused by a stupid human error of enormous consequence.

* * *

We notified the British embassy of Neeraj's sad outcome. A while later somebody called back to say that Neeraj should be cremated in Buenos Aires since they were unable to contact his relatives. We scheduled the cremation for the following day, and everyone on staff attended the ceremony to offer their respect. I was delegated to say a few words and officiate at the service. I could think of nothing better than to paraphrase Kipling's words in his famous poem:

... But when it comes to slaughter

You will do your work on water . . .
Yes. Din! Din! Din!
Neeraj, You brown-leather skin!
Though I've treated you and failed you,
By the livin' Gawd that made you,
You're a better man than I am, Gunga Din!

On the following Sunday, when we were both off-duty, Eva and I walked to the Costanera Avenue on the river bank and found a quiet area with no fishermen or children playing. A freighter was passing in the distance, while seagulls flew by towards the horizon. We opened the small box we carried, leaned over the balustrade and spread the ashes on the river, which the wind and waves scattered. Was Saraswati watching us from the shallow waters? As we were fulfilling our duty to Neeraj, a delicious odor surrounded us: the smoke from the chorizos grilling on the vending carts on the Costanera. The smell of cooking meat, so dear to the people of Argentina, reassured me that life would still go on.

* * *

At that time I didn't know that the arrival of this very special patient would be so important for all of us, and that it would change the course of my own life. I continued to learn from our tragic error, and eventually understood the intricacies of the metabolism of salt and water. But my concern for Neeraj and his unfortunate death inspired me to leave Argentina to study physiology and kidney diseases. Fortunately, I was granted a fellowship in nephrology and moved to Seattle in the United States. I could not have predicted that I would transmit my knowledge to young doctors years later in this country.

On the other hand, I didn't fully understand the philosophical dimension of Neeraj's end by water intoxication, and his calm attitude in the face of approaching death, until today, over forty years later, when I felt the need to write about it. The turning point arrived in the form of an online encounter with Dr. Nair, an erudite history professor in Trivandrum, India, author of a superb article on the central role of water in Hinduism. Our electronic contacts lead to an invitation to visit him in India, which I accepted last month.

Dr. Nair expected me at his comfortable home in Trivandrum. He was sixty years old, with a long white beard, and wearing a dark pair of pants and a white cotton shirt. Dr. Nair's wife greeted me warmly, and invited me to lunch with them, some typical Kerala dishes. After the meal, I was able to satisfy my curiosity:

"Dr. Nair, would you help me understand the importance of water in Hinduism?"

"To answer your question, we call nature *panchamahabutha*, which is composed of five elements: earth, water, fire, air and ether (the void or the sky). In our graphic description of nature, a circle, a symbol of fullness, represents water, which in India has always been an object of worship. I was quite touched by your telling me the story of Neeraj, who died of water intoxication. That's why I think it's important that you, as a physician, should study the work of Kirpal Singh, a spiritual teacher from the Punjab. He pointed out that while physiologists and physicians tell us a lot about the metabolism of living organisms, they cannot tell us what life itself is, and above all what consciousness is. Hindus believe all life is eternal, it continues in an endless cycle, appearing, disappearing and reappearing like waves and bubbles on the stream of time."

"According to this vision, what would be the meaning of death?

"The duality of death and life are but two sides of a coin rotating on its axis, as the soul will in due course pass on to another body."

"Is this view exclusive to Hinduism?"

"Not at all! It is well represented in the Gospels, where we read that: "Except a man be born again, he cannot see the Kingdom of God; except a man be born of water and of spirit, he cannot enter into the Kingdom of God" (John 3:3-8). Sometimes rebirth, given the ever-revolving wheel of life, may be an evolution towards a superior state and a higher level of consciousness. I certainly hope that

Neeraj's soul has found a way to reappear in an exalted state, as a superior being."

Hearing these words I suddenly remembered the old events, and I felt silent, as if paralyzed for a few seconds.

"I just remembered my last visit with Eva, Neeraj's nurse. Can I tell you what happened?"

"Sure, you had mentioned her on your emails. What do you know about her life?"

"After Neeraj's death, the pressures of the residency program left me little time for socializing, and somehow Eva and I did not make an effort to see each other. One year passed before I called her at the hospital. When we met again something very strange happened, which may put our story into perspective, especially now that I heard your comment about reincarnation.

For lack of a better idea, we agreed to meet at the very old-world Richmond Café, in those days a bourgeois location, with its ancient leather chairs and respectable-looking middle-aged couples. I sat at the only available table, facing the back of the room, and reserved the better seat for Eva. I had arrived early, with time to consider what we would talk about, what I would propose to her for the future.

When I feared she might never arrive, she approached me from behind, gave me a light tap on the shoulder, and said 'Hello!' I stood up to greet her, turned around and then sank again into the deep chair, shaken to my bones by the fact that she was not alone. She held a small, slender baby boy, judging by his blue-colored clothes, maybe three months old. How was I to know for sure? I am not a pediatrician. The baby's skin was darker than anyone else's in the room, not at all how a Danish baby might look. I congratulated her, but never had the courage to ask about the baby's father; neither did she tell me anything about him. The baby was quiet and well behaved, already interested in his surroundings, which he surveyed with great curiosity. Eva looked radiant, wearing the Karakul fur coat I knew so well. We chatted while drinking English tea with pastries. But I was feeling more and more restless, unable to ask Eva about her baby's father, and she never volunteered any information about that. Then I accidentally knocked off a glass of water from the table, which was spilling in slow motion over my shoe. I stayed in near shock for a few moments until she asked about me. I told her I had been granted a fellowship to study nephrology in the USA and was going to move to Seattle soon. Finally, we had nothing else to say to each other. I paid the waiter, while she quietly left the café with her baby, mingling with the crowd, but never bothering to look back."

"That is so interesting, and I should say: clear as water!", Dr. Nair concluded. "Maybe Neeraj found a way to continue being among us. At least he succeeded in having us talk about him and try to understand his life so many years later. This is another side of immortality, don't you think?" Perhaps the Ganga and the Río de la Plata are not so far apart after all!"

"Dr. Nair: I hope we will have many more chats in Seattle, a city I love, with many lakes. I found long ago that I love the proximity to water, and sea-kayaking is one of my favorite pastimes."

Note: this is a fictional story, inspired by an event that happened many years ago. Any similarity between the characters and any person, living or death, is purely coincidental. I am indebted to Dr. V. Sankaran Nair, for his kindness in answering my questions about the importance of water in Hinduism.

Swimming with Nazis in Argentina

In the summer of 1958, under a brilliant blue sky, a Nazi exile was drowning in the ocean, off the wide sandy beach of Villa Gesell in Argentina. It was early morning, a few years after the end of World War II, and the only person for miles watching the Nazi's desperate signals for help was a Jewish beach boy, paralyzed by indecision.

It was my first season as a beach attendant. The job offered me a paid vacation by the seaside and time to prepare for my medical school exams back in Buenos Aires. I was just a teenager, a competitive swimmer with no training as a lifeguard or in rescue experience. But now I ran for the life ring and rope my boss had optimistically placed under the weather flag, despite fearing for my life— I would have to swim out past the breaking waves, over the sandbar, to reach the struggling man. I had heard that it was safer to swim up to a drowning person from behind to avoid getting trapped in their grasp, and if they tried to hold on to you, to punch their heads first with all your might to disorient them or knock them out. Should I risk my life to save him? He was a Nazi after all.

As I sprinted towards the water, rapid-fire images of my childhood ran through my mind like in a movie during a high-speed car chase. I suddenly remembered family stories about my

Uncle Nathan's war experience in France, where he had been a truck driver for the Resistance in Lyon. Could the drowning man, an ex-German pilot, have been the one chasing Nathan's truck with machine-gun fire?

I decided I could not let the man drown. I took a deep breath and started on a brisk swim, diving under the waves as they surged above me. As I approached him, the man recognized me and begged me to throw him the life ring. I was deeply relieved I would not have to smack him in the head to quiet him down. Already exhausted from his attempts to save himself, he just put the ring over his head and arm and waved me towards the beach. He had swallowed tons of water after failing to swim across the sand bar against the wind and waves and accepted being towed in with relief.

When we reached the beach, both of us collapsed on the soft sand and lay there, winded. The man eventually stood up and told me his name was Werner. He shook my hand, grateful and more than a little ashamed, and said he would be back the next morning to thank me properly. He then walked toward the sand dunes, furtively looking around for potential witnesses. He must have been pleased no one else was there to see and later tell of his ordeal. I remained on the warm sand for some time, marveling at my own daring and exhilarated by the outcome of this adventure.

I knew Werner as the beach photographer. I

had frequently seen him on his rounds mingling with the tourists. Villa Gesell was then a sleepy resort founded by German immigrants, who usually spoke their own language rather than Spanish. My employer, a resort developer, had appointed me— untrained and unqualified as I was— as the only "lifeguard" on a miles-long beach. Presumably, I had gotten the job because I could swim faster, and was lighter and younger, than the man who had preceded me: a stocky, formidable gypsy ex-sailor everyone called Zigeuner. He was pleased with my arrival because he preferred the freedom of taking on odd jobs and chasing after the tourist's wives. He once told me that sailors washed their blue jeans in the ocean and then dried them in the sun to make them look professionally ironed! He made friends easily and was a great source of information about the town's diverse residents. He was the one who told me the photographer had been a pilot during the war.

The day after, Werner walked resolutely towards me with a smile as wide as the Atlantic Ocean. "Arghmando," he said in a strong Bavarian accent, "I can't thank you enough for your help yesterday. I could tell that you were having second thoughts because it took you a long time to jump in, but in the end you saved my life. That was brave, and I'm very grateful."

I remained silent, not wanting to explain the reason for my hesitation.

He continued: "What can I do for you in return? Is there anything I can help you with? Look, you are still new to Gesell. Let me introduce you to some of the restaurant and nightclub owners, maybe even the chief of police and other local personalities. This is a small town and knowing certain people could be useful to you."

Then he noticed me eyeing his bright, silver-colored camera, which had mysterious rotating dials like a high-precision instrument. "Are you interested in photography?" he asked.

"Oh, yes, it runs in the family. Some of our relatives were photographers in Europe before the war." I was a young student who had never handled expensive camera equipment, so I asked what kind of camera it was.

"This is a Leica that I kept after the war. It's the model the Luftwaffe gave its pilots for reconnaissance missions. It's small and unassuming, but it has very sharp lenses. Have you done much photography?"

"No, but I wish I could learn more about it. I have only ever used my father's Kodak 6 x 9, the one with bellows. But it had light leaks, and the negatives were fogged all the time." And then, in a sudden flash of intuition, I asked: "Can I shadow you as you work on the beach after I'm done working? It would be great to observe how you approach people and learn how to use the Leica. Maybe one day I'll be able to afford one like yours."

"Sure! I can show you how to use the camera and develop black-and-white pictures, which I do at lunchtime. I have to deliver prints to the tourists later in the evening." And then, to my surprise, he added, "One more thing. Would you like to go swimming together early in the morning before we get busy at the beach? It would be much safer to swim with a competent partner."

Although no longer an officer, Werner was still in excellent physical condition. A tall blond man with very light blue eyes, he could have been a poster boy for Nazi youth during the war. Yet, strangely enough, I found myself swimming with him, and occasionally a couple of his German military friends, several times a week. This was an unfamiliar, exhilarating environment. I had not expected to play such an adult role, and yet here I was being rewarded with the trust of professional soldiers. It puzzled me they did not object to swimming with a Jewish lifeguard but treated me with the same respect I showed them.

During our walks, Werner taught me the basics of photography: how to gauge the exposure without a light meter on a very bright beach; the rudiments of composition; and how to judge the moods of the tourists and the poses that would please them. The brightest moments came from learning how to handle and then actually shoot with the Leica, the historic Luftwaffe model that had seen action in the war.

Soon, I felt confident enough to ask Werner about his friends, and indirectly about his war experience. I was still unable to tell a Nazi apart from other Germans:

"Werner, what do you know about the tall, sexy woman who owns the Atlantic Theater? Why does she sneer when I pass by?"

"Because she is one of the Nazis who arrived twenty years ago when Gesell was founded. You are the only lifeguard in town and most people here know you are Jewish. Your last name could be German, but you don't speak German like other local guys your age!"

Sensing a good opportunity to dig for more information, I persisted. "Why does she need that powerful-looking radio antenna that's on top of the theater?"

"As everyone around here knows, Ursula used her radio to communicate with German submarines during the war. The Germans would surface nearby to purchase fuel and fresh supplies from the locals. Sometimes they would smuggle in Nazi officers, who would either stay in town, where they felt welcome, or go underground in Argentina or somewhere else in South America."

"That's amazing! How can these people live here openly when everyone knows who they are?"

"It's very simple: they feel protected! General Peron, who was president during the war, trained with Mussolini and was a Hitler sympathizer. Peron did not declare war on Germany until the day before the armistice was signed. He and his ministers let high-ranking Nazis enter the country in exchange for money or valuable secrets. Some of them ended up in Villa Gesell and now own some of the oldest businesses in town. They are not very friendly to me or some of my friends here."

"What's the story with the two people who swim with us sometimes?"

"My two friends were in the navy, and I was a pilot in the Luftwaffe, but we never joined the Nazi party. We are career officers who had no choice about being in the war." He was silent for a moment or two before proceeding.

"Have you heard of the Graf Spee? It was a Panzerschiff, the armored ship the British surrounded near Montevideo in the Battle of the River Plate. My two friends were amongst the officers who survived and escaped to Uruguay or Argentina. Langsdorff, their commander, was an honorable man who scuttled the ship to avoid it being captured. Afterwards, he went to a hotel in Buenos Aires where he dressed up in full uniform and then shot himself!"

I later met other German exiles but still could not actually tell if they were Nazis. And then one day I met the owner of Pensión Schwalbe, a small, delightful chalet in the outskirts of the pine forest. Its poetic name means "swallow bird." I had gone into the chalet to try and reserve a room for some friends who would be visiting. Mr. Schwalbe was standing behind the counter when I entered. I noticed most of the room keys were hanging from their hooks, so I knew the hotel was not at full capacity, even in season. Our conversation was short and to the point:

"What do you want here?" He said, clearly repelled by my presence.

"Mr. Schwalbe, I would like to reserve a room for the weekend for two friends from Buenos Aires. Do you have any vacancies?"

"I have rooms, but not for you and your Jewish friends. Go try somewhere else!"

I left the hotel shaken and disgusted by his answer. This was the first time I had met an aggressive Nazi and personally been a target of such blatant anti-Semitism. Now I know who you are, Mr. Schwalbe, I hope someday I will have a chance to get back at you! Who knows? You may go swimming one day and cramp badly out there beyond the sand bar. But I will go on eating my lunch behind the dunes, studying for my upcoming pathology exam, totally deaf to your cries for help.

Because of this incident and many others, I now realize my good fortune to have been born in Argentina and not in Europe during the chaotic years of the Second World War. As a young man I only had contact with suspected Nazis. With the passage of time, I learned to easily identify totalitarians, demagogues, and anti-Semites. Sadly, it is troubling to detect these tendencies in our own government and in large groups in the USA today.

* * *

When I mentioned to Werner that I was unable to make enough money as a beach boy, he took me to meet the owners of the Restaurant St. George. A delightful couple from Hamburg, Hans and Helga offered me a job as a dinner waiter. Hans was keen to tell me he could tolerate enough alcohol to supply all the hospitals in a large city. He introduced me to Aquavit, his favorite drink, and taught me the secret of knowing when to stop before getting drunk. You had to pinch your cheeks at the start, and then repeat the pinch after every drink until your cheeks started to feel a little numb. He and Helga had built their European oasis on a brick dome half encased in a sand dune. The acoustics were formidable, and I was allowed to listen to their classical music collection whenever the restaurant was closed. I could even bring a friend on lazy afternoons. The time I spent listening to Bach's Toccata and Fugue in this setting is still one of my most memorable musical experiences.

Hans had lost both his legs in separate horse-riding accidents. For a while, he was able to climb on the horse using a stepladder, but now he could no longer provide the sort of exercise his horse needed. To my great satisfaction, I was assigned the duty of running the horse bareback on the beach, a few times a week.

More importantly, it was at this time I met Han's chef, who took me under his wing, becoming first my instructor in the kitchen and eventually my mentor. He was a slightly overweight Hungarian Jew with grey hair and mustache, who had escaped from Europe during the war. He had been chef and maître d' in casinos and great hotels on the coast of Brazil and Argentina. Everyone respectfully called him "Meier-Baçi."

The chef was generous with all us waiters. I remember him teaching me his recipe for "Arroz a la Cubana," white rice topped by a fried egg and a ripe banana sautéed in butter with sugar. I still delight our son and grandchildren with this recipe many years later. The chef was a learned, world-traveled man, who was convinced of a relationship between Hungarian and the language of the Yaganes, an extinct tribe from Tierra del Fuego. Although I was not a linguist, he showed me a draft of his bilingual dictionary, and even I could see that some similarities were remarkable. He assumed that the Yaganes had migrated from Asia across the Bering Strait to finally settle at the tip of Patagonia. Meier-Baçi died a few years after my stay in Gesell. Although we kept in touch, I never learned the outcome of his fascinating dictionary. But I was inspired to learn more about the Yaganes in a remarkable historical book, Uttermost Part of the

Earth by Lucas Bridges, an Englishman whose father had founded the town of Ushuaia. By a strange coincidence, my parents are buried in Buenos Aires in a Jewish corner of the British cemetery, within a few feet of Lucas Bridge's grave.

Early one evening I accompanied Werner through the sandy streets of Gesell to deliver his photos in town. Suddenly, a tiny yellow sports car came speeding toward us, whipping up a whirlwind of sand and dust against the approaching sunset. It turned a corner at high speed and slid sideways before coming to a screeching halt in front of us. It was a convertible of a kind I had never seen before. The door opened, and a tall, aristocratic gentleman in his sixties got out waving wildly, before coming forward to greet us with an outstretched arm and a genial smile.

"Werner! Wie geht's? So nice to see you again after a whole year. I just arrived from BA to join my family."

"Hello, Baron Thyssen! A pleasure to see you too. Let me introduce my friend, our lifeguard Arghmando. I am still struggling as a beach photographer—not many planes to fly around here. But I could try flying your beautiful little car instead."

"So, you like my Karman Ghia? It's the only one in the country! My friends at customs gave me a hand at importing it.

After Thyssen left in another huge cloud of dust, Werner explained that he was an aristocrat and a very powerful industrialist whose family still owned one of the largest steel factories in Germany. With the Krupp family, they had supplied Hitler with steel for tanks and weapons during the war and had been essential to his military efforts. Then, as if guessing my thoughts, Werner added he was not sure whether Thyssen himself had been a Nazi, although he had certainly contributed to their military might. Now he had a vacation home in Argentina and possibly did business with the government.

The next morning on the beach, I saw a stern-looking Baron Thyssen approaching me. He requested (or rather demanded) that I place his wife's beach umbrella away from the rest of the tourists, very near the water where the sand was already wet. It crossed my mind to refuse, but I quickly realized that it would have been futile. The man was determined and used to being in charge. I would gain nothing if he went to my boss to complain. And to add to my surprise, he entrusted me with bodyguard duties for his five-year-old daughter and her friend.

"Mr. Armando, this little one is my daughter," he said, pointing to a cute girl in a pink swimsuit, "and I want you to watch over her at all times, especially if she goes near the water to play. Keep an eye also on her companion but consider my daughter's safety your most important duty for several weeks."

I later described the incident to Meier-Baçi, who had survived persecution in Europe, and with his longer life experience and intuition, could tell the Nazis from the decent Germans in the crowd. He felt that Thyssen was authoritarian and powerful because of his aristocratic background, but probably neither anti-Semitic nor a criminal. On one occasion, the chef came into the dining room to greet the baron and his wife and then prepared a special dessert for them. This diminished my doubts about Thyssen and his notorious war activities.

Interacting with the customers gave me an opportunity to meet other well-educated Germans and Europeans, and sometimes even make friends with them. This balanced out my acquaintance with others I suspected were Nazis. One lazy afternoon I was reclining in the sand under a beach umbrella to study for my exams at the end of summer. The ocean breeze was invigorating, making it easy to concentrate. Most of the tourists had left for their siesta and I was unaware I was whistling some classical music very loudly. Then, out of the blue came Gunther, a German Jew who had survived the war and migrated to Argentina with his family. He interrupted my reading with a jovial but pedantic complaint:

"Armando, excuse me, but you're driving me crazy! Could you whistle just one tune? In the last five minutes you gone through Beethoven's Fifth Symphony, the second movement of Mozart's Violin Concerto No.5, Bach's Brandenburg Concerto No. 2, and lastly to Liszt's second Hungarian Rhapsody. Please make up your mind!"

The German government was compensating Gunther for the loss of his textile factory in Frankfurt during the war. Like other German Jews, he was extremely patriotic, willing to defend all things German (except the Nazis), and nostalgic for the old country and its way of life. I had heard that Russian and Polish exiles resented this attitude and nicknamed German Jews as "yekes," a disparaging term in Yiddish. Gunther liked me because we both had a taste for classical music, and because I was working summers to help pay for my education. During one weekend break, Gunther and his family gave me a ride to Buenos Aires to see my parents. On the way back, Gunther, who had come from a drinks party, stopped the car in the middle of nowhere and fainted on the side of the road. My early medical studies were merely theoretical and so far useless when it actually came to providing care for anyone. Fortunately, a passing eighteen-wheeler stopped to help and ended up taking Gunther and his wife to a clinic in the nearest provincial town. Although I did not have a driver's license, nonetheless I had to drive the children on the dark dirt road back to Gesell—fortunately, the family Opel was an automatic. The family was grateful, of course, and later invited me to a home-cooked dinner, where it became clear how different we were. I did not speak their language or understand their customs. We never met again after their vacation was over.

Some of my acquaintances with other Germans in Gesell did not end any better. Another gentleman, who liked reading in the afternoon shade and used to chat with me, once surprised me by suggesting I take his daughter to a dance. She was a very attractive multilingual secretary who worked at the Dutch embassy but did not really know anyone in town. I could not believe my luck when I got to walk her to a nightclub, where I knew the band. We made quite the entrance. However, I only managed to get in a couple of dances with her. She became rapidly attached to the guitar player, a good-looking Frenchman, and I never got the chance to walk her back to her chalet.

When I told Meier-Baçi about my romantic tribulations, he listened sympathetically and promised to introduce me to other women regulars at the restaurant. But then, chance intervened, and I met a svelte Austrian athlete named Monika. The problem was, Monika behaved oddly, sulking under her beach canopy and refusing the usual invitations to play volleyball or swim with the other young tourists. As the beach attendant, I had a good excuse to engage her in conversation and, based on my regular readings of Freud's *The Psychopathology of Everyday Life*, I came up with the following diagnosis: Monika was depressed. Luckily, I persuaded her to follow me after dark to admire the noctilucas, a spectacle known only to a select few in town. You could observe the phosphorescence in two ways: by watching the sea sparkle on the breaking waves, or by scraping the wet sand with your sneakers. This magic light show delighted her and made her more willing to accept my company. Her mood continued to improve, which confirmed my hunch that a broken heart was the cause of her depression. Her family was grateful for my psychoanalytic contribution, and her uncle even loaned me his expensive fishing gear. Sadly, I never caught any fish since I managed to lose the line, weight, and lure at the first throw, and had to return the gear in shame to its owner.

My friendship with Monika continued to grow after we had returned to the capital, when Monika invited me to the German Club of Villa Ballester, a suburb of Buenos Aires. This town had such large German population that the Bundestag included their Argentine Hölter Schule as an official German school. Accepting her invitation to the club turned out to be a bad idea.

* * *

Despite this unpleasant incident, my experience in Gesell was an enriching one. My encounters with some of these characters impacted me in ways I could not have foreseen as a youth. For instance, when Baron Thyssen's family was returning to the capital at the end of the season, he wished me good luck on my medical studies and thanked me for watching over his little daughter. He also revealed his admiration for my work ethic, since I reminded him of his son in Germany, a medical student working summers to supplement his income! With great ceremony, he made a little bow, and presented me with a white envelope, which I opened only after he had left. The large sum inside left me open-mouthed: it would be sufficient for buying all of the textbooks I needed, and a navy blue (synthetic fabric) suit, which I wore with pride all the way to my graduation. Now, already retired from a medical career in another country, whenever I ride a "Thyssen-Krupp" elevator, I remember that historical episode and break into a smile.

When Werner showed me how to use his precious historical camera, little did we know that one distant day I would fulfill my dream of owning a Leica. In 1981 I went to a medical conference in Israel to report on my research. At the time, I was using an inexpensive Japanese SLR camera. After the meeting, I had a unique opportunity to go flying at low altitude to photograph the Jerusalem's Temple Mount, in restricted military airspace. The pilot, who had been a young man during the Second World War, was my mother's cousin, and an Israeli war hero. He tilted the plane to let me photograph the geographical center where the three monotheistic religions share their most sacred monuments. I was so excited that I could not stop shooting until I run out of film and we went back to town.

When I had the slides developed back home in Seattle, the result was catastrophic! Every image was either overexposed or out of focus. I was so disappointed that I grabbed the camera by its strap, circled it faster and faster over my head, and screaming my head off, I threw it in a perfect arc into Lake Washington in Seattle. It may still be home to innocent small fish. That same day I made a decision I never regretted: I bought a rangefinder Leica, a mechanical marvel that has never failed me. It has accompanied me on many trips, including a recent one to Myanmar. There I had the special opportunity of photographing the Rohinga, a Muslim group currently persecuted by the Buddhist majority. The images are collected in my book "Burmese Impressions," which would have impressed Werner, my photography tutor.

The experience with Meier-Baçi, my mentor during the Gesell years, came full circle when a young barista at my regular coffee shop came to chat as I was writing this story. A young Korean woman with huge prescription glasses and an engaging smile, she had observed me writing by hand with an elegant fountain pen while everyone else was typing on a computer or a phone.

"I'm Katherine. I would like to ask about your writing, what you write about, and so on. Can I hang out with you?"

"Sure, anytime, but why?"

"Because you must have many stories to tell, and I have no stories. I'm just a barista here and nothing happens to me. Can I join you for coffee next time?"

Since that surprising day, Katherine and I have met a few times to talk about our lives and experience. I have listened to her dreams and her projects for the future. She has now heard about "Swimming with Nazis in Argentina" and my other stories. This has brought home to me who I am: a silver-haired man with a mustache, a tweedy professor who writes in coffee shops with a fountain pen, and who has unexpectedly become a mentor to a bright young person. This more than rewarding relationship is also a shocking role reversal for the person I used to be when Meier-Baçi was my friend. Perhaps the story will repeat itself when Katherine, by then a gray-haired Korean lady, mentors an enthusiastic young person with a similar interest. I hope she will then remember with kindness, with pleasure and gratitude her interaction with Armando-Baçi.

The Taxi Ride from Hell

I had been exploring the ubiquitous book-stores all day and was exhausted. I dragged my feet toward the Café la Biela in Recoleta, looking for a taxi ride home. Deciding which taxi to climb into always makes me anxious, especially in a crowded and complicated city like Buenos Aires. This time, I took the third car in line, because I liked the driver's look: he was a solid criollo with short hair and a well-shaved face that inspired trust. As I opened the door and got into the cab, he studied me carefully, as if judging whether I, in turn, was an acceptable passenger. I had the fleeting premonition that this would be a very unusual taxi ride.

I asked him to take me down Avenida Luis María Campos to Belgrano, and he sped off, without giving me a second look or saying a word. When we stopped at the next traffic light and I looked to my right, toward the east, I was immediately alarmed at the sight of ominous dark clouds over the Río de la Plata. What could explain this sudden change in weather, when bright sunshine was still beaming down on the taxi? Then I noticed a passenger plane flying low under the clouds on its final approach to the airport. I thought about my upcoming return trip to the USA and worried about the possibility of heavy turbulence, actually feeling vertigo even though my flight was a long way off.

"Driver, can you tell me what the weather forecast is for today?" I asked anxiously.

"I haven't listened to the weather report since yesterday morning. I just couldn't!" he answered rudely, without even glancing at me through his rearview mirror. By now I had already classified him as uneducated and resentful, and I was also sure that he was lying. Taxi drivers spend hours in the car listening continuously to the radio, and the weather report is repeated on the hour (although it was true that his radio was turned off). Besides, drivers tend to be the best informed about what's happening in the city (and even in the rest of the world). So I insisted: "Excuse me, how come you don't listen to the forecast like other drivers do? Don't you care to know about possible traffic jams if it rains or there's a storm?"

"Look, maestro!" he said loudly and obviously upset—though I loved it that he called me maestro, an Argentine expression I had not heard for a long time. But that was not enough to make me forget his behavior. "I listen every day to the seven AM news and the weather report. But yesterday morning I was robbed and nearly killed! I haven't recovered yet. I haven't worked since I was assaulted, and today I could barely get up. I left home very late without hearing the news." His explanation instantly mollified me and made me ashamed to have spoken without knowing the full story. Why had I assumed he was disrespectful or rude just because he didn't want to tell me the forecast? But I recovered swiftly, expressed my sympathy for his ordeal, and voiced my relief that he was not hurt.

"What do you mean, not hurt!" he shouted. With no further comment, he took off as if hotly pursued by aliens, running the red light at the corner with Pueyrredón Avenue, putting the pedal to the metal for another hundred yards, and then suddenly hitting the brakes at the curb. Then he turned sideways to look at me, with an expression that was wild and sad at the same time, before pulling up his sweater and white shirt to show me the side of his chest. He had a horrible knife cut that was almost black at the entry point and ran down and forward for four inches, parallel to the ribs. The whole area was reddened and inflamed, and I recognized the start of a serious infection.

"I'm sorry, I didn't know about the attack! It must have been terrible. I know how you must feel. Fortunately, the knife must have slid along a rib without perforating your lung. Still, it would be better if you went to see a doctor to clean the wound and prescribe some antibiotics. It looks infected, you know. Tell me how it happened."

"I had barely started my shift, just after 6:30 AM, when I picked up a young couple who asked me to take them downtown. From the start, I thought they looked like junkies. You know the type? Skinny, pale, and a little smelly. A few minutes later the guy told me to stop on a side street, and right there the woman pulled a knife from her purse and stabbed me in the side of my chest! I tried to open the door and run away, but the guy put a pistol to my head and shouted:

"'Where do you think you're going, motherfucker? You're not getting out of here before you give us all the dough you collected last night. Give it to me right now or I'll blow your brains out!'

"I told him I had just eighty pesos because this was my first shift, but he did not believe me. He looked at me with hatred, and then he pulled the trigger anyway. It was a miracle the pistol did not go off! I think maybe his weapon wasn't loaded or maybe it just misfired. My eyes went cloudy, and I thought I was going to faint.

"The two of them then started arguing about what to do next. I was paralyzed with fear and couldn't move. Finally, the man took the knife from the woman, put it up against my neck, and ordered me to head for La Cava, the shantytown in San Isidro. I managed to restart the car and drove in that direction like they told me to. I guess you never heard of La Cava? It's one of the worst, a pit from Hell, where they survive by holding people up at gunpoint and selling drugs. When we got there, the woman made me stop and got out for a short time, while the man kept watching me with the knife at my neck. She came back empty handed because she didn't have enough money on her to make a deal. Afterwards, they forced me to drive back towards town and made me stop when we crossed the General Paz limit, where people on their way to work were waiting for colectivo mini-buses. Finally, the two got out of the car and quickly lost themselves in the crowd. I still can't believe they didn't kill me, and I'm alive to tell you the story now."

"It's amazing that you got away with just the knife wound. It's like a horror movie! But I can tell you your story reminds me of something that happened to me when I was a young trainee medical student at the emergency room in San Isidro. I know La Cava, same as you. One night late, we got a call to go pay a sick woman there a home visit. We parked the ambulance right outside the slum. The area was a giant pit in the mud, fifteen or twenty feet below ground, going for several uneven blocks, with makeshift houses of zinc and recycled cardboard barely standing up after the rains. The ambulance driver got out and told me to follow him. He slipped a revolver into his belt, just in case, because he knew the place quite well and didn't trust anyone to respect even the doctors they had called for help. After just a few feet of walking in the dark and slipping in the mud, someone suddenly started to shoot—the bullets went whistling passed us like in the movies! We couldn't tell if the shots were meant for us or someone else, but we sprinted back towards the ambulance, before the driver had a chance to respond with some shots of his own, since we could not see worth a damn. So, we both have had a great scare near La Cava. But your story is much more dramatic, and it happened just yesterday. I know how you must feel."

"Okay, boss. I guess you must know how life goes sometimes. Now, I better take you to Belgrano, where you wanted to go."

We continued riding in silence for a few minutes. Maybe he had calmed down a bit by the time we passed the central circle in Palermo, which was overflowing with magnificent jacaranda trees in bloom. The profusion of purple was surreal. It reminded me of other places where jacarandas are plentiful, like the Tigre delta where we used to go rowing, and I hoped the beauty of the trees would make him forget his horrible experience.

"I don't know what I'm going to do once I get back home!" the driver said, out of the blue, as if he had never even noticed the jacarandas.

" Do you have a family or friends to help you while you recover?

"I got to tell you, man! My wife left me a couple of weeks ago. I think she's living with a younger guy who works in the same factory." When I looked at him again I thought his criollo features were more intense than at the start of the trip. The hair on the back of his neck seemed blacker and sticking up a little, as he told his life story with a combination of fury and regret. I was becoming more pessimistic about the ride at every turn of the road. Better not to ask him any more indiscreet questions, especially during my vacation.

"I still have my two children," he continued in a lugubrious tone. "The girl is now grown up and left home almost a year ago. I never talk to her on the phone but should do that soon, before she forgets who I am. The boy is fifteen and living with me. When I got home after the robbery, the first thing I did was call my wife at the factory to ask her to come and help me. She answered the phone but told me she didn't believe a word I said, that I was calling so she would pity me, and right there she hung up, without saying goodbye. I don't get it! She knows that I never lie, that I am a hard worker, that I break my back to support them, ever since the day we left Formosa and I found this job as a driver in the city. I swear to you I never drink much, but at that moment I didn't know what to do, so I looked around the house and found a bottle of sugar cane liquor and gulped the whole thing down. I think I fell unconscious on the staircase, where my son found me lying when he came back from school. He helped me get up and cleaned my wound with alcohol, but I think it's infected anyway."

"This Formosan man is definitely going to ruin my whole day," I thought, "when all I wanted was a quiet trip back home. I better not ask him anything else!" I speculated he'd taken me for a priest and decided to confess, or maybe for his own doctor, now that he knew a little about my background. Why had I told him the story about La Cava? Maybe he found me receptive because of my age, my graying hair, my grandfatherly attitude. His story was giving me heartburn, palpitations, and a galloping anxiety. It was like that film by Jim Jarmusch, Life on Earth. I loved the episode with Roberto Benigni as the manic, talkative driver, whose passenger one night is a bishop. The Benigni character takes the opportunity to confess and tells the bishop a wild story involving bestiality with a lamb, and his other sins too, while the taxi races ever faster through the narrow streets of Rome. The passenger cannot take this aberrant story any longer and finally dies of a heart attack in the back seat.

I hoped not to have a copycat heart attack myself while my relentless driver continued describing his personal odyssey!

Fortunately, something happened that stopped my reflections. As the taxi turned a corner towards Cabildo, we found the street blocked by a mass of screaming picketers. They were furious factory workers who had heard the news that their factory was closing. Some of the workers had now occupied the building, while the demonstrators had blocked the traffic. The police, as usual, seemed to be doing nothing to prevent the mess. I knew we could be stuck here for hours, unable to move in any direction. Would the driver keep on hammering at me with his horror story? I had to do something about this. So I challenged his professionalism:

"Let's see, driver, what can you do to get us out of this mess? I cannot stay here all day!"

He looked at me angrily, but at the same time I noticed a hint of something like professional pride in his coal-dark eyes. Right then and there he lowered the window and pulled a white handkerchief from his pocket, which he then waved wildly out the window. He moved the taxi a few yards, only to stop in front of a yeti who was wearing a muscle shirt with the slogan "Chief of Picket Security" and wielding an iron bar.

"Come on, man, make way!" my driver shouted. "I'm taking this guy to the hospital. I think he's having a heart attack! Hurry up, damn it, he's not doing well at all!" He looked back at me and whispered urgently, "Look like you're dead, man, so maybe they'll let us out of here," and to be a good sport, I followed his orders and closed my eyes, clutching at my chest with both hands in a melodramatic display, Miraculously, the "chief of security" started to shout at the workers while swinging the iron bar over his head and managed to open up a path through the crowd like Moses parting the Red Sea. And so we escaped the riot with unprecedented speed. Who would have thought that this Formosan—at the end of his rope, clinically depressed, on the verge of suicide—would be capable of such a great feat?

Two blocks later I recovered my breath and cardiac health, and it occurred to me that both of us were in need of some sustenance and a stiff drink. Why not reward his deed with an espresso? Or, even better, a glass of wine? Although totally out of character for me, I invited him to stop for a minute at the nearest café bar. I told him not to worry about the meter, which he could leave running, and I would pay the difference upon arrival. As surprised as I was by my gesture, he allowed a shadow of a smile to cross his lips before stopping the car at the next corner café.

It was just a neighborhood joint, with billiard tables at one end and three drunken seniors sitting at a table closest to the bar. They were in a heated discussion about a goal Messi had made that had just played on TV. We sat down, and I asked the waiter for two glasses of red wine. The driver and I toasted our good health, clinking our glasses, downing the wine in great haste, and then letting out sighs of relief. The driver soon restarted his monologue, as I feared he would, although I hoped the wine would help him calm down. He said he had no idea how to repair his relationship with his children now that their mother was gone. He felt proud that the boy had helped him to dress his wound and was obviously worried about him after the robbery!

A few minutes later, the waiter arrived with the bill and I paid him in one-peso coins.

Unfortunately, I dropped one of the coins, which went rolling over the floor towards the drunken neighbors before disappearing under their table. When I went to look for it, I could not find it anywhere. Then, one of the rowdy fellows pointed his finger under the table and said loudly: "Acá estaaá, Acá estaaá" ("He-e-ere it is"). When I went over to pick it up, he put me totally to shame by singing the last stanza of the "National Flag" song, which we had all learned indelibly as children: "Acá estaaá la bandera idolatrada!" ("Here it is, the idolized flag...") His friends cracked themselves up at that, confirming that mocking others was a national sport.

Then the Formosan stood up before the group of winos, sticking out his chest and chin like a drill sergeant about to shout at some new recruits, and began scolding them for the bad joke.

"Stop bugging the man, you idiots! He never bothered you, and besides he is my client and nobody is going to touch him!" So, everybody went quiet, but I left the coin where it was and we discreetly returned to our table.

By now, I was starting to like the driver, who was a proud guy and a hard worker with a multitude of unexpected resources. He had put his imagination to excellent use when he got us past the workers' picket line. And how protective he had been in front of this drunken group! When would I learn not to judge others based on their appearance or the way they talked? I had been proven wrong before, like the time in Mexico in 1982 when a taxi driver taught me an unforgettable lesson on a ride back to my hotel. The driver seemed a little suspect, with his long, unkempt hair, a three-day beard, and what I felt was an unfriendly expression. He was driving uphill into the very steep, hilly streets of the old town, which was not the most direct route to my hotel. Letting my imagination run away with me, I was afraid of being robbed or kidnapped. However, the driver soon surprised me with his eloquence. Realizing I was from Argentina because I spoke like the actors on the soap operas he watched every Sunday on TV, he went on to discuss the Malvinas War and his views of how wars started. I was very ignorant about the subject, but he explained that the First World War began in 1914 when a Yugoslavian nationalist assassinated the Archduke Ferdinand of Austria, setting off a chain reaction in which millions of innocents died. It turned out the driver had been professor of history at the University in Guadalajara but had lost his job during the economic crisis and had come down to Vallarta to find another job. After he finished his lecture, he deposited me safely at my hotel. In reality, the man I had presumed to be robber or kidnapper was instead well educated, honest, and much better informed than I was. Now I could see that the conflicted Formosan also had a good side, which he had demonstrated several times since the beginning of our ride from hell.

Just when I was about to thank him for his help at the cafe, his mobile phone rang and he walked away towards the door, where I couldn't hear what he was saying. He returned a few minutes later, once again with his head bowed and his tail between his legs.

"Look, chief, we'd better get back to the cab and I'll take you home, because I need to go and take care of my family. That was my sister on the phone, calling from Formosa to give me some bad news about our father. She said he's had a stroke, is now in a coma, and they don't think he will live for long. Let's get going!"

I wasted no time rushing out to the cab, because the story of this guy's life was getting too hard to bear. Luckily, we were only a few minutes from my apartment. How was this man going to overcome all the blows that happened to him in such a short time? His misfortunes made me think of the French black comedy, L'Emmerdeur, in which innumerable mishaps happen to the main protagonist. But what could I do to help this guy stay sane (at least for the next few minutes until I got home) and not end up like in the movie? I decided I had to do something to help him out, or else we'd never make it to our destination. Maybe I could say something positive about his family?

"The news about your father is very sad, but hopefully, it won't be as serious as they say," I started, trying to inject a small dose of optimism. "And what you said about your son is very encouraging. He seems to be a great boy and very supportive of you. Have you thought about taking him to the soccer game this Sunday and spending some quality time together? Maybe after the game you could go to a pizzeria." As I threw out these suggestions, I forgot I was not supposed to get involved in his life. "I think it would be wise to take advantage of all that you have now, a couple of fabulous children, and be with them as much as possible." He looked at me a little surprised but didn't say anything and kept on driving. At that very moment, I noticed the sky had turned an impenetrable leaden gray and fat drops had started to rattle down on the car's roof like a machine gun. The rain was torrential by the time we arrived at my place, and I asked him to stop close to the front door. I managed to pay him what was on the meter and say farewell with a strong handshake and just a few words to wish him luck with everything, before I jumped out resolutely into the deluge.

I sighed deeply as I entered the apartment, as if asking for asylum in a church. I think it took me several days to recover from my experience. Yet I couldn't stop thinking about the Formosan driver, and I felt sorry I would never get to know the outcome of all his problems—whether he survived the knife wound, whether his wife returned home or left him for good. Above all, I was curious as to whether he was able to have a better relationship with his children.

About ten days later, the doorman rang the bell to deliver a white envelope with an inscription: To the doctor with the gray hair who lives in the USA. He had assumed it was for me, the only resident who fit that description. I opened it with curiosity and a little fear. I could not bear the thought that it might be from the driver, telling me about yet another tragedy. I found a short note inside, written in very proper handwriting in blue ink, on lined paper like you find in secondary school notebooks. It read:

Dear Doctor:

I'm sorry that I don't know your name, because we never introduced ourselves. But I'm sure the doorman will find you and give you this message.

I wanted to tell you that I ended up in the hospital for a couple of days, because the knife wound was badly infected. I was lucky and I got better, especially when the children came to keep me company and I was able to get home sooner. Just like you suggested, last Sunday I took my boy to the soccer match, and after the game we met up with his sister to go eat pizza together. It was the first time we had done anything like this, and they were happy. They didn't know how to thank me.

My father did not recover from the stroke and died before I could go north to see him. Now my sister, who has a furniture factory, decided she will help me and I can return to Formosa to work with her. The children said they also want to come and stay up there for a time, to see if they like life in the province more than in this lousy city.

Sincerely yours,

Facundo (your taxi driver from the other day)

The Parallel Death of Don Quijote

Don Quijote died at 1300 hours on the last Monday in September 1981. The forensic report concluded (unconvincingly) that a myocardial infarction had been the cause of death. But the coroner's trembling handwriting, and the text that had drifted inexorably towards the bottom of the page, revealed his painful internal struggle. He was unable to declare that the death had been due to a supernatural event. The diagnosis would be unacceptable on a death certificate.

Now I find myself searching for the critical factor that catapulted Don Quijote across the centuries to the small table by the lake where Emile and I had been having lunch. I could suggest the heat that befuddled us and the sunlight that blinded us—both unprecedented in autumn in the Pacific Northwest—were the two tangible elements that connected Seattle and La Mancha. But I prefer the idea that Emile and Don Quijote's obsession with chivalry and literature united them at that instant of total receptiveness that must arrive with death.

At first I attributed Emile's uncharacteristic emotional outburst to the bottle of Muscadet we had polished off in a familiar ritual between old friends. I was accustomed to his neurotic distractedness, and his mood swings. But during the meal his voice took on an unusual gravity, he became despondent, and I was alarmed by the depth and duration of his near trance, that seemed to last forever. Eventually, when he finally responded to my prompting, I was struck by how noticeable his foreign accent had become—he usually tried to conceal this, especially when speaking as one professional to another—and I realized that this sudden lack of pretension was a transparent symptom of distress. In response to my questions about how he was feeling, he uttered something incomprehensible:

"My life has changed so much in the last few weeks, and especially in the last few hours, that my feelings are no longer rational. Maybe the combination of the letters in my name can explain my distress. What do you think?"

"Emile, that's ridiculous! Are you suggesting that numerology and the Kabbalah will explain your despair? I think that a permutation of those letters is more likely to reveal the secret name of God or produce a golem."

"No, no, I believe that the name my father gave me predicted my adult personality. Like him, I had a classical education and suffered from a relentless romanticism. I believe he named me Emile in the magical expectation that his offspring, like Rousseau's creation, would embody the original goodness of man and be able to resist society's negative influences. Now it's clear that his intention failed! My reaction to Nathania's behavior shows that I remain naïve, forever an adolescent who's unable to cope with reality and falls deeper and deeper into the realm of dreams, where every one of our acts is a fiction."

"Stop there, Emile! I need to know the facts to be able to help you, or at least to be sympathetic to your plight. To begin with: I've never heard of this Nathania. Who is she?"

In the conversation that followed, Emile displayed undisguised emotion, which I found disturbing and unexpected since we were old friends, and usually cool-headed medical researchers. I confess I became more attentive to his body language and increasingly bizarre facial expressions than his narrative.

"I met Nathania only recently," he finally told me. "It was the first serious relationship I had since my wife left me seven years ago. She's a young, articulate woman, whose wisdom reminds me of the ancient oracle at Delphi. I find her poise and the dramatic impact of her beauty deeply disturbing. Her dark blue eyes, long brown hair, and intense demeanor are irresistible. I've never met anyone like her. Unlike the two of us, who toy with technology and science, she is an artist who's totally committed to her passions. Her poems have an obsessive rhythm that feels strangely synchronous with my own heartbeat."

He interrupted himself with a nervous, dry cough, and his breathing became uneven and labored, as if he were having an asthmatic attack.

"Our interaction was intense but of short duration, a mere few weeks, although we met frequently." Why was he using the past tense? Was their surprising relationship already over? "Sometimes we would go for a swim, or ride horses on the beach, cook mussels over a wood fire, and then sit under a tarp giggling like adolescents in a private forest. One night I brought her roses and a marvelous recording of Perlman performing a Brahms sonata, which we played on our CD player again and again. I was fascinated by the extreme contrast between the simplicity and joy of our meetings and the depth and drama of her poetry. Of course, sometimes we made love. To my delight I found her spirited, knowledgeable, and charged with imagination. She made allowances for my indecision, tentative behavior, and above all, inexperience. But her response to my orthodox lovemaking was lukewarm, and I suspected her pleasure never equaled mine."

"Emile, I cannot tell what's fact or imagination. Are you again letting your romanticism get the better of you?"

"You are right. My romantic nature imagined Nathania as an archetype, a composite of symbols and images that fundamentally define a woman for me. Soon my life became a struggle to satisfy my dreams of permanence and the illusion that I possessed her. Until last night, when I was shocked to discover that my liaison with Nathania was only possible in the world of fiction. I now know that... to remain together... forever, I must become a hero in the same literary universe as hers."

Emile paused, trying to fill his lungs with air. His speech had become more dysarthric as he grimaced and brought a clenched fist to his precordium. I could not refrain from estimating his probable blood pressure and heart rate. He seemed also to have become thinner and taller. How could that be possible? Unable to explain my impressions, I urged him to continue with his story.

"Last week we came across a dusty volume by Cervantes in a secondhand bookstore. When we examined the book back home, some of the narrative was unfamiliar, and appeared to be apocryphal, which excited our interest. Nathania seemed enraptured by one particular legend. Jealous of her fascination with the story, and feeling left out, I tried to caress and seduce her instead. But she rejected my attempts and threw herself back into her reading. I envied Cervantes's power to captivate her and resigned myself to our reading the story together throughout the night."

Emile looked sadder, slowing his discourse even further. Yet he sat more erect in his chair with his left hand clenched more tightly on his chest and began to tremble. His right hand, though, raised itself as though clasping a lance, which he then appeared to lift and shake vigorously. Although he himself seemed unaware of his movements, they alarmed a small dog seated under a woman's chair at a nearby table. It started to bark furiously at Emile, who turned his head and responded with this cryptic, soft-spoken sentence: "Let him bark. It's a sign it knows I'm on my way..."

I let the comment pass, trying to be practical, and instead inquired, "What was the subject that kept you both immersed in reading for hours? Why did it have such an effect on you?"

"It was about Don Quijote, a tireless reader of tales of chivalry, who was still living as a knight in armor at a time when all chivalry had ended in Spain. In this story, Don Quijote is befriended by one Mansour-al-Caliph, a Moor he once saved from drowning in a river. For nights on end the hero and the Moor play chess, savor liquors and sweets, and Don Quijote confides in the Moor about a recurrent dream: he envisions himself loved by a marvelous woman just before a battle that may be his last. Moved by his new friend's loneliness, Mansour offers his favorite slave, a Jewess of rare beauty and talents, to the hero for seven nights."

Emile's voice cracked and he paused again. The intense backlight from the lake surface prevented me from closely observing his face, but I noticed with dismay the streaming tears that refracted the sunlight, spreading it randomly over the tablecloth.

"When Don Quijote meets Nathania," Emile resumed, "she's draped dramatically in black veils, and he is paralyzed by her beauty." Did he say: Nathania? How could he not point out the name's coincidence? "She dances for him near a window that frames the bleak plains of La Mancha in the moonlight. His eyes tear uncontrollably as she plays the lute. She sings eloquently of the hero's prowess in war and of her gratitude for his saving the Moor's life. Don Quijote senses with implacable certainty that Nathania is the first woman to understand his chivalry, his soul, his life's philosophy. For six nights he lavishes her with gems, perfumes, and ancient books, the most precious of his belongings. On the seventh night, Nathania allows him to possess her body. He caresses the slave with inexperienced but tender moves. The revelation of physical love erases all sense of time, and he remains oblivious to the fact that the insane, dream-like week with Nathania has now reached its inevitable conclusion. The following night, consumed by an unbearable fire, and by the will to liberate Nathania from her master, he forcibly enters the slave's quarters..."

At this point Emile sighed deeply and once again broke off his tale in what seemed an interminable pause.

"Last night I returned unannounced to Nathania's home, eager to see her. I let myself in with the key she had given me, and quietly walked through the kitchen to her room. When I opened the door, I immediately saw the case from the Brahms

CD on the floor, lying in a puddle of coffee, and heard the brutal beat of metallic rock..."

There was now a tremor in his voice, and his face looked unusually thin and elongated. (No one would doubt the validity of my clinical observation). By now he seemed weather-beaten and wrinkled as though ravaged by extreme old age. I am willing to declare under oath that Emile's features grew longer, becoming blurred. He looked even taller than he had moments ago, and his shoulders drooped as he ended the story:

"And you know, Sancho, I could not see her face, but I found her mounted by the Moor, and I smelled the sweat of their sex, and I understood that her groans expressed the wholeness and the pleasure that she never had with me."

By the time I realized he had called me Sancho, Emile's head had fallen unnaturally to one side and his eyes had closed. The dog at the next table was no longer barking, and the restaurant grew silent, as if the other diners could sense that a tragedy had occurred nearby.

I know his death occurred a long time before the paramedics arrived at the restaurant. All our efforts at resuscitation failed, and they took him to the morgue. A few hours later, when I had partially recovered my composure, I felt strong enough to follow them to the county hospital. Unfortunately, my work shift happened to fall on the day of my friend's death. I would have preferred another coroner to have fulfilled this duty instead. Yet I completed my report and described that a curiously pointed beard had started to grow on his chin. I spent a long time considering what plausible alternatives to list as cause of death: heartbreak, despair, sudden loss of innocence, distorted perception, or even the transmigration of the soul of a literary figure. But I could not include these in my final report without tarnishing my professional reputation.

The Maharajah of Kapurthala

I concede that three passions rule my life: women (in particular), tango dancing, and precious stones. Psychoanalysis therapy made me realize the risk to my career, but I could not change my behavior, and I am still obsessed by the same desires. For instance, during the last incident I almost lost my job as a columnist for a local newspaper, since the editor refused to believe in the veracity of my narrative. He questioned my ethics, and my common sense.

Everything started at the *milonga*[1] 'El Arranque', an ancient theater in the center of Buenos Aires. I noticed her one evening, chatting in earnest with other women during the pause between two *tandas*.[2] Her dark complexion hinted she could be from a northern province. Soon she was dancing with an old geezer, one of many that pullulate in 'El Arranque.' I found her elegant posture, precise steps, and natural musicality, galvanizing. Like other *pescadores*[3], I love to supplement my meager journalist's income by enticing naïve women tourists into taking tango lessons after the milonga. We offer lower fees than accredited teachers who use their own studios.

---

[1] Milonga: a tango dance hall or event.

[2] Tanda: a set of four musical pieces by the same band or style.

[3] Pescadores: A nickname for people-catchers, or fishermen.

Later, I invited her to dance with a *cabeceo*[4], which she accepted with a slight smile. At a momentary chance for conversation, she said she would be in the Capital only for a short season. Her accent was clearly *porteño*[5] but I detected a modulation that was hard to identify. I couldn't help asking her if she spoke other languages.

"I speak English, if you prefer it to Spanish. But why would you? Since you are a porteño yourself," she said with conviction.

"I though you could be from the countryside, maybe from Salta or Tucumán. Am I mistaken?

"Yes, you are, because I was born in India."

"Really? That's fantastic and so uncommon here! Would you mind if we speak informally, and say 'vos,' like we do in the city?"

"I am not used to saying 'vos' and would prefer the more formal speech."

Later, when I managed to invite her again, I began in English—the language I learned from my grandparents—to try and hear better how she spoke.

"Please forgive my curiosity, but your English accent does not seem to be from India."

"I speak like an Australian because I've been in Sidney for many years. As I said, I lived in India

---

[4] Cabeceo: subtle eye signals used at a distance to invite someone to dance.
[5] Porteño: someone born or raised in Buenos Aires, a Port city.

since birth until I started the University."

"India is such a fascinating, but inscrutable country! Where were you born?

"I was born in the Punjab. Now I don't visit it too often, I prefer coming to Argentina to dance the tango and to do business here," she explained, enigmatically.

" My name is Gustavo, but they call me Tavo. And you?"

"My name is too complicated for the Argentines, and here everybody calls me Tia, my middle name."

I suddenly became aware she wore a marvelous ring on her right hand, mounted with a gigantic ruby.

"Congratulations for your good taste! Very few women wear a ring like yours, with a perfectly red ruby, maybe as heavy as half a carat."

"That's correct. You must be a connoisseur! I am a jewel importer, but I would prefer to keep this confidential. Better yet, let's keep dancing," she said impatiently.

By then, my tempestuous mind was building imaginary novels about the possibilities of this encounter. Nowadays, many Asians (especially from China or Japan) come to Buenos Aires to live or to dance the tango, but we rarely have people from India. I marveled at my good luck, getting to know this exotic broad, dressed to kill, good dancer, and a jewel's importer, on top! This is what my analyst would recommend for my depression!

"Please don't misunderstand me," I said optimistically, at the end of the song. "Maybe other dancers have tried to invite you out, either to help you perfect your tango (which is excellent, of course), or for personal reasons. But I assure you my case is different. I am a journalist. Your story is tantalizing and I would like to write it for the newspaper. Would you mind joining me for coffee nearby after the milonga?"

"Thank you, but that's not a good idea. I am quite familiar with the excuse of 'drinking coffee', between the *milongueros*[6] like you."

"No, no, I assure you that I intend only to describe the mystery of an Indian woman who is involved in our tango, and who speaks our language so well! Besides, jewels happen to be one of my interests. We could even contemplate some business together. What do you think?" She considered the option for a few seconds, watching me with curiosity, but in the end exhaling a deep sigh, she pronounced herself in an unexpected way:

"Look! I will come with you this time, something I hardly ever do. But don't get too hopeful, I just promise to answer your questions in more detail. However, I'm not interested in coffee. Instead, I'm very hungry after the dance. We should go to 'La Americana' around the corner, like other

---

[6] Milonguero: an inveterate tango dancer, a man of the night.

people after the milonga. I will feel more at ease there. I heard they make an excellent pizza. Do you agree?"

Once at the pizzeria, I was getting psyched up with the situation. Here I was, with this beautiful woman wearing a ring with an impeccable ruby! I could foresee literary, commercial, and romantic consequences for this new relationship. She pondered the menu, but she was familiar with the different pizzas and the diverse fillings in an *empanada!*[7]. She ordered a ham *fugazzetta*[8] and a Quilmes beer, and I felt an immense relief that she was not a vegetarian! For myself, I went for two *empanadas*, one with beef and one with *humita*[9], although I had no appetite in this mouth-watering situation. Talking with her was enough!

"Did you know?" I asked, between bites, "that people here may describe someone who is scandalously rich by saying: 'He thinks he is the Maharajah of Kapurthala', as they imagine a very exotic, faraway place, like from another planet." This comment shook her up and she nearly dropped her beer. She frowned, and I feared having said something inappropriate, but soon she relaxed again and we continued chatting.

---

[7] Empanada: a baked turnover, with optional fillings.
[8] Fugazzetta: An Argentine pizza with caramelized onion and melted cheese.
[9] Humita: a cream of corn filling with nutmeg.

"That's true, I come from a marvelous city of palaces and gardens, with a long history. It used to be a princedom in Northern India, but it lost importance after Independence. My parents took me to Australia when I was young. There I grew up, and married my present husband, an orthodox Jew from Sydney, but I remained faithful to my Sikh religion. I also went to the University and studied in a gemology school, which is my specialty."

When she mentioned gemology, my admiration went ballistic and ascended into the stratosphere! I have been mesmerized by precious stones ever since childhood, when my uncle Sigismund—who is a jeweler and an importer—taught me how to tell them apart. As we talked, her ring glittered with red wine-colored reflections of the pizzeria's lights, which somehow seemed inappropriate in this down–to-Earth venue.

"Isn't it a great coincidence that jewels have enchanted me since childhood? We will have much to talk about. But first, tell me how you became interested in tango, which must not be very popular in your country."

"Actually, I learned this music early in India from my father, who used to dance it well with a *canyengue*[10] style, when he was young. Sadly, he suffered a long illness, and died of an infection."

---

[10] Canyengue: An early style, typical of the suburban or marginal slums.

"So sorry to hear it! But, how did your father himself learn to dance tango in India? That blows me away!"

"This must stay between us. It would be better if you do not publish any of this. If you do, you will need to disguise people's names and the cities where it happened. Can I count on your good judgment and tact?"

"Of course, I promise you my most absolute discretion!"

"In this case, I will tell you how close you were to the truth a moment ago. It so happens that my father was the real Maharaja of Kapurthala!"

"That is amazing! Then, you are a true princess!

"Exactly, my name is Navpreet Tia. It means 'new love' and 'princess' in the Sikh language. My father was extremely rich, cultivated, and had multiple interests and a great curiosity. He had watched tango in the movies of Rodolfo Valentino, and later in Europe in the ones by Gardel, which made him want to learn how to dance it. He traveled extensively in India, and one day he made friends with some sailors from an Argentine freighter at a bar in Bombay Harbor, and they taught him the first tango steps. From then on, this dance became his obsession, and the contact with these people must have influenced his life, and possibly had an effect on his health."

At this moment, fleeting whirlpools of uncertainty were gyrating through my mind. Her story was fantastic and questionable, like Scheherazade narrating to the Persian King. Of course, my unbounded romanticism can counteract any aspect of reality, and this woman exhibited all the conditions to make me suspend my disbelief. It crossed my mind she was concocting a great hoax, but this vision was antagonized by more powerful ones of the old Maharajah cavorting in dark dives in Bombay Harbor, impenetrable with thick cigarette smoke, while dancing with Argentine sailors from the antipodes. Would he have paid them for their lessons, or was it just a cultural exchange? Did they know he was a magnate? Or, did he dress himself in simple clothes to hide his true status? I didn't think it would be prudent to inquire about these issues for the moment.

"I really appreciate all the confidential information you are providing!"

"Tonight it's getting late. Thank you for the delicious pizza! If you agree, we might continue this conversation in a café near Recoleta. We could talk a little about gems, my primary business, since you seem interested in them. So, I will give you a telephone number." With this suggestion, after a formal handshake, we went our separate ways.

For the next several days, my mind alternated at a high frequency between the possibilities of a romantic relationship—even though there were no basis for such an expectation—and the prospect of an import business opportunity in which I could involve my jeweler uncle. With extreme impatience, at the end of a week I phoned, in an example of correctness, to invite her for coffee. She replied quickly, with a businesswoman's attitude, but no signs of romanticism:

"Hi, Gustavo. If you agree, we could meet on Friday around six in the evening at the Café La Biela. Please find a quiet table near the end, because I would like to show you a few things I'm bringing to sell on this trip."

I arrived early to find an appropriate table, near a bright window light, but away from the crowds and tourists in Recoleta. I had in my pocket a compact 10x magnifying glass to examine some of the stones. I was smoking a cigarette when I saw her coming, with a rhythmic walk like on a syncopated tango, with elegance and self-possession. The collective gaze of some customers and waiters traced, with curiosity and transparent admiration, her trajectory as a satellite towards my table.

I stood up to hug her but she greeted me too formally, without the expected tango kisses, which made me lose confidence in my potential as a conqueror of the East Indies. But I quickly recovered and shook hands.

"Hello, Tia. A pleasure seeing you again!"
"Hello, Gustavo. You have a good memory."

"Well, your name is easy to remember."

"Yes, but don't forget that any names are not for publication, in case you do write an article about all this."

"Not to worry, I am well aware of your wishes. I'm happy to see you because I am obsessed with finding a pair of small precious stones at a good price. I would like to mount them on the cap of a Montlanc pen, the 'Agatha Christie' special edition. It has a snake with two little glasses for red eyes, which would look lovely if they were rubies instead."

"Today may be your lucky day! Let me show you what I'm bringing." After looking around to be sure there were no waiters nearby, she pulled from her purse a small, wine-colored velvet bag, which she opened over the table. I was obliged to repress a sigh when confronted with its contents. There were smaller bags inside, each containing one class of different stones, which shined with the luminosity of a kaleidoscope before a tropical sun. I could tell a small emerald, greener than a Brazilian parrot; several rubies of various sizes, and a pair of diamonds that reflected the café light in a surreal rainbow. "Do you think these rubies might be right for your pen cap? They are too small for a ring."

My heart melted at the jewel's sight, precisely what I was searching for. Tia mentioned a price in US dollars that was much less than expected, well within my budget. To be sure, I pulled the loupe from my pocket and confirmed that the rubies had a dramatic clarity; a flat faced cut that enhanced their brilliance, and a few inclusions that magnified their value.

"The rubies are admirable and I believe your price is fitting, but I would love to show them to my uncle who is a jeweler and has a studio nearby, on Ayacucho St. Would you mind coming to meet him for a moment after coffee? This may be the start of a solid commercial relationship."

"I knew you would love them! I brought them from India but they originate in Myanmar, where I have excellent contacts. Certainly, it's a good idea to go meet your uncle and show him the stones."

Of course, uncle Sigismund was marveled just as much by the apparition of an Indian princess in his studio, as by the gem's quality. He immediately advised that I buy the two rubies as a first step, and he produced the dollar payment from his safe.

"If an ongoing commercial relationship is attractive to you, I could propose a more substantial operation. Next month, I'm traveling to Australia and I could make a detour to my hometown in India for a few days, where I have a more extensive stock and excellent prices. If you both care to come along, I can invite you to stay at our family home, and then show you around Kapurthala. The profit from any transactions would largely compensate for your travel expenses."

When she left, my uncle Sigismund announced

that he did not like to fly, but he encouraged me to go instead. He would finance a larger operation, if I had the courage to follow Tia to Kapurthala. We knew we would never find rubies of the same quality and favorable price in our country, and he had enough prosperous clients in the area of '*Barrio Norte*'[11] to ensure the profits would be considerable. Moreover, the prospect of combining business with pleasure in a land of mystery, in the company of the opulent heir of a maharajah, already looked like a fairy tale. And then, there was the enticing history of her daddy with the Argentine sailors! If the family customs and genes had transferred to subsequent generations, this trip might include delightful personal consequences with the *milonguera princess*.

A month later we took off with Tia from Buenos Aires to New Delhi, flying 'Emirates', an airline that I had not known before. I was carrying a double-bottom bag, kindly stitched by my uncle's wife, loaded with 10,000 US $, the maximum allowed by customs. I had estimated triple profits at my return. We proceeded on a shorter flight to Amritsar, another Punjabi town, and finally in a limo with a private driver sent by Tia's family, to Kapurthala. We got in there at night, twenty-four hours later, dead tired, unable to see much in the

---

[11] Barrio Norte: a very affluent, traditional neighborhood of the Capital city.

dark. To my delight, Tia's old family palace was converted into a five-star hotel. I had never expected such a splendid display of riches. With a big smile, she installed me in her late father's bedroom, now called the 'honeymoon suite.' Obviously, the nocturnal habits of the maharajah were incomprehensible for a simple South American man. In spite of my fatigue, it was hard to fall asleep in that marvelous rosewood bed, inlayed with silver, with life-sized statues of nude women in each corner. The butler demonstrated a hidden mechanism that allowed the sculptures to blink their eyes and fan the guests. Disoriented by jet lag, I left the device on all night, and the soothing breeze help me to find my breath in the moist tropical heat.

Next morning I was summoned to breakfast with Tia on a gallery facing the gardens. She ordered good coffee with croissants, and fried eggs for me, but she had other questionable dishes herself, which she advised would be too spicy for a *porteño,* considering my lack of experience with exotic meals. She later offered to take me on a city tour to get my bearings. The first sight she pointed at was a smaller palace on the grounds of their property, the 'Sainir School,' with a striking architecture in the style of Versailles and Fontainebleau. She said she would have loved to study there when young, but they only accepted male students. We went on to visit the 'Shalimar Gardens' (a little run down, in my humble opinion, and less interesting than the

Palermo gardens in Buenos Aires), and then several temples of different religions. I liked most the prestigious 'Jagatjit Club,' built like the Parthenon in Athens. Sponsored by the princess, I was able to play a squash game with one of their instructors, who had no difficulty in destroying me with a score of five to nothing!

On the second day, we met in the hotel library to examine the gems Tia had selected. By then, I had rejected any remaining doubts regarding my new friend's legitimacy. She was who she said she was, and the palace was exactly as she had described during our flight. She conducted herself with poise as a true landlady, well respected by the hotel's staff. At this point, I was ready to conclude our business, and the impatience was chewing me up. My only regret was not detecting any signs of romantic interest on Tia's part. If we had a chance to dance a few good tangos, I could possibly change her mind!

Tia revealed some exceptional rubies of different sizes and spread them over an exquisite velvet fabric. I chose a group of six intensely red stones (maybe the ones called 'pigeon blood'), with impressive clarity, few if any inclusions, and an expert facet cut. Tia accepted my offer, a little disappointed that my budget was so limited, but we agreed that I would return with a larger capital for a more important purchase. I was rejoicing of my good fortune in meeting her, and the multiple possibilities opening up since that night at El Arranque. In this mood I returned to my room, where I carefully emptied half the contents of a Colgate toothpaste tube, then inserted the precious stones and refilled it with the paste, using a small plastic syringe I had carried in my suitcase, that I then discarded in the bathroom. The tube would go back in my cosmetics bag, inside my travel case.

Next day, although I had no touristic intentions, I felt like taking an exploratory walk by myself in the city center. Regrettably, I was unable to suffer the flies and the heat, the unspeakable crowd noise and the beggars pushing me around, which seemed worse than surviving a comparable outing to Plaza Once[12] (which is no mean feat!). Frightened out of my wits, I hired a rickshaw to get back to the hotel. An aged-looking Indian was pulling it with great effort—Although he looked very old, maybe he was not even thirty but prematurely worn out by his profession.

At my return, I quickly located the princess to explain my wishes to return home sooner and asked her to reserve me a flight in a couple of days. Confronted with the imminence of my departure, I thought of asking her about the chance of dancing a few tangos with the locals. She explained that few people would be interested, but to my surprise, she

---

[12] Plaza Once: A square by the train station of the same name in Buenos Aires.

organized a dinner party with friends, with an introductory tango lesson the night before my takeoff, in the magnificent dining room of the squash club.

The group included modern people in western attire, mostly involved in computing technology, which had studied or worked in the USA. We ate well (rice and expertly cooked veggies, but no meats since several were vegetarian). After dinner, I proposed a free tango lesson, hoping they would ask me to return and continue with a series of workshops on a future trip. I wished to supplement the profits from the jewel business, and possibly defray the travel expenses.

I was severely disappointed by the lesson's outcome. Except for the ex-Maharajah and his sailor friends, Indians (in their own country), did not seem receptive to this way of dancing. The women refused to practice the *'apilado* style' in a very tight embrace, and I could only show them the 'salon' style, keeping a decent distance between the partners. But Tia and I demonstrated how we do it in Buenos Aires, sticking close together, which they loved to watch. She exuded an intense scent that I had not perceived in Argentina, like an exotic wood or incense smoke. Her perfume reawakened lustful fantasies, which in the end were never satisfied. Tia conducted my visit as a master, in a purely commercial spirit.

The next day Tia escorted me to the airport,

and this time she bid me farewell more kindly, with an affectionate kiss on my cheek, wishing me a good trip and a quick return for another transaction. She hinted that she might spend a few days in Buenos Aires in a month, and perhaps I would see her at a milonga. The flight was long and uneventful. I dreamed about the profits we would make at my return, to be shared with my uncle. First, I would buy a new suit to go dancing, and go on vacation with a girlfriend for a few days on the beach at Cariló. I would also try and save some money for a future, more important stone purchase. In time, I would be able to buy a car and stop taking *colectivos*[13] and the *subte*[14], do away with their inconveniences and the risk of pickpockets.

When I arrived, after a quick shower and a shave, I called my uncle to let him know I was on my way with the gems. I went into his apartment with a triumphant smile from ear to ear, fanning the bag with the rubies before his face.

"Take a look, uncle, this time we hit the jackpot! Let's see what you think of my purchase in Kapurthala. It was really worth it." I then opened the bag and spread its contents over his desk, dying in expectation of his impression.

"Ah… Very beautiful, and of a very good size!"

---

[13] Colectivo: A colorful local minibus.
[14] Subte: The local nickname for the subway. ,

he exclaimed right away, as his eyes sparkled like the stones. Sitting at his workbench, he switched on a dark-field illuminated-microscope with a special light coming up from underneath the stone, and began a careful examination, looking for natural or unnatural inclusions. He wasn't talking, but his grin began to freeze in slow motion until it became a painful grimace. He finally raised his gaze towards me, with great sadness, to tell me: "Well, nephew, you were swindled! Some stones were over treated with heat to enhance their red color, and one has 'horsetails' inclusions, a sure synthetic corundum confirmation. These ones, for example, have interior bubbles and were possibly injected with glass or plastic. Others are of the red 'spinel' type, or tourmalines of lesser value. We could not sell them without telling the buyers their true identity and worth, and I don't like to lie about it. In retrospect, considering how little experience you have, I should have gone on the trip myself."

I was deeply humiliated, as I had brutally burst the balloon with all my dreams and ambitions. Somehow, I remembered one of La Fontaine's fables about 'Perrette and her pot of milk,' which I used to like as a child. Perrette was on her way to the market to sell the milk, while dreaming of the possible trades she would make with the earnings. As she is running and flying with happiness, she stumbles and the pot breaks, spilling the milk on the ground: Goodbye, lamb, and pig and cow of her dreams…! I was then feeling like Perrette, and made an undignified exit, with my tail between the legs.

A few weeks went by and little by little I started to pull through, until I felt like going back to dancing. One afternoon, I had a premonition and went into a pharmacy to buy a laxative, before arriving at the *milonga*[15]. I requested phenolphthalein, a colorless and tasteless fluid that is sold as easy to swallow capsules, which quickly dissolve in water. When I came in at El Arranque there was already a large collection of dancers and much confusion, but I managed to sit in my habitual place, with a good view of the room, to target potential dancing partners. In a distant corner in the back, hidden in the crowd, I caught a glimpse of my notorious princess drinking a soda, all alone since her women friends had not arrived as yet. She had a white fur coat on, too luxurious for a *milonga*. My first reaction was to get up to confront her face to face, but an alternative idea took hold in my mind. Instead, I walked to the restroom to negotiate with the attendant, who can also sell you cigarettes, chewing gum, condoms, and some illegitimate substances they can procure. When other people left the room, I purchased three small plastic bags with an innocent-looking white powder—which was his entire stock at the

---

[15] Milonga: a typical tango-dancing venue, a ballroom.

moment—and then returned to my table with no money left for even a bottle of mineral water.

A while later, Tia went up to dance with one of her favorite partners. I took advantage of the opportunity and moved to the table next to hers, contiguous to her chair. With surprising dexterity, I was able to drop the contents of the phenolphthalein capsules inside her soda, which instantly dissolved. Finally, I managed to insert the three white powder packages in the pocket of her fur coat, which hang on the chair, and then I nonchalantly left the room. On the way out, I stopped to chat with the police corporal, on duty as usual. I am in his good standing since the day I introduced him to one of my friends, a pretty woman dancer with a taste for adventure. He shook my hand warmly and entered the dance floor, while I quietly went back home.

A week later I presented to my editor a well-written column, entitled the 'Tribulations of an Indian Princess in Buenos Aires.' It began with her arrest in a popular *milonga* for possession of illegal drugs in amounts sufficient for their sale; it followed with a narrative of her violent behavior at the police station, where she caused a riotous disturbance, demanding a clean bathroom because of a severe attack of diarrhea and colicky pains. It went on to describe her life in Cochin, a historical city port that gained notoriety in past centuries with the Portuguese occupation. It made mention of her facility with languages and how she had learned to dance the tango with her father (possibly a Maharajah until the Indian Independence), a nobleman of questionable morality and suspicious habits. Finally, it reported her ability as a jeweler and precious stones importer. The police had searched her apartment without finding additional drugs, but they uncovered a safe full to the rim with a variety of gems, illegally imported, that awaited expert assessment of their authenticity. Of course, to maintain confidentiality neither the names used, or her city of origin were genuine—As I had agreed to do earlier, since promises are promises! Unfortunately, the editor demanded irrefutable evidence of the truthfulness of my story, which I was unable to produce. The beautiful red tourmaline stones I exhibited were insufficient proof to let me publish the column. I hold on dearly to them as a remembrance of my 'Innocent years.'

Svetlana and the Oligarch

The Russian oligarch's summons—an invitation Svetlana could not refuse— arrived on a typical rainy Seattle morning. The text message had been transmitted instantly, and with minimal effort, to her cell phone from an unidentified phone number in Vladivostok, the terminus for the Trans-Siberian railway. But, not so-long ago, it might have been hand-delivered by a postman, who would have stumbled over the wet, cobblestoned alley that curved downhill at the south end of Pike Place Market. Beyond the infamous tourist destination known as the "Gum Wall," he would have arrived at a half-visible entrance known only to the staff and students at the Russian-American Pilates Academy.

Svetlana, Sasha, and Sofia, the all-women training team, were former athletes at the prestigious Russian circus in St. Petersburg. Still in their prime and enviably fit, after retiring they had all trained at the Romana's Pilates in New York. Joseph Pilates, the legendary German gymnast and therapist, had invented a rehabilitation method for wounded soldiers during the First World War before leaving Germany to settle in the US. Among his early students were the renowned dancers Balanchine and Martha Graham, and more recently, our instructor Sasha had graduated from the school he started in New York City. As a long-time student and a recent apprentice at the Seattle Academy, I was in a good position to keep track of the comings and goings of its superlative staff. So, I was the first to notice Svetlana's agitation after receiving the text. I was also aware of the staff meeting that took place the next morning to coordinate schedules and find a substitute teacher, since Svetlana and her family would be absent for about a month, on assignment in Moscow and later in Washington DC. It would not be easy to come up with a suitable replacement for Svetlana, an amazing contortionist who was able to fit into the tightest of spaces and out through a bottleneck, like the sleek octopus at the Seattle aquarium.

After the staff meeting, Svetlana and I crossed the street to our usual hangout, the Storyville café, on the upper floor of a charming, old brick building. She wanted my opinion on the text and especially the coercion implied by its final paragraph. I suppose she trusted me because of my half-Russian ancestry. My maternal grandparents had escaped from the tsar's Cossack pogroms in the first years of the twentieth century. One of my grandmother's cousins had been a notorious anarchist, first in Odessa and later on in Argentina, so our family had some experience with resistance to oppression.

The message read:

Ms. Svetlana, President Putin was impressed with

your work during the G20 meetings in Bueno Aires, and he has requested that you and Maestro Houdinsky conduct a rehearsal in Москва for an official performance in Washington DC two or three weeks later. The formal event will be attended only by Mr. Putin and a guest during a private meeting. We will inform you in due course of the precise date and location as well as some specific requirements for the performance. The presentation will showcase your contortionist and gymnastic skills, combined with your husband's spectacular magic act. Your talented children can join you as assistants, but other performers will not be allowed. Once in Moscow, you will have time to make the large props for the magic act, which are hard to fly commercial from the USA. Later, we will transport these props by military plane to Washington DC for the official performance.

The pay will be generous, equivalent to a two-month professional income for each participant. We will reimburse the international business-class airfares, hotels and meals, as well as the material for the props. For security, the program details must remain confidential even from your closest family and the prop builders. Only need-to-know communication will apply.

Mr. Putin is aware that your parents' state pension is under review, and that your brother, a political journalist, is facing assignment to a re-education camp in Siberia. The president would look with interest into these issues following your successful performance in Washington DC.

Shimon Berditchevsky

"Now I see why you must accept this mobster's invitation!" I said, after reading the text message. "You will be well paid to perform for powerful people in Russia, including their creepy president. But I'm offended by the implied threats against your family if you refuse their request. It sounds fishy. There must be something special they want you and your husband to do, most likely during the magic act."

Svetlana gave me an intense, curious look while I delivered my concerned, grandfatherly speech. She slowly lifted her coffee cup to her lips with elegant, and studied, precision. But I detected a nearly invisible hand tremor that made me think she might be wondering what she and her husband were getting into.

"How did you meet this guy? Do you know him well enough to trust him?"

"We met him a few years ago at a circus party in Europe, where he knew many of the Russian artists. Our friends said he always kept his promises and paid contracts on time. He and Putin came to watch our act in Buenos Aires during the G20 conference last month. After the show, Berditchevsky suggested there might be a one-time, well-paid job for us in Russia. As you know, we're well established here, but we'll travel anywhere for a job with a reputable company. This gig is exciting because we get to see our parents, and we might meet other important people in business and politics. As it turned out, something like that happened during the G20 conference, because Putin's interpreter was staying at the same hotel and we had a friendly chat during breakfast. That's how we learned that Trump had a secret meeting in Putin's room. She told us no more than that, except that she was shocked there were no Americans present to translate or take notes."

"Just like we read in the news! Who knows what our president promised the Russians? And what was Berditchevsky doing there?"

"He's a major player in the global aluminum trade, a powerful industrialist, and Putin's close friend. You may have seen his name in the papers because he's one of the oligarchs hit by US sanctions. I think he must have friends or allies in Congress, since the Republicans want to remove his name from the blacklist."

"Forget him for a minute. Where did you perform in Buenos Aires? I grew up there, remember?"

"We had the honor of performing with other European colleagues at the re-opening of the Circo Sarrasani, an old institution in Argentina."

"I can't believe you worked at there! I remember, as a child in Buenos Aires, they had a huge tent only a few blocks from our home in Barracas. Did you know the circus was founded by German Jews in Dresden in 1901? By the end of the Second World War, when things got tough for them, they escaped to Argentina where they became favorites of President Peron and Evita. Our dictator loved the Sarrasani so much he changed its name to National Circus of Argentina. Our parents once took my brother and me to a show we'll never forget. What I loved best were their trained animals—elephants, horses, and especially chimpanzees."

"I hate to disappoint you, but nowadays it's no longer acceptable to have live animals in the circus. Instead, they use hi-tech laser lights and project an HD video of animals running free in the African savanna, and chimpanzee families in the forest. They still had a wild Mongolian horsemen's act."

"That's too bad, because I still remember the Sarrasani chimps! Can you believe they became part of Argentinian culture? There's even a darkly humorous tango song, 'El 31' by Juan D'Arienzo, where a man enters a café with a very unattractive girlfriend and his friends make fun of him by singing the lyrics, *'There goes Sarrasani with the chimp-an-zee.'"*

"How curious! I guess that might have been funny once, in Argentina. But the world has changed, I'm glad to say. Anyway, later

Berditchevsky came backstage to talk to us. He's very heavy and could hardly fit in his chair. He barely moves, like a couch potato who never practiced Pilates or even heard of it. I'm usually a good observer, but I couldn't tell if he had any muscles at all below all the flab. Still, he's sophisticated and seductive. He speaks slowly, maybe because of his large size. I think he belongs to the Russian-Jewish mafia, and he has the power to command others without raising his voice. In any case, he had no trouble convincing us to perform for Putin."

"How will you handle this assignment? Do you want me to check in on you? We could stay in contact with WhatsApp... The messages are encrypted, which may be safer for you."

"It's a deal. I'll keep you posted whenever I can, and I'll give you a complete report when we return," she said with a conspiratorial smile. Then we shared a hug and went our own way, each daydreaming about how this adventure would unfold. I had full confidence in my intrepid, athletic friend. She was known for being unconventional, like the day she arrived in Vegas for her wedding, already eight months' pregnant and wearing a fluffy pink tunic that floated on the wind. Fitting into a traditional dress would have been technically impossible even for a magician's partner. Yet none of their circus friends, who had converged in Vegas from many places around the globe, batted an eyelid at her rounded belly.

* * *

Svetlana and Maestro Houdinsky left Seattle next Saturday morning with Alex and Ludmilla, their two teenage children, in tow. Their flight plan took them via LA, on Air France and Aeroflot, on the shortest (and most expensive) route to Moscow—in business class, as promised by their handler. Berditchevsky had spared no expense, even selecting the first-class Baltschug Kempinski Hotel in Moscow. Usually, Svetlana stayed with her parents when she was in Russia, but Berditchevsky had insisted on putting them up at a central hotel with quick access to meetings with him and the president. To their surprise, the luxury hotel was just across the river from the Kremlin and Red Square, a few minutes on foot to a metro station (which they would barely have the chance to use since they were being picked up in a limo for most of their appointments). The hotel had good facilities—free wi-fi, a spa, and an elegant swimming pool—but it suffered from the common Russian practice of installing a concierge on every floor to keep a stern eye on the comings and goings of the hotel guests. As Russian citizens, the Houdinskys had to show their internal passports on request, which happened almost every time they left the hotel.

The rooms were large and the bathrooms modern and functional, but Svetlana found a dirty bathrobe with makeup on its sleeve, and then someone else's old underwear on the top shelf in the cupboard. As soon as she settled in, she phoned for an appointment at the Olga Burkova's Mind-Body Studio, where she was well-known from previous trips. The equipment was excellent, made by Gratz, the original 1928 manufacturer of Pilates apparatus in New York City. Everything she needed was there, from the Universal Reformer to the Guillotine Tower, which, given the context of their assignment, had nerve-wrecking connotations. She planned to go over daily to stay nimble for her contortionist act, which appeared to be one of the requirements for the job.

Another summons arrived the morning after their arrival. A limo would fetch Svetlana and her husband at the hotel at 1400 hours for a preliminary meeting with Berditchevsky. When they got to the lobby, they saw that a black Mercedes with tinted glass windows was already parked in front of the hotel. A tall, fit man, with a military bearing and pock-marked face, identified himself as Sergei, their driver. He signaled for them to get in and immediately departed towards a ritzy residential area, away from the Kremlin district. The Houdinskys knew that the most powerful people had moved from Rublevskoe Shosse to the city center. Sergei continued down Tverskaya Street, in the Arbat district, which was lined with souvenir shops and cafes, before turning into a tree-lined alley and stopping before a black metal gate with radio sensors for private access. The mansion inside was clearly old, with an aristocratic air that suggested a rich history. A butler took them into a tall, dark, wood-paneled library lined with thousands of leather-bound books, which they wondered if anybody ever read since there was no ladder to reach them. The gaudy décor and the tasteless modernist paintings suggested new money rather than an aristocratic past.

Suddenly the door at the opposite end opened as Berditchevsky made a slow and practiced entrance, as if looking to create a specific and perhaps intimidating effect. He went to the point, almost immediately.

"Welcome to Moscow, Svetlana, Maestro. I need to go over the general idea for your preliminary performance at the Kremlin. We want you to prepare an interesting program to entertain a guest with a very limited attention span. Not the complicated routine with its shocking twists you performed in Buenos Aires. Instead, I suggest a simpler series of short, colorful magic and gymnastic tricks, the kind that might impress young children or middle-schoolers rather than an adult. Lighting effects, card tricks, and even fire may be part of it, but animals, like rabbits or pigeons, cannot be used. The performance should include the Mechanical Doll, Svetlana's famous contortionist act, where she emerges from a wooden trunk and responds to remote commands. Then the main event that has Svetlana fitting tightly into a coffinlike box and you appearing to stab her over and over with a long sword through thin slots in the sides. The president will explain the objective for your performance at your next meeting, but you should start planning the program as we've discussed."

"When can we start working on the props?"

"Today. The rehearsal will happen in approximately ten days. Do you have a specific worker in mind? Otherwise, we can provide local artists."

"We've worked with our friend Vladimir, who's a talented metal artist and is familiar with our needs. He's available to start as soon as we contact him. We packed small props for the magic act in our luggage, and we can borrow any additional material from our friends at the Moscow Circus."

"Good. This will be all for today. Expect a notice to meet with the president in the next couple of days. These arrangements are confidential. Keep them to yourselves."

Afterward, they asked to be dropped off at the elegant Patisserie Café Pushkin near Arbat Street and the Pushkin monument, where they waited for Vladimir to join them. Svetlana went straight for the pistachio cake with yogurt shaped like a rose on top, while Houdinsky chose *medovik,* or honey cake, and a ginger tea. After all, the oligarch was paying! It took a while for the refreshments to arrive, so Houdinsky began drafting a program schedule. Svetlana used the extra time to text me her first WhatsApp message, which reflected her excitement and growing interest in the assignment.

Hi Apprentice!
Just done with our preliminary meeting with Mr. B. Visited his mansion and got general instructions. We are still in the dark about some special requirements for our act. Mr. B. wouldn't elaborate. Obviously, we feel compelled to accept whatever they want. We'll do it mostly to protect our parents and my brother. Now we have no choice. I hope these messages are encrypted, as you said...
On a lighter note, you'll be happy to know we'll be working with Vladimir, who you met when he visited Seattle. You felt he looked so much like your grandpa when he was young! They may even have come from the same area in the Bessarabia region. His grown-up daughters insisted he apply for a permanent visa to the USA. Amazingly, he won the visa lottery and they will be moving to Seattle. He will start over as a metal artist, and his daughters plan to use their experience as interior designers. I'm sure they will make you the best-looking metal railings for your living room.

Keep you posted!
S.

The time went by quickly, with training at the Pilates studio, planning the ideal program for the "unknown" guest with possible ADD, and working at Vladimir's metalworks studio. Then, the oligarch scheduled a meeting at the Kremlin (without the children), at 10 AM the following morning. Sergei was courteous but silent during their short trip across the river. He drove them through congested streets before entering the imposing complex from a side gate. Security was tight, with electronic sensors, mirrors, and sniffing dogs that ran obediently around the car, while the driver stood at attention. Finally, a tall, athletic man who introduced himself as "a secretary," led them through a long, slightly sinister hallway with almost no furniture and into a gray windowless room. After a tense half-hour wait, the secretary took the Houdinskys through double doors and into a more elegant baroque salon, where a heavily armed security guard was stationed by the main entrance. They sat for a while on comfortable cushioned chairs facing a mahogany desk with gilt legs and mother-of-pearl inlay. Suddenly, the door at the other end opened and in came a sweaty, flushed President Putin wearing an off-white judogi with a black belt. He stopped silently behind his desk and scrutinized the two visitors, who were now on their feet before him. Eventually, he produced an icy, expressionless half-smile and said:

"Master Houdinsky, Svetlana. I'm counting on your willingness to help the country you left many years ago. Before I describe your duties, I will remind you that everything we say here is highly confidential. There will be severe consequences if you discuss this program with anyone, especially people's names, or the locations and times of your performances. Now, do we understand each other? You may sit down." Svetlana was relieved that Houdinsky had remained quiet (as usual) during this alarming speech, and especially happy that he had agreed not to wear his favorite attire, an ankle-length, black leather coat. Usually, he enjoyed wearing it off stage as well as during work, because it added to his air of mystery and enhanced his forbidding appearance. "At your service, Mr. President," she replied, speaking for them both.

Still standing, Putin embarked on a military-style briefing:

"Your job will be to present a magic show and contortionist dance to a special guest in Washington. The main objective will be to set up a substitution act during the Maestro's performance. Your role, Svetlana, will be to mesmerize a powerful American executive, possibly during the Candle Dance, which made you famous in so many countries. The man should be focused on Svetlana's sensuous contortionist act, which should provide cover for the substitution."

"Mr. President." Houdinsky broke his customary silence. "What can you tell us about your special guest's personality?"

"All you need to know is that he's crude, unreliable, and a flirt. He may behave inappropriately and try touching your wife, even with you in the room. There will be more details after the rehearsal. You will do a practice show for me and a few officials in exactly one week."

"Sir, what's the size and shape of the object we need to switch?" asked Houdinsky, focusing on the main objective.

"It will be a standard-size Manila folder. We expect the guest to sign a document and place it in the folder, which will most likely sit on top of a coffee table very close to you during the performance. We will give you an identical folder with papers just before the rehearsal, when an officer unaware of our plot will play the role of official guest. We will give you a new folder with official documents just minutes prior to the show in Washington."

"Very well, Mr. President. I will decide the optimal time for the switch just before the performance. Now, Mr. Putin, may I voice a concern? Is there a legal risk for us for switching a folder with official documents in the USA?"

"You will be doing this show at our embassy in Washington DC, which is Russian territory. In

Russia, we decide what is legal and what is not." For a few moments, the silence in the room was absolute like the emptiness of space described by astronauts in orbit.

Houdinsky could sense Svetlana's fear and was astonished at his own assertiveness. Suddenly, Putin turned around, expressionless again. He adjusted his judogi belt and left the room with no further comment.

They instructed their handler to take them directly to Vladimir's workshop. They remained silent during the ride, because any comments could be recorded or overheard by the stony-faced Sergei. In any case, they needed no words to share how they were feeling. The main challenge was no longer technical, but psychological and diplomatic: how to handle a controlling, unscrupulous dictator and his unpredictable, powerful guest. They would need to put in play all their combined years of professional experience. Once at Vladimir's, they requested some changes to the metal box, which the puzzled metal artist had not seen in previous versions of the sword trick. But he did as they asked.

Once back at the Kempinski, they were forced to confront their floor's concierge, who was particularly nasty, demanding to see their internal passports yet again. The Maestro and Svetlana were powerless to refuse the president and the oligarch's demands, but the time had come to stand up to this arbitrary, exasperating employee. Houdinsky went back to their room, put on his signature trench coat, and loaded its secret pockets with magic paraphernalia. Followed by Alex and Ludmilla—who had spent a boring afternoon playing mediocre soccer with some kids in Gorky Park—the magician approached the concierge at a slow and threatening pace. He stopped in front of a huge No Smoking sign on the wall, looked at it with interest, and as he stretched his arm towards the woman, made a cigarette appear in his right hand. Before she could react, a tall flame shot out of his left hand. He lit the cigarette with it and immediately put the burning cigarette into his mouth, appearing to swallow it whole. Then, he pulled a small bouquet of flowers from one of his vest pockets and offered it to her with a flourish. But when she reached out to accept the gift, he quickly pulled back, and with a snap of his fingers, made it vanish. Instead, a tall flame burst by her face, but only for an instant, before tiny paper cuts showered down over her head like little twinkling stars, covering up her desk with a colorful blanket. Smiling sardonically, she tried to catch the paper cuts, but they quickly dissolved in front of her eyes as they fell, leaving nothing but a dirty, foul-smelling residue behind. Only then did the Maestro turn away, leaving her in shock but wishing he could have taken revenge against Putin and Berditchevsky instead. When they returned to the room, Alex and Ludmilla were no longer bored at all.

In the morning there was a new and succinct message from the oligarch:

The hotel's concierge reported an incident involving the maestro on her floor. We have notified her that your family is here on official duty and that no one should be disturbed. She received a severe reprimand. From now on, you will be able to go about your business without inconvenience.
On rehearsal day, please arrive two hours early to prepare your equipment. The palace technicians will move and install your props in the location you choose.
B.

Later, when Svetlana let me read this text, I realized how sad it was that Berditchevsky shared his name with one of the great Hassidic sages of the eighteenth century, the righteous Rabbi Itzhak Levi from Berditchev, the city of his birth. This *tzadik* with a channel to the divine, a tireless defender of the Jews, had tried to advocate for them before God himself. He was an inspiration for many generations of Hassidim. Could he have predicted that a Jewish mobster would be named after him two hundred years later?

The days passed quickly for the whole family as they prepared for rehearsal day. They were eager to perform. The children, especially, were astonished by the Kremlin, both the building and the strict security. The "secretary" delivered the

Manila folder, which Houdinsky placed in one of his secret pockets while they awaited their call to action. Half an hour later someone signaled it was time to begin the show and the Maestro, assisted by his children, took their places in front of a table where Putin sat talking intensely with an official they have never seen before. On the table was another Manila folder and an abundant supply of vodka and some small dishes. As requested, Houdinsky went through a series of short routines involving cigarettes, smoke, and fire, and disappearing objects, but he intentionally avoided complicated or especially long sequences. Then Svetlana proceeded with her Marionette Act, materializing from inside the wooden box the children wheeled in before the guests. The magician controlled her jerky but perfectly executed mechanical movements with a remote similar to that for a TV. Then followed her sensuous Candle Dance, during which she balanced a lighted candle on her head, then on her abdomen, and then on her lower back. Dressed in a fluid, translucent robe that left little to the imagination, she delivered a rapturous, trancelike performance. At last, they went on to the final act, with Svetlana fitting into a tight box with side slots, where the Maestro appeared to stab her repeatedly with a long sword. She eventually reemerged unhurt, slowly stretching out from her tight compartment. They bowed to the enthusiastic, boozy audience, though they never managed more than an approving gaze from the stony-faced president.

Once back at the hotel. Houdinsky reassured the family that all had gone well. These acts were their bread and butter, and he was not anxious about their success. Any distress came from the potential consequences for their family, which depended on Putin's satisfaction after their next performance.

The next text message from Berditchevsky arrived in good time. It read:

Well done. The president approved your covert substitution, and neither the main guest nor any of the observers were aware it had occurred during the performance. We will now move the props to Washington DC for the official event. The airline tickets are ready for your return to the USA at the scheduled time. Our driver will take you to your hotel. On the day of the performance, when you arrive at the embassy in DC, we will provide you with a new Manila folder with documents. You will need to be on site three hours beforehand, for both security reasons and final performance details. You will be told at last minute whether this will happen during lunch or dinner. Don't hesitate to contact me with any questions.
B.

Now, finally, they felt ready to visit Svetlana's parents for lunch. On the phone, her mother asked the question Svetlana knew was coming: "What would you all like to eat? We never have a chance to see you, and Dad and I want to be sure you are happy here."

"Mom, everything you make is delicious! But my husband would love to try your special *kholodets*. He is crazy for aspic. And the children and I would be happy with your warm borscht with *smetana*. We can't find this kind of sour cream in the US, and I miss it badly."

Lunch went well, but her parents refrained from mentioning their plight with the state pension. Svetlana's brother had not heard yet whether he would be sent to the re-education camp, although other journalists in the opposition had already been detained. All Svetlana could say at the moment was that they were using their contacts and were hopeful somehow these issues would be resolved.

****

The hotel in DC was near Dupont circle, less than three miles from the Russian Embassy on Wisconsin Ave., which was located on Alto Hill, one of the highest points in the city, with a view of the White House and the Capitol. When the summons came, they gathered up their small props and costumes and arrived three hours early to familiarize themselves with the surroundings and assess their location, doors and drapes placement, available exits, and so on. An officer took them up a splendid marble staircase to the second floor and across to the big ballroom, where receptions and concerts were held. They checked the Petrovskiy (Blue Room), dedicated to the Russian emperor Peter I, who had built the Russian fleet. They were more at ease when told the reception would be in the Red Hall next door, a cozier environment sometimes used for small groups or for lunches. It would be ideal for their act. Other employees had placed their big props near one of the several doors, as the Maestro had requested, so they moved backstage to change clothes and wait patiently for the call to action.

When it came and they re-entered the Red Hall, Putin was already seated, chatting with his special guest, President Trump. This was no surprise given the advanced description of his personality and the request for a program with shorter sketches. As they expected after the earlier meeting in Argentina, there were no other assistants or translators present. President Putin was drinking substantial amounts of vodka, while Trump helped himself to his usual Diet Coke. Both men sampled the colorful but simple dishes. A Manila envelope had been placed on the table in front of the only guest.

The show began with the usual cigarette tricks, and the making of a short tube with old newspapers. The Maestro then pulled out an endless string of concentric smaller tubes, which grew and grew improbably to nearly the ornate ceiling and crystal chandeliers. Later, he really held his audience's attention as he opened a two-meter square black cloth before him, and while holding it at arm's length, seemed to levitate behind it, moving slowly up and down by as much as a foot—to both presidents' amazement. This was followed by the children wheeling in the large wooden box and stopping before Houdinsky. He lifted the top and Svetlana rose slowly, moving like a mechanical doll in response to remote commands from the magician's hand-held gadget. At the end of the act, she went back into the box, pretending to fall back into a doll's sleep as the lid was closed.

They now had the full concentration of their audience of two. Time to proceed with the first of two major sketches: Svetlana's Candle Dance, a repeat of her performance in Russia and one of Putin's favorites. The sensuous flow and the remarkable movement of the lit candle from one part of her body to the next brought Trump to attention: as though in a dream, he tried to catch the dancer by her waist and low back. But she deftly turned and swirled out of reach until the candles were snuffed out and she returned backstage. Meanwhile, the Manila folder appeared untouched.

The final act involved the arrival of a three-foot-long metal box, open on all sides at first, and then closed sequentially on three sides, to allow

Svetlana to slip in, however improbably, into such a tight space. Then the lid was closed and Houdinsky stabbed at the box through the slits with his long Japanese sword. This time the children held a tall post with multicolored theatrical lights that cycled on and off. Suddenly, white smoke surrounded the box, which then exploded open on all sides to reveal it was completely empty, as if the contortionist had evaporated with the smoke. Trump stood up, confused and maybe disappointed that Svetlana had disappeared. Again, there was no sign the Manila folder had been disturbed at all.

By the time Houdinsky and the children brought their clothes and small props back to the embassy car and opened the door, Svetlana was crouched on the floor in the back, smiling mischievously up at her artistic family and invisible to the outside world.

****

One week later, Svetlana was back teaching again at the Seattle Russian-American Pilates Academy when a final text from Berditchevsky arrived:

Well done! The President was fascinated by your dance performance and by the Maestro's stealth in the substitution act. He is looking at your family's difficulties in Russia, and they should hear

soon about developments. We may request your services again someday in the future.
Regards,
B.

I was totally proud of my friend's accomplishment and curious about its possible consequences. I suppose we'd never hear about these. But that night I had a particularly vivid, realistic dream: *The New York Times* exposed President Trump's recent financial agreement with Russia. Deutsche Bank was subpoenaed to release related documents about a money-laundering scheme between the two countries. This resulted in a wave of desertions by the Republican members of Congress, who agreed to demands for impeachment proceedings. The president resigned shortly thereafter.

The Quantum Café

Foreword

My exposure to coffee drinking and café life started in childhood, and my fascination with this infusion continues unabated to this day. Over the years, coffee-related "quanta" (snippets or granules) have had important effects on my life and inspired me to write these short stories. I have changed some names and/or locations, sometimes to protect the innocent.

Quantum 1
Barracas

Carlitos Laborde, a classmate of mine from secondary school, came to visit with me for the first time on a Sunday morning. The son of a prominent land developer, he might well have felt out of place in our small apartment in Barracas, a working-class barrio in Buenos Aires. But, whatever his feelings, it did not take long for his natural sense of curiosity to assert itself as he discovered and then took to some of my family's customs. Even so, none of us could have predicted then that he would develop such an obsessive taste for coffee that eventually determined his economic and romantic future.

My father delighted in listening to his modest collection of classical music when he relaxed at home at the weekend. On this first visit, Carlitos was immediately intrigued by the unfamiliar music streaming from our 33 1/3 RPM vinyl record player, one of the few in our neighborhood. It was a duet from the Magic Flute—though Mozart was by no means the musical fashion on our block. In fact, through the open window, we could hear the syncopated rhythms of D'Arienzo, a popular band from the Golden Age of Tango, which our ground-floor neighbor, a car mechanic, broadcast at full blast over huge speakers, so ensuring the entire building was his captive audience.—In Barracas, Mozart was no competition for D'Arienzo, and Carlitos was witnessing at first-hand the battle of musical styles between my father and our insufferable neighbor.

Frustrated by the sonic attack, my father resorted to his foolproof remedy for any adversity: his ritual of drinking the best possible coffee, followed by a tiny sip of cognac, and then a cigarette, possibly the only one that day. The emphasis was on the coffee, but the ritual had to include all three elements in sequence. So, he started making a Turkish coffee, an odd choice since we had no Turks in our family or among our friends. Carlitos and I followed him into the kitchen, where we saw him take out a small brass pot that was wider at the bottom and had a long handle that extended at 45 degrees from the base. He called this pot a cezve, without explaining how he knew the name. Carlitos watched, mesmerized, as my father filled it with cold water before adding very fine coffee grounds from a colorful can with Arabesque designs, followed by a teaspoon of sugar. He stirred the mix and put it on to boil. "No more mixing after this," he said with confidence. The moment the water boiled, he poured the coffee into two demitasse cups, one for himself and another for Carlitos as a welcome gesture, telling him to wait for the foam and coffee grounds to settle while the coffee cooled a little. My friend was familiar only with the filtered coffee his family made, and you would have thought, from the delighted expression on his face, that he was going through a mystical experience.

Carlitos, a spitting image of Sherlock Holmes, was probing the mysterious tar-pit sludge at the cup's bottom when we heard an insistent pounding on the door. It announced the energetic arrival of our next-door neighbor, an exuberant middle-aged woman with frenzied frizzled hair, eyes dark as blackberries, and an olive complexion.

"Hello, everybody! I'm bringing you some home-made lahmejoon straight from the oven. Eat it while it's still hot," she commanded. "I didn't make the pizza too spicy. I know you people in Argentina don't eat spicy food like we do in Armenia. Don Marcelo, how wonderful, you're making

Armenian coffee! Would you make one for me too? But please remember never to call it Turkish coffee again."

"I'd be happy to, Maryam! I'll make it not too sweet, just as you like it." My father and I shared a quick glance as he caught himself nearly uttering the unspeakable T word. Carlitos noticed this too but kept his cool. After Maryam had left, he filled Carlitos in. "The first time our neighbors came to visit, we treated them to coffee, but we stupidly referred to it as Turkish. They were so upset that we got a long but well-deserved history lesson."

My father went on to explain that the troubles between the Turks and Armenians went back a long time. In 1915, just before the fall of the Ottoman empire, the Turks feared that the Armenians, who were Catholics, would conspire with the Russian tsar to overthrow the Ottoman forces in the East. The Turks rounded up and deported the entire Armenian population to the deserts of Syria and Mesopotamia. The result was the mass murder of more than a million Armenians. Somehow, Maryam and her family escaped the genocide. Then, in a cruel reversal, when Armenia became part of the Soviet Socialist Republic, it was Stalin who slaughtered the Armenians in an effort to crush what he considered a political and intellectual elite and curtail the influence of the church. Thousands of survivors emigrated to Lebanon, Syria, France and the Americas, including

Argentina. Maryam and her husband escaped to Buenos Aires.

Maryam's family was by now well established in the city, where they owned one of several Armenian tanneries that processed and marketed attractive leather goods. I relished visiting their workshop for its unusual animal smells, the foreignness of a profession that was unlike any I knew at the time, and its Spanish name, marroquinería, which evoked the sights and smells of distant lands. One afternoon I asked Carlitos to join me at this exotic store. Maryam was so touched by our visit, she offered us traditional Armenian sweets and a package of halva, one of their national dishes, to take home. We shared them in Barracas, which gave my father the perfect excuse to brew Armenian coffee for everyone.

As the weeks went by, Carlitos grew even fonder of my father's coffee, his classical music, and the Armenian dishes Maryam shared with us. But I suspected he was really bewitched by Maryam herself, her shapely figure and intense dark eyes, her charm, and her talents as a chef. The affection was mutual, because Maryam had no children and she enjoyed Carlitos's undisguised admiration. We had all become her extended family. She also enjoyed my mother's Jewish cooking including specialties like buckwheat kasha. It reminded her of the old country, which she still missed in spite of its tragic history. Strangely, the family on my mother's side might have lived side by side with the Armenians in Bessarabia, now known as Moldova. Both families had suffered Russian persecution and pogroms and had escaped to Argentina at about the same time. The two ethnic groups, the Russian Jews and the Catholic Armenians, coexisted in the same barrios in Buenos Aires. We also shared a taste for Russian tea with lemon, made in a samovar that, like its owners, had survived the long ocean trip to find a place in my grandparents' home.

Our home was just a few blocks from the stadium of La Bombonera, the Boca Junior's fútbol club. Yet our parents never took us to watch the Sunday matches, because they felt the fans were too rough and rowdy, even dangerous. One boring Sunday, when my Mom was away visiting relatives, my father came up with a different idea: "Do you guys want to go to a rugby match? The French and Argentine national teams are playing in town, and I'd like to go cheer for Old Country. After the game we can all go downtown to check out a good Italian espresso place I know." We shouted "Yes!" without a moment's hesitation.

Of course, the very organized French team easily won the rugby match, with its admirable line of quick-witted players who almost never missed a pass. Soon afterwards, we were on a bus downtown, getting off at a popular intersection on Calle Lavalle to look for Café Le Caravelle, which was frequented by Northern Italians. Inside, the cigarette smoke was as dense as fog over the Golden Gate bridge on a wintery night. The fashionable customers were dressed as though they were going for a stroll on the Milano Gallery, and we felt completely underdressed in our sports attire. But the café's unforgettable espresso—prepared from imported beans by a barista in a white jacket and black bow tie—was elegant and smooth to the palate, with a very delicate flavor and a long-lasting, delicious aftertaste. Carlitos and I secretly agreed (though we never said so aloud), that the Caravelle's espresso was superior to my father's home-made coffee. It became our standard of reference from then on.

"Is this the best there is, Don Marcelo? What do you think of the Brazilian coffee made by our neighbors to the north?" Carlitos asked with a naïve expression.

My father needed no further provocation to take us all on a mad dash up Calle Suipacha to a place I had never seen before: The Casa do Brazil. It comprised a narrow room with a counter at least 10 meters long, where three to four rows of customers moved forward at lightning speed toward the counter and their caffeine fix. There, the most competent and sure-fisted baristas were delivering cafezinhos, the Brazilian version of a single-shot espresso, in tiny white demitasses. No one would dare think of adding milk or of requesting a cappuccino or a latte. The point was to delight in the undiluted coffee flavor. We were surprised by how quickly the customers sipped their small shots, thanked the barista with a small tip, and immediately took off, apparently without any desire to linger in this mad equivalent of the Willie Wonka Chocolate Factory.

In time, the Casa do Brazil disappeared from downtown, and Le Caravelle lost both its character and high standards to become a shadow of its former self. Both places fell victim to political turmoil, multiple currency devaluations, and a lack of high-quality, imported beans. But the memory of the taste that we were privileged to experience in our youth has stayed with me. It was the basis for a lifetime of learning about what makes a great coffee.

When we got home, my father played music that would have been appropriate in church but much more joyful and lively. We could not put a name to it. "No, this isn't religious music! I knew I'd get you with this one," he said, laughing. "It's 'The Coffee Cantata,' which Bach wrote around 1735, when coffee had just arrived in Germany and became an instant success. Up until then, people used to drink beer with breakfast, but coffee became popular because it helped to sober you up. It was particularly attractive to young women, who for the first time were allowed into coffee houses. In this short comic opera, the father tells his coffee-addicted daughter to quiet down and stop chattering! The words he sings in German,

'Schweight Stille, Plaudert Nicht,' became the cantata's name."

My father and I would occasionally go out together, developing strong bonds between us. Around the corner from our home there was a rough neighborhood café, on a tree-lined street on the corner of Coronel Salvadores with Montes de Oca. Sometimes my father would take me there to drink a soda, while he gratified himself with an espresso, followed by a shot of Hesperidina. This was a unique Argentine liquor, made with bitters and sweet orange peels. This liquor was advertised with a musical rhyme in Spanish that even today makes me smile. We would then stare at the neighborhood bums playing billiards for small bills. Only adults could play billiards and drink alcohol, but children were allowed to sit and watch with their parents. I never saw a woman there, except when coming to fetch her idle husband. The day I became an adult, at twenty-one, my dad suggested we go for a walk in the neighborhood, as if he had something in mind to talk about. And then he shocked me by sitting with me at the corner bar, where he treated me to my first Hesperidina. Then I had a lesson at playing billiards, proud to be joining the older crowd, while the bums kept watching over us with a sneer. To my surprise, Dad was pretty good at it, for a brainy chess-player, who I had thought was just an observer of billiards and gambling at the café. He could have given the customers a run for their money!

My father had a strong influence also on my friend Carlitos. Together with his taste for coffee and good music, Carlitos learned to appreciate the company of desirable foreign women. He loved the spices Maryam used with Armenian food, her lavash bread and, of course, her pizza with eggplant and chick peas. He was also a huge fan of favas or peas in tomato sauce with garlic, parsley and mint. And then, a few years later at the University, he met Maryam's niece, Natalie, and his future was sealed. Natalie seemed like a younger version of her aunt: with her intense gaze, sexy curves, and talents as a cook. She was intelligent and was applying to the School of Architecture. It was clear that Carlitos and Natalie were falling for each other, and his attraction for her increased side by side with his love of coffee. All went well until his father, a rich Argentine nationalist, became alarmed by his son's foreign preferences. First, Carlitos had offended his father by complaining that the filtered coffee he made at home was tasteless. He then compounded the insult by refusing to eat with his family at a traditional neighborhood pizzeria. He insisted that lahmejoon was far superior to their fugazzetta, and even better than the pizza at Guerrín, the best pizzeria in Buenos Aires. These comparisons were tantamount to heresy. The father retorted caustically that "your friends' only redeeming feature is that at least they are Catholic." Enraged and out of control, he even repeated the racist, unfounded rumor he had heard among the least-educated in their family, that "Armenian and Turkish women tend to get very heavy and grow a beard after they marry."

Carlitos and I stopped seeing each other once we became interested in different careers. He went to business school, stayed in the country, and kept in contact with our old neighbors in Barracas. I, on the other hand, entered medical school at the University of Buenos Aires and eventually left Argentina for post-graduate training at the University of Oklahoma. I don't remember much about that period, except that Oklahoma was a state with red soil and few trees in the center of the Bible belt; there was no coffee worth drinking to be found anywhere; and the caption on the state's car license plate read—unjustifiably—"Oklahoma is OK." Since it was a dry state in those days, you had to be careful not to order "coffee" in a certain Italian restaurant or risk being furtively served wine in a coffee cup instead. The first time this happened to me, I innocently added sugar to the coffee cup and ruined a very good Chianti. Never again!

After graduating from Medical School and moving to the USA, during my medicine residence I made a very short trip to see my parents in Buenos Aires. I took a taxi from the airport directly to a downtown hotel, because my parents then lived in a very small apartment. As soon as I arrived, I dropped off my suitcase and gave in to the urge to walk at random through the well-travelled streets that I had known so well in my childhood. So much had changed. I could no longer find the old cafés I had frequented with my father. I slowly cruised through the Microcenter, feeling the strangeness of those who return home after a long absence. Everything now seemed older and shabbier, pointing to the lack of maintenance common in underdeveloped countries. I was obviously rejecting my fellow countrymen's irrational belief that Argentina, and particularly Buenos Aires, was the center of the universe.

My pilgrimage took me to Calle Corrientes and the front of the Gran Rex Theater, where I had watched my father shed nostalgic tears during an Edith Piaf concert; past the ancient pizzeria Las Cuartetas, where he and his brother Charles had first tasted dulce de leche just after arriving from France; and then to the myriad downtown bookstores, usually opened till late at night to cater to the cultural needs of the porteños, the people of Buenos Aires. Eventually I found myself wandering on Calle Lavalle, with its many movie houses, record stores, and eating places. And then, the shock of memory nearly made my heart stop. I was passing by the steakhouse that had almost made me late for my wedding. They used to make the best steak with soufflé potatoes I had ever tasted anywhere, and I had been forced to wait anxiously for the meal until just minutes before the wedding! But I did get married to Diana, and two days later we were on a plane back to the USA to complete our medical residencies.

On the next block I came across a restaurant sign that read "Eraván," the name of a capital city I wouldn't have expected in this part of town. It was inconsistent with the Spanish names of the other venues. What was this place doing in downtown Buenos Aires, far away from the traditional barrios like Palermo or Barracas usually preferred by Armenians? My curiosity was stronger than my feet, and I was inexorably pulled into the cavernous building. It was crowded inside, but I managed to push my way to the end of the salon, where behind a clear glass wall criollo cooks were making lahmejoon.

Waiters briskly carried steaming trays to tables of regular-looking Argentines. On the left side of the room was a long counter with two smart baristas dressed in white coats and wearing black bow ties. A flashing neon sign offered a choice of Armenian coffee, espresso, or French press, all from imported roasted beans. On the wall behind the counter a painting of an intense-looking woman with very dark eyes seemed to supervise the whole operation. The Armenian coffee was very tasty, not too sweet, and paired with the delicious pastries I remembered from my youth in Barracas: classic halva and my favorite, nazook, made with sour cream, sugar, vanilla and eggs, and sometimes filled with walnuts. The sight of them made me feel guilty for not having gone to my parents' home first, before my tour of the city. Now it was too late. I resolved to go see them first thing in the morning.

As I approached the counter to pay my bill, the cashier raised her eyes and we both stared at each other, astounded by our mutual recognition: "Armando!" "Natalie!" we said in unison before embracing warmly. She immediately called for the head waiter to fill in for her at the counter and then, taking me by the elbow, led me to her office in the back. The room was larger than I expected, with an ornate desk and an antique leather sofa on top of an exquisite woven rug with ancient Armenian religious symbols.

Predictably, my first question was: "Are you still seeing Carlitos"?

"Of course, you haven't heard ... we married three years ago! The wedding was at St. Gregory Illuminator, the Orthodox Armenian Cathedral in Palermo. Later the same day the Laborde family priest blessed us at a private ceremony in Barracas. So, we honored the wishes of both families."

"What happened to your interest in Architecture?" I asked.

"I graduated, of course, but never had a chance to work on this field because the economic crisis nearly stopped the building of high-end houses. Fortunately, we were able to open this new restaurant and we both work here full-time. Carlitos will be so sad he didn't meet up with you—he's scouting for a new restaurant location in the USA. This one was his idea, but the project was developed with my aunt Maryam, who's our executive chef, with financial help from Carlitos's father."

"Wait a minute! Wasn't his father very nationalistic and suspicious of foreigners? I knew he was opposed to your friendship."

"Precisely," she said. "Until Maryam and I charmed him with Old World hospitality, good manners, and the taste of our cooking. Once he heard the details of Maryam's family escape from Stalin's Armenia, and got to appreciate their business expertise and the success of the marroquinería, he became a fan. In fact, he was the original owner of this property before signing it over to us so we could open a restaurant—that was his wedding present. He was convinced that Carlitos's love for coffee and his background as an economist, together with Maryam's expertise in the kitchen, would ensure our success. The restaurant had a rough beginning because people in this city have narrow-minded culinary interests. Steak and potatoes still reign supreme. But we have created a new culture in a part of town where we are a novelty. And now you can see the results! Argentines are coming in droves and responding well to our originality and high quality, our tasty food and the best coffee."

I spent the rest of my short trip with my parents before returning to Seattle to resume my work. Later on, we learned from visiting friends that Eraván's exotic attractions were short-lived. It had been sold to local investors who, unsurprisingly, turned it into a parrilla, a typical Argentine steak house. Carlitos and Natalie had moved to the USA, where they opened the first "Armenian Resto-Café" in Miami.

Reflecting on my life, and the memory of events that had contributed to my passion for good coffee, I was helped by the words of Maimonides, the Jewish philosopher and physician, who observed back in the thirteenth century that "Time is composed of atoms, that is to say of many parts that cannot be further subdivided, on account of their short duration." Today, we call these particles "quanta," which can occur simultaneously in two different and even very distant states. Modern physics would accept that a quantum of my coffee life has become "concrete" and suggests the probable locations of each particle's state: one was in Barracas, Buenos Aires, and the other exists now in Seattle, WA, in one of an infinite number of universes known as a multiverse.

The Quantum Café

Quantum 2: Le Procope

It took my father forty years after leaving military service in France to return to his birthplace in Paris. He longed to be reunited there with his brother Nathan, a blue-collar worker, painter, writer, and French Foreign Legion veteran. As it happened, my wife, Diana, and I had the chance to invite Dad to join us on a trip to Paris, where we shared in the brothers' emotional reunion. The precise location where we celebrated this event marked an important quantum in my life, and in my coffee universe.

The epic reunion began at Nathan's own *terrasse*, a newspaper kiosk at a corner of Rue Montorgueil, in the heart of the original marketplace of Les Halles. Though developers have since erased the market from the map, it was a vibrant scene at the time, and today's neighborhood of malls and fashion boutiques pales in comparison. The brothers' reunion was apparently the event of the year, as the neighboring butchers, grocers and fishmongers, who all knew my uncle, came out of their shops to watch. The rubicund owner of a nearby wine store came over with several small glasses of Macon-Villages and then made an exuberant and ceremonial toast to us right there on the street.

We quickly discovered that Nathan's was not just another kiosk: he himself was a neighborhood character, and some of his clients included local philosophers and writers like Sartre and Camus (who had become his friend). They usually dropped by for the morning papers, exchanged a few comments, and then sometimes joined him for a cup of coffee or even a glass of white wine at a bar on the same street.

After a while, Nathan closed up shop and offered to take us all for lunch at a typical neighborhood bistro, the kind that is so hard to find nowadays. I thought he was heading towards an eye-catching sign with a huge golden snail twenty-five feet above the entrance to a restaurant named L'Escargot d'Or. But I was mistaken.

"We're not going to L'Escargot," Nathan said. "It isn't like it was in the old days when Marcel Proust or Sarah Bernhard used to go there for dinner. Now it's just a place for tourists, who are impressed by the opulent decor that was fashionable during the reign of Napoleon III. I don't want you to feel we're having lunch at the opera! Instead, I'd like to show you another side of Paris at an authentic working-class bistro with much better food."

We followed him to the next corner and a smaller place named Le Zinc for its hundred-year-old, pewter-colored zinc countertop. It had simple cream-colored walls, vaulted ceilings, and shelves replete with bottles of famous vintages covered with dust and the occasional spider web. After some brief introductions, the proud owner and his bartender produced a carafe of Chiroubles from a cask that, we were informed, had just arrived from the Beaujolais countryside. Our first course was unforgettable: a subtle preparation of eggs poached in that very red wine, or *oeufs en meurette*, a dish from Burgundy. But the rest of the meal was dominated by the life story of our uncle, who delighted us with an endless series of anecdotes and experiences. During the Second World War, he had been a truck driver for the French Resistance—he pulled an old photograph from his wallet, showing how he had fallen with his truck into a ravine near Lyon when escaping from German fire. Later, he served with the Foreign Legion in Indochina, up until the final stages of the war when the Viet Minh attack at Dien Bien Phou left the surviving French army in disarray. And finally, he was also active in Algeria, though he preferred not to remember that time in his life.

Exhausted from an emotional first day in Paris, we drifted towards our hotel for the night. But we saw Nathan again on Saturday morning, though not at his kiosk, which was closed for the day. We had arranged to meet up with him at the well-known Boule d'Or, located near the fountain at St. Michel. He referred to this café as his "headquarters," and we found him sitting regally by the window, writing. He told us he loved this proletarian café in the Latin quarter, where he was king. He claimed they made some of the best *café crème* in the city and at reasonable prices too. Although he worked hard at the kiosk, he could not have afforded the more expensive Les Deux Magots and Café de Flore in Saint Germain, frequented by Sartre and Simone de Beauvoir. Since Nathan was working on the first draft of his *History of the Literary Cafés in France,* whenever he could he researched other places like the Closerie des Lilas in Montparnasse, favored by the 19th-century poets Baudelaire and Paul Verlaine, and later on by Hemingway and Beckett. I don't know whether he ever finished the book, because most of his papers were discarded after he died, and by then we were too far away in the USA to do anything about it.

After a round of coffee for everyone, and a couple of cigarettes for the brothers, Nathan took us on a long tour through the streets of Paris, primarily on the left bank, but also to Le Marais, one of his favorite areas, on the right bank. We must have made quite an impression on the neighborhood as we followed this smallish but vibrant man in a long, dark-blue coat—the distinctive uniform of the French working class—who gesticulated and pointed out at all the historical landmarks along the way. And so began our informal education about Paris, its secret corners and extensive history, as told by one of the best-informed Parisians around.

He knew each cobblestone and the façades of many houses. At one point he stopped in front of a college on a cheerful little street to show us a touching memorial plaque with the names of many Jewish children the Germans had sent to concentration camps during the war. Nathan brought them back to life with his vivid description of wartime events. By the time we approached the river on our walk through Le Marais, we felt transported to a different Paris, not only of a few decades past but from as far back as medieval times. We realized that the city contained innumerable secrets, and that we were slowly entering a universe that was dramatically different from the one most tourists observed.

As we neared the Seine on Rue du Pont Louis-Phillipe, we were suddenly overtaken by an energetic young man wearing a short black cape and carrying an unusual walking stick—it was chest height and had a series of colored rings near the top. He walked with determination towards a large, gray-stone building, right next to a beautiful ancient church. Sensing a chance to emulate the great Cartier Bresson by capturing a "decisive moment," I ran after the man intent on taking his photograph, when he suddenly disappeared into the building. As I stood there perplexed, Nathan ran up to me and explained that the man was a *compagnon,* a member of a Masonic order dating back centuries. "Their name comes from Old French, and it means someone with whom one breaks bread." And then, in a surprise move, my uncle took us all inside the order's headquarters for a simple but delicious lunch.

The tall, rectangular building was like the refectory in a monastery from the Middle Ages, with high wooden beams and a long communal table, where the young man I had pursued had already joined other members for the meal. We sat very near the group to share the healthy but tasty lunch, and later we offered an appropriate donation. I managed to move even closer to the young man and actually engage him in conversation. I learned that his walking stick was primarily a badge used by pilgrims everywhere. Above the colored rings I had noticed earlier was an ivory top engraved with secret symbols— a set square, compass, and mortise axe—plus the letters U V G T, emblems of the carpenters' guild, one of the associations of artisans the order had been overseeing and teaching for centuries. He had apparently received his ceremonial staff on completing his education and internship. Tradition required he now go on the road for one or more years, either in France or in a foreign country. Although this used to mean making a pilgrimage on foot, he was in fact getting ready to fly for on-the-job training with an established carpentry master in Denmark. Other branches taught the culinary arts, baking or pastry making, all to a high level of expertise. One of my most admired chefs, Joël Robuchon, possibly the foremost chef in France, had trained as a *compagnon.*

At this point, Nathan cut in to exhibit his vast knowledge of French history. He described the order's ancient origins and the legend of Maître Jacques, a sage from Provence, who had reached Jerusalem near 970 BCE and was then hired by King Solomon as a stone carver to help build the First Temple. His followers had kept his teachings secret up until modern times, and many had become the master builders, or *masons,* of great monuments. And, mysteriously, a different story placed Maître Jacques in Orleans, where he built the towers of the great cathedral in 1401.

As we left the building, Nathan pointed next door to the church of St. Gervais. Its cemetery supposedly held the relics and bones of other famous *compagnons*, the stone cutters and carpenters who had built Nôtre Dame cathedral. Nathan explained that the order had a long history of being persecuted by the papacy, by other governments, and also by the Germans during the war, all of whom disliked and mistrusted the Masons for their secrecy. Even today the order has its political challenges, since it is a competitor of the powerful General Labor Union (CGT).

Sunday, the day scheduled for a full-fledged family reunion, finally arrived. After a light breakfast, we dressed for a party knowing that Nathan's grown-up children and their families would be there. At noon, we arrived for a banquet at historical Café Procope, on Rue de L'Ancienne Comédie. It was a formal venue with crystal chandeliers and multiple portraits of illustrious people, which we had no chance to investigate, since a jubilant crowd was expecting us at the entrance to the main dining room. A radiant Nathan announced our arrival to the whole family, and all fifty of them, still unknown to us, lined up in some sort of predetermined order to greet us with the four kisses, two on each side, as is expected among members of the same family in France. First in line was tiny Sophie, Nathan's Romanian wife, a featherweight dynamo who stuck by our sides chatting brightly till the end of the receiving line. This included their three children, grand-children, wives and second cousins, none of whose names we managed to remember. A bright young woman, a distant cousin of about fourteen, also accompanied us while practicing her rudimentary English.

With faces colored by makeup from several cousin's faces, taken aback by the size of our extended family, we proceeded to climb the stairs to the second floor for a group photo on the balcony, taken from across the street by a professional photographer. But the balcony, now burdened with the weight of the entire Lindner family, began to vibrate ominously, threatening to collapse and pitch us all into the street below. I immediately voiced my alarm, like a good citizen, but Sophie replied in her cute French-Romanian accent: "Stay still! If this building has held for three hundred years, it will hold for the next three minutes while we take this photograph."

Lunch was a six-hour affair with multiple courses orchestrated by Nathan in my dad's honor, and innumerable speeches by both brothers and multiple family members. In between courses, I managed several visits to the antique bathroom. Finally, a several-feet-tall "gateau St. Honoré," the *pièce de résistance,* put an end to the official celebrations. I was then able to explore the striking building and to read some of the historical posters on the walls and brochures on the tables. Nathan had chosen the perfect location for this reunion: Café Procope had been the first literary café in France, and it was only much later that it became a restaurant.

The history of coffee drinking in Europe was a subject close to my heart. Because of our unforgettable family reunion, I was inspired to learn more about this subject. I discovered that in 1669 during Louis XIV kingdom, Soliman-Agha the ambassador to the *Sublime Porte,* the government of the Ottoman Empire, had introduced coffee drinking in France. Shortly afterwards, an Armenian named Pascal opened a coffee shop at the site of the market in St. Germain. When his small establishment was about to go broke, an adventurous Sicilian by the name of Procope re-imagined the possibility of opening the present-day facility across the street from the original. Here, gentlemen fell into the habit of drinking coffee, which until Le Procope opened had only been served in taverns. Sorbets were also offered in tiny porcelain cups by waiters in exotic "Armenian" garb. Soon Le Procope would attract the best and most illustrious company of philosophers, writers, and politicians.

As I toured Le Procope, I discovered small tables with brass plates dedicated to the original customers: Rousseau, Voltaire, Napoleon III, and the encyclopedist Diderot. I sat in awe at some of these tables, day-dreaming about drinking Turkish coffee with someone like Voltaire, who drank as many as forty cups of coffee mixed with chocolate a day! It was at Le Procope that Voltaire met Benjamin Franklin and Thomas Jefferson. During the French Revolution, the Phrygian (or "liberty") cap made its debut at the café, where Robespierre, Danton, and Marat were all regular customers. Later, the café became popular with writers like Alfred de Musset, George Sand, and Anatole France, and also with politicians and orators like Leon Gambetta, who learned the art of public speaking there. Sitting at Voltaire's table, I felt surrounded by their spirit as I meditated on the effects of coffee on creativity and awakening the mind.

I knew that Nathan was writing his manuscript at the Boule d'Or, but I never imagined that one day I would imitate this behavior by studying for my medical exams at a corner café near the School of Medicine in Buenos Aires. And today I record these events at another café, the Storyville in Seattle's Pike Place Market. I am grateful to the Ethiopian farmer who discovered how to roast and extract the illuminating nectar from a tiny red bean. And God bless the Yemenite who learned to grow the most delicate and flavorful variety of coffee, which we call "Arabica" helped to create a habit that later spread through Arabia and Turkey, eventually landing on European shores and finally in America.

My interest in coffee has never faded, but over the years changes in the café world have influenced my own coffee quanta. For instance, the Café Procope itself was refurbished in 1988 in an 18th-century style, with Pompeian red walls, a tinkly piano, and waiters dressed in pseudo-revolutionary uniform. I returned to Le Procope once and was disappointed by these changes. Robespierre would have objected strongly to them all and the guillotine would have been busy once again! I also read that the ladies who were escorted to Café Procope in its earliest days soon disappeared, and for a long time afterwards no one remarked on the absence of women from coffee houses. I'm glad this situation has been reversed, of course, but not so happy about the young woman singing and humming the same song over and over in the next chair next to mine at Storyville today while composing music for her school.

For all these reasons, Café Procope is an important quantum in my coffee life. This was really brought home to me when I received a message on Facebook from an unknown person who goes by the name "Domino-Domino." She claimed to be a second cousin! This sounded like a phishing expedition, but it turned out to be true. She explained she was one of Nathan's granddaughters and had been at the banquet for my father! She was then a fourteen-year-old-girl who had tried practicing her English on us. We have since met up again in person and have even had coffee together at in Paris, across from the Pompidou Center, very near the place we first met. Just like it took my dad forty years to return to France, it took the same length of time for Dominique (her real name) and me to find each other through Facebook. Le Procope is now firmly established as a stable particle in my coffee universe.

The Quantum Café

Quantum 3: Café Florian

My third quantum materialized in Venice, where Turkish merchants had introduced coffee in the 16th century. It was unexpected because the position of quanta, like that of electrons, is undetermined and so we cannot predict where they will turn up. They only become "concrete" when they interact with something else. In this case, the particle found me when I was with my family at the historic Café Florian, established in 1720. I was getting my camera ready to capture the scene in the extravagant Senate Room, when we saw a middle-aged couple come in, looking stern and forbidding. They sat themselves down at a table in a corner that was dimly lit and overlooked the Piazza San Marco, so our first impression of them was that they were part of a film, like The Third Man, which starred Orson Welles and was set in 1949 Vienna. Interestingly, the cut and style of their clothes suggested they were from Eastern Europe: Austria or more likely in East Germany.

Out of respect, whenever I photograph people I like to make myself known to them or ask their permission. That day, something prompted me to take the photo brazenly and against the clear wishes of the mysterious couple. I still have the slide, an Agfachrome of very florid colors, that shows them looking astonished and indignant because of my boldness. And a huge copy still hangs, many years later, in a prominent place in our dining room. It is a lasting memory of the adventure which involved our son, Serge, when he was 12 years old.

I mounted my camera on a small tabletop tripod and aimed. The woman lit a cigarette, and the two turned to look at us, appearing both incredulous and uneasy. I snapped the shutter while pretending to talk with my family. The two stared at me with loathing for the rest of the evening. It was annoying, almost frightening, but at the same time it got our imaginations going. Could they be spies or Stasi agents? They say that some of them are currently highly active in several European countries.

The arrival of our waiter, in an elegant black tuxedo and bow tie, distracted us. He was tall, thin, and serious, and would have gone unnoticed at a state dinner in any country in Europe. We ordered a Negroni for Diana, an espresso for me, and a Virgin Bellini with fresh peaches for Serge. From our ornate marble table, our son looked around admiringly. The opulent room was decorated with excessively elaborate paintings by a certain Giacomo Casa. One of them, "Civilization educating the nations," had incomprehensible Masonic signs, for instance an angel touching a rock with the number XIX on it. From our modern cultural perspective, it seemed very pretentious. When the waiter returned with the drinks, Serge took the opportunity to ask: "Excuse me, sir. Is it true that the Florian has been open nonstop since 1720?"

"That's right, young man," the waiter answered in excellent English. "We were only forced to close for a few days in 1918, during World War I, when troops from Germany and Austria were closing in on us from the east, and we had to evacuate the city. But venetians relocated most of the city's residents to other parts of Italy, with great efficiency and for free. The bombs fell near here on the Bridge of Sighs but fortunately did not destroy the café."

"Why is it called Florian"?

"During the French Revolution, the Jacobins, who were republicans opposed to all foreign influence, gathered here. The original name of the café was Triumphant Venice, but when French troops entered the city, that seemed inappropriate. That's why they changed it to Florian, the name of the owner at the time."

"So much history!" replied Serge. "I like this place. I'm sure a lot of important people came here."

"You're very young. Do you know our writer Goldoni? Goethe, Charles Dickens, and Marcel Proust also came here. I'm sure you haven't heard of Casanova, who was a regular customer because we were the only café that allowed women in at the time," he said with a conspiratorial little smile.

While we had our drinks, the people at the

nearby table continued to look at me in a disconcerting way. But that did not prevent me from savoring the quality of the espresso, made with a mixture of beans called "Venezia 1720," and its intense but balanced aroma. The waiter explained imperiously that the coffee had excellent "organoleptic" properties.

After leaving the Florian, we walked for a bit through the narrow alleys and over their many bridges and took a charming and very touristy vaporetto (although the locals do not appreciate having to compete with foreigners for seats). We continued to explore after dinner. It got dark. The windows and stained glass lit up, and the city felt like the backdrop on a stage. Soon a thick fog rose, and we found ourselves in a maze of dark passageways and narrow sidewalks that went under the bridges spanning a canal behind La Fenice Opera House. As we passed calle de Caffetier, the mist thickened and the city seemed desolate to us, as though it existed in a strangely empty and dark world like Chernobyl after the explosion. We were about to go back to the hotel when we saw a couple ahead of us in the distance. Almost in unison we said, "Aren't they the spies from the café?" We followed them through the mist for about a hundred meters without being absolutely sure of their identity. To our surprise, they disappeared through a side door in front of the canaletto, which turned out to be the pier and entrance for the boats going to the Hotel Luna. We looked cautiously inside but could only see the employees at reception and an elegant baroque lounge, with tapestries and numerous paintings in gold frames. No sign at all of our alleged spies!

Back at the hotel, Serge surprised us by asking: "Can I go out on my own tomorrow to take a look around the city? I won't get lost."

We thought about it carefully; the idea unsettled us. We were always overprotective of him, but it seemed appropriate to let him have this experience by himself this one time. Armed with a map that showed the location of the hotel, he would have no problem in this quiet and friendly city. Although not entirely comfortable with the idea, we finally gave him permission.

"Great! Here's the hotel, here are the canals, and here are the boat stops," he said, pointing them out on the map, "and in case I'm not sure, the Venetians surely understand some Spanish."

Serge left next morning after breakfast. We told him a thousand times to come back in time for dinner and gave him money for lunch and to buy a souvenir.

There was still a lot for us to explore. We visited galleries, glass factories, medieval corners of the city. At the Café Segafreddo, the espresso was smooth and the people friendly. We soon felt as though we had been born in that narrow alley and would know some of the neighbors: the tall, elegant woman in somewhat bohemian clothes walking a little wooly white dog; the gray-bearded old man reading the fables of Italo Calvino; the housewife loaded down with provisions and fish from the market behind the Rialto; and the kids running around with balloons of very color. From our angle, we could see the vaporetto stop, and as dusk fell we saw a beaming Serge reappear, carefully carrying a small brown parcel in his right hand.

"Hello, Serge! How'd it go? You seem really happy."

"It was awesome! I only got lost once near the Accademia, but a waiter at a cafe told me how to find the vaporetto. They understand a lot Spanish in Venice and even say calle instead of via. But look what I bought!"

There and then he opened the parcel, and very proudly set down on the table a collection of ten crystal swans on the table, placing them in a straight line, largest to smallest, behind the mother swan.

"What else did you do?"

"First I crossed the Rialto and went to see the fish market. I've never seen so many different shapes and sizes of seafood... but what impressed me the most were the shouting fishermen competing with one another in their dialect. I understood enough to get the idea. The seafood made me hungry, so I ate a slice of pizza on a street corner." He turned red, feeling a little guilty, since at that time, he was still chubby.

"Our rabbi and the cantor who is getting me ready for my bar mitzvah said I should visit the old Guetto, the ancient quarter, where there are no posters or signs. But a very friendly old man from the neighborhood accompanied me to the entrance of the 'Great German School,' the first Ashkenazi synagogue in Venice, founded around the 1500s. Too bad I couldn't take a picture to show the cantor. I liked the decorations, the bimah, and the Ten Commandments inscribed in gold. Oh, and the gallery upstairs was just for women!"

"What a nice experience to be in such a historic place! They're going to love it when you tell them about it."

"You're going to laugh at me! From one corner came a delicious smell of pasta. I loved the name on the door: Osteria ai Quaranta Ladroni, like the forty thieves of Ali Baba. The menu was really cheap. As Dad says, "You have to follow your nose," and so I went in to eat. The thieves were gone, but they did give me some amazing linguini con salsa di pomidoro!" Then he took a long pause and, with an impish smile, refused to tell us anything else. "I'm saving the most interesting thing for the end."

"Come on, don't be so mysterious!"

"When I took the vaporetto back from the Guetto, I saw the spies of Café Florian again! Luckily, they didn't recognize me. I was sitting in the middle of the boat and saw them pass by and sit at the front, on the opposite side, next to a man who was already there. Why did they choose that seat seeing the vaporetto was almost empty? The man carried a Herald Tribune, but the strange thing was, when he got off two stops later he no longer had it. Instead, the man who had been next to him rushed to get off at the Accademia station and had the same paper in his hands! I decided to get off there too and follow him. He seemed to know that part of town well. He went down a little side street, zigzagging through parts that were covered and darker. I followed behind at about twenty meters. There were few people around and it scared me a little. But he soon walked out onto a sidewalk next to a canal that flowed into an exceptionally large one, the Giudecca, according to the map. There were more people, and since the guy didn't know me, I decided to follow him at a distance. I mean, who would suspect a tourist kid?"

"Serge, that's crazy, how did you come up with such an idea? How far did you go?"

"Before arriving at the Giudecca, he went into a bar where they sell cicchetti, the Venetian tapas. The guy stood by the counter, bought one, and ordered a glass of white wine. I got up the courage to go in and look around. The cicchetti had the price written on them. Even though I wasn't hungry anymore, as a cover I ordered one of polenta with prawns. I went to eat it outside in front of the bar by a railing where there were other people. On the other side of that narrow canal, people were working in an old gondola factory, and I stood for a while watching them."

"What about the guy?"

"He was inside. No, I didn't lose sight of him. Soon a fat man came in, with a few days' worth of stubble and sort of dirty, like the actor in Topkapi. He looked foreign, but he didn't look around like a tourist would. He also ate something at the counter, near the guy from the vaporetto. When they left on their own and a minute apart... You will not believe it. The fat one had the copy of the Herald Tribune. I bet it was the same one. I must be the only one who realized they had passed it between them."

Serge looked at us, waiting for a reaction.

"Maybe they're just two tourists, and we're making the whole thing up," said Diana.

"But, Mom, don't you think it's weird about them having the same newspaper? Maybe they're Stasi spies? Too bad we don't know anyone in the government or the police, even though they'd laugh at us."

After a while, I had a thought.

"Do you remember my friend George, the State Department diplomat? Before our trip, I asked him for a reliable contact in Venice in case we had any problems or needed advice about events or interesting places. I have the consulate number and could call him. His name is Phillips."

We arranged to meet the next day at the

Florian along with the cultural attaché. We ordered an aperitif and waited for it in the Sala Orientale, which featured a painting of Marco Polo (one of Serge's heroes) among other notable Venetians. A man who could only be an American soon came in. He was about 40 years old and wore a light grey suit, sky-blue shirt without a tie, a nondescript expression, and a somewhat fake smile that seemed out of place in this café. Someone forgettable who would go unnoticed anywhere. He recognized us immediately and sat down to join us.

"Nice to meet you! I haven't heard from George for a while. We worked together in Europe. What do you think of Venice? I often come to the Florian." We talked a bit about the history of the place, and then he got to the point "How can I help you...?"

We explained the reason for our call and let Serge tell him in detail about his adventures. Phillips looked at him a little curiously, but he remained expressionless, poker-faced. But I could see his eyes light up when Serge said the guy at the cicchetti bar looked like Peter Ustinov.

"Did he have a dark beard and a wart on his nose?" he asked casually.

"That's right!" Serge answered immediately.

He had turned out to be an even better observer than we thought.

"You say you took a picture of the couple in

this café?" he unexpectedly asked me. "Did you have a copy?"

"No, sorry. I'm taking all the slides back to Seattle to develop them there. We're going back soon."

"Well!" said Phillips." Many thanks for the story. It's impossible to know if this is of any importance—we'll look into it—but I appreciate you taking the trouble to tell us what you saw. Have a good visit in Venice."

We never had a chance to ask him to suggest any sights. We were left wondering what his real occupation was at the consulate. His comments and behavior seemed to have nothing to do with culture.

Over the next two days we visited the Lido and spent a few hours at the beach. We couldn't miss the famous Sent sisters' factory in Murano, known for its contemporary glass jewelry. We ended our visit with a traditional lunch at Ai Frati, a Venetian dish of pasta with scampi and liver. Many great Murano glass artists eat there. From time to time, the image of the couple from the Florian would come to mind.

The morning before we left, we found a copy of the Venice English News on the breakfast table. A front-page article caught our attention:

"Night police activity at the Luna Hotel: Last night, at about 23 hours, hotel staff confirmed that federal police had come looking for a couple of foreigners, who were registered under the name

Morgenthaler. They could not be found in their room, but a moment later, to the loud sound of marine engines, a boat sped off from the side exit into to the Grand Canal and was soon lost to sight. The boat did not have its regulatory lights on, so it could not be determined whether it was a water taxi or a private boat. It is presumed the guests had registered under a false name, and that thanks to their successful river escape, the police were unable to locate them. Details of the activities of the two people and the reasons for the police presence are unknown."

The photo of the mysterious couple that I rashly took on that trip to Venice remains unchanged in its special place in our dining room, well lit by a strong LED light. Very close to it, in its own niche on a shelf, an exquisite family of crystal swans seems to float over the waters of the historic lagoon.

The Florian Café is still open, as it has been almost continuously since 1720, without any knowledge whatsoever that an essential quantum of my coffee life happened there with indelible consequences.

Santa Claus's Doctor

I knew I should write this story when an eight-year-old girl asked me very innocently if it were true that I was Santa Claus's doctor. During a dinner with friends, she listened, fascinated, to the story of an experience I'd had with a patient. Her question startled me because young people tend to speak the truth and that made me confront the doubts that I had long had about the boundaries between what is real and what is imaginary.

I met Santa in early December '99, the same day it started snowing furiously. The vast field looked like a sheet of white dunes, a large extension of the bed at my temporary housing.

I had agreed to substitute for a local doctor for a month while he was on vacation. It was my first time in Idaho and also in a small country town. I soon found myself surrounded by the children and grandchildren of former Basque immigrants who were sheep farmers and producers of the region's famous potatoes. Some still played jai alai, a kind of Basque ballgame, in a court. I also discovered that among my patients were several survivalists obsessed with living through a hypothetical catastrophe and already prepared for the end of the world. Some built underground shelters stocked with enough food to last them for months and weapons more powerful than the Taliban's. A sign in the waiting room reminded them that they were prohibited from entering the clinic with firearms or knives more than four inches long. I can't say whether Santa had settled in that region because he felt comfortable among them or he wanted to assure them that the world would go on as before after the turn of the millennium.

That morning the clinic was full of people and the waiting room looked like a train station on a national holiday. On the patient list I saw that one Nicholas Claus was the next person up. To save time, I stepped out and called:

"Mr. Claus, please come in!"

I waited a few seconds and, since no one stood up, I repeated, "Mr. Nicholas Claus," with no result.

I wondered if he didn't understand me because of my accent, or maybe the bad weather had prevented him from coming in, even though in the area people were used to snow. The nurse explained that she remembered him from an earlier visit, but that you had to ask for him in another way—and she went out to call him herself, loudly and assertively:

"Is Santa in the waiting room?"

Immediately a large, older man got to his feet. He had a dazzling smile set in an enormous beard that was as white as the snow I could see from the window.

He walked to my office in a leisurely manner. Although somewhat overweight, his body looked as solid as a professional wrestler's. But his demeanor was sweet and calm. He was wearing jeans and a red-checked shirt, which were traditional clothes in these parts. He also sported a sleeveless vest of soft brown wool. I couldn't tell what animal it was from, but I knew it wasn't sheep's wool.

When he sat down, I noticed he was somewhat worried, so I introduced myself and began by asking him the reason for his visit.

"Nice to meet you, Doctor Moguilevski. Look, I'm not feeling well. I've got extremely high blood pressure and a headache, and I've lost my appetite. My legs are a bit swollen, and when I walk I feel short of breath. I haven't seen a doctor in a while, and I'm not currently taking anything. The discomfort interferes with my activity and it's less than a month away from Christmas. I'm way behind with my preparations: I have to read people's letters and get the things they're asking for."

He spoke in a deep tenor's voice that was serious and enigmatic, with the accent common among the farmers of the area. His symptoms were easy to diagnose, but his comments about the activities and preparations for Christmas baffled me. I couldn't think what his occupation might be but did not want to delve into it at that moment.

"Well, Mr. Claus, I'd like to examine you and see whether I can work out why you're feeling the way you are. Take off your shirt, please, I'm going to take your blood pressure and listen to your chest."

"Doctor, call me Santa like everyone else," he said softly, sitting down in front of me with the agility of a younger man.

Considering he looked like a farmer or a sailor, I was surprised that he spoke with such precision and moved with an elegance that was hard to describe.

When I first saw him, he reminded me of the Alaskan fishermen I'd recently seen in a video. They conveyed the strength, determination and great courage needed to navigate those stormy seas; unlike me, they did not suffer from seasickness in the incessant pitching and swaying. When I asked him if he came from Alaska, he said yes and that he had been a fisherman in his youth. He was only passing through Idaho and had stayed here to rest when his health worsened.

I confessed that I envied his vest, that I really liked it. Then he explained that it was wool from his flock of reindeer. I imagined what a luxury it would be go out for a walk or into a café downtown when I got home in January. What surprised me was that, though there were deer in Idaho, at no point did I ever hear anyone mention reindeer, which were more typical of Lapland. I'm sure he had brought it from Alaska.

I proceeded to take his blood pressure. While he was taking off his vest and rolling up his shirt sleeve, I noticed that on his left wrist he wore a huge solid gold bracelet, perhaps 18-karat. In the center was inscribed "Santa" in large print letters. I had no choice but to ask him about that. He explained that a great friend, a miner in Alaska, had discovered a gold vein the previous Christmas and had had the bracelet made as a gift.

"But Santa"—I had begun calling him this seeing as he only responded to that name—"it must be worth a fortune! Aren't you afraid you might be mugged?"

"Don't worry, Doctor, people are fond of me, and nothing has ever happened to me. Actually, I confess that I feel a certain weakness for jewelry and, until the moment I hand it over to the new owner, I like to have it around so I can admire it. Let me show you. See what you think."

Although he was still wearing the blood pressure cuff, he stretched out his arm and grabbed his backpack from which he extracted a black silk bag the size of a football. From there he began to take out jewelry of all kinds: rings with rubies, rings with aquamarines, sophisticated Swiss watches made of white gold, and strings of exotic black pearls. One necklace, made of several strands of pale gold and precious gemstones, resembled the one in the Tutankhamen exhibition I had seen at the Museum of Art.

All this greatly alarmed me. I don't know whether I was surprised by the overwhelming display of jewelry or by its incongruity in this small clinic on the Idaho prairie. I wondered if he had stolen the jewelry, but he looked nothing like a thief. Nor did he look like a wealthy rancher or an executive at one of the big tech companies of the neighboring Pacific Coast states. In any case, I insisted he put it away under the pretext of continuing the physical exam. I began to wonder whether this man needed psychological rather than high blood pressure treatment. Besides, I could smell the slightest whiff of vodka or gin, although maybe I only imagined it. But the jewels were real: I had touched them with my own hands. Neither being a madman nor an alcoholic could adequately explain the treasures he had shown me so enthusiastically and so candidly.

I wanted to continue with the examination. Shortly afterwards, I sent him to the lab for immediate testing and asked him to wait in the room until he got the results. He didn't protest and left quietly with his backpack over his shoulder.

An hour later, when the results came up on my computer, I asked him back in to tell him about his diagnosis and treatment.

"Well, Santa, I'm glad you came in. You have several problems that need solving. Your blood pressure has gone untreated for quite some time and that affects the heart and kidneys. That's why your head hurts and your feet swell. The situation carries considerable risk, and I would like us to agree to start treatment today. It consists of going on a diet, reducing your consumption of beer and other alcohol, and taking several medications. But the important thing is that you accept responsibility for helping yourself."

"I'm going to do everything you recommend, although the beer thing is very difficult. But I'd like you to assure me that I'm going to feel better in the next few days. Can you imagine the disappointment if Christmas arrives and people don't find anything in their stockings when they wake up? I have a huge box full of letters with requests, including some that other patients here at the clinic gave me. Swollen and lacking in energy like this, I'm in no shape to go down chimneys—you have to help me. I don't even feel strong enough to care for and feed the reindeer!"

I thought that he was hallucinating and I would have to arrange for a psychiatric consult later on. Some chronic drinkers can reach a state of dementia, such as Wernicke Syndrome, in which they lose their memory but constantly make things up. Luckily, Santa had a good memory, for now. Whatever his problem was, it was important to lower his blood pressure and help him feel better.

"Look, Santa, I'd like you to start on a diet of fresh vegetables and fruit, only a little salt, and no frozen or canned food at all. I'm going to give you a diuretic for your swollen legs, and another medication to lower your blood pressure and protect your kidneys at the same time. But I want to see you again soon to check how you're doing and make any adjustments. Since you've never been treated, I can't predict how you will respond to these changes. I'm going to make you an appointment for next week, but phone if questions arise or you get worse. Please stop by the lab for tests again two hours or so before you see me."

As I left, I noticed he was flirting with the receptionists and that the nurse furtively handed him a white envelope. I called her in on some pretext and got up the nerve to ask her what she had given him, whether it was the date of his next appointment or something else. She blushed and said that, just in case this patient was the real Santa, she wouldn't lose anything by asking him for something. Not for her but rather for her teenage daughter, who had never seen the sea and dreamed of a fine, white, sandy beach. While I found the idea of the letter with her request amusing, her dream did not seem far-fetched considering the Idaho winter was suitable only for the descendants of Basque highlanders.

When I saw him heading for the exit it occurred to me that this man was really strange and seemed able to induce magical thinking or superstition in certain people as was the case with the nurse. That's why I excused myself as though I needed to go to the bathroom and then causally made my way towards the exit. I saw him leave as the automatic door closed again. When I got to the main entrance, I looked toward the parking lot, where the cars were almost completely covered in snow, but I couldn't see Santa or anything moving at all. Nor did I see any recent footprints in the snow. I waited outside for almost five minutes and saw only a couple of people going to their cars. In the end, I began shivering with cold and had to return to my office without working out how this man had left without leaving a trace.

The following week went by quickly. There was a lot of work to do, and I didn't get around to thinking about my patient until the day I saw his name on the list again. I found him sitting in the waiting room holding his head as if it hurt, with a compress to his forehead. He seemed more worried than on his first visit. I asked him in right away, and he told me what had happened.

"Hi, Doctor. I've just come from the emergency room. They had to put a few stitches in my forehead because this morning I fell off the sleigh and got cut. I've followed all your directions, but the treatment lowered my blood pressure too much. Overall, I feel better. I don't get tired and I walk fine. But today I was carrying the sleigh, and when I raised my head I got dizzy—everything spun around me and I lost my balance. When I got up, my forehead was bleeding and I had to go to emergency fast. Luckily, it's nothing. But, look, it's two weeks till Christmas and I still can't get organized. I'm afraid this will be the first time I haven't been ready to make the many people who are looking forward to me happy! Do you think I'll be in shape soon?"

"I'm sure you will. Luckily, your blood pressure has dropped quickly, though I'm sorry you got dizzy and cut your forehead. That shouldn't have happened. On the other hand, I notice you've lost weight and no longer have swollen legs. The results of your tests are also improved and your kidneys are working well again. I think you'll be ready to do whatever you need to do for Christmas."

"Thank you very much, Doctor Moguilevski. You're giving me confidence. But let me ask you a question. Your name tells me you must be Jewish and may not know our traditions. Do you celebrate something at Christmas? Do you believe in miracles?"

"Not to worry, I understand and respect you. As for miracles, we believe in some, but they're different from yours. Do you know the meaning of Hanukkah, the Festival of Lights? We celebrate the Maccabee rebellion, when a small group of warriors defeated the Roman troops and restored the Second Temple in Jerusalem. And the second miracle was that, when they entered the temple, they found a lamp that had only a little oil and yet it stayed lit for eight days. That's why we observe the holiday now by lighting a new candle every day. We also respect the miracles others accept. As far as your treatment is concerned, I don't need to share your beliefs. I'll still do everything I can to make you better so you can meet your obligations in time for Christmas. From now on, cut the dosage of your medicines in half and come back in a week. If they're really working, I'll be happy to discharge you."

Over the following nights I had nightmares in which Santa, as though drunk, drove his sleigh in an unchecked rage and whipped the reindeer to make them jump higher and higher from one snowy roof to another. At one point, he completely lost control and fell from a great height, slowly, as though he were floating in the clouds, until he landed and cut his forehead when he collided with his sleigh. I got out of bed anxious and upset. Another night, however, I dreamed that I saw many young people enjoying themselves and jumping with joy over their new toys, as the reflection of Hanukkah candles flickered on the windows of neighboring houses. In my dreams, the festivities were all mixed up.

As I had asked, Santa returned on December 23. He seemed younger and less worried, as though he had regained his confidence. He walked briskly and breathed without difficulty, and his wound had healed up well, leaving no scar on his forehead. He seemed taller than on his first visit. This time, I could not detect alcohol on his breath. I examined him and noted with satisfaction that his blood pressure was back to normal and that his heart was now beating with the strength of a young runner's. As promised, I discharged him, convinced that his improvement showed a new attitude and augured a healthier future. As he listened to me, Santa let out a big sigh of relief and smiled broadly again from ear to ear. Then he said something unexpected:

"Doctor, I am incredibly grateful for what you've done for me even though you did not entirely believe what I told you. Of course, you are a skeptic and a rational man. I know you are an expert in your field and helping me will also make a lot of other people happy. That's why I'd like to give you a present, without having to go down your fireplace. I think you're going to like this!"

And so, without further ado, he took off his impressive vest of reindeer wool and offered it to me with both hands, in a vaguely Asian gesture, similar to what a Korean might do when delivering a letter. I was excited, although I did not know if it was right to accept gifts from a patient in a society so concerned with the appearance of propriety. In the end, I accepted it with reservations but convinced that if this man could now celebrate Christmas by fulfilling his purpose, real or imaginary, then I deserved his thanks.

"I wish you a happy holiday! Remember that we met. May life bring you many pleasant surprises!" he said kindly. He turned away and left the office with a steady step.

The 25th dawned clear and cold. I was grateful I did not have to go to the clinic early and I only had a few days left of work before going back to my family, and daily routine, in Portland. I shaved slowly and then, feeling quite hungry, started heating up breakfast. I'd had no nightmares the night before and was in a good mood. I went to the bedroom to get dressed and put on my brand-new vest, something I never would have imagined before coming to substitute for a doctor in Idaho. I looked admiringly at myself in the mirror: it fitted me perfectly. Once it had been dry cleaned, it would look like new. I knew it would give my friends in Portland a lot to talk about. But at the same time I was consumed with curiosity about who exactly this special patient was. Was he really a psychotic or just a rich rancher, someone eccentric but kind who gave away his possessions to people in need? I would never be able to put my doubts to rest, nor did I think I would see him again.

The next day I went to the clinic, and fortunately there were by far fewer patients. I was proudly wearing my impressive fur vest when the nurse came out with a big smile to give me a hug.

"Doctor, how good to see you dress as though you were from this town! The vest is divine. But let me tell you: my daughter received an unexpected gift for Christmas. She found a promotional certificate for a flight and free accommodation for two at a state-of-the-art hotel in Cancun. I'm going to join her very soon. She's finally going to get to know the sea!"

A few days later I returned to Portland wearing my new vest.

Several years have passed since my strange stint as a substitute in Idaho. The millennium ended without a newsflash or cataclysm (surely to the great disappointment of the survivalists I met on that trip). Now I am grateful to the girl who asked me her innocent question and reminded me of my mysterious patient. The vest is still my favorite garment and is very warm. I don't take it off even on the hottest summer days.

II - ESPAÑOL

Matsumoto-san y el pañuelo
de seda blanca

En un memorable atardecer luminoso en nuestra costa del Pacífico, Matsumoto-san, una consumada tanguera, se dejó por descuido un pañuelo blanco en la milonga. Este olvido insignificante fue suficiente para lanzarme a una búsqueda sobre los orígenes de ese pañuelo. Más aun, para intentar explicar la capacidad asombrosa de su dueña de mejorar el estado del tiempo.

El pañuelo era de seda blanca, con un brillo y una suavidad poco comunes, con un diseño monocromático muy elegante, y pensé que sería japonés, como su dueña. Además de la belleza de la seda, me sorprendió un detalle inusitado. Tejida en una esquina de la tela había una pequeña inscripción con caracteres negros irregulares, en un idioma que no supe reconocer.

Luego llamé a Matsumoto-san para contarle que había encontrado su pañuelo. Por el tono de su voz, me pareció preocupadísima por haber extraviado ese chal que le había encomendado su familia. Por eso le sugerí que nos encontráramos bien pronto en el café del Parque Olímpico de escultura, frente al malecón de Seattle. Esperaba un lindo día. Mi optimismo se basaba en un hecho especulativo: nuestros amigos habían observado que cuando planeábamos una salida con ella para una caminata por el bosque o un paseo en kayak, podíamos contar con la certeza de días soleados.

El sábado siguiente estábamos sentados a una mesa afuera, en el café, disfrutando desde la colina de la vista de la bahía, bajo un brillante cielo azul. De pronto vimos aparecer entre la niebla del Puget Sound, por detrás de las barcazas y los ferris enmarcados por las montañas Olímpicas, otra gran superficie de agua con bordes irregulares y un río que allí desembocaba, rodeado de rascacielos en la orilla opuesta. Los dos pensamos en el mismo instante en un espejismo: la muy lejana bahía de Tokio, un paisaje familiar para Matsumoto-san, pero que yo solo había visitado una vez.

En cuanto el mozo nos sirvió un ahumado té oolong, lamentablemente en tazas de plástico, le pedí a Matsumoto-san que me hablara de la historia de su exquisito pañuelo. Aparentemente estaba ansiosa por contármelo y, sin más, comenzó:

—Te cuento, Maurice, que me lo regaló mi madre cuando dejé Japón para un trabajo en los Estados Unidos. El 17 de julio de 1999 estábamos en Kioto para el festival Obon. Hay una tradición en nuestra familia de transferir el pañuelo de la madre a su hija mayor en esa ocasión, y mantuvimos esta costumbre por muchas generaciones. Creo que la calidad exquisita de la seda y el cuidado que tuvieron sus dueñas han contribuido a que se conserve así.

—Me llama la atención la inscripción que

tiene en una esquina. ¿Sabés lo que significa?

—Mi madre y yo también teníamos curiosidad por saberlo. Seguramente no es una etiqueta o una marca registrada y no está escrita en japonés. Es muy frustrante no identificar esos caracteres.

—¿Qué podrías contarme sobre tu madre y las tradiciones de la familia?

—Mi madre es una persona algo rara. Sufre de un síndrome compulsivo y te confieso que lo heredé también un poco. Por ejemplo, tiene una gran pasión por la limpieza, se lava las manos todo el tiempo, evita tocar picaportes o asideros en el transporte público. Le gusta "purificar" los suelos del baño y la cocina con agua y sal, igual que otros a la entrada de funerarias, o cuando los luchadores de sumo echan sal en el ring antes del combate.

Hizo una pausa, un poco avergonzada por la descripción de su madre, pero al fin continuó, algo más calmada:

—Tenía otra costumbre que no he visto en otras casas en Japón. Los viernes, a la hora del crepúsculo, le gustaba cubrirse la cabeza con un pañuelo blanco y encender velas mientras susurraba una melodía aprendida de niña de mi abuela. A veces estuve a punto de continuar con ese hábito familiar, porque me trae una sensación de calma y alegría después de una semana de mucho trabajo. También me siento así cuando estoy en una ceremonia sintoísta. No te vas a sorprender, siendo un buen bailarín, si te digo que me satisface tanto como si hubiera bailado un buen tango con una pareja experta. Es lo mismo que experimenté durante la última milonga y eso explica que olvidara mi precioso pañuelo.

Entonces examinamos los desconocidos caracteres tejidos en la tela. La letra manuscrita mostraba una mezcla de un texto sinuoso con unas ramas laterales rectas que no se asemejaba a nada que hubiésemos visto antes. Pensé que podían ser letras hebreas, pero fui incapaz de descifrarlas, dado mi conocimiento rudimentario de ese idioma. Enfrentados a esta extraña inscripción, se me ocurrió imaginar que podrían ser muy antiguas y tener alguna conexión con los rituales de su familia, de modo que le propuse consultar con un experto en el tema.

—¡Sería estupendo! —me dijo Matsumoto-san—. Nunca tuve ocasión de investigar este misterio, pero no quisiera que perdieras mucho tiempo en esto y que descuidases tus asuntos. Yo sé que tu curiosidad no tiene límites, pero no abandones tus estudios sobre los efectos terapéuticos del tango en el sistema neurológico.

Su preocupación no me sorprendió, ya que ella es psiquiatra y una investigadora muy escéptica. También admiro sus modales suaves y su simpatía, que la ayudan a extraer información íntima de la gente y muchos no se dan cuenta de que se trata de un interrogatorio directo y muy preciso.

—No te preocupes, de vez en cuando necesito apartarme un poco de mi trabajo y me vendría bien una corta pausa para investigar el misterio de tu familia.

Quizá me apresuré un poco en contestarle, porque más tarde descubrí que este curioso asunto iba a requerir un gran esfuerzo. Realmente, yo admiro a los que aceptan un desafío intelectual y, al igual que Matsumoto-san, soy ante todo un investigador. Esta era mi oportunidad para enfocarme en un tema diferente sin sentirme culpable.

Aprovechando mi gran red de conocidos, pude conseguir una cita con el ya centenario y aun lúcido rabino Moshé Bensimón, respetado erudito y líder de la comunidad sefardita, especialista en historia y tradiciones judías. También era coautor de un conocido diccionario hebreo-inglés.

La casa del rabino, cerca del Seward Park, era pequeña y acogedora, con un jardín muy imaginativo de flores y hierbas salvajes que me recordaban a algunos de Haifa. El interior estaba decorado con numerosas fotos de familia, mapas antiguos y grabados. Una anciana envuelta en un chal negro nos abrió la puerta y nos saludó con un ligero acento del Medio Oriente, antes de dirigirse a la cocina a preparar un café turco muy dulce y aromático que nos sirvió mientras esperábamos a Bensimón.

Cuando el rabino se presentó, fue directamente al grano. Primero le describimos las costumbres de la familia de Matsumoto-san y le mostramos el pañuelo. Bensimón acarició la elegante prenda de seda con los dedos, muy retorcidos por la artritis. Entonces se puso un anticuado par de anteojos de lentes gruesos para examinar la inscripción. Al poco rato exclamó:

—¡Amigos, ustedes han venido al sitio justo! Me traen algo muy curioso y fascinante para alguien de mi edad. Primero les diré que este texto no está escrito en hebreo, sino en arameo. ¡Es un idioma con tres mil años de historia, el mismo que hablaba Jesucristo! También lo usaban sus discípulos para difundir su mensaje. Es el lenguaje original usado en el Talmud antes de que fuese traducido al hebreo que leemos hoy en día. Lamento mucho no entender estas palabras que no puedo traducir, pero, en cambio, trataré de pronunciarlas.

Se puso a mascullar en voz alta durante un ratito y al final se arregló para articular unas palabras que hicieron casi saltar a Matsumoto-san de su silla al oírlas. En forma inesperada comenzó a repetir las palabras del rabino, en su propia entonación:

—Ama-te-ra-su o-mi-ka-mi, amaterasu-omikami... ¡Este es el nombre de la diosa-sol en la mitología japonesa! —dijo Matsumoto-san. Y siguió repitiendo estas palabras sin parar, como iluminada, mientras su cara parecía irradiar una luz interior.

—¡Esta coincidencia es notable! —dijo entonces el rabino que estaba de pie junto a Matsumoto-san, imitando la pronunciación de estas palabras en japonés.

—Por favor, cuéntenos lo que sepa sobre la diosa-sol.

—Amaterasu debe ser la kami, una deidad sintoísta, la más importante porque es considerada la antepasada ancestral de la Casa Imperial de Japón. La celebramos cada 17 de julio, el día en que recibí el pañuelo de mi madre, con unas procesiones, y también el 21 de diciembre, en el solsticio de invierno. Todavía recuerdo una versión de este mito que aprendí en mi infancia:

"Amaterasu tenía un hermano llamado Susanoo, que era bastante travieso. Un día Susanoo, que era el dios de las tormentas, decidió demostrar sus poderes desatando una tempestad que enfrió y oscureció el mundo, con fuertes vientos que dispersaron las cosechas y las flores que amaba su hermana. Amaterasu, desesperada, se escondió en una cueva negándose a salir, de modo que el mundo permaneció helado y triste. Como la situación era insostenible, el pueblo japonés se unió con ocho mil kamis para bailar y cantar a la entrada de su cueva, rogándole que saliera. Finalmente, un kami pudo persuadirla para que reapareciera, poniendo un espejo afuera de la cueva entre dos grietas en las rocas para que ella pudiera admirar su propia belleza. Cuando la diosa abandonó su reclusión, una brillante luz de sol volvió a iluminar el universo y por eso la idolatramos por su amor y compasión".

Matsumoto-san hizo una pausa para recordar detalles y darnos más información.

—Lo increíble para mí es que parece haber una correlación con la tela de mi pañuelo, porque la diosa había descubierto el uso de los gusanos de seda y nos inspiró a tejer con un telar.

Cuando Matsumoto-san consideró otros detalles de la leyenda, moderó su entusiasmo y se dirigió al rabino:

— Señor, ahora creo que todo esto debe ser solo una coincidencia. No puedo aceptar que exista una conexión entre un kami japonés y sus viejas tradiciones judías y, menos aún, una relación con mi familia.

El rabino Bensimón se levantó deprisa, sin preocuparse por sus articulaciones anquilosadas por la edad. Parecía más alerta y rejuvenecido que al principio de nuestra visita. Entonces recomenzó la charla con notable energía:

—¡Fíjese, amiga mía, la historia extraordinaria de este mito y las costumbres de su familia me iluminan y hasta se me aflojaron las coyunturas! Ante todo, creo que el uso del arameo en la inscripción es de suma importancia. Es lógico especular que los ancianos israelitas visitaron su país hace muchos siglos y dejaron una huella indeleble en algunos japoneses. Otra cosa increíble es la coincidencia de las fechas: usted recibió ese pañuelo el día 17 del séptimo mes durante el festival Ubon. Ese mismo día celebramos la cosecha en la tradición judía de Sucot.

El rabino estaba gozando a raudales con nuestra visita y hablando más lentamente para saborear cada palabra mientras hurgaba en su memoria. Al rato continuó con un entusiasmo renovado:

—Les quiero contar una historia que escuché de mis maestros cuando era un joven seminarista en la yeshiva de Estambul. Durante el reino del rey Salomón, en el siglo X a. C., las doce tribus de Israel habían llegado al sumun de su prosperidad.

Hablaba más despacio, buscando las palabras exactas:

—Las dos tribus en la región sur de Judea eventualmente dieron origen al pueblo judío actual. Pero la zona norte, llamada Samaría, fue conquistada en el siglo XVIII A. C. por el ejército asirio, obligando a las diez tribus restantes a partir hacia el exilio, perdiéndose en la historia. Algunos de mis maestros creen que emigraron hacia el norte cruzando el río Éufrates, donde hoy se encuentran Irak y el Kurdistán. Durante su marcha épica por varios siglos, cruzaron varias montañas y países siguiendo la Ruta de la Seda para atravesar China y llegar hasta el océano. Nuestros antepasados eran buenos marineros y no sería nada sorprendente que hubieran llegado hasta Corea y Japón.

Cuando el rabino se detuvo por un momento, Matsumoto-san, que hasta ahora parecía nerviosa pero callada, no pudo contenerse e interrumpió al rabino. Estaba realmente incrédula:

—Perdóneme, rabino. La historia que ha relatado es fascinante, pero uno necesitaría pruebas concretas de que estas tribus perdidas atravesaron todos esos países y se relacionaron con otros pueblos. Lo que nos cuenta me resulta exagerado y poco convincente —soltó (y yo pensé que era un poco irreverente).

—¿Me permite que le dé algunos ejemplos convincentes? Puede verificar que los pastunes de Afganistán y Pakistán, que son musulmanes, tienen muchas costumbres similares a las judías: practican la circuncisión en el octavo día del bebé; tienen leyes dietéticas similares; y algún se ponen en la frente una cajita negra de cuero, llamada tefilín o filacteria, con los preceptos sagrados e inscripciones de la Torá en su interior. Usted debe saber que esta es una costumbre de los yamabushi en Japón. Son una secta de monjes ascéticos que viven en las montañas y practican el Shugendō, una religión que mezcla el sintoísmo con elementos budistas.

—¡Eso sí que es interesante! Le debo confesar que su mención de los yamabushi me trae algunos recuerdos. Hace muchos años salimos de vacaciones con mi madre a las montañas sagradas de Kumano y Omine. Al llegar nos recibió un pariente que era un sacerdote yamabushi y tenía en la frente una cajita negra como esa. En nuestro honor, durante una ceremonia, él se puso a soplar el horagai, que es un cuerno en forma de caracol.

—Ahora soy yo el sorprendido. Aunque sea usted muy escéptica, eso es bastante semejante al shofar, el cuerno de oveja que soplamos los judíos durante las ceremonias del año nuevo en la sinagoga. Ya veo que usted es difícil de convencer, pero esto parece más que una coincidencia. Entonces, déjeme contarle otra cosa: una de nuestras tribus, los Menashe, fueron expulsados de Persia en el año 361 a. C. por Alejandro Magno. La tribu escapó hacia la frontera de India con Birmania, en donde cambiaron de nombre a Shinlung y se hicieron musulmanes o idólatras en algunos casos. Hoy, debe haber uno o dos millones de personas en esa región que tienen idea de su herencia judía. Otros siguieron hasta la frontera de China con Tíbet y son los antepasados de los actuales Chiang-Min, una pequeña tribu de la provincia de Szechuan. Fue la única tribu monoteísta que no conocía la palabra "dios" hasta que ellos llegaron.

Estábamos maravillados de la capacidad del rabino para recordar todas estas historias aprendidas en su juventud, pero el hombre parecía fatigado por el esfuerzo. Cuando nos despedíamos agradeciéndole calurosamente su contribución y nos preparamos para salir, Bensimón nos hizo otro comentario inesperado de una persona casi centenaria:

—A diferencia de las fuentes tradicionales, como mi yeshiva o cualquier universidad, pienso que las bibliotecas de hoy en el espacio cibernético son tan vastas que podríamos decir que son infinitas. Como bien saben, fue Borges, el escritor argentino, quien imaginó este concepto ya en 1941, en su cuento "La biblioteca de Babel". Por eso creo que deberían buscar más detalles en Internet sobre la inscripción en arameo.

Después de nuestra entrevista con el anciano sabio, salimos a caminar por la costa del lago Washington, asimilando toda la nueva información. Matsumoto-san estaba algo silenciosa, pero eventualmente se puso a charlar en voz alta:

—Estoy emocionada con la erudición del rabino y las posibles conexiones que sugirió con las tradiciones de mi familia, pero hay algo me molesta. ¿Te das cuenta de que, si estas revelaciones son correctas, podrían cambiar drásticamente mis ideas sobre mis antepasados, mi comportamiento y mis habilidades?

A medida que caminábamos, mi amiga se iba desplazando cada vez con más determinación, iba acelerando y casi marchaba, forzándome a ajustar mis pasos a los suyos. De pronto nos topamos con una banda de muchachos ruidosos cargando latas de cerveza, que nos obligaron agresivamente a abrirles camino y dejarlos pasar, hasta acorralarnos en un angosto pasaje. No me sorprendí cuando Matsumoto-san adoptó una pose marcial, algo que yo había observado antes. Entonces se movió de costado, primero avanzando con su pierna derecha y después con la izquierda, con su peso distribuido sólidamente en tierra para lanzar a gran velocidad unos ataques decididos hacia arriba y abajo, y luego para adelante con ambos brazos, tras lo cual el grupo se dispersó sin tener que pegarle a nadie, pero dándoles un mensaje clarísimo: "¡Conmigo no se metan!". Esto nos dejó el camino libre, mientras la patota se dispersaba con temor, sin discutir y en gran desorden.

Enseguida me miró algo avergonzada, como pidiendo perdón por haber actuado tan agresivamente.

—Discúlpame si te asusté al reaccionar así con la banda. No sé si alguna vez te conté que los del clan Matsumoto pertenecemos a la casta de los samuráis. Cuando estaba en la Secundaria ya practicaba aikido y kendo y, cuando alguien me agrede, no puedo evitar defenderme así. Por eso me impresionó cuando el rabino habló de los yamabushi, que suelen ser guerreros feroces, y algunos creen que hasta tienen poderes sobrenaturales. ¡No vayas a pensar que yo también los tengo! Yo aprendí en el colegio y sigo practicando artes marciales hasta el día de hoy.

Bensimón había previsto que iba a encontrar más información en las bibliotecas infinitas de Internet. Pero él no mencionó que no bastarían los hechos históricos para explicar la conducta de mi amiga o su capacidad para mejorar el tiempo. En todo caso, dados mis antecedentes judíos, estaba intrigado por la posible llegada de los antiguos israelitas a Japón de modo que, siguiendo las sugerencias del rabino, me metí con gran curiosidad en Internet.

Fui altamente recompensado al encontrar un buen contacto en el mismo Japón, un erudito en la Biblia con el nombre improbable de "Kubo", que afirmaba tener evidencia sobre la conexión entre los dos pueblos. Al principio me distrajo la sonoridad de su nombre y me lo imaginé como un pequeño personaje, de formas geométricas, pero muy estudioso, sentado en un cuartucho de apenas tres esteras de ancho bajo unas luces fluorescentes. Primero tuve sospechas de hallarme ante un evangelista con una actitud poco científica, adepto a grandes vuelos de la imaginación y a las conjeturas. Pero a medida que ahondaba en sus escritos, me di cuenta de que estaba equivocado, ya que era un hombre bien informado y cuya mente inquisitiva merecía respeto. Al fin, me conquistó con sus buenas maneras y sus respuestas diplomáticas a mis preguntas por correo electrónico. Terminaba siempre sus mensajes con un respetuoso y cautivador "Shalom, desde Tokio".

El señor Kubo me aconsejó un libro que resultó ser especialmente convincente y que pude encontrar en la Universidad de Washington. Al entrar al bello edificio de la biblioteca Suzzallo, de estilo gótico-renacentista, me dirigí al salón de los Viejos Manuscritos y me impactó la luminosidad que emanaba de sus vitrales y coloreaba las estanterías con libros. Esta atmósfera casi religiosa me desconcertó un poco, porque venía con serias inquietudes científicas.

Al rato me descubrí admirando un volumen: Los japoneses y las diez tribus perdidas de Israel, publicado en 1980 por Joseph Eidelberg, un judío que había visitado Japón y se quedó durante muchos años viviendo en un monasterio sintoísta. El libro enumeraba cientos de palabras japonesas con un sonido y significado similar a otras en hebreo. Por ejemplo: el hebreo goy, ¿un no-judío o un extranjero?, es parecido al japonés gaijin; daver, 'hablar', en hebreo, es como daberu, 'conversar', en japonés. La similitud entre el hebreo shamar, o 'proteger', y el japonés samurái, 'servir o cuidar', entre los nobles, era también muy persuasiva.

Siguiendo las sugerencias de mi interlocutor cibernético, el sabelotodo pero oscuro señor Kubo, me puse a estudiar una teoría publicada en las revistas de biología molecular sobre el origen genético de los japoneses. Había muchas correlaciones entre los grupos sanguíneos japoneses y judíos, y ciertas características en el

ADN eran exclusivas entre ellos y nunca observadas entre los chinos o los coreanos. Era fácil especular que algunos israelitas llegados por la Ruta de la Seda al principio de la historia pudieron dejar una marca indeleble en el ácido nucleico en la muy aislada población de la isla de Japón.

Estando en eso, hubo un cambio en los reflejos sobre la mesa y los manuscritos que quebró mi concentración. Mirando hacia los ventanales, noté una luz encantadora: un flujo continuo de gotas de lluvia se deslizaba sobre el vidrio, que la gravedad forzaba en un curioso diseño en ramas, repetido de manera interminable mientras caían hacia el umbral. La forma de este modelo fractal (en que cada gota era idéntica a la precedente) me sugirió una imagen análoga en la que los genes de la diosa Amaterasu iban resbalando hacia abajo entre las futuras generaciones. Si aceptamos la premisa de una interacción entre los hebreos visitantes y los japoneses, y con el trono imperial y la jerarquía de la religión sintoísta, bien podemos imaginar que este íntimo contacto permitió la penetración de características genéticas hasta la actual familia de los Matsumoto.

Inmerso en el ilustrado ambiente de la biblioteca Suzzallo, comencé a soñar despierto y a tejer una madeja de posibles relaciones entre las tribus israelitas migratorias y el pueblo japonés, y especialmente con las cualidades y andanzas espectaculares de mi amiga, Matsumoto-san. En eso me acordé de una cita de Borges, que había observado que "toda colaboración es misteriosa". Él daba ejemplos de interacciones a través de los tiempos y de espacios geográficos y, a veces, dentro de un sueño. Por ejemplo, un emperador mongol en la India del siglo XIII soñó con un palacio fabuloso y lo construyó para su mujer. A su vez, Coleridge, en 1797, soñó con este mismo palacio y al despertarse compuso, con lo poco que recordaba del sueño, un fragmento del poema lírico "Kubla Kan". En otra colaboración similar, una japonesa de Seattle, en 2007, poseída por un poder inexplicable de mejorar el tiempo, extravía un pañuelo blanco de seda. La curiosidad de un buen amigo la ayuda a descubrir una posible relación ancestral con el Kami más venerado en la mitología japonesa y quizá con una de las perdidas tribus de Israel.

Al tomar conciencia, a través de los vitrales, de que el cielo se oscurecía súbitamente, desperté de mi ensoñación. De pronto comenzó a soplar un viento poderoso que torcía las copas de los árboles y que empezaba a destruir los jardines de la Escuela Forestal. Un diluvio inundó los pisos de ladrillo de la Plaza Roja. Esta tormenta extraordinaria parecía interminable.

Mientras esperaba que amainara el temporal, llamé por teléfono a Matsumoto-san para describirle mis hallazgos y para quejarme del mal tiempo inesperado e inapropiado para la estación. Cuando la encontré, me contó que estaba en una cabaña cavernosa en la isla López, para considerar las consecuencias de nuestra visita reciente al rabino Bensimón. Dijo estar deprimida tratando de comprender la historia de su familia, y que no tenía ganas de volver a la ciudad por un tiempo. Preocupado por su aislamiento, quise ayudarla y se me ocurrió una solución inspirada por el mito japonés de Amaterasu que nos había contado. Traté de persuadirla para salir a caminar por el bosque detrás de la cabaña y buscar su estanque favorito para observar los peces de colores. Yo calculaba que, si por casualidad daba una ojeada a la superficie del charco, se encontraría con la sorpresa y el placer de ver su propio reflejo en el agua. Finalmente, intenté convencerla de volver a citarnos en nuestro café favorito. En especial, le pedí que trajera puesto su extraordinario pañuelo blanco. Confiaba en que todo esto la ayudaría a recuperar su personalidad habitual y a ser más comprensiva ante las nuevas posibilidades que había revelado la visita al rabino.

A la mañana siguiente, justo antes de nuestro encuentro, se abrió un cielo azul esplendoroso sobre la "ciudad esmeralda" y un sol brillante iluminó las fachadas de ladrillo en la Plaza de los Pioneros. Amaterasu, quiero decir, Matsumoto-san, llegó antes y ya estaba sentada, esperándome en una mesa de afuera, con un capuchino humeante y una expresión bastante menos escéptica. El pañuelo blanco descansaba sobre sus hombros, flotando levemente por la suave brisa de la mañana.

Las excesivas aguas del Río de la Plata

Neeraj Prasad, un marinero hindú, apareció en Buenos Aires un día de invierno de 1965 para ser tratado con diálisis en el hospital donde yo era residente. La llegada sorpresiva de un extranjero muy delgado y moreno, vestido solo con pantalones de algodón blanco y una camisa larga hasta las rodillas, nos impactó por su exotismo. Para mí, un joven médico, y un budista apenas en teoría, que nunca había salido del país, examinar a un hombre de la India era un honor y una oportunidad para relacionarme con alguien muy fuera de lo común en la Argentina. Este encuentro, que luego se convertiría en un misterio médico, iba a expandir mi perspectiva en áreas tan inconexas como el metabolismo del agua y los electrolitos, la importancia del agua para el hinduismo, el poder predictivo de la astrología y lo impredecible del romance.

Mi estupor aumentó al ver que a Neeraj lo sostenía por el brazo una mujer rubia de ojos azules, que irradiaba seguridad y buena salud; ella iba envuelta en un tapado negro de piel de caracul (mi abuela rusa lo hubiera llamado "astracán"). Los dueños del Southern Cross —el barco en que Neeraj era tripulante—, que eran ingleses, habían contratado a esta enfermera danesa multilingüe para traducir y asistirlo durante su internación. Suspiré aliviado (y admirado por el porte y la elegancia de la mujer) cuando nos informó de que nos ayudaría.

Neeraj parecía temeroso del ambiente extraño que lo rodeaba, pero Eva consiguió que se le adjudicara una habitación individual, mientras yo esperaba para tomar su historia clínica y examinarlo. Él traía pocas pertenencias dentro de una bolsa de arpillera, de donde sacó una curiosa vasija de metal, que llamó "kindi", y nos dijo que era algo que se usa en la mayoría de los hogares hindúes. Era pequeña y circular y tenía un cuello largo que se extendía en ángulo desde la panza. Neeraj pidió que le trajeran agua limpia y llenó su vasija. Luego bebió un largo trago directamente del pico y se lavó el rostro y las manos. Apoyó la vasija sobre la mesa de luz de tal forma que no mirara hacia el sur, ya que —según su creencia— "podría invitar a la muerte de un ser querido".

Al rato Neeraj se sentó cómodamente sobre la cama, con las piernas cruzadas y con el torso desnudo, ajeno al efecto que esa imagen chocante producía en la fría habitación del hospital. Le hablé, en un inglés inarticulado (su inglés era mejor que el mío), sobre su traslado a nuestro hospital.

—Señor Prasad, ¿qué pasó cuando se enfermó en el barco?

—Sí, doctor Sahib, por favor, llámeme Neeraj. Traíamos una carga de Bombay. Bordeamos la punta de África y cruzamos el Atlántico hacia Argentina. Me sentí enfermo en cuanto entramos en un mar distinto, con agua barrosa, de color marrón. Recogí un poco con mi balde y me impactó que no fuera salada. Los otros marineros me dijeron que era el River Plate. Navegábamos sobre un canal dragado, marcado por frecuentes boyas, cuando de pronto me encontré débil y vomité sangre de un rojo brillante sobre la reluciente cubierta que había fregado durante horas.

—¿Era la primera vez que le sangraba el estómago? ¿No estaba mal antes?

—Sí, doctor, me sangró una vez un poquito al ir de cuerpo. Ya hacía un tiempo que tenía náuseas y andaba tristón por culpa del contramaestre. Me tenía entre ojos, ¿sabe? No me quería nada, seguro que porque soy hindú. Este inglés que le digo, odiaba a los hindúes y maltrataba a los marineros. A mí me obligaba a pasar el día entero fregando la cubierta con holystone. ¿Sabe, doctor, lo que es el holystone? Es un pedazo de arenisca que se usa para restregar las cubiertas de madera de los barcos. Además me hacía pintar mamparos, lustrar bronces y engrasar las cadenas del ancla. Bueno, esto me afectó. Tenía gusto ácido en la boca y me ardía el pecho.

—Disculpe, doctor —intervino Eva— , Neeraj se desmayó y lo trajeron a la enfermería en estado de shock. No había sangre disponible para transfundirlo. El barco tardó dos días en llegar al puerto y en traerlo al hospital en que trabajo. Para entonces, ya casi no orinaba, ya que había desarrollado insuficiencia renal aguda. Lo trasladaron aquí para que lo trataran con diálisis, sabiendo que hace poco tiempo que se usa esta técnica en Argentina. Yo estoy encargada de cuidarlo durante la noche. Ahora debo irme, pero volveré a las ocho.

Eva se arropó en su llamativo tapado negro, saludó a Neeraj con un cálido apretón en el hombro y nos dejó solos.

Cuando revisé a Neeraj, vi las callosidades sobre sus rodillas color chocolate, causadas por su duro trabajo en el barco. Después de terminar su examen, pasé el resto del día con mis colegas en un torbellino de tareas, preparándonos para su primera diálisis.

Nuestra poca experiencia con este nuevo tratamiento se compensaba con un fuerte entusiasmo. Íbamos a utilizar un equipo que se había inventado hacía poco tiempo en Europa. El primer paso fue colocarle catéteres en las venas del brazo para hacer circular la sangre por el aparato. Estos tubos estaban rodeados por un baño de agua (el dializado) que contenía sales y otras sustancias para limpiar impurezas y normalizar la composición de su sangre.

Luego de la diálisis, Neeraj pareció responder bien desde el punto de vista médico, pero él no se encontraba mejor. No le gustaban los repetidos pinchazos con los que tomábamos las muestras de sangre, pero nunca mostró una expresión de queja ni de frustración; mantenía la calma y su enigmática sonrisa. Después de cada tratamiento, Neeraj bebía tres pequeños sorbos de agua de su *kindi,* mientras repetía un nombre en voz baja (ritual que reiteraba después de bañarse o de comer). Decía que estaba haciendo *"achamana"* para recordar a Dios y para volverse más puro. A mí me resultó curioso que precisamente la purificación era lo que nosotros, los médicos occidentales, intentábamos lograr con la diálisis.

Eva volvió a las ocho, como había prometido. Esta vez, con un vestido más convencional y el característico delantal de enfermera. Ayudó a Neeraj con la cena, aunque él no tenía apetito. Esa noche, logré unirme a su conversación, una oportunidad para relacionarme con mi extraordinario paciente y su enfermera danesa. Conversadora y con algo de coquetería, y su personalidad escandinava muy liberada, Eva se fue haciendo amiga mía de a poco, y tuvimos ocasión de compartir la fascinación por nuestro paciente en común, y también algunos momentos de intimidad. (Pero más tarde me enteré de que tenía competidores para conseguir su atención, como en el caso de Giovanni, un hombre de piel clara, descendiente de inmigrantes italianos, que trabajaba en mantenimiento durante la noche). Eva cuidaba a Neeraj con suavidad y eficiencia, y yo, disimulando mi admiración por la fluidez de sus movimientos, le pregunté a Neeraj por su pasado, con ayuda de Eva, que nos traducía a ratos.

—Nací en Benarés, doctor, a orillas del río Ganges. Mi madre contaba que cuando nací, mi tío roció mi piel con gotas de agua de este río sagrado para purificarme, para que algún día fuera como él. Como es costumbre en mi país, llamaron a un astrólogo para que calculara mi horóscopo. Luego de hacerlo, su expresión se volvió seria y les dijo que el agua iba a influir mi vida, desde mi nacimiento hasta mi último aliento. Mi familia aceptó su predicción al pie de la letra, porque nosotros los hindúes consideramos el agua el pilar de la vida de todos los seres. Por eso mis padres me llamaron Neeraj, que en hindi significa 'nacido del agua', como la flor de loto o las perlas.

Yo no podía controlar mi curiosidad sobre este paciente tan poco común, de modo que le pregunté si pensaba que este horóscopo realmente predijo cosas que le sucedieron, y si creía que su vida había sido influida por el agua. Nos contó que de niño conocía a personas en las orillas del Ganges. Un pescador lo tomó bajo su ala y lo hizo su aprendiz; vendían lo que pescaban en los mercados cercanos. Cada vez que dejaban tierra firme, él tenía que vaciar un recipiente de arcilla lleno de agua sobre la proa del bote para traer suerte en la pesca. Le encantaba el contacto con el río, pero la ganancia era muy baja y tuvo que buscar otro trabajo. Entonces lo contrataron para ayudar a un viejo fabricante de perfumes en una callecita de Benarés. Su tarea era mezclar los aceites y fragancias de las fórmulas secretas que él había perfeccionado. Usaban aceites como sándalo, cardamomo, jazmín, rosas, hinojo e incienso — nombres que todavía podía oler en su memoria. Un día, el maestro le dio una muestra de su mejor creación: "Esencia del Ganges", que le pidió llevara consigo para siempre, y que un día él mismo se la regalara a la persona que más quisiera.

Luego de contarnos esto, Neeraj tomó su bolsa de arpillera y sacó un pequeño perfumero marrón que nos ofreció a Eva y a mí para que lo oliéramos. Su olor punzante exudaba río, tierra mojada y cenizas; un olor que sugería muerte. Tuvo el efecto opuesto en Eva, quien tocó la mano de Neeraj con más ternura de lo que Florence Nightingale hubiera prescrito, pensé, mientras Neeraj proseguía su relato.

—Un amigo me llevó a Bombay, donde me ofrecieron un puesto de marinero de cubierta en un buque de carga. He viajado a muchos lugares y una vez fui a Copenhague, una ciudad que recuerdo con cariño. Mi única mala experiencia en años ha sido con el contramaestre del Southern Cross; pero todavía no me siento a gusto siendo marinero. Los viejos brahmanes hablaban de una antigua prohibición que impedía a los hindúes cruzar el océano. A veces temo que lo que me pasa es un castigo por haber desobedecido esta vieja prohibición. Por otro lado, esta regla benefició a los musulmanes, que podían transportar pimienta y otras especias desde la India.

Cuando me estaba yendo de su habitación, me di cuenta de que Neeraj era increíblemente parecido a Gunga Din, el porteador de agua y héroe de una vieja película basada en el poema de Rudyard Kipling, con Douglas Fairbanks y Cary Grant.

* * *

La segunda diálisis de Neeraj no tuvo complicaciones, y los análisis mostraron que la composición de su sangre se estaba normalizando. Él estaba más despierto y comunicativo, se relacionaba bien con Eva, quien lo acompañaba cada noche. Una de esas noches, cuando la sala estaba en silencio y la mayoría de los pacientes dormía, noté que su habitación estaba apenas iluminada y que había una vela encendida en su mesita de luz (probablemente contra las normas de seguridad). Él le contaba a Eva sobre su vida en la India mientras, en la otra cama, ella se había recostado de lado, con la cadera y el brazo derecho extendidos, y con los pies recogidos detrás de las rodillas. Desde nuestros puntos de vista privilegiados y opuestos, Neeraj y yo la observábamos con admiración, reconociendo al mismo tiempo que nos había evocado la misma visión: ¡la sirena! La pose de Eva era sorprendentemente similar a la estatua en el puerto de Copenhague, que Neeraj había descubierto desde el muelle. Como muchos otros marineros, se había enamorado de ella (literalmente). Por mi parte, solo la había visto en fotos y había leído que, en el pasado, si un marinero miraba la estatua tenía que mojarse la cabeza y el pecho, y enfriar sus pies en el agua, para evitar el encantamiento de la sirena. En ese momento, sentí mi mente como un torbellino, un leve mareo, como si yo hubiera estado en Copenhague y caído igualmente bajo su hechizo.

Esa noche, soñé que bajaba por una oscura escalera del hospital, de la mano de una mujer rubia que se parecía a la sirena. Entramos en un cuarto oscuro de fotografía, en donde la única iluminación provenía de la luz roja de seguridad. Yo subí mucho la temperatura en el tanque de lavado, haciéndolo despedir vapor, que se esparció por toda la pieza. Entonces nos confundimos en un íntimo abrazo, mientras nos invadía una niebla roja y espesa. Ese recuerdo es tan intenso y persistente que no puedo asegurar que haya sido solo un sueño.

* * *

Un día invité a Eva a acompañarme a una milonga, a tomar un trago y a observar a los milongueros. Nos sentamos bien cerca, viendo pasar a los bailarines en un abrazo apretado y con los ojos a menudo cerrados. Le expliqué que para esta gente "la vida es un tango". Eva observó como el público se invitaba a bailar con señales casi invisibles de sus ojos, como hablando otro lenguaje para ella incomprensible. Le encantó comprobar que el baile contribuía a que se relacionaran más íntimamente.

—Eso me encanta en mi profesión, le expliqué: poder comprender mejor el cuerpo humano. Por eso necesito estudiar con buenos maestros. Haber conocido a Neeraj me está motivando a viajar a Estados Unidos para especializarme en mi materia. Además, la situación política del país se pone cada día más difícil y tendría que hacerlo pronto. No tengo novia; solo buenos amigos y mi familia, que me retiene.

—¡Quizá pueda descubrir una buena razón para que te quedes! —manifestó, inesperadamente—. Pero tengo que ir a descansar, mañana nos espera un día de mucho trabajo con nuestro paciente.

Después de las siguientes sesiones de diálisis, Neeraj empeoró, le sobrevinieron fuertes dolores de cabeza. Prefería sentarse en la cama, la espalda recta y con las piernas cruzadas, y seguir la antigua práctica de yoga que consistía en bajar y torcer la cabeza y verter agua salada del *kindi* dentro de cada orificio nasal en forma alternativa, y luego drenarlo por el lado opuesto, para así aliviar el dolor de cabeza y purificar los senos nasales.

Nuestro equipo médico estaba preocupado y sorprendido por estas prácticas, pero le permitió continuarlas.

Neeraj empezó a aumentar de peso y su rostro y párpados se hincharon visiblemente; dormía mucho y hablaba poco. Eva le limpiaba la frente transpirada y le masajeaba los brazos y las piernas con aceite. Una tarde leímos un asombroso informe de laboratorio: la concentración de sodio en la sangre de Neeraj estaba bajando, lo que significaba que el contenido de agua en su cuerpo excedía lo normal, el sesenta por ciento del peso. Esto explicaba sus dolores de cabeza, ya que las células del cerebro, sobrecargadas de agua, no tenían sitio para expandirse dentro del rígido cráneo. Dado que una función de la diálisis era la de extraer agua, estos resultados eran por demás paradójicos.

Nuestro jefe de nefrología, sin encontrar una explicación para el exceso de agua después de la diálisis, ordenó que todos los médicos nos reuniéramos para intentar aclarar el misterio. Después de escuchar nuestros comentarios, resumió las posibles interpretaciones. Neeraj sufría de insuficiencia renal y era incapaz de producir orina. Sin embargo, para justificar el exceso, también debía existir un ingreso masivo de agua, aunque no podíamos determinar su origen, ya que su ingesta se limitaba a 500 ml por día. Por otro lado, el volumen de agua en el tanque de diálisis así como la cantidad de sales agregadas eran siempre iguales. El jefe de técnicos lo había confirmado usando una balanza de laboratorio muy precisa.

—A menos que a alguno se le ocurra algo mejor, el tratamiento tendrá que ser la diálisis diaria, por dos o tres horas adicionales, comenzando ya mismo. ¡Vamos, a trabajar! —ordenó.

Hicimos lo que se nos indicó, esperando una mejoría. Sin embargo, durante los próximos tres días, nuestro paciente se volvió más letárgico, a veces decía incoherencias y sufrió dos pequeñas convulsiones que lo dejaron confundido durante unas horas. La concentración de sodio en sangre era cada vez más baja, a pesar de nuestros esfuerzos. En un momento, Neeraj comenzó a mirar hacia todos lados, como si escuchara una voz o alguien que lo llamaba, y pronunció varias veces el nombre "Saraswati". Finalmente, nos llamó a Eva y a mí.

—Doctor Sahib, espero que me cure con la diálisis, pero en mi país, cuando una persona siente que el fin de la vida está cerca, decimos que ha llegado 'mi tiempo de agua y arroz'. Cuando así sea, mi deseo es que ustedes sigan las costumbres hindúes.

Se detuvo, tomó el perfumero con Esencia del Ganges, sosteniéndolo frente a nosotros:

—Cuando esté por morir, por favor, derramen unas gotas de agua sagrada dentro de mi boca. Luego, deseo ofrecer a Eva lo que quede de agua en el frasco.

A continuación volvió a poner el pequeño perfumero en su bolsa de arpillera y comenzó a meditar. Poco después, su respiración se hizo más lenta y profunda, y ya no sabíamos con seguridad si él advertía nuestra presencia. Eva sostuvo su mano por unos momentos y luego la soltó con suavidad; juntos, nos fuimos de la habitación.

—Eva, me siento tan mal. Creo que hemos hecho todos lo posible por Neeraj, pero temo que todo haya sido inútil.

—No te preocupes tanto, todavía hay esperanzas, ¿no?

—No soy supersticioso, Eva. Yo hago mi trabajo y me concentro en cuestiones técnicas, pero no sé por qué me obsesiona tanto lo del horóscopo de Neeraj. Fijate vos que predijo su relación vital, repetida con el agua: su nacimiento a la orilla del sagrado Ganges; su trabajo de marinero; su malestar en el gran Río de la Plata; y ahora, su intoxicación por agua, tan misteriosa e intratable. ¿Será que su destino ya estaba determinado y que no importa cuánto nos esforcemos?

—Alberto, comparto tus sentimientos acerca de su predestinación. Ya no estoy pensando como enfermera, y mis emociones le están ganando a mis ideas más racionales. Yo también temo que estemos perdiendo la batalla. Pero sin embargo, Neeraj se mantiene calmo a pesar de estar empeorando.

Desde su punto de vista, el agua es símbolo de purificación y fertilidad, y participa tanto de la generación de la vida como de la muerte.

—¿Viste, Eva, que Neeraj está extrañamente tranquilo, aunque sospeche que el fin de su vida puede estar cerca? Quizá sus creencias religiosas lo ayuden a aceptar su destino. Pero es irónico que el agua, 'el sostén de la vida de todos los seres', según el hinduismo, también pueda ser excesiva y llegar, literalmente, a ahogar a una persona en sus propios fluidos. Él está empeorando, como si tuviera adentro una fuerza imparable.

—Ahora sí que pareces supersticioso. ¿En qué fuerza estás pensando?

—Eva, pasó algo muy extraño. Buscando en la Enciclopedia Británica encontré que Saraswati, el nombre que Neeraj repitió luego de despertar de la convulsión, como si alguien lo estuviera llamando, era la diosa de los Ríos en el *Rigveda,* el más antiguo de los textos escritos en sánscrito. Me enteré de que el sagrado río del mismo nombre se había secado y que ahora nadie sabe dónde está. ¿Habrá salido a la superficie en el Río de la Plata?

—¿Cómo te puede parecer sagrado? Es un río fangoso y hediondo, que aspira a ser un océano. Es como para darte náuseas. Yo extraño el mar Báltico y sus aguas claras, la región donde crecí.

* * *

Durante el siguiente y último tratamiento de Neeraj, todos nosotros controlábamos continuamente los procedimientos para asegurarnos de que nada saliera mal. El jefe de nefrología caminaba obsesionado, en círculos alrededor del aparato de diálisis, observando cada detalle. Pero para desesperanza de todos, Neeraj comenzó a tener náuseas, un fuerte dolor de cabeza y finalmente sufrió una convulsión severa, obligándonos a interrumpir la diálisis. Recordé su deseo en caso de que se acercara la muerte, y salí disparado hacia su habitación para buscar su preciado perfumero. Volví corriendo como un loco y, con una temblorosa mano derecha, rocié unas gotas de la sagrada Esencia del Ganges en la boca de Neeraj. Luego le di la botellita a Eva. Lamentablemente, Neeraj no volvió a despertar de su profundo sueño y murió en paz unas horas más tarde.

Luego de ese final devastador, me desplomé en una silla en mi habitación, con la cabeza hundida entre las manos, buscando una explicación para la muerte de Neeraj. Mi mente oscilaba en ciclos entre causas racionales y sobrenaturales. ¿Éramos culpables de una ignorancia colectiva sobre la diálisis, o era ese su ineludible destino? El horóscopo de Neeraj había predicho que el agua influiría en su vida hasta el amargo final. Pero ¿cómo podía ser que el agua, "el sustrato de toda vida", fuera el instrumento del fin de su existencia? Desconocía la respuesta. Y no entendería los aspectos espirituales de esta experiencia hasta muchos años después.

Ese mismo día, mientras Eva se preparaba para volver a su trabajo habitual en el otro hospital, se le acercó Giovanni, el hombre de mantenimiento, y le habló en privado:

—Señorita Eva, antes de que se vaya, hay algo que me gustaría decirle. Espero que me pueda aconsejar sobre lo que tengo que hacer. No me decido a contarle a mi supervisor lo que he hecho.

—¿Qué has hecho, Giovanni? ¿Tiene que ver con la muerte del paciente?

—No lo sé, señorita Eva, pero quizá haya cometido un error la semana pasada cuando estaba trabajando en el cuarto de diálisis. Yo soy el responsable de limpiar todo, incluyendo el tanque de agua de la máquina de diálisis. Es de acero inoxidable y se producen calcificaciones después de cada uso, así que la froto a fondo con un cepillo metálico. Hace seis noches, estaba fregando como siempre cuando una cinta blanca se desprendió del interior del tanque. Yo no sabía dónde iba exactamente, así que la reemplacé con otra cinta en el lugar donde pensé que iría. Estaba confundido y tenía miedo de contárselo a alguien. Tengo familia y no quiero perder mi trabajo. ¿Qué debo hacer ahora?

Eva sabía que algo terrible había pasado, aunque no era totalmente consciente de su relevancia. Vino a buscarme, me apartó en un rincón y me refirió con detalle la conversación.

Con el corazón destrozado, fuimos a buscar

al jefe de nefrología para relatarle la triste información que nos dio Giovanni. Todos marchamos de inmediato al cuarto de diálisis para investigar. Nos horrorizamos al ver que la cinta que marca el nivel de agua ahora estaba mucho más arriba de donde debía. ¡El excesivo volumen de agua había diluido las sales a una baja concentración, causando un ingreso severo de agua en el paciente, en lugar de extraerla! No era culpa de Giovanni, sino nuestra, ya que nunca deberíamos haber usado un sistema tan primitivo como la cinta para marcar el nivel de agua. Habíamos resuelto el misterio médico, pero con profunda tristeza, nos dimos cuenta de que era demasiado tarde para ayudar a Neeraj.

* * *

Notificamos a la embajada británica el funesto final de Neeraj. Un rato después, alguien nos llamó para indicarnos que Neeraj tendría que ser cremado en Buenos Aires, ya que no habían podido contactar con ningún familiar. Lo cremamos al día siguiente, y todo el equipo médico asistió a la ceremonia para ofrecer su respeto. Me eligieron para que pronunciara unas palabras y para oficiar el servicio. No se me ocurrió nada mejor que parafrasear las palabras del famoso poema de Kipling:

Pero si hablamos de matanza
harás tu tarea en el agua...
Sí. ¡Din! ¡Din! ¡Din!
¡Neeraj, tu piel de cuero achocolatado!
Aunque te he tratado y te he fallado,
juro por el Dios que te ha creado,
que eres mejor hombre que yo, ¡Gunga Din!

El domingo siguiente, cuando los dos estábamos libres, Eva y yo caminamos por la Costanera y encontramos un lugar tranquilo, sin pescadores o niños jugando. Abrimos la cajita, nos asomamos sobre la baranda y arrojamos las cenizas al río, que el viento y las olas desparramaron. ¿Nos observaría Saraswati desde las aguas bajas? Mientras despedíamos a Neeraj, un delicioso aroma nos envolvió: el humo de los chorizos en los puestos de la Costanera. El olor a carne cocinándose me reconfortó y me hizo recordar que la vida continuaba.

Con el paso del tiempo seguí aprendiendo de nuestro trágico error y, finalmente, entendí lo intrincado del metabolismo de la sal y el agua. La experiencia con Neeraj cambió mi vida por completo, ya que me decidió a viajar a Estados Unidos para especializarme en nefrología y radicarme allí. No podría haber predicho que en un futuro yo les transmitiría mi conocimiento a otros jóvenes médicos y especialistas en este país extranjero.

Por el contrario, no entendí hasta muchos años más tarde la dimensión filosófica de la muerte de Neeraj a causa de intoxicación por exceso de agua, y la actitud de calma en su rostro mientras se acercaba la muerte. Esta comprensión me inspiró para escribir sobre estas cosas. El momento crucial llegó en la forma de un encuentro *online* con el doctor Nair, un erudito historiador de Trivandrum, India, autor de un gran artículo sobre el papel central que tiene el agua en el hinduismo. El mes pasado acepté su invitación a visitarlo en la India.

El doctor Nair me esperaba en su confortable vivienda en Trivandrum. Tendría unos sesenta años, una larga barba blanca y llevaba un pantalón oscuro y camisa de algodón blanco. Su mujer me saludó amablemente y me convidaron a almorzar una típica comida de Kerala. Luego de comer, pude finalmente satisfacer mi curiosidad:

—Nosotros creemos que *panchamahabutha*, la naturaleza, consiste en cinco elementos: la tierra, el agua, el fuego, el aire y el éter (el vacío o el cielo). El agua la representamos con un círculo, símbolo de plenitud, como un objeto de veneración. Su relato de la muerte de Neeraj por un exceso de agua me afectó profundamente. Por eso le sugiero que, como médico, podría estudiar los escritos de Kirpal Singh, un maestro espiritual de Punjab. Singh había señalado que, si bien los fisiólogos y los médicos nos explican el metabolismo de los organismos vivos, no nos pueden decir qué es la vida misma y, sobre todo, qué es la consciencia. Los hindúes creen que la vida, en cualquiera de sus formas, es eterna; que continúa en un ciclo infinito, apareciendo, desapareciendo y reapareciendo como olas y burbujas en la corriente del tiempo.

—En ese caso, ¿cuál sería el significado de la muerte?

—La dualidad de la vida y la muerte no son otra cosa que dos caras de una moneda que rota en su eje, ya que el alma pasará a otro cuerpo en su debido momento. Esta visión no es exclusiva del hinduismo; está bien representada en los Evangelios: "...Excepto que un hombre nazca de nuevo, no puede ver el Reino de Dios; excepto que un hombre nazca de agua y de espíritu, no puede entrar en el Reino de Dios..." (Juan 3:3-8). Renacer, dado el incesante girar de la rueda de la vida, puede ser una evolución hacia un estado superior y un estado más elevado de la consciencia. Yo espero que el alma de Neeraj haya encontrado una forma de reaparecer en un estado elevado, como un ser superior.

Después de la muerte de Neeraj, las presiones de la residencia me dejaron poco tiempo para socializar y, además, por alguna razón, Eva y yo no hicimos ningún esfuerzo por vernos. Pasó un año hasta que la llamé al hospital. No tuve mejor idea que encontrarnos en el viejo café Richmond, un lugar burgués para esos tiempos, con sus antiguas sillas de cuero y sus características parejas de mediana edad y de aspecto respetable. Me senté a la única mesa libre, que miraba hacia el fondo del bar, y le reservé a Eva el mejor lugar. Había llegado temprano, con tiempo para pensar de qué íbamos a hablar; qué le iba a proponer para el futuro.

Cuando temía que ella ya no vendría, se acercó desde atrás, me dio una suave palmada en el hombro, y dijo:

—¡Hola!

Me levanté para saludarla; me di la vuelta y volví a hundirme en la silla, temblando hasta los huesos al ver que no estaba sola. Sostenía en sus brazos un bebé delgado, vestido con una ropita celeste, que tendría unos tres meses. La piel del bebé era más oscura que la de cualquier otra persona del lugar; nada parecido a un típico bebé danés. La felicité, pero no tuve el coraje de preguntarle quién era el padre y ella tampoco comentó nada sobre él. El bebé era tranquilo y se portaba bien, interesado en sus alrededores, que examinaba con curiosidad. Eva se veía radiante, con su tapado de piel de caracul que yo conocía tan bien. Hablamos un poco, tomando té inglés con galletitas. Pude contarle que la experiencia con Neeraj me había decidido a salir del país para avanzar en mi profesión, y ella me alentó para hacerlo, y mi partida no pareció perturbarla demasiado. Al rato, mientras yo le pagaba al mozo, ella se levantó suavemente y comenzó a retirarse del café, en silencio, y con su bebé en brazos, sin ni siquiera molestarse en mirar hacia atrás.

Nota: esta es una historia de ficción, inspirada en un hecho ocurrido hace muchos años. Cualquier semejanza entre los personajes y alguna persona, viva o muerta, es pura coincidencia. Estoy agradecido al doctor V. Sankaran Nair por su amabilidad por responder a mis preguntas sobre la importancia del agua para el hinduismo.

Nadando con nazis en Argentina

En el verano de 1958, bajo un brillante cielo azul, un exiliado nazi se estaba ahogando en mar afuera de la ancha playa de arena de Villa Gesell, Argentina. Era temprano por la mañana, y el único testigo, en muchos kilómetros, de sus desesperados gritos de ayuda era un joven bañero judío paralizado por la indecisión.

Era mi primera temporada como bañero improvisado. El trabajo me ofrecía vacaciones pagas en la costa atlántica y tiempo para preparar mis exámenes de la Facultad de Medicina de Buenos Aires. A los dieciocho años, yo era un nadador de competición sin entrenamiento ni experiencia en salvatajes. Pero ese día de 1958, a pesar del miedo por mi vida, corrí a buscar la soga y el anillo salvavidas que mi jefe había colgado, con mucho optimismo, bajo la bandera de la playa. Iba a tener que nadar hasta afuera de la rompiente, pasando la barra de arena, para llegar hasta el hombre que luchaba contra las olas. Yo había oído decir que, en esas circunstancias, era más seguro acercarse al sujeto desde atrás para que no te atrape en sus brazos. Pero que si eso sucedía, había que darle un fuerte puñetazo en la cabeza para desorientarlo o desmayarlo. ¿Iba a arriesgar mi vida para salvarlo? Después de todo, se trataba de un nazi.

Mientras corría hacia el agua a todo vapor, algunas imágenes de mi niñez se dibujaban rapidísimo en mi mente como en una película de carreras de auto. Me acordé de historias sobre mi tío Nathan y su experiencia en Francia durante la Guerra, cuando él conducía camiones para la resistencia en Lyon. El hombre que se ahogaba, un expiloto alemán, ¿no habría sido el mismo que ametrallaba desde el aire el camión de Nathan?

Al fin decidí que no podía dejar que se ahogara. Respiré hondo y comencé a nadar con rapidez para zambullirme bajo las fuertes olas que rompían frente a mí. Al acercarme, el hombre me reconoció e hizo gestos para que le tirara el salvavidas. Me alivié muchísimo al no tener que pegarle en la cabeza para calmarlo. Se lo veía exhausto por el esfuerzo. Apenas pudo pasar el brazo y la cabeza dentro del salvavidas y me indicó por señas que lo remolcara hacia la playa. Al ser incapaz de cruzar la rompiente, había tragado una tonelada de agua luchando contra el viento y las olas, de modo que se dejó arrastrar sin protestar.

Cuando alcanzamos la orilla, los dos colapsamos sobre la arena blanda y quedamos tirados y sin aliento. Finalmente, el hombre se alzó y me explicó que se llamaba Werner. Me dio un fuerte apretón de manos, agradecido y también algo avergonzado, diciendo que volvería por la mañana para darme las gracias más formalmente. Entonces se fue caminando hacia las dunas, mirando con cautela para no encontrar a ningún conocido que pudiese contar su desventura. Yo permanecí recostado sobre la arena caliente por un rato, maravillado por mi audacia y alborozado por el resultado de la aventura.

Sabía que Werner era el fotógrafo de la playa. Lo había visto a menudo dando vueltas para mezclarse con los turistas. En esa época, Villa Gesell era apenas un balneario soñoliento, fundado por inmigrantes alemanes que preferían hablar su propio idioma más que en español.

Mi jefe, un promotor inmobiliario, me había contratado —aun sin experiencia— como el único bañero en una playa de muchos kilómetros de extensión. Supongo que mis únicos méritos eran el de ser más joven, más delgado y más rápido nadador que mi predecesor: un gitano imponente y forzudo, ex marinero, a quien todos llamaban "Zigeuner". Él se alegró de mi llegada porque prefería la libertad de tomar trabajitos y de correrles detrás a las esposas de los turistas. Una vez me enseñó cómo los marineros lavaban sus blue jeans en el mar y después los secaban al sol para dejarlos planchados e impecables. Hacía amigos con facilidad y era una fuente de información sobre los variados residentes del pueblo. Él fue quien me contó que el fotógrafo había sido piloto de guerra en Alemania.

Al día siguiente, Werner se acercó caminando con firmeza y una sonrisa más ancha que el océano Atlántico.

—Arghmando —me dijo con su fuerte acento de Bavaria—, no sé cómo agradecerle su ayuda de ayer. Yo vi que usted no se decidía, porque tardó bastante en tirarse al mar, pero al fin me salvó la vida. Tuvo mucho coraje y le estoy más que agradecido.

Me quedé callado. No quise explicarle las razones de mi titubeo.

—¿Qué puedo hacer por usted? —me preguntó—. ¿En qué puedo ayudarlo? Sé que usted es nuevo en el pueblo. Si me permite, quisiera presentarle a algunas personas, como los dueños de algunos restaurantes y discotecas, o también al jefe de policía y otra gente importante. Este es un pueblo chico y le podría ser útil conocerlos.

Werner se dio cuenta de que yo miraba con gran curiosidad su cámara fotográfica plateada, que tenía unos misteriosos diales rotativos y parecía un instrumento de precisión.

—¿Le interesa la fotografía? —me preguntó.

—¡Muchísimo! Algunos de mis parientes en Europa eran fotógrafos antes de la Guerra.

Yo era entonces un joven estudiante y nunca había usado un equipo fotográfico tan lujoso, de modo que me interesé por varios detalles.

—Esta cámara es una Leica que me guardé al terminar la Guerra. Es el modelo que le daban a los pilotos de la Luftwaffe para las misiones de reconocimiento. Es pequeña, pero el mecanismo es infalible y tiene lentes muy nítidas. ¿Usted ha trabajado en fotografía?

—No, pero me gustaría mucho. Solo tuve ocasión de usar una Kodak 6 x 9 de mi padre. Lástima que el fuelle tenía agujeritos y le entraba luz, ¡ya se figura usted cuántos negativos terminaban velados! —En ese momento se me encendió una lamparita y le pedí algo mayúsculo—: ¿No me dejaría seguirlo mientras trabaja en la playa, al terminar mi turno? Sería genial poder observar cómo toma contacto con la gente y aprender a usar la Leica. ¿Quién sabe? Quizá algún día tenga recursos para comprar una como la suya...

—¡Cómo no! Puedo mostrarle cómo utilizar la cámara y también cómo revelar fotos en blanco y negro a la hora del almuerzo. Tengo que entregarlas a los turistas al atardecer —y entonces, para mi gran sorpresa, agregó una sugerencia—: Otra cosa, ¿no le gustaría salir a nadar juntos por las mañanas temprano, antes de que empecemos el trabajo en la playa? Es mucho más seguro nadar con otros, sobre todo, con expertos.

Aunque ya no era un militar en activo, Werner se mantenía en un estado físico excelente. Era alto, rubio y de ojos azules, podía haber pasado fácilmente por un modelo de la juventud nazi.

Lo más extraño fue que, efectivamente, comenzamos a nadar juntos con frecuencia; y a veces también con un par de amigos suyos, exmilitares alemanes. Este ambiente nuevo, tan poco familiar para mí, era muy estimulante. No me esperaba actuar en un rol tan adulto, aunque me sentía recompensado por la confianza de estos militares profesionales. Pero me desconcertaba que no les molestara nadar con un bañero judío y que me trataran con el mismo respeto que les demostraba yo.

Mientras caminábamos sobre la arena, Werner me enseñaba los rudimentos de la fotografía: cómo calcular la intensidad de la luz en una playa brillante sin un fotómetro, cómo interpretar el talante de los turistas y cuáles serían sus poses favoritas. Lo más memorable fue que me ensañara a manejar y a tomar fotos con su Leica, el modelo de la Luftwaffe que había usado durante la Guerra.

Pronto tuve confianza como para preguntar a Werner sobre sus amigos e, indirectamente, sobre su experiencia bélica. Todavía me era difícil identificar a un nazi entre otros alemanes:

—Werner, ¿qué sabe de esa mujer alta y atractiva que creo que es la dueña del Cine Atlántico? ¿Por qué me pone mala cara cuando paso por allí?

—Porque ella es una de los nazis que llegaron hace como veinte años, cuando se fundó Villa Gesell. Acá todo el mundo sabe que usted es el único bañero del pueblo y que es judío. ¡Usted tiene un apellido germánico, pero no habla alemán como los otros muchachos de su edad de por aquí!

Aprovechando la oportunidad de extraer más información, le pregunté para qué usaba ella esa antena de radio tan impresionante que veíamos sobre el tejado del cine:

—Como es sabido, gracias a la radio Úrsula se comunicaba durante la Guerra con los submarinos alemanes que salían a la superficie para comprar combustible y provisiones frescas de la gente local. A veces hasta permitían el desembarco de oficiales nazis, que podían quedarse en el pueblo, donde eran bienvenidos, o podían seguir para ocultarse en otras partes de Argentina u otros países de Sudamérica.

—¡Eso es increíble! ¿Cómo pueden vivir aquí abiertamente, cuando todos saben quiénes son?

—Es muy sencillo: se sienten protegidos porque el general Perón, presidente durante la Guerra, era un admirador de Hitler, y había aprendido sus tácticas con Mussolini. Como sabrá, Perón no declaró la guerra contra Alemania hasta un día antes del armisticio. Él y sus ministros permitieron la entrada de numerosos nazis de alto rango a cambio de dinero y secretos de valor. Algunos de ellos terminaron aquí, en Villa Gesell, y suelen ser dueños de los negocios más antiguos del pueblo. Pero no tienen buenas relaciones ni conmigo ni con algunos de mis amigos.

—¿Cuál es la historia de los dos hombres que a veces salen a nadar con nosotros?

—Mis dos amigos estaban en la marina, y yo era piloto de la Luftwaffe, pero nunca fuimos miembros del partido. Éramos oficiales de carrera y no teníamos otra opción que participar en las hostilidades.

Werner se quedó callado por un rato, antes de continuar:

—¿Ha oído hablar del Graf Spee? Era un Panzerschiff, o sea un acorazado que los ingleses acorralaron cerca de Montevideo, en la batalla del Río de la Plata. Mis amigos estaban entre los primeros oficiales sobrevivientes que pudieron escapar al Uruguay o a la Argentina. Langsdorff, que había sido su comandante y era una persona honorable, decidió hundir el barco para evitar que lo capturaran. Después de la batalla, se fue a un hotel de lujo en Buenos Aires, ¡se vistió con el uniforme de gala y se pegó un tiro!

Más adelante me encontré a otros alemanes exiliados, pero me era difícil saber si eran o no nazis. Hasta que un día conocí al dueño de la pensión Schwalbe, un chalecito encantador en las afueras del bosque de pinos. Tenía un nombre poético que significa 'golondrina'. Yo me había presentado allá para tratar de reservar habitación para unos amigos visitantes. Cuando entré, el señor Schwalbe estaba parado detrás del mostrador. Pude ver que la mayoría de las llaves de los cuartos estaban colgadas en la pared detrás suyo, lo que indicaba que el hotel no estaba lleno, aunque era plena temporada. Nuestra conversación fue muy corta y directa:

—¿Qué anda buscando por aquí? —me dijo sin preámbulos, disgustado por mi visita.

—Señor Schwalbe, quisiera reservar una habitación para el fin de semana, para dos amigos de Buenos Aires. ¿Tendría alguna libre?

—Tengo habitaciones libres, pero no para usted y sus amigos judíos. ¡Vaya a buscar a otra parte!

Salí del hotel alterado y asqueado por su respuesta. Era la primera vez que encontraba a un nazi abiertamente agresivo, y que yo era el blanco de un ataque antisemita tan flagrante. "¡Ahora sé quién es Schwalbe y espero poder pagarle la que me hizo! ¿Quién sabe? Un día puede estar nadando y que le dé un calambre allá afuera de la rompiente. Pero yo pienso seguir comiendo mi almuerzo detrás de las dunas, estudiando para el próximo examen de patología, completamente sordo a sus gritos de ayuda."

Gracias a este incidente y a muchos otros, tomé conciencia de mi buena suerte al haber nacido en la Argentina y no en Europa durante los años caóticos de la Segunda Guerra Mundial. De joven solo tomé contacto con presuntos nazis, pero aprendí a identificar con facilidad a los antisemitas, así como a otros demagogos y totalitarios. Es triste y alarmante que ahora, después de tantas décadas, vuelva a detectar estas tendencias en nuestros gobernantes, así como en otros grupos en los Estados Unidos, mi país adoptivo.

* * *

Cuando le mencioné a Werner que no ganaba lo suficiente como bañero en la playa, me llevó a conocer a los dueños del Restaurant San George. Hans y Helga eran una pareja encantadora de Hamburgo y me ofrecieron trabajo como mozo a la hora de la cena. Hans estaba ansioso por demonstrar que su tolerancia para la bebida era superior a todo el alcohol que podrían usar en un día en los hospitales de una gran ciudad. Me hizo conocer el Aquavit, su bebida favorita, y me reveló su secreto de cómo saber cuándo parar antes de estar borracho por completo. Había que pellizcarse (subrepticiamente) las mejillas entre dos dedos al empezar a beber y repetir eso después de cada trago hasta que las mejillas comenzaran a entumecer. Hans y Helga habían construido su oasis europeo en una cúpula de ladrillo recubierta en parte por un médano. Tenía una acústica formidable y me daban permiso para escuchar su colección de música clásica cuando el restaurante estaba cerrado. Podía incluso traer a amigos en una tarde descansada. La escucha de la Tocata y fuga de Bach en este ambiente sigue siendo una de mis experiencias musicales más memorables.

Hans había perdido sus piernas en dos

accidentes aislados montando a caballo. Ya no podía ejercitar su caballo como hacía falta y ni siquiera tenía montura. Para mi gran deleite, me pidieron que hiciera correr al caballo en pelo sobre la playa, varias veces por semana. Por esa época tuve la suerte de conocer al cocinero del restaurante, que me tomó como su protegido y ayudante de cocina, y fue mi amigo y mentor. Era un judío húngaro algo rechoncho, de pelo y bigote grises, que se había escapado de Europa durante la Guerra. Había sido chef y maître de los casinos y grandes hoteles de la costa en Brasil y en Argentina. Todos lo llamaban respetuosamente "Meier-Baçi".

Este chef era muy generoso con el personal de cocina y con los mozos. Recuerdo cuando me enseñó la receta del arroz a la cubana, un arroz blanco topado con un huevo frito y banana madura, salteada en mantequilla con azúcar. Hoy día aun puedo deleitar a mis nietos con esta receta. El chef había viajado mucho y era un hombre culto, convencido de que había una conexión entre el húngaro y el idioma de los yaganes, la tribu ya desaparecida de Tierra del Fuego. Aunque yo no fuese lingüista, me había mostrado un borrador de su diccionario bilingüe y pude ver que el parecido era notable. Él creía que los yaganes habían emigrado del Asia a través del estrecho de Bering para, finalmente, establecerse en el extremo de la Patagonia.

Meier-Baçi falleció unos años después de mi estadía en Villa Gesell. Aunque nos mantuvimos en contacto, nunca supe el destino de su fascinante diccionario. Pero eso me inspiró a leer más sobre los yaganes en un notable libro histórico: El último confín de la Tierra, de Lucas Bridges, un inglés cuyo padre fue el fundador de Ushuaia. Por una extraña coincidencia, mis padres están enterrados en Buenos Aires en un rincón judío del cementerio británico, a pocos pasos de la tumba de Lucas Bridges.

* * *

Una tardecita, mientras acompañaba a Werner a entregar sus fotos en el pueblo, se nos apareció a la carrera un autito deportivo amarillo, levantando un remolino de arena y tierra frente al sol poniente. Dobló la esquina a toda velocidad y, derrapando de costado, paró con un gran chirrido enfrente nuestro. Abrió la puerta para salir un hombre alto, muy aristocrático, de unos sesenta años, saludando efusivamente con un brazo estirado y una sonrisa brillante.

—¡Werner! Wie geht's? ¡Qué bueno encontrarte después de un año entero! Recién llego de Buenos Aires para estar con mi familia.

—¡Hola, barón Thyssen! ¡Qué placer verlo! Permítame presentarle a mi amigo Arghmando, el nuevo bañero. Yo estoy aun luchando como fotógrafo en la playa. Como sabrá, no hay muchos aviones para pilotar en la Villa, pero, en cambio, podría hacer volar su hermoso autito.

—Parece que te gusta mi Karman Ghia. Es el único del país. Mis amigos de la aduana me ayudaron a importarlo.

Después de que el barón se alejara envuelto en otra gran nube de polvo, Werner me explicó que se trataba de un aristócrata y poderoso industrial cuya familia era aún propietaria de una de las más grandes fábricas de acero en Alemania. Junto con los Krupp, habían provisto a Hitler del acero para sus tanques y armamento, algo esencial para su capacidad bélica. Y como si adivinara mis pensamientos, Werner agregó que no estaba seguro si Thyssen era también un nazi, aunque sí había contribuido al poderío militar germánico. Ahora tenía una casa de vacaciones en Argentina y posiblemente estaba en negocios con el Gobierno.

Al día siguiente, en la playa, vi acercarse con determinación y mirada severa al barón Thyssen. Me pidió (o quizá me ordenó) que pusiera la sombrilla para su esposa alejada del resto de los turistas, muy cerca del agua, sobre la arena mojada. Se me pasó por la mente que debería negarme, pero me di cuenta de que eso sería fútil. El hombre venía decidido y estaba acostumbrado a que lo obedecieran. No ganaría nada si él iba a quejarse a mi jefe. Pero para mi sorpresa, me confió asimismo que cuidara especialmente a su hija, de cinco años y a su amiguita.

—Don Armando, esta nena es mi hija —me anunció, apuntando a una chiquita muy simpática, con una brillante malla de baño rosada— y quiero que la vigile constantemente, en especial si se acerca al mar para jugar. También cuide a su amiguita, pero la seguridad de mi hija debería ser su preocupación principal por las próximas semanas.

Más tarde conté este incidente a Meier-Baçi, quien había sobrevivido a la persecución en Europa, y con su larga experiencia e intuición era capaz de distinguir a un nazi en una multitud. Él opinaba que Thyssen era autoritario y algo arrogante, en parte por su ascendencia aristocrática, pero que probablemente no era ni antisemita ni criminal. En una ocasión mi amigo el chef se presentó en el salón-comedor para saludar al barón y a su esposa, ya que les había preparado un postre especial. Con este gesto pude reducir mis dudas respecto al barón Thyssen y sus bien conocidas actividades durante la Guerra.

***

Al relacionarme con los clientes tuve oportunidad de conocer a otros alemanes y europeos cultos, y hasta de hacer nuevas amistades. Esto balanceaba mis encuentros con otros que despertaban mis sospechas de ser nazis.

245

Una tarde me encontraba recostado en la arena bajo una sombrilla de la playa estudiando para los exámenes del fin del verano. Las brisas marinas eran estimulantes y mejoraban la concentración. Muchos de los turistas se habían ido a dormir la siesta y yo no tenía consciencia de estar silbando muy fuerte alguna música clásica. De pronto vi venir a Gunther, un judío alemán sobreviviente de la Guerra que había emigrado a la Argentina con su familia. Él me interrumpió la lectura (y los silbidos) con un comentario jovial, pero algo pedante:

—Disculpe, Armando, pero ¡usted me está volviendo loco! ¿No podría silbar una sola tonada? En los últimos cinco minutos pasó por la Quinta sinfonía, de Beethoven; por el Concierto No. 5 para violín, de Mozart; por el Brandenburgués No. 2, de Bach; y terminó con la Rapsodia húngara, de Liszt. ¡Por favor, decídase de una vez!

El Gobierno alemán compensaba a Gunther por la pérdida de su fábrica textil en Frankfurt durante la Guerra. Igual que muchos otros judíos alemanes, Gunther era muy patriótico, capaz de defender todo lo que fuese alemán (excepto a los nazis), y tenía nostalgia por su país y el modo de vida. Pero yo había escuchado a otros judíos rusos o polacos decir que ellos no compartían esa actitud, y usaban el apodo de "yekes" para los alemanes, un término despectivo en yidish.

Gunther me apreciaba porque teníamos un gusto parecido en música clásica y porque yo trabajaba durante el verano para pagar mis estudios en la facultad. Un fin de semana que tuve libre, mi amigo y su familia me llevaron en su auto hasta Buenos Aires para ver a mis padres. Cuando volvíamos al pueblo, Gunther se detuvo de repente al lado de la ruta, en el medio de la nada, se bajó y allí mismo se desmayó, quizá por un exceso de vino en una fiesta. Mi conocimiento médico era solo teórico e inútil si se trataba de ayudar a alguien. Por fortuna, con ademanes desesperados conseguí que parara el único camión de transporte visible a esa hora tardía. El conductor se ofreció a llevar al enfermo con su mujer a una clínica de una ciudad cercana. Aun sin licencia, no tuve más remedio que manejar el auto con los niños durante muchos kilómetros en una oscura ruta de tierra hasta Gesell. Por suerte, el Opel de la familia era automático. Al día siguiente, cuando el enfermo se repuso, regresaron en un taxi. Estaban muy agradecidos por mi iniciativa y luego me invitaron a una deliciosa comida casera. Pero durante la cena resultó evidente que me consideraban muy diferente a ellos. Creo que opinaron que si yo no hablaba ni entendía el alemán, sería muy difícil que llegara a ser amigo de la familia. En resumen, nunca más volvimos a vernos después del fin de las vacaciones.

Hubo otros encuentros con los alemanes de Gesell que tampoco acabaron bien. Por ejemplo, un caballero que gustaba de leer en la playa bajo una sombrilla por las tardes y que solía conversar conmigo, un día me sorprendió con la sugerencia de que llevara a su hija a un baile. Se trataba de una atractiva secretaria multilingüe que trabajaba para la embajada de Holanda, pero que no conocía a nadie en el pueblo. Yo no podía creer en mi buena suerte cuando caminamos juntos a un club nocturno en donde yo tenía amigos en la banda. Hicimos una entrada triunfal. Sin embargo, solo conseguí bailar con ella un par de piezas. Mi pareja simpatizó de inmediato con el guitarrista, un francés muy buen mozo, y así se esfumaron mis chances de volver con ella a su cabaña.

Cuando le conté a Meier-Baçi mis tribulaciones románticas, me escuchó con simpatía y prometió presentarme a otras chicas que frecuentaban el restaurante. Pero antes de eso tuve la suerte de conocer a una esbelta atleta austríaca. El problema fue que Monika, así se llamaba, era muy rara, enfurruñada bajo la lona de su carpa en la playa, y rechazaba las invitaciones de jugar al vóley o de ir a nadar con otros turistas. Como yo era el encargado de la playa, tenía una buena excusa para entrar en conversación, y basado en mis lecturas de Freud, La psicopatología de la vida cotidiana, no dudé de que se trataba de una depresión. Por suerte, conseguí convencerla para que me acompañara por la noche a admirar las noctilucas, un espectáculo que conocíamos solo unos pocos entendidos en el pueblo. Se podía observar la fosforescencia de dos maneras: viendo el brillo de las olas en la rompiente, o simplemente raspando la arena mojada al borde del mar. Esta exhibición brillante y mágica la cautivó y jugó en mi favor: desde entonces comenzamos a salir juntos. Su humor siguió mejorando, lo que sugería que un desengaño amoroso había causado la depresión. Su familia quedó muy agradecida por mi contribución psicoanalítica y un tío hasta me prestó su carísima caña de pescar. Lo triste es que nunca alcancé a pescar nada, ya que perdí la línea, el anzuelo y la carnada al primer intento, y tuve que devolver muy avergonzado el equipo de pesca a su dueño.

Mi amistad con Monika siguió prosperando después de la temporada, al volver a la capital, y ella me invitó a conocer el Club de Villa Ballester, un suburbio de Buenos Aires. La población alemana era tan numerosa en ese barrio que el Bundestag había aceptado a la Hölter Schule Argentina como una escuela alemana oficial. Pero fue muy mala idea que yo aceptara esta invitación.

Llegué al club un domingo por la mañana después de un traqueteado viaje en tren. Jugamos un rato al básquet con unos muchachotes que no parecían interesados en mi existencia, y después de salir a correr por la zona fuimos a comer con los padres de Monika un almuerzo muy poco inspirado (sándwiches de salchichas, chucrut y papas fritas). Yo no tenía nada en común con su familia y la conversación se vino abajo muy pronto. Como era un día de calor, después de comer fui a darme un baño antes de volver a la ciudad. Apenas me puse bajo la ducha colectiva, los otros miembros reaccionaron como si hubiera entrado un extraterrestre en el vestuario, su actitud se volvió glacial, y noté que todos tenían fija la mirada sobre mis genitales: ¡habían descubierto que estaba circuncidado! En la Argentina de aquella época, eso te identificaba automáticamente como "judío". Para evitar un incidente violento, me sequé lo más rápido posible, haciendo como que no había pasado nada. Así que saludé muy apresurado a la familia y salí disparado hacia la estación del tren, para terminar sano y salvo mi imprudente visita al Club Alemán.

* * *

A pesar de estos episodios desagradables, mi experiencia en Gesell fue enriquecedora. Y mis encuentros con algunos de estos personajes me impactaron de un modo que no podía predecir en mi juventud. A propósito de esto, cuando la familia del barón Thyssen regresaba a la capital al fin de temporada, él se acercó para desearme suerte con mis estudios universitarios y para agradecerme por haber cuidado a su hijita. También me demostró su admiración por mi ética profesional, ya que le recordaba a su hijo, estudiante de medicina en Alemania, que "¡trabajaba durante los veranos para suplementar sus ingresos!". Entonces, muy ceremonioso y con una pequeña reverencia, me entregó un sobre blanco que abrí solo después de que se había ido. Quedé boquiabierto al encontrar que su regalo sería suficiente para comprar todos los libros de texto necesarios y un traje azul marino (de fibra sintética) que pude vestir con orgullo muchas veces hasta mi graduación. Ahora, ya jubilado de mi carrera médica y en otro país, cada vez que subo a un ascensor de marca Thyssen-Krupp, recuerdo este episodio y se me dibuja una gran sonrisa.

Cuando Werner me mostró cómo usar su famosa cámara de fotos, no me imaginaba que un día lejano iba a satisfacer mi sueño de tener una Leica. Así es que en 1981 fui invitado a Israel para presentar mis resultados en una conferencia científica. Por esos tiempos yo tenía una cámara japonesa SLR de poco valor, y usaba diapositivas en color. Al terminar el congreso tuve la oportunidad única de tomar fotos aéreas de Jerusalén. Iba invitado por un famoso piloto de pruebas, un primo de mi madre considerado un héroe en Israel. Para ayudarme a fotografiar las mejores vistas nos hizo pasar a baja altura por encima del antiguo Templo del rey Salomón y del Muro Occidental (antes llamado "de los Lamentos"), una zona militar por donde pocos tienen permiso para volar. Entonces él inclinó el avión de lado para que se viese mejor el centro geográfico en donde las tres religiones monoteístas comparten sus monumentos más sagrados. Mi excitación fue tan grande que no paré de disparar hasta quedarme sin película, y entonces regresamos al aeropuerto.

Al volver a Seattle mandé revelar las diapositivas y, para mi horrible sorpresa, el resultado fue una catástrofe: ¡todas las fotos habían salido sobreexpuestas y fuera de foco! Nunca supe si eso se debía a errores míos causados por la ansiedad, o a fallas técnicas de la cámara. El hecho es que fue más fácil echarle la culpa al aparato. Furioso y descontrolado, tomé la cámara por la correa haciéndola girar sobre mi cabeza en círculos cada vez más rápido y al fin, vociferando de rabia y frustración, la dejé volar en un arco perfecto hasta caer en el lago Washington. Creo que hasta hoy, muchos años más tarde, debe servir de hogar a muchos pescaditos de colores. Ese mismo día decidí algo de lo que nunca me arrepentiré: ¡compré una Leica M con telémetro, una maravilla mecánica que no me ha fallado nunca! Incluso la llevé conmigo en un viaje reciente hasta Myanmar, un país exótico y poco desarrollado. Allí tuve ocasión de fotografiar a los rohingya, un grupo étnico musulmán, perseguido por la mayoría budista. Estas fotos las presenté en un libro, Impresiones birmanas, que creo le hubiera impresionado bien a Werner, mi primer maestro de fotografía.

Mi experiencia con Meier-Baçi, mi mentor durante los años en Gesell, me volvió a la mente cuando una barista del café en que habitualmente escribo mis historias se acercó para conversar. Era una joven coreana con grandes anteojos de aumento y una sonrisa encantadora. Me había observado escribir a mano con una lapicera de tinta muy elegante, mientras todos los demás escribían en una computadora o en sus teléfonos.

—Hola, soy Katherine. Quisiera preguntarle sobre su escritura, sobre los temas que le interesan y por qué escribe aquí a menudo. ¿Le molestaría si lo acompaño?

—Por supuesto que no, siéntese si gusta. Pero ¿por qué quiere conversar?

—Porque usted debe tener muchas historias para contar. ¡En cambio yo no tengo ninguna! Soy solo una barista y acá nunca pasa nada. ¿Podríamos tomar un cafecito la próxima vez que venga?

Desde ese día inesperado, Katherine y yo nos encontramos a veces para discutir sobre nuestras vidas y experiencias. Yo escuché con atención sobre sus sueños y proyectos para el futuro. Ella, por su parte, me oyó hablar de mi cuento "Nadando con nazis en Argentina" y otras de mis historias. Esto me hizo reflexionar sobre mí mismo y sobre quién soy: "Un profesor vestido un poco a la antigua, de pelo y bigote ya plateados, que escribe en los cafés con una lapicera de tinta, y que, por sorpresa, terminó siendo mentor de una joven entusiasta e inteligente". Esta relación es muy gratificante, y es una inversión de roles sorprendente porque yo era muy joven cuando Meier-Baçi era mi amigo. Quizá la historia se repita algún día, cuando Katherine, ya una gran señora coreana de cabellos grises, se transforme en mentora de otra joven entusiasta con intereses parecidos a los suyos. Confío en que entonces ella recuerde con placer y gratitud sus tempranos encuentros con Armando-Baçi.

La infernal historia de taxi

Algo cansado de explorar tantas librerías, me acerqué a la esquina del café La Biela en Recoleta, buscando un taxi para regresar a casa de mi familia. La elección de un taxi siempre me produce un poco de ansiedad, sabiendo que esto puede terminar en una aventura, especialmente en Buenos Aires, ciudad populosa y complicada. Elegí el tercero de la cola porque me gustó la pinta del chofer, un criollazo sólido, de pelo corto y bien afeitado, que me inspiró confianza. Abrí la puerta para entrar y me miró apenas, como para cerciorarse de que yo también era un pasajero aceptable. En ese instante tuve el presentimiento fugaz de que este viaje iba a ser muy distinto de muchos otros en mi memoria.

Le pedí que me llevara a Belgrano por la avenida Luis María Campos y partió en seguida, sin mirarme ni decir más nada. Al llegar al primer semáforo rojo nos detuvimos y pude mirar hacia el este, a mi derecha, en donde me alarmó la vista de unas nubes muy negras de tormenta sobre el Río de la Plata, mientras comenzaba su aterrizaje un avión de pasajeros sobre el Aeroparque cercano. Pensé en mi futuro vuelo de regreso a EE. UU. y sentí un poco de vértigo al imaginar la posible turbulencia. Me sorprendió el cambio de tiempo, ya que brillaba un sol casi cegador sobre nuestro auto.

—Dígame, chofer —le dije, ya preocupado—,

¿no sabe el pronóstico del tiempo para hoy?

—No escuché nada ni ayer ni hoy, ¡porque no pude! —contestó bruscamente y sin mirar para atrás por el espejito.

De inmediato lo clasifiqué como un maleducado o un resentido; me pareció que me estaba macaneando, ya que un chofer que pasa horas en su auto es normal que escuche la radio sin parar y el pronóstico lo repiten a cada rato, aunque su radio estaba apagada. Un taxista suele estar bien informado sobre todo lo que pasa en la ciudad y, a veces, en el mundo entero, de modo que insistí:

—Perdóneme, pero ¿cómo es que usted no escucha el pronóstico por la radio, para enterarse de lo que va a pasar con el tráfico, en caso de lluvia o tormenta, como hacen muchos otros taxistas?

—Mire, maestro —me dijo, muy irritado (me encantó que me llamara maestro, una expresión argentina que hacía rato que no oía, pero eso no fue suficiente para quitarme el enojo por su conducta)—, lo que me pasó fue que anteayer me asaltaron y casi me matan. Todavía no estoy recuperado. Ayer no trabajé del todo y hoy apenas si me pude levantar y salí muy atrasado, después que pasaran las noticias de las siete, las que siempre escucho.

Con ese comentario se me pasó la furia de repente y quedé hasta algo avergonzado por haber hablado sin conocimiento de causa y por presumir que era un irrespetuoso, al no querer responderme sobre el pronóstico.

—¡No me diga! ¿En serio lo asaltaron? Por suerte que no lo lastimaron.

—¿Cómo que no me lastimaron? —me contestó con un grito.

Y sin decir más, arrancó el auto y saltó la luz roja de la esquina de Pueyrredón, le metió a fondo por unos cien metros, frenó de golpe en la otra cuadra y apagó el motor. Allí mismo giró el cuerpo hacia mí, como enfurecido, y se levantó el pulóver y la camisa blanca para mostrarme el costado. Le vi una horrible cuchillada, con punto de entrada casi negro y bien abajo, que seguía hacia adelante por unos 10 cm, paralela a las costillas. Toda la zona estaba enrojecida, inflamada, con un principio de celulitis.

—Perdóneme, ¡por supuesto que ahora le creo! Siento mucho lo que le pasó. Por suerte que el cuchillo se debe haber encontrado con una costilla y no le perforó el pulmón. A lo mejor debería ver a algún médico para que lo curen y le den una receta para antibióticos. ¿Cómo fue que ocurrió?

—Eran apenas las 6.30 de la mañana cuando subió una pareja para que los lleve hacia el centro. No me gustaron de entrada, tenían pinta de pichicateros. A los pocos minutos de marcha el tipo me dijo que pare a un costado de la calle, la mujer sacó un cuchillo y, sin avisarme, trató de clavármelo en el costado. Yo intenté abrir la puerta para rajarme, pero no pude porque el tipo me puso un revólver en la sien y me gritó: "¿Adónde querés ir, hijo de puta? ¡De acá no salís sin darnos toda la guita que juntaste esta noche y me la das ahora mismo o te reviento el mate!

"Le dije que llevaba solamente unos 80 pesos de cambio porque recién había empezado a trabajar y el desgraciado me miró con odio y apretó el gatillo. De milagro no salió la bala, no sé si falló el tiro, o si el revólver no estaba cargado. Me dio como un vahído, se me nubló la vista y creí que me iba a desmayar.

"Los dos empezaron a discutir y al fin me pusieron de nuevo el cuchillo en la yugular y me dijeron: "—Arrancá y llevános por San Isidro a una de las villas". Y tuve que arrancar y llevarlos a una de las peores, a la Cava, que usted no debe conocer, pero ahí venden drogas. Allí la mujer se bajó por un ratito pero volvió sin nada, no le había alcanzado la plata. Al final me hicieron manejar de vuelta hacia la ciudad y parar en la General Paz, en donde había ya mucha gente aglomerada esperando colectivos. Me dijeron que pare el auto y se bajaron para mezclarse con la muchedumbre. No puedo creer que no me hayan matado y que pueda contarle la historia.

—¡Es de terror! Lo que le ocurrió es impresionante y entiendo cómo se siente. Pero le cuento que me hizo recordar algo que me pasó hace muchos años cuando era un pibe, practicante de medicina en la Asistencia Pública de San Isidro. ¡Yo también conozco la Cava! Una noche nos llamaron de la villa para ir a ver a una señora enferma y al llegar estacionamos la ambulancia afuera. Era un pozo enorme en el barro, de muchas cuadras de largo, a varios metros por debajo del nivel de la calle, con casitas de zinc y de cartón que apenas si se mantenían en pie. Bajamos con el chofer de la Asistencia, que se puso una pistola en la cintura, por si acaso. Él conocía bien ese ambiente. A los pocos metros de camino en la oscuridad, de repente empezaron los balazos. No veíamos a nadie y no sabíamos si los tiros eran para nosotros, pero nos volvimos corriendo a la ambulancia, como en las películas, sin que el chofer tenga tiempo de responder con un tiro, porque igual no veíamos de qué se trataba. Parece que usted y yo tuvimos un gran susto en esa misma villa, con muchos años de diferencia. Pero lo de usted es realmente un drama y le pasó apenitas hace dos días.

—Bueno, jefe, me parece que usted también se las sabe todas. Mejor que sigamos el viaje a Belgrano.

Continuamos en silencio por unos minutos. Pensé que se había calmado un poco, sobre todo al pasar por Palermo, en donde la plazoleta estaba abarrotada por unos magníficos jacarandás en flor, deslumbrantes en una densidad púrpura casi surrealista, y tuve la esperanza de que eso lo hiciera olvidar su horrible experiencia. A mí esos árboles me recordaron antiguos paseos en bote de remo por el Delta, y me despertaron sueños de visitar un día otros sitios famosos por la presencia de jacarandás. Pero confiaba que la belleza de esos árboles le hiciera olvidar un poco su horrible experiencia.

—Y ahora no sé qué voy a hacer cuando vuelva a casa —me lanzó de pronto, despertándome de mis fantasías, como si él no hubiese visto los jacarandás.

—¿No tiene familia, mujer, alguien que lo ayude a recuperarse?

—Mire, mi mujer me dejó hace unas dos semanas; creo que está viviendo con otro tipo, uno más joven que trabajaba en la misma fábrica.

Al mirarlo, lo encontré más aindiado que al principio. Me pareció que sus pelos de la nuca eran más negros de lo que había notado y que se le paraban un poco cuando me contaba eso con bastante furia. Me di cuenta de que el viajecito y la tarde no se presentaban muy optimistas y que era mejor no hacer preguntas indiscretas, ni adentro ni afuera de un taxi. Menos aun cuando estás de vacaciones.

—Todavía me quedan mis dos hijos —siguió en un tono lúgubre de circunstancias—. La chica es ya mayorcita y se fue de casa hace un año, casi nunca la llamo, pero debería hacerlo, ya ni se acuerda de mí. Pero el pibe tiene unos 15 años y vive conmigo. Al llegar a casa después del asalto, lo primero que hice fue llamar a mi mujer a la fábrica para pedirle que viniese a ayudarme. Atendió el teléfono, pero me dijo que no me creía, que la llamaba para que ella me tuviese lástima, y allí mismo me cortó sin despedirse. ¡Pero si ella sabe que yo no miento, que soy muy laburador y me rompo el culo para mantenerlos desde el día que nos fuimos de Formosa y conseguí acá este trabajo de taxi! Le juro que nunca fui bebedor, pero en ese momento no supe más qué hacer, busqué algo para tomar y cuando encontré una botella de caña me la bajé entera. Parece que me caí por la escalera, en donde quedé tirado por varias horas. Me encontró mi hijo cuando volvió tarde de la escuela, me ayudó a levantarme y a lavar la herida con alcohol, pero creo que está infectada lo mismo.

¡Este formoseño me está arruinando el día! —pensé—. ¡Si yo solo quería hacer un viajecito tranquilo, mejor no preguntarle más nada! Parece que me tomó por cura y decidió confesarse conmigo. ¿Podría ser que yo le resulte receptivo por mi edad, mis pelos grises o una actitud anticuada de abuelito? Creo que su historia ya me dio acidez, una ansiedad desmesurada y alguna que otra palpitación. Esto me recuerda una película de Jim Jarmusch, *Noche en la Tierra,* con cinco episodios de viajes en taxi en distintos países. En uno de ellos, Roberto Benigni actúa de chofer maníaco y verborrágico, cuando sube al auto un obispo en el asiento de atrás. Aprovechando la oportunidad de una confesión gratuita, el chofer le cuenta su propia historia descabellada, con todos los detalles de su bestialismo con una oveja y otros pecados, mientras corre desenfrenado por las angostas calles de Roma. El obispo se desespera más y más al escuchar esta historia truculenta y al rato se muere de un infarto en el taxi. ¡Espero no dar motivo para el guion de otra película con la odisea que este hombre implacable me sigue contando!

Lo que me sacó de estas elucubraciones fue cuando, al doblar una esquina por Cabildo, nos encontramos de pronto con la calle bloqueada por una manifestación. Había cientos de obreros furiosos por la noticia del cierre de su fábrica, queriendo tomar posesión del edificio. La policía no parecía estar haciendo nada y dejaba que los piqueteros bloquearan el paso de los vehículos sin intervenir. Supe que nos íbamos a quedar colgados allí por horas, sin poder movernos ni para atrás ni para delante, con la certeza de seguir escuchando historias de terror.

—A ver, chofer, ¿qué se le ocurre ahora para sacarnos de este despelote? No puedo quedarme aquí toda la tarde.

Me miró con bronca y, al mismo tiempo, le noté un resplandor de orgullo profesional en la mirada. Allí mismo sacó un pañuelo blanco del bolsillo, bajó la ventanilla y, agitando su pañuelo, movió el taxi unos metros hasta pararlo justo delante de un energúmeno con una barra de hierro en la mano y una camiseta que lo designaba como "jefe de seguridad" de los piqueteros, y comenzó a gritarle desaforado:

—¡A ver si me abren paso, llevo a un hombre al hospital, que parece que le dio un ataque al corazón! Apúrese, por favor, que está muy mal —se dio vuelta para mirarme y me dijo muy bajito—: Hágase el muerto, a ver si nos dejan salir de acá.

Le hice caso, cerré los ojos, agarrándome el pecho con una habilidad histriónica digna de Marcello Mastroiani. Milagrosamente, el piquetero empezó a moverse y a gritar cosas a la gente, girando la barra de hierro por encima de su cabeza, y consiguió que los manifestantes nos abrieran camino como si fuese el centro del mar Rojo, y así nos salimos del escándalo con una facilidad nunca vista. ¿Quién hubiera imaginado que este formoseño meado por los perros y deprimido casi hasta el suicidio fuese capaz de semejante hazaña?

Dos cuadras más adelante recuperé el aliento y la salud cardíaca, y se me ocurrió que los dos necesitábamos tonificarnos un poquito y parar el auto por unos minutos. Entonces me sorprendí a mí mismo con una propuesta inesperada y fuera de carácter:

—Oiga, chofer, este viaje se está poniendo muy difícil. ¿Qué le parece si me deja invitarlo a un café o una copa de vino? Los dos lo andamos necesitando. Mire, allí en la esquina hay un café y podríamos parar por unos minutos. No importa si deja andando el taxímetro, yo le pago la diferencia.

—Tiene razón, señor, un vasito de vino nos

va a venir bien a los dos. No se preocupe por el precio del viaje, después lo arreglamos al llegar.

Era un café de barrio, con unos billares al fondo y tres borrachitos sentados a una mesa cercana al bar, hablando a los gritos de un gol de Messi que pasaban por la tele. Nos sentamos y le pedí al mozo dos vasitos de vino tinto.

—¡Salud! —dijimos al mismo tiempo, y nos bajamos el vino con un suspiro, tomándolo un poco más rápido de lo recomendable.

—El vino me va a calmar un poco, pero igual no tengo idea de lo que voy a hacer ahora con mi familia, especialmente con los chicos, desde que se les fue la madre. Yo no me ocupaba demasiado de ellos. ¡Pero fue grandioso que el pibe me ayudó a curar la herida y se preocupó por mí después del asalto!

Justo en ese momento llegó el mozo con la cuenta y le pagué con monedas de un peso. Solo que dejé caer una sin querer, y comenzó a rodar por el suelo hasta desaparecer cerca de la mesa de los borrachitos. Me levanté a buscarla, pero no la veía. En ese momento uno de ellos apuntó con el dedo hacia el suelo, debajo de la mesa, y empezó a decir en voz alta: "Acá estáaaa, acá estáaaa"; y cuando me acerqué a buscarla me remató con una canción para terminar la estrofa: "Acá estáaa la bandera idolatraaaada, la enseña que Belgrano nos legó..." (La famosa letra del himno a la Bandera Nacional), mientras se mataba de risa con sus amigotes por la cargada que me habían hecho.

En eso se levantó el formoseño, que se plantó frente al grupito con el pecho adelante y una actitud marcial de sargento castigando a sus colimbas y les reprochó con fuerza la burla que se mandaron (lo que es prácticamente un deporte nacional o, por lo menos, muy porteño):

—¡A ver si dejan de joder a la gente, manga de vagos! El señor no les hizo nada y además es mi cliente y nadie lo va a molestar.

Con lo cual se callaron todos, dejé perder la moneda y nos volvimos tranquilitos hacia la mesa.

Reconozco que en los últimos minutos me había empezado a gustar más el tipo, un trabajador con orgullo y lleno de recursos. ¡No puedo creer la imaginación que desplegó al sacarnos del lío con los piqueteros! ¡Y cómo me defendió recién frente a los borrachos! No debería juzgar a otros por su apariencia o su forma de expresarse. La prueba de mis prejuicios me la dieron hace ya muchos años, en 1982, en México, cuando recibí una lección inolvidable en otro taxi en Puerto Vallarta. Yo quería regresar al hotel, a varios kilómetros al norte por la playa. Me tocó un conductor de mala facha, con pelos largos y desaliñados, con una barba sin afeitar por varios días y una expresión de pocos amigos. Salimos y en la otra esquina lo paró un chamaquito que entró y se sentó a su lado en el asiento del pasajero. El chofer comenzó a subir las colinas muy empinadas del pueblo viejo, doblando a derecha e izquierda por un laberinto de callecitas empedradas, que no era la ruta más directa hacia la playa. Mi imaginación desenfrenada comenzó a analizar posibilidades de un robo, o un secuestro, pero al llegar a un barrio modesto, el chico se bajó luego de darle un par de pesos, una fracción de lo que yo iba a tener que pagar como turista. Era evidente que no había razón para alarmarse. El chico no quería subir tantas cuadras a pie y el chofer aprovechó para llevarlo, sabiendo que los turistas no se enojan en estos casos.

Ya solo conmigo, empezó a darme conversación. Se dio cuenta enseguida de que era argentino (porque hablaba igual que en las telenovelas que miran los domingos) y a preguntarme por la guerra de la Malvinas, que venía de empezar. Le respondí algo banal, como "que el Gobierno militar quiso usar un enemigo externo para distraer a la gente y no protestar por tantos años de terror y de dictadura". Pero en cambio él me salió con algo mucho más sorprendente: ¡me explicó que a veces las guerras empiezan de un modo inesperado, con el ejemplo de que, en 1914, un nacionalista yugoslavo en Sarajevo asesinó al archiduque Fernando de Austria y así comenzó la Primera Guerra Mundial, en la que murieron tantos millones de inocentes, y Europa quedó dividida en muchos estados más pequeños!

Su memoria y su erudición me dejaron pasmado y lo felicité. Resultó que él era tapatío.

Antes de venir a Vallarta era profesor de historia en la Universidad de Guadalajara, pero con la crisis económica se quedó sin trabajo y tuvo que buscar otra forma de mantener a su familia. ¡Así descubrí que mi presunto asesino en serie, el desaliñado pero elocuente chofer de Vallarta, resultó ser educado, honesto y mucho mejor informado que yo! Ahora debo reconocer que también el formoseño conflictuado tiene su lado bueno y ya me sorprendió varias veces desde el principio de este viajecito infernal.

Justo cuando estaba por agradecerle su ayuda con los borrachitos, comenzó a sonar su teléfono celular. Se fue caminando hacia la puerta y no pude oír de qué se trataba, pero vi que hablaba con alguien con agitación creciente. Al cabo de un par de minutos le colgó y volvió para la mesa con el rabo entre las piernas.

—Mire, jefe, mejor que sigamos viaje, voy a tener que llevarlo de una vez porque necesito volver y ocuparme de mis cosas, de familia. Recién acaba de llamar mi hermana desde Formosa para contarme que tenemos malas noticias sobre mi padre. Parece que tuvo un derrame cerebral. Está inconsciente y no creen que pueda sobrevivir por mucho tiempo. Vamos saliendo.

Entré al auto apurado, porque faltaban pocos minutos para llegar a destino y la historia de su vida se estaba poniendo intolerable para los dos. No sabía cómo este hombre iba a poder sobreponerse a todas las tragedias que le ocurrieron en tan poco tiempo. ¡Ni siquiera en el cine, como en la comedia francesa *L'Emmerdeur* ocurren tantas cosas! Cuando a Jacques Brel se le escapa la mujer con un médico amigo, él se quiere suicidar, con tal mala suerte que nada le resulta. Para colmo, Lino Ventura, que es un asesino a sueldo, tampoco quiere que su vecino se suicide y se lo impide para que no venga la policía. Pero en mi caso corrí el riesgo de echar más leña al fuego y, con gran imprudencia, retomé el tema de su familia:

—¡Qué triste lo que me cuenta de su papá! Ojalá no sea tan grave como piensan —comencé, tratando de inyectar una gota de optimismo positivista—. Pero, por suerte, lo que me decía de su hijo es muy lindo. Parece ser un muchacho cariñoso. Debería llevarlo al fútbol este domingo y tratar de hacerse más amigos entre ustedes. A lo mejor también los quiere encontrar su hija después del partido para ir todos juntos a una pizzería —se me ocurrió sugerirle, olvidando otra vez que no debería meterme o interferir en su vida—. Quizá sea muy sabio aprovechar lo que ya tiene, un par de hijos formidables, y estar con ellos en todo lo posible.

Me miró con interés, un poco sorprendido, sin decir nada, y siguió manejando. En ese momento, noté que el cielo había cambiado brutalmente a un impenetrable gris plomizo y unas gotas gordas empezaron a caer con un traqueteo metálico de ametralladora sobre el techo del auto. La lluvia era torrencial justo cuando llegamos y le pedí que pare frente al edificio. Alcancé a pagarle lo que decía el taxímetro y me despedí con un apretón de manos y pocas palabras:

—Suerte con todo, ¡especialmente con los hijos! —y salí corriendo para no quedar empapado en el chaparrón casi tropical.

Respiré hondo y, con un gran suspiro, entré al departamento como si fuese un refugio. Creo que tardé varios días en reponerme de semejante aventura, pero me quedé pensando en el formoseño y me dio lástima que no iba a poder enterarme nunca del desenlace, de saber si sobrevivió a la infección de su cuchillada, si su mujer volvió a casa o lo abandonó para siempre. Sobre todo, tenía curiosidad por saber si él llegó a mejorar la relación con sus hijos, pero decidí olvidarme poco a poco del asunto y seguir mi vida normal.

Unos diez días más tarde sonó el timbre y apareció el portero para entregarme un sobre blanco con la inscripción: "Para el doctor de pelo blanco que vive en Estados Unidos". El portero comprendió que era para mí, el único vecino con esa descripción. La abrí con curiosidad y algo temeroso, pues no quería aceptar la posibilidad de que fuera algo de mi chofer para contarme otra nueva tragedia que se le había quedado en el tintero. La abrí enseguida y encontré que era una nota corta, con letra bastante prolija en tinta azul, en un papel rayado como si fueran los deberes para un colegio secundario. Decía:

Estimado doctor:

Perdone que no sepa su nombre, nunca nos presentamos, pero seguro que el portero lo va a encontrar para darle mi mensaje.

Le cuento que terminé un par de días en el hospital por culpa de la infección de la cuchillada. Por suerte, mis hijos vinieron a acompañarme y regresé a casa pronto. Como usted me dijo que hiciera, el domingo lo llevé al pibe al fútbol y al terminar el partido nos encontramos con su hermana para comer una pizza los tres juntos. Era la primera vez que lo hacíamos y quedaron muy contentos, no sabían cómo agradecerme.

Mi padre no pudo recuperarse de su derrame y falleció sin que yo pudiera llegar a verlo. Ahora mi hermanita, que tiene una fábrica de muebles, decidió ayudarme y puedo regresar a Formosa a trabajar con ella. Parece que mis chicos quieren hacer la prueba de venir conmigo y quedarse allí por un tiempito a ver si les gusta más que esta Capital de porquería.

Lo saluda muy atte.,

Facundo, su chofer del taxi del otro día

La muerte paralela de don Quijote

Don Quijote murió el último lunes de septiembre de 1981, a las 13 horas. El informe patológico concluyó (sin certeza) que, a causa de un infarto de miocardio, pero la caligrafía temblorosa del forense y la lenta caída del texto hacia el fondo de la página eran testigos de su lucha interior con un dilema. Era incapaz de declarar su convicción de que la muerte se debía a razones sobrenaturales. Ese diagnóstico hubiera sido inaceptable en el certificado de defunción.

Ahora busco en vano aquel factor crítico que pudo catapultar a don Quijote a través de los siglos a la pequeña mesa junto al lago en que Emile y yo estábamos almorzando. Podría sugerir que el calor apabullante y el sol que nos cegaba (ambos sin precedente en otoño en esta región del noroeste) fueron elementos tangibles que podrían haber conectado Seattle con La Mancha. Pero prefiero especular que la obsesión de Emile y don Quijote con la literatura y las novelas de caballería pudo haberlos unido en ese instante de sensibilidad total que ocurre al llegar la muerte.

Así es que me sorprendió profundamente la reacción emocional tan poco característica que tuvo Emile. Al principio se lo achaqué a la botella de Muscadet que nos habíamos tomado en un ritual común entre viejos amigos. Yo estaba acostumbrado a sus ausencias, su tendencia a la distracción y su ciclotimia, pero durante la comida su voz fue adquiriendo un tono grave, dejó de hablar y cayó en un aparente trance que me alarmó sobremanera. Cuando al fin respondió a mis preguntas, me impresionó que su acento extranjero se hubiese vuelto tan marcado (algo que él normalmente disimulaba, sobre todo, en sus relaciones profesionales). Era obvio que esa falta de pretensiones, una fractura en su máscara de esnob, era síntoma visible de su angustia. Cuando le pregunté cómo estaba, contestó algo casi incomprensible:

—Mi vida se transformó tanto en las últimas semanas, especialmente en las últimas horas, que se ha vuelto intolerable. Lo que siento es casi irracional. ¿Crees que la combinación de las letras de mi nombre podría ayudarme a explicar mi ansiedad?

—¡Emile, eso es ridículo! ¿Cómo se te ocurre que la numerología y la cábala puedan esclarecer tu angustia? Me parece más probable que una permutación de las letras de tu nombre pueda revelar el nombre secreto de Dios, o de crear un golem.

—No se trata de eso. Opino que el nombre que me dio mi padre pudo predecir mi personalidad de adulto. Tanto él como yo recibimos una educación clásica y sufrimos de un romanticismo implacable. Por eso supongo que me llamó 'Emile' con la esperanza mágica de que su descendiente, como la creación de Rousseau, pudiese incorporar la bondad original del hombre y así resistir las influencias negativas de la sociedad. ¡Pero es evidente que sus intenciones no dieron el resultado esperado! Como ves por mi reacción al comportamiento de Nathania, está claro que sigo siendo un ingenuo, un eterno adolescente incapaz de hacer frente a la realidad. En cambio, me deslizo más hondo en el mundo de los sueños, donde cada uno de nuestros actos es ficción.

—A ver, Emile, para poder ayudarte y comprender tu difícil situación, tendrías que contarme cómo ocurrieron los hechos. Para empezar, ¿quién es Nathania, a la que nunca habías mencionado?

A partir de ese momento noté que a Emile le embargaba una emoción exagerada e inesperada que me perturbó. Éramos viejos amigos y nos conocíamos bien como científicos con la cabeza sentada y analítica. Confieso que comencé a interesarme más por su lenguaje corporal y sus raras expresiones faciales que por su historia.

—Conocí a Nathania hace poco —me dijo finalmente—. Fue la primera relación seria que tuve desde que me dejara mi mujer, hace siete años. Es una mujer joven, muy elocuente, y su sabiduría me trae a la mente a las pitonisas del antiguo oráculo de Delfos. Su porte transmite dramatismo y su belleza es enorme e inquietante. Encuentro irresistibles sus ojos azul oscuro, su pelo lacio y castaño, su intensidad. En resumen, nunca conocí a alguien como ella. Al contrario que nosotros dos, que nos manejamos en el terreno de la ciencia, ella es una artista comprometida totalmente con las cosas que le apasionan. Sus poemas tienen un ritmo obsesivo, que siento sincrónico con los latidos y el ritmo de mi corazón.

Lo interrumpió una tos nerviosa y seca, y su respiración se volvió irregular y trabajosa, como si sufriera un ataque de asma.

—Nuestra relación fue intensa y frecuente, aunque solo duró unas pocas semanas.

Me pregunté por qué estaba usando el tiempo pasado, como si su relación ya hubiese terminado.

—A veces íbamos a nadar o a cabalgar por la playa; cocíamos mejillones recién pescados sobre un fuego en la arena y luego nos escondíamos bajo una lona, riendo como adolescentes en un bosque secreto. Una noche le regalé unas rosas y un disco de Pearlman interpretando una sonata de Brahms, que tocamos en su casa hasta el cansancio. Me fascinaba el contraste enorme entre la simple felicidad y alegría de nuestros encuentros y la profundidad y el dramatismo de sus poemas. Por supuesto, a veces hacíamos el amor. En eso, descubrí con gran placer que era enérgica, hábil e imaginativa. Daba la impresión de que no le importaran mucho mi indecisión, mis dudas o mi inexperiencia. Pero estoy seguro de que no la impresionó mi estilo, menos técnico y apasionado, y pienso que su placer nunca fue tan grande como el mío.

—Emile, ya no sé cuáles son los hechos y cuál tu imaginación. ¿No te estarás dejando llevar de nuevo por el romanticismo?

—Es cierto, con mi espíritu platónico, imaginé a Nathania como un arquetipo, un conjunto de símbolos e imágenes que para mí definen, de un modo fundamental, lo que es una mujer. De ese modo, mi vida se transformó en una batalla para satisfacer mis sueños de permanencia y mi ilusión de que la poseía. Así fue hasta ayer por la noche, cuando descubrí con terrible sorpresa que mi relación con Nathania solo es posible en el mundo ficticio de la literatura. Ahora entiendo que para seguir juntos... para siempre... me debo convertir en un héroe en el mismo universo literario en que ella existe.

Emile hizo una pausa, tratando con dificultad de llenar sus pulmones. Su discurso se había vuelto disártrico, hacía muecas raras y se apretaba con fuerza un puño sobre el corazón. No pude controlar mi tendencia de querer adivinar su presión arterial y la frecuencia de su pulso. Entonces observé que parecía volverse más flaco y más alto, como estirado. ¿Cómo era posible? Pensé que lo estaba imaginando. Incapaz de explicar mis impresiones, le pedí que, por favor, continuara con su relato.

—Hace una semana encontramos un volumen de Cervantes muy usado y polvoriento, en una librería de segunda mano. Ya en la casa, cuando lo examinamos con detenimiento, vimos algo raro en un relato que desconocíamos, y que nos pareció ser apócrifo. Naturalmente, eso nos despertó un fuerte interés. Especialmente a Nathania, que quedó embelesada por ese cuento en particular. Me molestó su profundo entusiasmo con el libro y su fascinación por esa historia. Me sentí abandonado. Intenté seducirla con caricias, pero me rechazó sin miramientos y continuó leyendo con gran concentración. El poder cautivador que Cervantes ejercía en ella me dio envidia, pero tuve que resignarme a que siguiéramos leyendo juntos ese cuento durante la noche.

Emile se veía cada vez más triste y su monólogo se fue volviendo progresivamente más lento. Permanecía derecho sobre la silla, pero yo veía como apretaba el puño izquierdo sobre el pecho. Comenzó a temblar, pero su brazo derecho estaba erguido bien alto, como si tuviera en la mano una lanza que sacudía con fuerza. Él no parecía consciente de estas sacudidas, que consiguieron alarmar a un perrito blanco que dormitaba debajo de la silla de una señora, en la mesa a su derecha. El perro se puso a ladrarle furiosamente, pero Emile solo ladeó la cabeza y pronunció un comentario muy críptico:

—¡Dejadlo que ladre, sabe que voy por buen

camino!

Yo dejé pasar su comentario, para evitar distracciones, y le pregunté:

—¿De qué trataba el cuento que los tuvo ocupados leyendo juntos por horas? ¿Cómo te afectó?

—Se refería a don Quijote, un lector empedernido de novelas de caballería, ya sabés, que continuaba viviendo como un caballero medieval cuando esa época había terminado en España ya hacía tiempo. En este episodio, don Quijote traba amistad con un tal Mansour-al-Caliph, un moro al cual había salvado una vez de ahogarse en un río. Durante largas noches, el héroe y el moro saborean dulces y licores, juegan largas partidas de ajedrez, y don Quijote le confía a su nuevo amigo que tiene un sueño recurrente: imagina ser amado por una mujer maravillosa justo antes de la que podría ser su última batalla. Conmovido por la soledad de su huésped, Mansour le ofrece a su esclava favorita, una judía de rara belleza y talento artístico, para acompañar al héroe durante siete noches.

La voz de Emile sonaba resquebrajada y la falta de aliento lo obligó a hacer una nueva pausa. El contraluz intenso que me deslumbraba en el lago detrás suyo me hacía difícil observar su rostro con detalle, pero sí noté con inquietud un torrente de lágrimas que refractaban los rayos de sol y repartían sus imágenes al azar sobre el mantel en la mesa.

Al rato, Emile pudo continuar:

—Cuando don Quijote se encuentra por primera vez con Nathania, esta se le aparece drapeada dramáticamente en velos negros y él queda paralizado por su belleza.

¿Nathania, dijo? ¿Cómo es posible que no mencione la coincidencia de nombres?

—La esclava interpreta para él una danza oriental frente a una ventana que enmarca la llanura desolada de La Mancha iluminada por la luna. Los ojos del Quijote lagrimean sin control mientras ella acaricia una melodía en un laúd. Le canta con elocuencia, celebrando su destreza y valentía en las guerras, y su gratitud por haber salvado la vida del moro. Don Quijote percibe con implacable certidumbre que Nathania es la primera mujer que ha podido comprender su caballerosidad y heroísmo, su alma y su filosofía. Durante seis noches, le regala joyas, perfumes y antiguos libros, sus más preciosas pertenencias. En la última, Nathania le permite poseerla. Acaricia a la esclava con ternura a pesar de su inexperiencia. La revelación del amor físico le hace perder todo sentido del tiempo y permanece ajeno al hecho de que la semana enloquecida y de ensueño con Nathania ha llegado a su inevitable conclusión. De modo que la próxima noche, consumido por un fuego insoportable y por su voluntad de liberar a Nathania de su esclavitud, entra por la fuerza en los recintos del harem.

En este momento, Emile suspiró profundamente e interrumpió su relato con una pausa que me resultó interminable, hasta retomar la narración con voz más débil:

—Anoche llegué sin anunciarme a casa de Nathania, ilusionado por verla. Accedí con la llave que ella me había dado y me acerqué en silencio, a través de la cocina, hacia su dormitorio. Al abrir la puerta, vislumbré de inmediato la cubierta del disco de Brahms tirada por el piso en un charco de café y escuché el ritmo brutal de rock metálico.

Para entonces, su voz se había vuelto muy temblorosa, mientras que su cara parecía increíblemente enjuta y alargada. (Nadie podría dudar de mi experta observación clínica.) El rostro estaba arrugado y apergaminado como el de alguien extremadamente viejo. Estoy dispuesto a declarar bajo juramento que sus facciones se estiraron y desdibujaron aun más. Me pareció, si es posible, más alto que un momento antes y dejó caer los hombros mientras terminaba de narrar su historia:

—Te cuento, Sancho, que no pude ver su cara porque el moro la estaba montando, pero percibí el sudor de su sexo. Y comprendí que sus gruñidos expresaban el placer total que nunca había experimentado conmigo.

Cuando tomé conciencia de que me había llamado "Sancho", la cabeza de Emile ya había caído anormalmente hacia un costado y tenía los ojos cerrados. El perro de la mesa de al lado había dejado de ladrar y en el restaurante reinaba un silencio sepulcral, como si los otros comensales hubieran palpado la tragedia en el aire.

Estoy seguro de que su muerte ocurrió bastante antes de que llegara la ambulancia de primeros auxilios. Por supuesto, no me fue posible resucitarlo y lo condujeron directamente a la morgue del hospital.

Unas horas más tarde, cuando pude recuperar mi entereza, tuve fuerza para ir a mi trabajo. Por desgracia, ese día tenía turno de guardia en el mismo hospital. Hubiese preferido que otro patólogo se ocupara de cumplir con esta obligación, pero igualmente tuve que completar el informe e incluso describir que una barbita curiosamente puntiaguda había comenzado a crecer en su mentón. Pasé mucho tiempo considerando las posibles causas de su muerte: un desengaño amoroso, desesperación, percepción distorsionada, pérdida súbita de la inocencia o aun, la transmigración del alma de una figura literaria. Por supuesto, no hubiese podido incluir ninguna de estas alternativas en el certificado de defunción, sin empañar gravemente mi reputación profesional.

El marajá de Kapurthala

Reconozco tener tres pasiones: las mujeres, el tango y las piedras preciosas. El psicoanálisis me ayudó a comprender el riesgo que presentan para mi carrera, pero nunca pude cambiar mi comportamiento y sigo obsesionado por las mismas cosas. El último incidente es un ejemplo, ya que casi pierdo mi empleo como columnista en un conocido diario local. El editor no creía que los eventos que quise publicar fueran verdaderos y cuestionó la ética de mi conducta y, más aun, mi sentido común.

Todo empezó en El Arranque, la milonga en un antiguo teatro en el centro de Buenos Aires. La vi una tarde, sentada con un grupo de mujeres que charlaban animadamente durante el intervalo entre dos tandas. Tenía facciones morenas, algo indiana. "¿Será del interior, de alguna provincia del norte?", pensé, curioso por identificarla. Bailaba con uno de esos vejestorios que pululan por El Arranque y, al verla, me impactaron su postura elegante, sus pasos precisos y su musicalidad tan natural. Me gusta bailar allí porque es fácil entusiasmar a las turistas incautas para darles clases después de la milonga. Igual que otros "pescadores", eso me sirve para suplementar mis escasos ingresos de periodista independiente. Ofrecemos clases a un precio más bajo que el de los maestros acreditados que tienen estudio propio.

Al rato me decidí a cabecearla y aceptó con una leve sonrisa. Como es costumbre, dijimos simplemente "hola" y nos largamos en una emotiva tanda de Di Sarli. Durante una pausa entre dos canciones me contó que estaba en la Capital solo por una temporada. Pronunciaba con un acento bien porteño, pero me pareció escuchar un tono subyacente que no pude identificar. Creí que podría ser de Salta o Tucumán. Mi intriga fue muy fuerte y le pregunté si hablaba otros idiomas. A regañadientes, porque quería bailar y no conversar mucho, me explicó que había nacido en la India y que además hablaba inglés, pero con acento australiano, ya que vivía hace tiempo en Sídney. Cuando traté de tutearla, como hacemos normalmente los porteños, se negó "porque no estaba acostumbrada a eso". De modo que seguimos hablando en inglés (la lengua que aprendí con mis abuelos). En ese poco rato decidí que era una compañera de baile muy poco común. Se me escapó una frase inocente:

—¿En serio? Nunca estuve en la India, ¡qué país fascinante e inescrutable! ¿De qué parte viene?

—Soy nacida en el norte, en el Punjab. Pero ahora voy menos de visita, prefiero venir a Buenos Aires a bailar y a hacer negocios —me explicó con una sonrisita enigmática.

—Me llamo Gustavo, pero me dicen Tavo. ¿Y usted?

—Mi nombre es un poco complicado para los

argentinos y acá todos me llaman Tia, mi segundo nombre.

Al recomenzar el baile observé que llevaba un anillo maravilloso en la mano derecha, engarzado con un rubí que me pareció gigantesco y la felicité por su buen gusto. Pocas mujeres tienen un anillo así, con un rubí rojísimo, como de medio quilate. Le sorprendió que alguien en la milonga fuese conocedor de piedras preciosas y me contó que ella era importadora de joyas. Pero enseguida aclaró, con un poco de desparpajo, que eso era confidencial y que sería mejor seguir bailando.

A esa altura, mi imaginación descontrolada interfería con mi baile y me hacía novelas sobre las posibilidades de este encuentro tan imprevisto. Si bien ahora llegan asiáticos (especialmente chinos y coreanos) para vivir o para bailar tango, en Buenos Aires siempre ha habido muy poca gente de la India, y a alguien con turbante puede que lo sigan por la calle porque nunca han visto a nadie tan misterioso. ¡Pero una mina así, exótica y bien vestida, con tanto mundo, que además es importadora de joyas! ¡Esto es lo que me recomendaría el analista que pagaban mis padres cuando era más joven, para aumentar mi autoestima! Así es que decidí de inmediato recurrir al chamuyo, una de mis especialidades en el tango y en la vida.

—No tome a mal lo que le voy a sugerir —le dije con optimismo al terminar la canción—. Yo soy periodista. Su historia es extraordinaria y quisiera conocer los detalles para escribir sobre el misterio de una mujer de la India que ama nuestro tango y que habla tan bien nuestro idioma. ¿No me permitiría invitarla a un cafecito acá cerca al terminar la milonga?

—Gracias, pero no me parece buena idea. Conozco bien la excusa del cafecito de ustedes los milongueros.

—No, no, además de un artículo, el tema de la importación de gemas es justamente uno de mis intereses. Quizá podamos considerar algún negocio. ¿Qué opina? —dudó algunos segundos, mirándome con curiosidad, dio un suspiro y al final se pronunció con algo inesperado:

—Mire, lo voy a acompañar por esta vez, algo que no acostumbro a hacer, pero no se haga ilusiones, solo le prometo contestar con más detalle a sus preguntas. Eso sí, le comento que el café no me interesa, pero sí tengo hambre después de tanto baile. Mejor vayamos a La Americana, que queda acá en la esquina. Allí van otros conocidos del tango, de modo que me voy a sentir más cómoda, ¿de acuerdo?

Ya en la pizzería, me alegraba comprobar lo bien que se estaban dando las cosas. ¡Yo aquí sentado con esta hermosura, con su anillo de rubí impecable! Presentía que esta relación podía tener consecuencias literarias, comerciales o aun románticas. Cuando miró el menú, agradecí mi suerte al no tener que explicarle la diferencia entre pizza y empanadas, o los diferentes rellenos, porque los conocía todos. Pidió una *fugazzetta* con jamón ("¡No es vegetariana, qué maravilla!", pensé con alivio) y una cerveza Quilmes, y yo me decidí por dos empanadas, una de carne y otra de humita, aunque no tenía el más mínimo apetito en ese momento. Solo quería seguir hablando con ella. Mientras esperábamos la comida, me contó algo aun más inesperado: dijo que venía de Kapurthala, ese nombre tan sonoro y conocido hasta en nuestras tierras. Me encantó saberlo y le expliqué que hasta tenemos una expresión para describir a alguien escandalosamente rico: "¡Se cree el marajá de Kapurthala!". Pero mi comentario la sobresaltó y casi tira la cerveza, frunció el ceño y yo temí haber dicho algo inapropiado, pero al fin se relajó un poco y continuamos hablando. Me explicó que esa es una ciudad maravillosa de palacios y jardines, con una larga historia, un principado en el norte de la India, que quedó muy disminuida luego de la independencia. Parece que, cuando era joven, sus padres decidieron llevarla a Australia. Allí creció y se casó con su marido actual, un judío ortodoxo de Sídney, aunque conserva su religión: el sijismo. Allí también estudió en la universidad y fue a una escuela de gemología, que es su especialidad.

Cuando mencionó la gemología, mi admiración se elevó a la estratosfera. Desde chico me cautivaban las piedras preciosas, cuando me las daba a conocer mi tío Segismundo, que es joyero e importador de diamantes y otras gemas. Había aprendido su profesión en Varsovia, antes de venir a la Argentina. Entretanto, el anillo de Tia lanzaba destellos de un rojo profundo, reflejando las luces de la pizzería, lo que me resultó un poco inapropiado para ese local tan popular.

—¡Qué gran coincidencia que tengamos intereses en común! Las joyas son una de mis pasiones, y luego tendremos que hablar de eso. Pero primero me come la curiosidad de por qué le interesó el tango, que no debe ser habitual en su país.

—En realidad aprendí a bailar esta música en la India, cuando era chica, ya que mi padre lo practicaba desde joven, muy bien y muy canyengue. Fue él quien me enseñó los movimientos básicos.

—Pero ¿cómo aprendió su padre el tango en la India? Eso es más sorprendente aún.

—Mire, yo quisiera que lo que le cuento quede entre nosotros. Me tiene que prometer que si lo publica va a cambiar los nombres de la gente y las ciudades. ¿Puedo contar con su discreción?

—Por supuesto, le prometo una discreción absoluta.

—En ese caso, le explico que usted dijo algo inocente, sin saber que estaba tan cerca de la verdad. Resulta que mi padre fue el mismo marajá de Kapurthala, algo que, en general, no creo necesario contar.

—¡No me diga! ¡Entonces usted es realmente una princesa!

—Claro, me llamo Navpreet Tia. El primer nombre significa 'nuevo amor' y Tia, justamente, quiere decir 'princesa', en la lengua panyabí. Mi padre era sumamente rico y educado, con intereses múltiples y gran curiosidad. Había visto el tango en películas de Rodolfo Valentino y Gardel en Europa, y le dieron deseos de aprender a bailarlo. Él viajaba mucho por la India y en algún bar del puerto de Bombay conoció a unos marineros de un carguero argentino, se hicieron amigos y ellos le enseñaron los primeros pasos. Desde ese momento el tango fue su obsesión, que yo comparto, aunque a mí nunca me gustó el contacto con esa gente.

En ese momento giraron por mi mente remolinos fugaces de incertidumbre. Todo me parecía entre fantástico y dudoso, como un relato de Scheherazade al rey de Persia. Claro que mi romanticismo desaforado puede ganarle a la realidad, y esta mina tenía todas las condiciones para suspender mi incredulidad. Se me cruzó por la mente que me quería hacer el cuento del tío, pero esa visión competía con otras más poderosas del viejo marajá en tugurios tenebrosos de Bombay, impenetrables de humo de cigarrillos, bailando con unos marineros argentinos con costumbres de las antípodas. ¿Les pagaría por las clases? ¿Era solo un intercambio cultural entre desconocidos? ¿Sabrían que era un potentado o a lo mejor se vestía con sencillez para ocultar su verdadera posición? Consideré que no era prudente abordar estos temas por el momento y le agradecí su confianza por contarme esos detalles de familia.

Terminadas las empanadas y la pizza, como se hacía un poco tarde decidimos parar la charla. Conseguí su promesa de volver a encontrarnos pronto en algún café de la Recoleta para hablar de joyas, que nos interesaban tanto a los dos. Recibí con un ligero temblor, que traté de disimular, un papelito con su número de teléfono y nos separamos con un formal apretón de manos.

Por varios días mi mente alternaba con alta frecuencia entre las posibilidades de una relación romántica (aunque no tenía motivos para pensar en eso) y un negocio de importación en el que quizá pudiese involucrar a mi tío joyero. Mi impaciencia no tuvo límites y, al cabo de una semana, creí oportuno invitarla con una llamada telefónica que traté fuese bien correcta. Respondió pronto, con la estrategia de un buen negociante, pero sin señales de romanticismo, y propuso vernos el viernes, a las 6 de la tarde, en el café la Biela. Me pidió que buscara una mesa tranquila por el fondo, porque quería mostrarme algunas cosas que traía para exhibir en Buenos Aires.

Llegué tempranito al café para asegurarme de conseguir una mesa apropiada, cerca de una ventana con luz, pero lejos de la muchedumbre y de los turistas de la Recoleta. Traía en el bolsillo una lupa compacta de 10 aumentos, para examinar algunas piedras. Me senté a fumar un pucho cuando desde la ventana la vi llegar, caminando con elegancia y desenvoltura, con un ritmo de tango sincopado. Alguna gente y los mozos del café reaccionaron con una mirada colectiva al verla entrar, y los ojos siguieron su trayectoria satelital hasta mi mesa, con un poco de curiosidad y bastante admiración. Me saludó formalmente, nada de besitos tangueros, lo que me hizo perder un poco la confianza en mi capacidad de conquistador de las Indias Orientales. Pero pude reaccionar con rapidez para estrechar su mano y mencionar su nombre. Allí mismo me recordó que estos nombres no son para publicar, en caso de que escribiera un relato sobre estas cosas, y le aseguré que eso lo tenía bien presente.

—Me alegro de verla, ya que estoy obsesionado por encontrar un par de piedras preciosas pequeñas, pero a buen precio. Las necesito para engarzar en una lapicera Montblanc, modelo Agatha Christie. En el capuchón tiene una serpiente con dos ojitos rojos de vidrio, pero quedaría divina si la cambio por dos rubíes.

—¡Pues está de suerte! Déjeme mostrarle algunos ejemplos de lo que traigo.

Luego de observar los alrededores para asegurarse de que no pasaba ningún mozo cerca, sacó de su cartera una bolsita de terciopelo color vino, que abrió sobre la mesa. Tuve que ahogar un suspiro al ver el contenido del paquete. Traía adentro otras bolsitas que contenían, cada una, piedras de distinto tipo, de diversos colores, pero con la luminosidad de un caleidoscopio frente a un sol tropical. Reconocí una pequeña esmeralda más verde que una cotorra del Brasil, varios rubíes de distinto tamaño y un par de diamantes que reflejaban las luces del café en un arcoíris surrealista.

—¿Le parece que estos rubíes podrían servir para su lapicera? Son muy chiquitos para un anillo.

Mi alma se derritió al verlos. Era precisamente lo que buscaba para ese capuchón. Anunció un precio en dólares que estaba por debajo de lo esperado y bien dentro de mi presupuesto. Para asegurarme, saqué del bolsillo mi lupa y comprobé que tenían mucha claridad, un corte en facetas planas perfecto para favorecer el juego de la luz y unas pocas inclusiones que aumentaban su valor.

—Los rubíes me interesan mucho, pero quisiera mostrárselos a mi tío, que es joyero, y tiene su taller a pocas cuadras, sobre la calle Ayacucho. ¿Qué le parece si pasamos por allí un momento después del café? Considero que el precio es adecuado, y esto puede ser el principio de una sólida relación comercial.

—Sabía que le iban a gustar. Los traje de la India, pero vienen de Birmania, en donde tengo excelentes contactos. Estoy de acuerdo en que pasemos un momento a mostrarle estas piedras a su tío.

Por supuesto que el tío Segismundo quedó maravillado, tanto por la presencia de una princesa india en su local, como por la calidad de las gemas. De inmediato aconsejó que comprara los dos rubíes, como primer paso, lo que hice en ese momento, pagándole en dólares que él tenía en su caja fuerte. Luego le preguntó si podía volver para mostrarle las esmeraldas que había traído. Nos despedimos por el momento, y tanto él como yo quedamos fascinados por esta relación que había caído del cielo.

En unos días, Tia volvió a encontrarse con nosotros dos en el taller y disculpándose por el surtido limitado que tenía para mostrar en Buenos Aires; le vendió a Segismundo, a muy buen precio, una hermosa esmeralda que él necesitaba para un pendiente de una señora adinerada. Gracias a la inclinación creciente que mostrábamos, Tia nos sugirió otra curiosa idea:

—Si les interesa continuar esta relación comercial, podríamos hablar de una operación más importante. Viajaré a Australia el mes próximo, pero no sería difícil hacer un desvío y pasar unos días en nuestra casa familiar en Kapurthala, en donde tengo un surtido de joyas muy extenso, especialmente rubíes, a precios excelentes. Incluso, si quieren acompañarme, podría mostrarles mi ciudad natal. La ganancia en esta operación iría a compensar fácilmente el costo de su viaje.

Cuando ella se fue, mi tío Segismundo afirmó que a él no le gustaba volar, pero me estimuló a que lo hiciera yo en este caso. Barajando posibilidades, nos pusimos de acuerdo en que él me podía financiar una operación más grande, si yo me animaba a seguirla hasta Kapurthala. En nuestro país no encontraríamos jamás rubíes de esa calidad a bajo precio y él tenía suficientes clientes acaudalados en barrio Norte para asegurar su venta con enormes ganancias. Además, la idea de combinarlo con un viaje a ese país de misterio, en compañía de una rica heredera del marajá, se presentaba como un cuento de hadas. No dejaba de considerar la historia del papá con los marineros argentinos. Si los genes y costumbres de su familia eran duraderos, este viaje podría tener ramificaciones muy personales con la princesa milonguera.

Un mes más tarde Tia y yo partimos de Buenos Aires a New Delhi, en un vuelo de Emirates, una aerolínea en la que nunca había viajado. Llevaba un bolso con doble fondo, hecho con cariño por la mujer de mi tío, cargado con 10 000 dólares, el máximo que me atreví a llevar sin declarar en la aduana. Calculaba poder triplicar las ganancias a mi regreso. Seguimos en un vuelo más corto hasta Amritsar, una ciudad del Punjab, y de allí en un auto con chofer enviado por la familia de Tia hasta Kapurthala. Llegamos de noche 24 horas más tarde, muertos de cansancio, sin poder ver nada en la oscuridad.

Tia propuso alojarme gratis en el antiguo palacio de su familia, en la actualidad convertido en un hotel de cinco estrellas. Nunca hubiese esperado un despliegue tan enorme de riquezas. Muy sonriente, ella me ofreció ocupar la antigua cámara de su padre, ahora transformada en la *suite* para recién casados *(honeymoon suite)*. Era evidente que las costumbres nocturnas del marajá eran de un gusto incomprensible para un vulgar sudamericano. A pesar del cansancio, me costó dormir en esa maravillosa cama de palisandro, con incrustaciones en plata, con columnas en cada ángulo, talladas en forma de mujeres desnudas y pintadas de color piel. Tenían un mecanismo oculto, que me mostró el camarero, que les permitía guiñar los ojos y abanicarme. Desorientado por la fatiga del viaje, lo dejé encendido toda la noche sin darme cuenta y la brisa de los abanicos me ayudó a respirar en esa atmósfera húmeda y tropical.

Por la mañana desayunamos en una galería frente al jardín. Tia me hizo servir un buen café con medialunas y huevos fritos, pera ella comió otras cosas de aspecto desagradable, que me advirtió serían demasiado picantes para un porteño, dada mi falta de experiencia en ese tipo de comidas. Luego se ofreció a darme un paseo por la ciudad para ambientarme. Lo primero que me mostró dentro de los jardines de la propiedad fue otro palacio más pequeño, el sitio de una escuela llamada Sainir, de una arquitectura espléndida, inspirada en los palacios de Versalles y Fontainebleau. Dijo que le hubiese gustado estudiar allí de joven, pero que solo aceptaban varones. Continuamos visitando los jardines de Shalimar (bastante descuidados y menos interesantes que los de Palermo en Buenos Aires, en mi opinión poco ilustrada) y algunos templos de varias religiones. Lo que más me gustó fue el antiguo pero prestigioso club Jagatjit, parecido al Partenón de Atenas. Patrocinado por la princesa, pude jugar un partido de *squash* con uno de los instructores, que me destruyó sin dificultad en ¡cinco a cero!

El segundo día nos encontramos en la biblioteca del hotel para evaluar las joyas disponibles, de acuerdo con mi presupuesto. Ya había eliminado cualquier duda sobre la legitimidad de mi nueva amiga la princesa. Era quien decía y el palacio transformado en hotel era como me había contado durante el vuelo. Se manejaba como dueña de casa, con gran respeto de toda la servidumbre. Solo me faltaba concluir el negocio y me carcomía la impaciencia. El único inconveniente era la falta de intereses románticos por parte de la princesa. ¿Quizá pudiese hacerla cambiar de opinión bailando unos lindos tangos?

Encima del escritorio desplegó unas joyas excepcionales, de distintos tamaños, sobre una manta enrollada de fieltro exquisito. De acuerdo con mis posibilidades pude elegir un grupo de seis rubíes de hermoso color rojo intenso, gran claridad, pocas inclusiones y un corte facetado muy experto. Aceptó mi oferta algo desilusionada porque el presupuesto era limitado, pero quedamos en que podría volver en otro viaje con más capital para una inversión de mayor importancia. Yo me regocijaba por mi buena fortuna al haberla conocido y las posibilidades que se habían abierto desde esa noche en El Arranque. Luego en mi cuarto vacié con cuidado la mitad de la pasta dentífrica de un tubo de Colgate, introduje las piedras preciosas y volví a rellenarlo con la misma pasta, usando una jeringa que traía en la maleta y que luego descarté en el baño. El tubo iría en la bolsita de cosméticos en mi maletín.

Yo venía sin intereses turísticos y con planes para una estadía corta de tres o cuatro días. Pero al día siguiente me decidí a caminar solo por una horita por el centro de la ciudad. Lástima que las moscas y el calor, el ruido infernal de la muchedumbre y los empujones de los pordioseros me resultaron inaguantables, peores que los de cualquier día de semana en Plaza Once (lo que no es moco de pavo). Volví al hotel aterrorizado, en un *rickshaw* del que tiraba un indio de aspecto muy viejo, pero que quizá no tuviese ni treinta años, desgastado prematuramente por su oficio.

Al llegar, busqué a la princesa y le expliqué

que me gustaría partir en un par de días hacia Buenos Aires y que, por favor, me reservara un boleto. Pero antes, le pregunté si no habría una posibilidad de bailar unos tanguitos con la gente local. Me explicó que allí no había mucha gente interesada, pero para mi sorpresa, aceptó llamar a unos pocos amigos y organizar una comida y una clase de introducción al tango la noche anterior a mi regreso, en un salón fastuoso del club de *squash*.

Era un grupo simpático de gente moderna, vestida a la occidental, sobre todo profesionales o técnicos de la industria de computación y varios habían estudiado o trabajado en EE. UU. Comimos bien (arroz hecho de varias maneras y verduras bien cocidas, pero sin carne, ya que había algunos vegetarianos). Luego de cenar les propuse darles una clase gratuita de tango, confiado en poder llegar a interesarlos y que me pidieran que continuara con un curso en un futuro viaje. Eso podría suplementar las ganancias del negocio de las joyas y, a lo mejor, pagarme el costo del viaje.

Fue una desilusión. Aparte del exmarajá y sus marineros, el resto de los indios (en su propia patria) no fueron receptivos a este baile. Todas las mujeres se negaron a practicar el estilo "apilado" que tiene un abrazo muy apretado y solo pude mostrarles algo de estilo "salón", guardando distancia con la pareja. Pero hicimos una demostración con Tia de cómo lo bailábamos en Buenos Aires, bien pegaditos, que les encantó. Ella diseminaba un perfume muy intenso que no le conocí en Argentina, que me recordaba la madera o el humo de incienso. Eso volvió a despertarme imágenes lujuriosas, pero que al fin no llegaron a nada. Tia manejaba mi visita con maestría en un espíritu puramente comercial.

El día siguiente, Tia me acompañó al aeropuerto y, esta vez, se despidió un poco más cariñosamente con un besito en la mejilla, deseándome un buen viaje y un regreso pronto para otra transacción. Me dijo que estaría por unos días en Buenos Aires el mes próximo y que quizá la viera en alguna milonga. El vuelo fue largo, pero sin dificultades. Soñé mucho con la idea de la ganancia por realizar a mi llegada, que repartiría con mi tío Segismundo. Primero necesitaba un traje nuevo para ir a las milongas y un descanso de pocos días en la playa de Cariló con alguna amiga. Además debía aumentar mis ahorros para otra futura compra de joyas de más valor. Eventualmente iba a poder comprar un auto y dejar de viajar en colectivos y en el subte, con todos sus inconvenientes y riesgos de carteristas.

A mi llegada, pasé sin inconvenientes la aduana, felicitándome a mí mismo por el éxito del procedimiento. (Tenía en reserva el nombre de un despachante de aduana que en otras ocasiones había ayudado a gente amiga, pero no fue necesario que se ocupara.) Previa una ducha y afeitada rápidas, llamé al tío para avisarle de que venía con las joyas. Entré en su departamento con una sonrisa triunfadora de oreja a oreja, abanicando la bolsita con los rubíes frente a su cara.

—Mirá, tío, ¡esta vez nos salió una buena! A ver qué te parece mi compra en Kapurthala. Creo que valió la pena el viaje y tu inversión.

Abrí la bolsita sobre su escritorio, con gran expectativa por su respuesta.

—Ah, muy lindas y de buen tamaño —comentó de inmediato, sonriendo. Encendió un microscopio de campo oscuro, equipado con una lámpara especial para iluminar las piedras desde abajo y las examinó con cuidado, buscando inclusiones naturales o artificiales. No decía nada, pero noté que su sonrisa se iba congelando de a poco, hasta transformarse en una mueca. Finalmente, levantó la vista y me miró con tristeza, diciéndome—: ¡Te estafaron, sobrino! Estas son piedras tratadas con exceso de calor para realzar el tono rojo. Hay una que tiene inclusiones en "cola de caballo", un signo indudable de que es un corindón sintético. Otras tienen burbujas en la piedra, como si las hubiesen rellenado con vidrio de plomo. La mayoría son del tipo de "espinel" rojo, de muy poco valor, o de turmalina. No podemos venderlas sin informar al comprador de qué se trata, de su origen y valor, porque no quisiera mentirles. ¿Por qué no fui yo mismo a ese viaje? ¡Qué tarado, me dejé cegar por la princesa y no pensé en tu falta de experiencia!

No solo yo moría de vergüenza, sino que se

me pinchó brutalmente el globo con todos mis sueños y ambiciones. Recordé una fábula de La Fontaine, que conocía desde chico, sobre "Perrette y su jarrón de leche", en camino al mercado para venderla. Iba soñando en todos los animales que compraría con la ganancia, corriendo y saltando de alegría. Pero de pronto tropieza, dejando correr la leche por tierra y… "Adiós cordero, cerdo y vaca de sus sueños". Me sentía como Perrette y, sin decir más nada, me retiré con el rabo entre las patas.

Transcurrieron algunas semanas y poco a poco me fui recuperando y comencé a volver por las milongas. Una tarde tuve un presentimiento y antes de llegar pasé por una farmacia a comprar un purgante. Me decidí por la fenolftaleína, un líquido sin color ni gusto, que viene en capsulitas fáciles de tragar o de disolver en agua. Las guardé en mi bolsillo por el momento. Al entrar en El Arranque ya había mucha gente y bastante confusión, pero igual me senté en mi sitio de costumbre, donde era fácil ver la sala y cabecear a alguna milonguera. En un ángulo bien atrás, descubrí a mi famosa princesa tomando un refresco, pero esta vez sola, ya que su grupo de amigas no había llegado todavía. Llevaba un sacón de piel de color blanco, bastante lujoso para la milonga. Mi primera reacción fue acercarme e interpelarla, pero recordé que no tenía evidencia alguna para denunciarla a la policía y, menos aun, sin comprometerme a mí mismo por las joyas importadas ilegalmente. De modo que puse en práctica una idea que venía elucubrando por varios días. Entonces fui hacia el baño a hablar con uno de los cuidadores, que además venden cigarrillos, chicles, preservativos o condones y alguna que otra sustancia menos legítima a la que tienen acceso. Cuando se fueron del baño otros bailarines, le compré tres sobrecitos de plástico con un polvito blanco de aspecto inocente, todo su surtido en ese momento, y volví a mi mesa casi sin un centavo para pagar mi agua mineral.

Al rato, Tia salió a bailar con uno de sus compañeros favoritos. Aproveché la ocasión para moverme a la mesa de al lado, bien pegadita a la suya. Con una destreza que me sorprendió a mí mismo, dejé caer el contenido de las cápsulas de fenolftaleína en su refresco, que se disolvieron al instante. Luego me di maña para meter las tres bolsitas blancas en el bolsillo de su sacón, que estaba colgado en la silla vecina, y salí con calma de la milonga. Al pasar, charlé unas palabras con el cabo de policía, de guardia en la puerta como siempre, con quien tengo buenas relaciones desde que le presenté a una chica del tango, muy amiga y en busca de aventuras. Me saludó con un caluroso apretón de manos y se dirigió hacia el interior mientras yo me retiraba tranquilo para la casa.

Una semana más tarde le presenté a mi editor del diario una columna, que me pareció muy bien escrita, titulada: "Tribulaciones de una princesa india en Buenos Aires". Comenzaba con su arresto en una popular milonga porteña por posesión de drogas en cantidades suficientes para la venta; seguía con su reacción violenta en la comisaría, en donde causó una escena y griterío, reclamando un baño limpio por tener un severo ataque de cólicos y diarrea. Continuaba un relato de su vida en Cochín, una ciudad y puerto históricos que ganó fama gracias a la ocupación portuguesa en siglos pasados. Luego mencionaba su facilidad para los idiomas y aprendizaje del tango en la India con su padre (posiblemente un marajá hasta el momento de la independencia), un noble con costumbres y moralidad muy sospechosas. Finalmente, comentaba sobre su habilidad como joyera e importadora de piedras preciosas. En su departamento, la policía no descubrió drogas, pero sí una caja fuerte repleta de gemas, importadas ilegalmente y cuya autenticidad debía ser estudiada por los expertos. Por supuesto, en la columna que presenté, ni los nombres ni la ciudad de origen eran genuinos, para mantener la confidencialidad (como le había prometido a Tia al escuchar su historia, ya que ¡promesas son promesas!). Lamentablemente, el editor solicitó pruebas contundentes sobre la veracidad de la historia, que yo no podía proporcionarle, y la vista de unas hermosas piedras de turmalina que le mostré no fueron suficiente evidencia para dejarme publicar la columna. Estas piedras las conservo como recuerdo de mis años de inocencia.

Svetlana y el oligarca

La invitación del oligarca —una convocatoria que Svetlana no hubiera podido rechazar— llegó a Seattle en una típica mañana lluviosa. La transmisión del correo electrónico a su teléfono celular fue instantánea desde un número no identificado de Vladivostok, la terminal del ferrocarril Transiberiano. Antes, el mensaje lo hubiera entregado en mano un cartero, resbalando sobre los adoquines mojados de un pasaje que descendía en apretada curva desde el extremo sur del mercado de Pike Place. Una vez pasado el "muro del chicle", de triste fama turística, llegaría por fin a una entrada apenas visible, conocida solamente por los estudiantes y maestros de la Academia ruso-americana de pilates.

Svetlana, Sasha y Sofía, nuestras entrenadoras, habían sido gimnastas en el prestigioso Circo Ruso de San Petersburgo. Aun en la cumbre de sus carreras y en un estado físico impecable, se habían graduado como docentes en el célebre Instituto Romana Pilates de Nueva York. Su fundador era Joseph Pilates, el legendario gimnasta y terapista alemán que, antes de escapar de su país para radicarse en los Estados Unidos, había inventado un método de rehabilitación para los soldados heridos durante la Primera Guerra Mundial. Entre sus primeros alumnos había bailarines de renombre, como Balanchine y Martha Graham. Como estudiante avanzado en la Academia de Seattle, yo estaba bien ubicado para observar las idas y venidas de nuestras excepcionales maestras. Así es que fui el primero en notar la agitación de Svetlana luego de recibir el mensaje. También fui testigo de la conferencia que tuvo lugar al día siguiente para coordinar el programa de clases y para buscar a un maestro sustituto, ya que Svetlana y su familia se iban por un mes a Moscú y a Washington DC. No iba a ser fácil encontrar un sustituto adecuado para Svetlana, una contorsionista asombrosa, capaz de meterse por los vericuetos más estrechos y salir por el cuello de una botella, como el pulpo del Acuario de Seattle.

Después de la reunión del personal, Svetlana y yo cruzamos la calle hacia el café Storyville, que nos encantaba, situado en el piso superior de un antiguo edificio de ladrillos. Quería saber mi opinión respecto al mensaje recién recibido y, en especial, sobre su último párrafo, en que la reclutaban por la fuerza. Creo que confiaba en mí porque tengo algunos antepasados rusos. Mis abuelos maternos habían escapado de los pogroms, las masacres de los cosacos del zar a principios del siglo XX. Además, un primo de mi abuela había sido un anarquista notorio, primero en Odesa y más tarde en Argentina, de modo que nuestra familia tenía experiencia en resistir a la opresión.

El mensaje decía así:

Señora Svetlana:

El presidente Putin quedó bien impresionado por su actuación durante la cumbre del G20 en Buenos Aires y ha solicitado su presencia, junto con el maestro

Houdinski, para un ensayo en Moscú antes de una actuación oficial, dos o tres semanas más tarde, en Washington DC.

En el evento oficial estarán presentes el señor Putin y un solo invitado durante una reunión privada. Ya le informaremos sobre la fecha exacta y el sitio de la reunión, así como de algunos requerimientos específicos para su actuación. Esta debe exhibir sus habilidades gimnásticas y de contorsionista, así como el espectáculo de magia de su marido. Las únicas personas que pueden participar son sus dos hijos, que podrían venir como asistentes. Ya en Moscú, tendrán tiempo de preparar la utilería de gran tamaño para el número de magia, ya que sería difícil de transportar en vuelos comerciales desde los Estados Unidos. Más tarde mandaríamos estos accesorios en avión militar a Washington DC para la representación oficial.

Su remuneración será generosa, equivalente a dos meses de ingresos profesionales para cada participante. Vamos a reembolsar los boletos de avión en primera clase, hoteles y comidas, así como los materiales de utilería. Por seguridad, los detalles del programa deben ser confidenciales aun con su propia familia y los fabricantes de accesorios. Solo puede comunicarles detalles obligatorios y por necesidad.

El señor Putin está informado de que la jubilación de sus padres está bajo discusión y de que su hermano, un periodista político, podría participar en un programa de reeducación en Siberia. El *presidente va a considerar estos factores con interés luego de su actuación en Washington DC.*

Shimon Berditchevsky

—¡Ahora entiendo por qué estás obligada a aceptar la invitación de este mafioso! —le comenté después de leer el mensaje—. Les van a pagar bien para actuar ante un grupo de gente poderosa en Rusia, incluyendo a su repulsivo presidente. Pero encuentro ofensivo que los amenacen con represalias contra tu familia si rechazás la propuesta. Me suena todo muy sucio. Deben querer que hagas algún truco especial, posiblemente durante el número de magia con tu marido.

Svetlana me miraba con curiosidad mientras yo recitaba mi discurso paternal. Levantó lentamente la taza de café a los labios con precisión y su elegancia habitual. Sin embargo, pude detectar un temblor casi invisible de su mano, lo que me hizo pensar en qué lío estarían por meterse ella y su marido.

—¿Cómo encontraste a este tipo? ¿Lo conocés bastante para tenerle confianza?

—Lo conocí hace unos años en una fiesta del circo en Europa, en donde él tenía relaciones con muchos artistas rusos. Mis amigos me aseguraron que él cumplía sus promesas y pagaba los contratos sin demoras. El mes pasado vino con Putin a ver nuestro espectáculo en Buenos Aires durante la conferencia del G20. Después del mismo,

Berditchevsky me dio a entender que podría ofrecernos un trabajo temporario en Rusia, muy bien pagado. Como sabrás, estamos bastante bien relacionados en este país, pero cuando se trata de una oferta de una empresa reputada, estamos dispuestos a viajar a donde sea. En este caso, podríamos ver a nuestros padres y conocer a gente importante de los negocios y la política. Algo así nos ocurrió durante el G20, porque el intérprete de Putin estaba en el mismo hotel que nosotros y tuvimos una linda charla durante el desayuno. Entonces nos contó que Trump había estado en una reunión secreta en la habitación de Putin. No quiso decirnos nada más, pero estaba estupefacto porque no hubo ningún otro estadounidense presente para traducir o tomar notas.

—¡Exactamente como leímos en los diarios! ¿Quién sabe qué les habrá prometido nuestro presidente a los rusos? ¿Y qué estaría haciendo Berditchevsky con ellos?

—Es un industrial poderoso, un agente importante en el comercio internacional del aluminio y amigo de Putin. Ya habrás visto su nombre en los diarios porque es uno de los oligarcas sancionados por el Gobierno americano. Debe tener amigos o aliados en el Congreso porque los Republicanos están tratando de eliminar su nombre de la lista negra.

—Dejémoslo tranquilo por el momento. Mejor hablemos de tu trabajo en Buenos Aires. ¿Te acordás que yo nací allí? ¿Dónde representaron el espectáculo?

—Tuvimos el honor de actuar con colegas europeos en la reapertura del Circo Sarrasani, una vieja institución en la Argentina.

—¡No te lo puedo creer! Todavía me acuerdo de cuando era chico y tenían una enorme carpa a pocas cuadras de nuestra casa en Barracas. Como sabrás, el circo lo fundaron unos judíos alemanes en Dresde, en 1901. Para el fin de la Segunda Guerra Mundial, cuando las cosas se pusieron difíciles, se exilaron en la Argentina, en donde fueron los favoritos del presidente Perón y Evita. Perón estaba fascinado por el Sarrasani y le cambió el nombre a Circo Nacional Argentino. Una vez mis padres nos llevaron con mi hermanito a ver una función inolvidable. Lo que más me impresionó fueron los animales amaestrados: elefantes, caballos y, especialmente, los chimpancés.

—Lamento decepcionarte, pero hoy en día es inaceptable usar animales vivos en el circo. En cambio, recurren a rayos láser y proyectan un vídeo en alta definición con animales que corren libres por la sabana africana y familias de chimpancés en la selva. Pero todavía aceptan un acto muy desenfrenado con jinetes de Mongolia.

—¡Qué lástima, yo todavía recuerdo a los chimpancés del Sarrasani! ¿Podés creer que se incorporaron a la cultura popular en la Argentina? Hasta hay un tango de humor negro llamado "El

31", grabado por Juan D'Arienzo, en el que un tipo entra al café con una mujer muy fea y sus amigos se burlan cantándole el estribillo: "Ahí llega Sarrasani con el chim-pan-cé...".

—¡Qué increíble! ¿Puede ser que eso lo consideraran divertido alguna vez en Argentina? Me alegro de que el mundo haya cambiado. En todo caso, Berditchevsky vino a vernos después de la función. Estaba muy gordo y casi no cabía en su silla. Apenas si se movía, como si fuera una bolsa de papas.——Aun así, me pareció sofisticado y persuasivo. Hablaba lentamente, a lo mejor por su tamaño. Creo que pertenece a la mafia judía rusa y tiene el poder de ordenar a la gente sin levantar la voz. Como ves, no tuvo dificultad para convencernos de trabajar para Putin.

—¿Cómo vas a manejar esta misión? Si te parece bien podemos seguir en contacto a través del WhatsApp. Los mensajes están cifrados y lo encuentro más seguro para vos.

—De acuerdo. Te mantendré al tanto cuando pueda y cuando vuelva te daré un informe más completo —me dijo, con una sonrisa conspiratoria.

Nos dimos un abrazo y cada uno salió por su lado, soñando despiertos sobre el posible curso de esta aventura. Yo tenía confianza total en mi intrépida y atlética amiga. Era conocida por ser poco convencional, como el día en que se presentó a su casamiento en Las Vegas ya embarazada de ocho meses, vestida con una vaporosa túnica de color rosado, flotando con la brisa. Le hubiera sido técnicamente imposible meterse dentro de un vestido tradicional, aun siendo la futura esposa de un mago. Pero ninguno de sus amigos del circo, que habían convergido en Las Vegas para la fiesta, demostró sorpresa alguna al ver su panza redonda y prominente.

* * *

Svetlana y su marido, el maestro Houdinsky, partieron de Seattle el siguiente sábado por la mañana, acompañados por Alex y Ludmila, sus dos hijos adolescentes. La ruta pasaba por Los Ángeles, volando con Air France y Aeroflot, el trayecto más corto (y el más caro) hacia Moscú. Estaban en primera, como les había prometido Berditchevsky, quien no reparó en gastos, incluyendo la estadía en un hotel excepcional, el Baltschug Kempinski de Moscú. Generalmente, cuando Svetlana estaba en Rusia le gustaba dormir en casa de sus padres. Pero esta vez, Berditchevsky había insistido en que se quedaran en un hotel céntrico para tener acceso rápidamente a las reuniones con él y con el presidente. Por sorpresa, el hotel estaba justo al otro lado del río del Kremlin y la Plaza Roja, a pocos minutos a pie de una estación del metro (que apenas tendrían ocasión de tomar, ya que casi siempre vendrían a buscarlos en una limusina). El hotel tenía muy buenas instalaciones —wifi gratuito, un spa y una elegante piscina—, pero padecía de la práctica frecuente en Rusia de poner en cada piso a un conserje para vigilar, con ojos de águila, las idas y venidas de los huéspedes. Al ser ciudadanos rusos, los Houdinsky estaban obligados a mostrar su pasaporte si se lo pedían, como ocurría cada vez que entraban o salían del hotel.

Las habitaciones eran bien grandes y los baños modernos y funcionales, pero Svetlana encontró una bata manchada de maquillaje en una manga y, después, una vieja ropa interior que alguien había olvidado en el estante superior en el armario. Apenas instalados en el hotel, hizo una llamada telefónica para pedir cita en el estudio Cuerpo y Mente de Olga Burkova, en donde la conocían bien de otros viajes. Los aparatos eran excelentes, de marca Gratz, el fabricante original desde 1928 de equipos para pilates en Nueva York. Tenían todo lo que ella pudiera necesitar, desde el "reformer universal" a la "torre de guillotina", un nombre con connotaciones enervantes, considerando su misión en Moscú. Hizo planes para asistir diariamente a entrenarse y estar flexible para su número de contorsionismo, uno de los requerimientos de este trabajo.

La mañana siguiente a su llegada, recibió otra convocatoria. Una limusina vendría a buscarla con su marido al hotel a las 14 horas para una reunión preliminar con Berditchevsky. Cuando salieron al vestíbulo vieron que una Mercedes negra con vidrios ahumados ya los estaba esperando frente al hotel. Un tipo alto, en buen estado físico y postura militar, con la cara marcada de viruela, se identificó como Sergei, su conductor. Este les indicó que entraran al auto y partió de inmediato hacia una zona residencial muy lujosa, alejada del barrio del Kremlin. Los Houdinsky sabían que la gente más influyente se había mudado de Rublevskoe Shosse hacia el centro de la ciudad. Sergei continuó por la calle Tverskaya, en el barrio de Arbat, una zona de cafés y negocios turísticos para, finalmente, doblar en una callecita arbolada y detenerse frente a un portal metálico negro en su entrada privada. La mansión, ubicada dentro del parque, tenía sus años y un aire aristocrático con mucha historia detrás. Un mayordomo los acompañó a un salón-biblioteca con altos muros de madera oscura y miles de libros encuadernados en cuero y se preguntaron si alguien los leería, ya que no vieron una escalera para alcanzarlos. La decoración llamativa y el paupérrimo gusto de las pinturas modernistas impresionaban mal, como a plata nueva, más que a un pasado aristocrático.

De pronto se abrió una puerta en el extremo opuesto de la sala, para dejar entrar a Berditchevsky, quien caminaba lentamente, en una actitud muy estudiada para crear un efecto específico e intimidarlos. Fue al grano:

—Bienvenidos a Moscú, Svetlana y maestro. Quiero darles una idea general sobre el ensayo preliminar en el Kremlin. Tienen que preparar un programa interesante para entretener a un invitado con la atención muy limitada. No debe tener rutinas complicadas con muchas vueltas y sorpresas como las que presentaron en Buenos Aires. En cambio, les sugiero una serie de episodios cortos y coloridos de magia y de gimnasia, algo para impresionar a chicos jóvenes, como de Secundaria, más que a un adulto. Podrían usar trucos de cartas, efectos luminosos y hasta con fuego, pero no pueden traer animales vivos como conejos o palomas. El espectáculo podría incluir la muñeca mecánica, el famoso número de contorsiones de Svetlana, en que sale de un cofre de madera y responde a un control remoto. Luego pueden seguir con el acto principal en que ella se acomoda en un espacio muy apretado en un cajón parecido a un ataúd y el maestro le clava muchas espadas a través de las paredes laterales. El señor presidente les va a explicar los objetivos de este acto ilusionista en su próxima reunión, pero quiero que comiencen ya mismo a planear el programa que acabo de explicarles.

—¿Cuándo podemos comenzar a trabajar en la utilería?

—Hoy mismo. El ensayo está programado para dentro de diez días. ¿Tienen algún fabricante en mente? Si es necesario, podemos proporcionarles artesanos locales.

—Otras veces hemos trabajado muy bien con nuestro amigo Vladimir, un artista metalúrgico muy talentoso, que conoce bien nuestras necesidades. Está disponible para empezar apenas lo llamemos. También trajimos en las maletas algunos artículos pequeños para el acto de magia y si fuera necesario podemos pedir prestadas otras cosas a nuestros amigos del circo de Moscú.

—Perfecto. Entonces, eso será todo por el momento. Esperen noticias mías para encontrarse con el presidente en un par de días. Les recuerdo que estos arreglos son confidenciales. No los pueden compartir con nadie.

Más tarde, le pidieron al conductor que los dejara frente a la elegante Patisserie Café Pushkin, cerca de la calle Arbat y del monumento a Pushkin, para esperar a Vladimir. Svetlana ordenó de inmediato el pastel de pistacho decorado con yogur en forma de rosa, mientras Houdinsky se deleitó con un *medovik*, un pastel de miel y un té de jengibre. De todos modos, ¡pagaba el oligarca! Al rato llegaron las delicias y Houdinsky comenzó a esbozar un programa para el espectáculo. Svetlana aprovechó el tiempo libre para enviarme su primer mensaje por wasap, que reflejaba su entusiasmo e interés creciente por el proyecto.

¡Hola, aprendiz!

Recién terminamos nuestra reunión preliminar en la mansión del señor 'B' para recibir instrucciones generales. Aun nos mantiene en la oscuridad y se niega a discutir detalles. Obviamente, estamos obligados a aceptar lo que se le ocurra. Debemos hacerlo para proteger a mis padres y a mi hermano. Ya no tenemos elección. ¡Quiero creer que este mensaje esté cifrado, como me dijiste…!

Cambiando de tema, te cuento que vamos a trabajar con Vladimir, al que conociste cuando visitó Seattle. ¡Tú creías que se parecía mucho a tu abuelo de joven! A lo mejor vinieron los dos de la misma zona en la región de Bessarabia. Sus hijas ya grandes insistieron en que solicitara una visa permanente para los Estados Unidos, y no lo vas a creer: ¡se ganó la lotería de la visa y ahora se mudan a Seattle! Va a comenzar de cero como artista metalúrgico, y sus hijas piensan usar su experiencia como diseñadoras de interiores. Seguro que van a fabricar las barandas más elegantes para tu salón comedor.

Hasta pronto.

El tiempo pasó rápido con los entrenamientos en el estudio de pilates; planeando el mejor programa para un huésped "desconocido" con atención deficiente y trabajando con Vladimir en su taller metalúrgico. Finalmente, el oligarca les informó de un encuentro en el Kremlin (sin los hijos), programado para el día siguiente a las 10 a.m. Sergei se mostró cortés, pero silencioso, durante el corto viaje sobre el río. Atravesaron calles bastante concurridas hasta que por fin entraron en un complejo imponente por una puerta lateral.

Había un fuerte dispositivo de seguridad, con sensores electrónicos, espejos y perros olfateando muy obedientes alrededor del auto, mientras el conductor se mantenía en posición de firme al lado de su puerta. Finalmente, un hombre alto y atlético, que se presentó como "un secretario", los llevó a lo largo de un corredor un poco siniestro y casi sin muebles hasta un salón gris y sin ventanas. Después de una tensa media hora de ablandamiento, el secretario los hizo pasar hasta un salón barroco muy elegante en donde otro guardia, armado hasta los dientes, se estacionó junto a la puerta principal. Se sentaron por un rato en sillas muy acolchadas frente a un escritorio de caoba con patas doradas e incrustaciones de madreperla. De pronto, se abrió la puerta al otro extremo de la sala para dejar entrar a un enrojecido y sudoroso presidente Putin, envuelto en un kimono blanco de judo con un cinturón negro. Se paró en silencio detrás de una mesa escrutando a sus visitantes, que se habían puesto de pie frente a él. Al fin, con la mirada inexpresiva y una sonrisa glacial, les dijo:

—Maestro Houdinsky y Svetlana, cuento con que ustedes quieran ayudar a este país que dejaron hace muchos años. Antes de explicarles sus obligaciones, les recuerdo que lo hablado acá es totalmente confidencial. Las consecuencias serían severas si mencionan este programa a alguien, especialmente el nombre de los participantes, la ubicación y la hora de su actuación. ¿Nos entendemos? Ya pueden sentarse.

Svetlana se tranquilizó al ver que Houdinsky se había callado (como de costumbre) durante ese discurso alarmante y se alegró en particular de que él no se hubiera puesto su atuendo favorito: un sobretodo de cuero negro largo hasta los tobillos. Generalmente le agradaba usarlo aun fuera de su trabajo, porque le daba un aire misterioso e intimidante.

—A su servicio, señor presidente —respondió, hablando por los dos.

Siempre de pie, Putin lanzó su encargo en un estilo militar:

—Su misión será presentar un espectáculo de magia y baile con contorsiones para un invitado especial, en Washington. El objetivo principal es sustituir un objeto por otro durante el acto del maestro. Svetlana, su trabajo consistirá en cautivar a un poderoso ejecutivo estadounidense, quizá durante el "baile de la vela" que la ha hecho famosa en tantos países. El invitado debería estar subyugado por el baile sensual y las contorsiones de Svetlana para que la sustitución pase desapercibida.

—Señor presidente —interrumpió Houdinsky rompiendo su silencio habitual—, ¿qué nos puede contar sobre la personalidad de su invitado?

—Solo necesitan saber que es grosero, poco fiable y que le gusta flirtear. Podría comportarse de modo inapropiado e intentar toquetear a su mujer, aun en su presencia. Ya les daremos más detalles después del ensayo. Entonces quiero que nos demuestren su plan exactamente dentro de una semana durante una representación para mí y varios funcionarios.

—Señor, ¿de qué forma y tamaño sería el objeto que hay que sustituir? —preguntó Houdinsky, enfocando en el objetivo principal.

—Va a ser una carpeta marrón de medida estándar. Calculamos que el invitado va a firmar un documento y ponerlo dentro de la carpeta, que probablemente esté sobre una mesita de café muy cerca de ustedes durante la función. Les vamos a dar una carpeta idéntica con documentos justo antes del ensayo, y un funcionario no informado de su papel hará la parte de invitado oficial. Justo antes del número principal en Washington, les vamos a entregar un nuevo sobre con documentos oficiales para sustituirlo.

—Muy bien, señor presidente. Ya decidiremos antes de la función el momento justo para hacer el intercambio. Si me permite una pregunta, hay algo que nos inquieta: ¿cuál sería el riesgo legal para nosotros en los Estados Unidos al sustituir una carpeta con documentos oficiales?

—Ustedes darán este espectáculo en nuestra embajada en Washington DC, que es territorio ruso. ¡En Rusia, nosotros decidimos lo que es legal y lo que no lo es!

Por un instante, el silencio en la sala fue absoluto, como el vacío descrito por los astronautas en órbita espacial.

Houdinsky se dio cuenta del miedo palpable de Svetlana y se asustó de su propia audacia. De repente, Putin giró por completo sobre sus talones, totalmente inexpresivo. Se ajustó el cinturón negro sobre su kimono de judo y abandonó la sala sin comentario alguno.

Al salir, le pidieron al conductor que los llevara directamente al taller de Vladimir. Viajaron en silencio porque cualquier comentario podría ser grabado o escuchado por Sergei, que parecía impávido. De todos modos, no necesitaban palabras para compartir sus sentimientos. El desafío ya no era solo técnico, sino psicológico y diplomático: cómo manejar a un dictador sin escrúpulos y a su invitado imprevisible. Era necesario poner en juego su dilatada experiencia profesional. Una vez llegados a lo de Vladimir, le pidieron que hiciera unos cambios en la caja metálica, lo cual sorprendió al artesano porque no lo habían hecho así en las versiones previas del truco de las espadas. Pero les obedeció sin discusión.

Ya de vuelta en el Kempinski se vieron obligados a confrontar a la conserje de su piso, que se puso especialmente desagradable e insistió en examinar de nuevo sus pasaportes rusos. Tanto el maestro como Svetlana se sentían impotentes para rechazar las demandas del presidente y del oligarca, pero decidieron que había llegado el momento de darle una lección a esta empleada arbitraria e irritante. Entonces volvieron a su habitación, en donde Houdinsky se puso su característico abrigo de cuero y comenzó a cargar sus bolsillos secretos gigantes con todos sus trastos e implementos para la magia. Seguido por Alex y Ludmila —que habían pasado una tarde aburrida jugando un fútbol mediocre con otros chicos en el parque Gorky—, el mago se acercó a la conserje lentamente, con un paso amenazante. Se paró deliberadamente frente a una enorme señal en la pared que decía "No fumar", la miró con curiosidad y, mientras estiraba un brazo hacia la mujer, hizo aparecer un cigarrillo en su mano derecha. Antes de que ella pudiese reaccionar, una llamarada explotó desde su mano izquierda. Prendió el cigarrillo con la llama y, de inmediato, se lo metió en la boca, como si se lo fuera a comer. A continuación, sacó un ramo de flores de uno de sus grandes bolsillos y se lo ofreció a la conserje con una reverencia. Pero cuando ella hizo ademán de recibir el regalo, él lo retiró bruscamente y, con un chasquido de los dedos, lo hizo desaparecer. En cambio, una gran llama pareció salir de su rostro por un instante, antes de que una llovizna de papelitos de colores cayera sobre la cabeza de la mujer como estrellitas titilantes, cubriendo su escritorio de un manto multicolor. Con una sonrisita sardónica, la mujer hizo ademán de atrapar los papelitos en el aire, pero se disolvían dejando solo un sucio residuo maloliente. Solo entonces, viéndola al borde del colapso, el maestro se dio media vuelta, pensando qué lindo hubiera sido vengarse así de Putin y Berditchevsky. Cuando volvieron a su habitación, Alex y Ludmila no daban más señales de aburrimiento.

Por la mañana llegó un corto mensaje del oligarca:

La conserje del hotel pasó un informe sobre el incidente con el maestro en su piso. Ya le hemos notificado que su familia se encuentra acá en misión oficial y que no debe ser incomodada. Recibió una severa amonestación. De ahora en adelante, ustedes podrán ir y venir sin inconvenientes.

Por favor, lleguen con dos horas de adelanto el día del ensayo para preparar sus materiales. Los técnicos del palacio pueden ayudarlos a mover la utilería al sitio más conveniente.

Cuando luego Svetlana me dejó leer ese mensaje, me pareció triste que Berditchevsky fuera tocayo de uno de los grandes sabios jasídicos del siglo XVIII, el virtuoso rabino Itzhak Levi de Berditchev, la ciudad en que nació. El *tzadik* con acceso a lo divino, un defensor infatigable de los judíos, había tratado de interceder por ellos ante el mismo Dios. Por generaciones, fue una gran inspiración para sus *jasidim*. ¿Quién hubiera previsto que un mafioso judío iba a llevar el mismo nombre doscientos años más tarde?

El tiempo pasó volando para la familia mientras se preparaban para el ensayo. Estaban ansiosos por actuar. Los chicos en especial estaban fascinados por el Kremlin, tanto por el edificio como por la seguridad estricta. El "secretario" les entregó una carpeta, que Houdinsky puso en uno de sus bolsillos secretos, mientras esperaban para entrar en escena. Media hora más tarde les avisaron de que comenzaran el espectáculo y el maestro, asistido por sus dos hijos, tomó posición frente a la mesa de Putin, que estaba hablando con vehemencia con un funcionario a quien no habían visto nunca. En la mesa había otra carpeta marrón y vodka en abundancia, así como varios aperitivos.

Como le habían pedido, Houdinsky comenzó una serie de cortas rutinas usando cigarrillos, humo y fuego, haciendo desaparecer objetos, pero evitando secuencias complicadas o demasiado largas. Entonces se presentó Svetlana con su número de la "muñeca mecánica", saliendo de una gran caja de madera que los chicos empujaron frente a los invitados. El mago dirigía sus movimientos entrecortados a la perfección por medio de un control remoto similar a uno de la tele. A continuación, ella presentó su sensual "danza de la vela" en la que balanceaba una vela encendida primero sobre la cabeza, después en el abdomen y finalmente por detrás, sobre el coxis. Estaba vestida con una bata transparente y vaporosa, que dejaba poco espacio a la imaginación, y les entregó una actuación extasiada, como en un trance. Finalmente pasaron todos al último acto, en que Svetlana se infiltra en un apretado cajón con ranuras en los lados, mientras el maestro parece acuchillarla con largas espadas a través de las paredes. Eventualmente vuelve a salir ilesa, estirándose con lentitud fuera del apretado encierro. La audiencia, algo alcoholizada, los aplaudió con gran entusiasmo, aunque apenas consiguieron una mirada de aprobación del impasible presidente.

Una vez en el hotel, Houdinsky se esmeró en asegurarle a su familia que todo había salido bien. Estos actos eran su pan de cada día y no había razón para preocuparse. Pero por dentro pensaba en las posibles consecuencias para su familia en Rusia, que dependían de la satisfacción de Putin luego del próximo espectáculo.

El mensaje siguiente de Berditchevsky llegó bien pronto:

Muy buen trabajo. El presidente aprobó la sustitución, ya que ninguno de los observadores ni el invitado principal se dieron cuenta de que había ocurrido durante la función. Ahora podemos mudar la utilería a Washington DC para la función clave. Los boletos de avión ya están listos para su regreso a los Estados Unidos de acuerdo con el programa. Nuestro conductor los llevará de regreso al hotel.

Cuando lleguen a nuestra embajada en Washington, el día del evento, les vamos a entregar una nueva carpeta marrón con documentos. Deben acudir al sitio tres horas antes de la representación por razones de seguridad y para hablar sobre los detalles. Ya les diremos en el último momento si la función será durante el almuerzo o la cena. No duden en comunicarse conmigo por cualquier pregunta.

Finalmente, se sintieron listos para compartir con los padres de Svetlana un almuerzo. Por teléfono, su madre le hizo la pregunta tan esperada: "¿Qué les gustaría comer? Nunca tenemos oportunidad de verlos, y papá quiere asegurarse de que van a estar felices aquí con nosotros".

—Mamá, ¡todo lo que hagas estará delicioso! Pero mi marido se vuelve loco por comer tu especialidad: el *kholodets*. Le encantan las carnes en gelatina. Y tanto yo como los chicos estaríamos muy contentos con tu *borscht con smetana*. Extraño mucho esa crema agria y no puedo encontrarla en los Estados Unidos.

El almuerzo fue muy exitoso, pero sus padres trataron de ocultar su ansiedad respecto a la jubilación. Tampoco su hermano había oído si lo iban a mandar a la rehabilitación en Siberia, ya que habían detenido a otros periodistas de la oposición. Svetlana solo pudo asegurarles que estaba recurriendo a todos sus contactos para ayudarlos y que tenía esperanzas de que las cosas se iban a resolver.

****

El hotel en Washington quedaba cerca de la rotonda Dupont, a menos de tres millas de la embajada rusa, en la avenida Wisconsin de Alto Hill, uno de los puntos más altos de la ciudad, con vistas de la Casa Blanca y del Capitolio. Cuando les llegó la convocatoria, reunieron todos los artículos y disfraces para llegar tres horas antes a fin de familiarizarse con el edificio, las puertas de acceso y las salidas; el lugar de las puertas y ventanas, cortinas y demás. Un funcionario los acompañó por una escalera de mármol espléndida al segundo piso, a través de un gran salón de baile usado para las recepciones y conciertos, y fueron a inspeccionar el salón Petrovskiy (la Sala Azul dedicada al emperador Pedro I, el que había construido la flota naval rusa). Sintieron alivio al saber que la recepción sería al lado, en el Salón Rojo, un ambiente más acogedor que se destinaba para almuerzos con grupos pequeños, ideal para sus propósitos. Mientras otros empleados colocaban los accesorios cerca de una de las puertas como había pedido el maestro, ellos fueron a vestirse y a esperar con paciencia la llamada a la acción.

Cuando llegó el momento de entrar en el

Salón Rojo, Putin ya estaba sentado charlando con su invitado especial: el presidente Trump. No resultó una sorpresa, ya que lo delataba la descripción previa de su personalidad y el pedido de un programa con episodios cortos. Como era de esperar después de lo ocurrido en la Argentina, no había otros huéspedes presentes. El presidente Putin parecía consumir cantidades apreciables de vodka, mientras que Trump se servía su favorita: Coca dieta. Los dos saboreaban aperitivos sencillos y multicolores dispuestos en una bandeja. Sobre la mesa frente al único huésped había una prominente carpeta marrón.

La función comenzó con los típicos trucos con cigarrillos y luego el maestro se puso a fabricar un corto tubo hecho de papeles de diario viejos. De allí dentro empezó a desenrollar una serie interminable de tubos concéntricos que crecían y crecían de un modo incomprensible hasta llegar al techo florido y con candelabros de cristal. Después cautivó a su audiencia desplegando una tela negra de unos dos metros cuadrados que sostenía frente a él a la altura de sus hombros, y por detrás de ella parecía bajar y subir lentamente hasta un pie de altura, como si levitara —con gran asombro de ambos presidentes. A continuación, los chicos hicieron rodar una enorme caja de madera que pusieron frente a Houdinsky. Este levantó la tapa para dejar salir lentamente a Svetlana, que se movía como una muñeca mecánica, respondiendo a los comandos del mago desde un artilugio que tenía en sus manos. Al terminar el acto, ella volvió a entrar en la caja, pretendiendo caer en un sueño profundo de muñeca a medida que la tapa se iba cerrando.

Para entonces, Houdinsky tenía la atención completa de su audiencia. Había llegado la ocasión de repetir el acto favorito de Putin: el baile de Svetlana con la vela. Los movimientos sensuales y fluidos de la vela encendida que pasaba de una parte de su cuerpo a la otra pusieron a Trump en un estado de alerta y agitación: como en un ensueño, trataba de capturar a la bailarina por la cintura y por las caderas. Pero ella se le escapaba, girando como un torbellino, hasta que apagó la vela para, finalmente, regresar entre bambalinas. Entretanto, la carpeta marrón no parecía haber sido tocada ni movida de su lugar.

El acto final comprendía la llegada de una caja metálica de tres pies de largo, al principio abierta por tres de sus lados, para dejar entrar a Svetlana, de un modo muy improbable, en ese espacio tan estrecho. Houdinsky fue cerrando cada costado de la caja y luego comenzó a dar fuertes estocadas con una larga espada japonesa por las rendijas laterales. Entonces reaparecieron los chicos sosteniendo un poste muy alto con luces teatrales de varios colores que se prendían y apagaban alternativamente. De pronto, la caja fue rodeada de un humo blanco espeso y hubo una serie de explosiones al abrirse súbitamente por sus cuatro lados y revelar que estaba vacía, como si la contorsionista se hubiese evaporado junto con el humo. Trump se levantó confuso y quizá desilusionado por la desaparición de Svetlana. Nuevamente, no se notaba ningún cambio en la posición de la carpeta marrón.

Para el momento en que Houdinsky y los chicos se habían cambiado de ropa y recogido todos los materiales pequeños para trasladarlos al auto de la embajada, al abrir la puerta se encontraron con Svetlana recostada en el piso frente al asiento de atrás, sonriendo muy traviesa a su artística familia, pero invisible para el mundo exterior.

****

Una semana más tarde, Svetlana estaba nuevamente en Seattle, enseñando en la Academia ruso-americana de pilates, cuando recibió el último mensaje electrónico de Berditchevsky:

¡Muy buen trabajo! El presidente quedó fascinado por su baile espectacular y por el sigilo con que el maestro efectuó la sustitución de las carpetas. Ahora está investigando las dificultades de su familia en Rusia, y creo que pronto van a tener novedades al respecto. Es muy probable que el presidente vuelva a solicitar sus servicios en el futuro. Muchos saludos.

Yo me sentía orgulloso por los éxitos de mi amiga y tenía curiosidad por las posibles consecuencias de su acto. Creo que nunca sabremos cómo terminó eso. Pero esa noche tuve un sueño muy vívido y realista: un artículo en el *New York Times* ponía en evidencia los arreglos financieros del presidente Trump con Rusia. El departamento de Justicia había citado al Deutsche Bank para presentar todos los documentos relacionados con un lavado de capitales entre los dos países. Acto seguido, comenzó una ola de deserciones de los miembros Republicanos del Congreso que ahora aceptaban las demandas de procesar al presidente Trump, quien anunciaba su renuncia de inmediato.

El Café Quántico

Mi experiencia con el café comenzó durante la infancia y, hasta el día de hoy, no ha disminuido mi fascinación por situaciones y lugares conectados con esta bebida. Con los años, muchos "quanta" (gránulos o episodios) relacionados con el café han influido en mi vida. Esto me ha inspirado para escribir algunos relatos cortos. En ciertos casos he cambiado los nombres de personas y de sitios para proteger a posibles inocentes.

Quantum No. 1: Barracas

Carlitos Laborde, mi compañero de clase en la Secundaria, vino a visitarme por primera vez un domingo por la mañana. Hijo de un conocido promotor inmobiliario, es posible que se sintiera desubicado en nuestro pequeño departamento en Barracas, un barrio trabajador de Buenos Aires. Pero, independientemente de sus impresiones, su curiosidad natural se impuso y pronto descubrió y adoptó algunas costumbres de mi familia. Aun así, nadie hubiera podido predecir que él revelaría un gusto obsesivo por el café que iba a determinar su futuro económico y sentimental.

A papá le encantaba escuchar su modesta colección de música clásica cuando descansaba en casa los fines de semana. Ya en su primera visita, a Carlitos le intrigó la música poco habitual que surgía de nuestro tocadiscos de vinilo de 33 revoluciones, uno de los pocos en el barrio. Escuchábamos un dueto de La flauta mágica. En cambio, por la ventana abierta entraban los ritmos sincopados de D'Arienzo, una orquesta popular de la época de oro del tango, que nuestro vecino de abajo, un mecánico de autos, difundía a todo vapor con sus inmensos altoparlantes, para asegurar que todo el edificio lo escuchaba. En Barracas, Mozart no era competencia para D'Arienzo, y Carlitos fue testigo de la batalla de estilos musicales entre mi padre y nuestro inaguantable vecino.

Frustrado por el ataque sonoro, mi padre recurrió a un remedio infalible para cualquier adversidad: su ritual de beber el mejor café posible, seguido de un pequeño sorbo de coñac y luego un cigarrillo, posiblemente el único de ese día. El énfasis estaba en el café, pero el ritual debía incluir los tres elementos en secuencia. Entonces, comenzó a hacer un café turco, una elección extraña, ya que no había turcos en nuestra familia o entre nuestros amigos.

Carlitos y yo lo seguimos a la cocina, donde lo vimos sacar una pequeña olla de latón que era más ancha en la parte inferior y tenía un mango largo que se extendía a 45 grados desde la base. Dijo que esta olla era un cezve, sin explicar cómo sabía su nombre. Carlitos observó, hipnotizado, cómo mi padre lo llenaba con agua fría antes de agregar café molido muy fino de una lata colorida con diseños arabescos, seguido de una cucharadita de azúcar. Agitó la mezcla y la puso a hervir.

—A partir de ahora, no hay que mezclarlo más —dijo con confianza.

En el momento en que el agua hirvió, sirvió el café en dos tacitas de café, una para él y otra para Carlitos, como un gesto de bienvenida, y le aconsejó que esperara a que la espuma y el café molido se asentaran mientras el café se enfriaba un poco. Mi amigo solo conocía el café filtrado que se preparaba en su familia, y uno hubiera creído, por la satisfacción en su rostro, que estaba pasando por una experiencia mística.

Carlitos, una viva imagen de Sherlock Holmes, estaba sondeando el misterioso lodo de alquitrán en el fondo de la taza cuando escuchamos un golpeteo insistente en la puerta. Era un anuncio enérgico de la visita de nuestra vecina, una mujer exuberante de mediana edad con el cabello encrespado y con rulos, ojos oscuros como moras y una tez verde oliva.

—¡Hola a todos! Les traigo un poco de lehmeyún casero directamente del horno. Cómanlo mientras esté caliente —ordenó—. No hice la pizza demasiado sazonada. Sé que a ustedes los argentinos no les gusta la comida picante como en Armenia. Don Marcelo, ¡qué bueno, está haciendo café armenio! ¿No haría también uno para mí? Pero, por favor, que no se le ocurra volver a llamarlo "café turco".

—¡Con todo gusto, Maryam! Ya te hago un café t…, espero que no sea demasiado dulce, como te gusta.

Papá y yo cruzamos una mirada cómplice cuando él casi pronuncia la palabra "t…" prohibida. Carlitos también se dio cuenta, pero se hizo el tonto. Después de que Maryam se fuera, papá le aclaró a Carlitos:

—Cuando nuestros vecinos vinieron a visitarnos por primera vez, los invitamos con café, pero estúpidamente lo llamé "café turco". Estaban tan incómodos que tuvimos que aguantarnos una larga pero bien merecida lección de historia.

Mi padre le explicó que los problemas entre los turcos y los armenios se remontaban mucho tiempo atrás. En 1915, justo antes de la caída del Imperio otomano, los turcos temían que los armenios, que eran católicos, conspiraran con el zar ruso para derrocar a las fuerzas otomanas en el este. Los turcos juntaron y deportaron a toda la población armenia a los desiertos de Siria y Mesopotamia. El resultado fue la exterminación en masa de más de un millón de refugiados. De algún modo, Maryam y su familia escaparon del genocidio. Pero luego, en una inversión cruel, cuando Armenia se convirtió en una República Socialista Soviética, Stalin masacró a los armenios para eliminar lo que él consideraba una élite política e intelectual y reducir la influencia de la iglesia. Miles de sobrevivientes emigraron al Líbano,

Siria, Francia, Estados Unidos e, incluso, a la Argentina. Maryam y su esposo escaparon a Buenos Aires.

La familia de Maryam ya estaba bien establecida en la ciudad; eran dueños de una de las curtiembres para procesar y comercializar atractivos artículos de cuero. Me encantaba visitar su taller por sus olores animales tan raros; por lo extraño de una profesión que no conocía hasta entonces y por su nombre en español, "marroquinería", que evocaba imágenes y aromas de tierras lejanas.

Una tarde le pedí a Carlitos que me acompañara a visitar esta tienda exótica. Maryam estaba tan conmovida por nuestra visita que nos ofreció dulces y un paquete de halvá, uno de sus dulces tradicionales, para llevar a casa. Los compartimos en Barracas, lo que le dio a mi padre la excusa perfecta para preparar café armenio para todos.

A medida que pasaban las semanas, Carlitos se aficionó al café de mi padre, su música clásica y los platos armenios que Maryam compartía con nosotros. Pero yo sospechaba que fue Maryam quién lo hechizó, con su figura atractiva y sus bellos ojos oscuros, su encanto y su talento como chef. El afecto era mutuo, porque ella no tenía hijos y disfrutaba de la admiración no disimulada de Carlitos. Todos nos habíamos convertido en su familia extensa. Ella también apreciaba la cocina judía de mi madre, incluyendo especialidades como el kasha, de trigo sarraceno. Le recordaba al viejo país, que todavía echaba de menos a pesar de su trágica historia. Curiosamente, la familia del lado de mi madre podría haber coexistido con los armenios en Besarabia, ahora conocida como Moldavia. Ambas familias habían sufrido persecución y pogromos rusos y habían escapado a Argentina casi al mismo tiempo. Los dos grupos étnicos, los judíos rusos y los armenios católicos, ahora cohabitaban en los mismos barrios de Buenos Aires. También compartíamos el gusto por el té ruso con limón, hecho en un samovar que, como sus dueños, había sobrevivido al largo viaje por el océano para encontrar un sitio en la casa de mis abuelos.

Nuestra casa estaba a solo unas cuadras del estadio de La Bombonera, el club de fútbol de Boca Juniors. Sin embargo, nuestros padres nunca nos llevaron a ver los partidos del domingo, porque sentían que los fanáticos eran demasiado rudos y maleducados, incluso hasta peligrosos. Un domingo aburrido, cuando mi mamá estaba visitando a unos familiares, a mi padre se le ocurrió una idea diferente:

—¿Quieren ir a un partido de rugby? Los equipos nacionales francés y argentino están jugando en la ciudad y me gustaría ir para apoyar a mi antigua patria. Después del partido, podemos ir todos al centro, a un buen lugar de expreso italiano que conozco.

—¡Sí! —gritamos sin dudarlo un instante.

Por supuesto, el partido de rugby lo ganó fácilmente el equipo francés, muy organizado y con una admirable línea de jugadores ingeniosos que casi nunca perdieron un pase. Poco después, estábamos en un autobús camino al centro y bajamos en una esquina de la calle Lavalle para buscar el café Le Caravelle, que frecuentaban los italianos del norte. En el interior, el humo del cigarrillo era tan denso como la niebla sobre el puente Golden Gate en una noche de invierno. Los clientes estaban vestidos a la moda, como para pasear por la Galería de Milán, lo que nos hizo sentir incómodos con nuestro atuendo deportivo. Pero el café expreso del Caravelle, hecho con granos importados por un barista con chaqueta blanca y un moño negro, fue inolvidable, elegante y suave al paladar, con un sabor muy delicado y un regusto delicioso. Carlitos y yo comentamos en secreto (aunque nunca lo dijimos en voz alta) que el café expreso del Caravelle era superior al café casero de mi padre. Desde entonces se convirtió en nuestro estándar de referencia.

—¿Es esto lo mejor que hay, don Marcelo? ¿Qué opina del café hecho por nuestros vecinos del norte? —preguntó Carlitos con una expresión ingenua.

Esa provocación bastó para que mi padre nos llevara a la carrera por la calle Suipacha a un lugar que yo nunca había visto antes: la "Casa do Brazil". Se trataba de una sala muy angosta, con un mostrador de al menos 10 metros de largo, donde tres o cuatro filas de clientes avanzaban a velocidad del rayo hacia el mostrador por su dosis de cafeína. Allí, los baristas más expertos ofrecían cafezinhos, la versión brasileña de un café expreso simple, en pequeñas tacitas blancas. Nadie se atrevería ni a pensar en agregarle leche o a pedir un capuchino o un café con leche. El objetivo era deleitarse con el puro sabor del café sin diluir. La rapidez con que los clientes tomaban sus pequeños tragos era sorprendente. Luego agradecían al barista con una pequeña propina y se marchaban de inmediato, sin ganas de quedarse en este equivalente de la fábrica de chocolate enloquecida de Willie Wonka.

Con el tiempo, la Casa do Brazil desapareció del centro de la ciudad y Le Caravelle perdió tanto su carácter como sus altos estándares para convertirse en una sombra de lo que fue. Ambos lugares fueron víctimas de la agitación política, las devaluaciones monetarias múltiples y la falta de granos importados de alta calidad. Pero la memoria del gusto que fue un privilegio probar en nuestra juventud se ha quedado conmigo. Fue la base de toda una vida de aprendizaje sobre lo que hace a un gran café.

Cuando llegamos a casa, papá tocó una música que nos parecía apropiada para la iglesia, pero mucho más alegre y animada. No pudimos identificarla.

—¡No, esto no es música religiosa! Sabía que los iba a agarrar con esto —dijo, riendo—. Es la Cantata del café, que Bach escribió alrededor de 1735, cuando esta bebida acababa de llegar a Alemania y se convirtió en un éxito instantáneo. Hasta entonces, la gente solía tomar cerveza con el desayuno, pero el café se hizo popular porque ayudaba a recuperar la sobriedad. Resultó particularmente atractivo para las mujeres jóvenes, a quienes por primera vez se les permitió entrar en las cafeterías. En esta breve ópera cómica, el padre le dice a su hija adicta al café que se calle y deje de argumentar. Las palabras que canta en alemán, "Schweight Stille, Plaudert Nicht", se convirtieron en el nombre de la cantata.

Mi padre y yo a veces salíamos juntos y creamos fuertes lazos entre nosotros. A la vuelta de la esquina de nuestra casa había un café ordinario, en una calle arbolada en la esquina de Coronel Salvadores con Montes de Oca. Mientras yo me contentaba con un refresco, él se gratificaba con un café expreso, seguido de un trago de Hesperidina. Este era un licor argentino único, hecho con amargos y cáscaras de naranja dulce. Esta bebida la anunciaban con una rima musical en español que incluso hoy me hace sonreír. Luego mirábamos a los vagos del vecindario jugando al billar por poca plata. Solo los adultos podían jugar al billar y beber alcohol, pero a los niños se les permitía sentarse y mirar con sus padres. Nunca vi a una mujer allí, excepto cuando una venía a buscar a su marido ocioso.

El día que me hice adulto, a los veintiún años, mi padre sugirió que saliéramos a caminar por el vecindario, como si tuviera algo en mente de qué hablar. Y luego me sorprendió al sentarse conmigo en el bar de la esquina, donde me convidó a mi primera Hesperidina. A continuación me dio una lección de billar, y yo, orgulloso de sentirme gente grande, mientras los vagos nos vigilaban con desprecio. Para mi sorpresa, papá era bastante bueno en eso (yo sabía que era un buen ajedrecista), y yo pensaba que era solo un observador de billar y juegos de cartas en el café. ¡Hubiese podido hacerles muy buen partido a los otros clientes!

Mi padre también ejerció una fuerte influencia en mi amigo Carlitos. Junto con su gusto por el café y la buena música, Carlitos aprendió a apreciar la compañía de mujeres extranjeras atractivas. Le encantaban las especias que Maryam usaba en la comida armenia, su pan lavash y, por supuesto, su pizza con berenjenas y garbanzos. También era un gran fanático de las habas o arvejas en salsa de tomate con ajo, perejil y menta.

Cuando unos años más tarde, en la universidad, Carlitos conoció a Natalie, la sobrina de Maryam, su futuro quedó sellado. Natalie parecía una versión más joven de su tía: con su mirada intensa, curvas sexis y talento como cocinera. Ella era inteligente y estaba por ingresar a la Facultad de Arquitectura. Era evidente que Carlitos y Natalie se estaban enamorando, y su atracción por ella aumentó junto con su amor por el café. Todo salió bien hasta que el padre de mi amigo, un rico nacionalista argentino, se alarmó por las preferencias extranjeras de su hijo. Primero, Carlitos había ofendido a su padre al quejarse de que el café filtrado que hacía en casa no tenía sabor. Luego agravó el insulto al negarse a comer con su familia en una pizzería tradicional del vecindario. Insistió en que la lehmeyún era muy superior a su fugazzetta, e incluso mejor que la pizza de Guerrín, la mejor pizzería de Buenos Aires. Estas comparaciones eran equivalentes a una herejía. El padre replicó con ironía que "al menos tus amigos son católicos, porque no tienen otra característica redentora". Furioso y fuera de control, incluso repitió el rumor racista e infundado que había escuchado entre los menos educados de su familia, que "las mujeres turcas y armenias tienden a ponerse muy pesadas y les crece la barba después de casarse".

Carlitos y yo dejamos de vernos una vez que nos interesamos en diferentes carreras. Él estudió finanzas, se quedó en el país y se mantuvo en contacto con nuestros viejos vecinos en Barracas. Yo, por otro lado, ingresé a la Facultad de Medicina y, finalmente, abandoné la Argentina para capacitarme en un posgrado en la Universidad de

Oklahoma.

No recuerdo mucho sobre ese período, excepto que Oklahoma era un estado con tierra roja y pocos árboles en el centro del "cinturón bíblico"; no había café que valiera la pena en ningún lado; y la placa de matrícula en los autos decía, injustificadamente: "Oklahoma es ok". Dado que en ese estado estaba prohibida la venta de alcohol, uno tenía que cuidarse de no pedir "café" en cierto restaurante italiano por el peligro de que te sirvieran furtivamente vino tinto en una taza de café. La primera vez que me sucedió esto, inocentemente agregué azúcar a la taza y arruiné un muy buen Chianti. ¡Nunca más!

Durante mi residencia en medicina en los Estados Unidos me dieron unos pocos días de vacaciones e hice un viaje muy corto para ver a mis padres en Buenos Aires. Desde el aeropuerto, tomé un taxi directamente a un hotel del centro porque mis padres entonces vivían en un departamento bastante pequeño. Tan pronto como llegué, largué mi maleta y me dejé llevar por el impulso de andar al azar por las calles transitadas que conocía tan bien desde mi infancia. Habían cambiado mucho. Ya no podía encontrar los viejos cafés que frecuentaba con mi padre. Crucé lentamente el microcentro, sintiendo la extrañeza de quienes regresan a casa después de una larga ausencia. Ahora todo parecía más viejo y descuidado, quizá por la falta de mantenimiento común en los países subdesarrollados. Esto me hizo rechazar la creencia irracional de algunos de mis compatriotas de que Argentina y, en particular Buenos Aires, eran el centro del universo.

Mi peregrinación me llevó a la calle Corrientes y frente al Teatro Gran Rex, donde había visto a mi padre lagrimear con nostalgia durante un concierto de Edith Piaf; pasé por la antigua pizzería Las Cuartetas, donde él y su hermano Charles habían probado el dulce de leche por primera vez, apenas llegados de Francia; y me asombré otra vez por las innumerables librerías del centro, generalmente abiertas hasta altas horas de la noche, y por la inquietud cultural de los porteños, la gente de Buenos Aires. Al final, me encontré deambulando por la calle Lavalle, con sus numerosas salas de cine, tiendas de discos y lugares para comer. Y de pronto, una imagen de mi memoria casi hizo parar mi corazón: estaba pasando por el asador que casi me había hecho llegar tarde a mi casamiento. Solían hacer el mejor bistec con papas suflés que había probado en mi vida, ¡y me obligaron a esperar, con gran ansiedad por mi parte, la comida hasta solo unos minutos antes de mi boda! Pero me casé con Diana, y dos días después estábamos en un avión de regreso a los Estados Unidos para completar nuestras residencias médicas.

En la siguiente cuadra me encontré con el letrero de un restaurante, que decía "Eraván", un nombre inesperado en esta parte de la ciudad, ya que chocaba con los nombres españoles de los otros negocios. ¿Qué estaba haciendo este lugar en el centro de Buenos Aires, lejos de los barrios tradicionales como Palermo o Barracas, generalmente preferidos por los armenios? Mi curiosidad era más fuerte que mis pies, y me arrastró, de forma inexorable, al cavernoso edificio. Estaba lleno de gente, pero me las arreglé para abrirme camino hasta el final del salón donde, detrás de un vidrio transparente, vi a cocineros criollos preparando lehmeyún.

Los camareros llevaban enérgicamente bandejas humeantes con estas delicias exóticas a mesas de argentinos de aspecto normal. En el lado izquierdo de la sala había un largo mostrador con dos elegantes baristas vestidos con sacos blancos y moñitos negros. Un letrero de neón parpadeante ofrecía una variedad de cafés: armenio, expreso o prensa francesa, todo de granos tostados importados. En la pared de detrás del mostrador, una pintura de una mujer intensa y de ojos muy oscuros parecía supervisar toda la operación. El café armenio era muy sabroso, no demasiado dulce, y combinaba con los deliciosos pasteles que recordaba de mi juventud en Barracas: el clásico halvá y mi favorito, el nazook, hecho con crema agria, azúcar, vainilla y huevos y, algunas veces, relleno de nueces. Al probarlos me sentí culpable por no haber ido primero a la casa de mis padres.

Ahora era demasiado tarde. Resolví ir a visitarlos a primera hora de la mañana.

Cuando me acerqué a la caja para pagar la cuenta, la cajera levantó los ojos y ambos nos miramos, asombrados:

—¡Armando!

—¡Natalie!

Dijimos al unísono antes de abrazarnos calurosamente. De inmediato llamó al jefe de camareros para que la reemplazara en el mostrador y luego, tomándome del codo, me llevó a su oficina en la parte de atrás. La habitación era más grande de lo que esperaba, con un escritorio elaborado y un sofá de cuero antiguo sobre una exquisita alfombra tejida, con antiguos símbolos religiosos armenios.

Como era de esperar, mi primera pregunta fue:

—¿Sigues viendo a Carlitos?

—Por supuesto. ¿No lo sabías? ¡Nos casamos hace tres años! La boda fue en St. Gregory Illuminator, la Catedral Ortodoxa Armenia en Palermo. Más tarde, el mismo día, el sacerdote de la familia Laborde nos bendijo en una ceremonia privada en Barracas. Por lo tanto, honramos los deseos y creencias de las dos familias.

—¿Qué pasó con tu interés por la arquitectura? —pregunté.

—Por supuesto, me gradué, pero nunca tuve la oportunidad de trabajar en este campo porque la crisis económica casi paró la construcción de casas de alta gama. Por suerte, pudimos abrir este nuevo restaurante y ambos trabajamos aquí a tiempo completo. Carlitos estará triste por no haberse encontrado con vos, está buscando abrir un restaurante en los Estados Unidos. Eraván fue idea suya, pero el proyecto lo desarrollamos con mi tía Maryam, quien es nuestra chef ejecutiva, y con la ayuda financiera de mi suegro.

—¡Esperá un minuto! ¿No era muy nacionalista y desconfiaba de los extranjeros? Sabía que se oponía a tu relación con Carlitos.

—Precisamente —dijo—, hasta que Maryam y yo lo cautivamos con la hospitalidad del Viejo Mundo, los buenos modales y el sabor de nuestra cocina. Una vez que escuchó los detalles de cómo escapó la familia de Maryam de la Armenia de Stalin y comenzó a apreciar su experiencia comercial y el éxito de la marroquinería, se convirtió en un fanático nuestro. De hecho, él era el propietario de este edificio antes de firmar para que pudiéramos abrir un restaurante, fue su regalo de bodas. Estaba convencido de que el amor de Carlitos por el café y su formación como economista, junto con la experiencia de Maryam en la cocina, garantizarían nuestro éxito. El restaurante tuvo un comienzo difícil porque las personas en esta ciudad tienen gustos culinarios limitados. Acá siguen reinando el churrasco y las papas fritas. Pero hemos creado una nueva cultura en una parte de la ciudad en donde somos una novedad. ¡Y este es el resultado! Los argentinos vienen en masa, respondiendo a nuestra originalidad y alta calidad, la sabrosa comida y el mejor café.

Pasé el resto del corto viaje con mis padres antes de regresar a Seattle para reanudar mi trabajo. Más tarde, unos argentinos visitantes nos contaron que el éxito del exótico Eraván había durado poco. Lo habían vendido a inversores locales que, como era de esperar, lo convirtieron en una parrilla, un típico asador. Carlitos y Natalie se habían mudado a los Estados Unidos, en donde abrieron el primer Resto-Café Armenio en Miami.

Al reflexionar sobre mi vida y hacer memoria de mi pasión por el buen café, me ayudaron las ideas de Maimónides, el filósofo y médico judío que observó en el siglo XIII que "el tiempo está compuesto de átomos, es decir, de muchas partes que no pueden subdividirse aún más, debido a su corta duración".

Hoy llamamos a estas partículas "quánta", las que pueden existir simultáneamente en dos estados diferentes e incluso muy distantes. La física moderna aceptaría que un quántum de mi vida en el café se ha vuelto "concreto", lo que permite conocer las ubicaciones probables y el estado de cada partícula: la primera estaría en el barrio de Barracas (Buenos Aires) y la otra, ahora en Seattle (Washington), dentro de un número infinito de universos posibles, denominado el "multiverso".

El café quántico

Quantum No. 2: El Procope

Cuando mi padre terminó el servicio militar y se fue de Francia, tardó cuarenta años en regresar a París, la ciudad en que había nacido. Soñaba con volver a ver a su hermano Nathan, un hombre trabajador, pintor y escritor, veterano de la Legión Extranjera Francesa. Un día mi esposa y yo tuvimos la oportunidad de invitar a mi padre, quien vivía en Buenos Aires, a acompañarnos a visitar París, en donde compartimos el reencuentro muy emotivo de los dos hermanos. El lugar exacto en que celebramos este acontecimiento pasó a ser un quantum importante en mi vida, así como en mi universo cafetero.

El legendario reencuentro comenzó en el kiosco de diarios y revistas (La Terrasse) de Nathan en la calle Montorgueil, en el corazón del antiguo mercado de Les Halles. Aun cuando los promotores inmobiliarios hayan borrado este mercado del mapa, en aquel momento era un escenario importante de la vida en París, y las galerías y boutiques de moda de hoy en día palidecen en comparación. La reunión de los hermanos parecía el acontecimiento del año, ya que los vecinos carniceros, verduleros y pescaderos salieron de sus negocios para observarlos. El rubicundo dueño de una bodega cercana se acercó con varios vasitos de

Mâcon-Villages y nos ofreció un caluroso brindis en la misma calle.

Pronto descubrimos que Nathan era mucho más que dueño de un kiosco: era un personaje del barrio, y entre sus clientes del pasado hubo filósofos y escritores como Sartre y Camus (quien llegó a ser su amigo). Solían detenerse para comprar el diario por la mañana, intercambiar algunos comentarios y, a veces, hasta acompañarlo con un café o un vasito de vino blanco en un bar de la esquina.

Al rato Nathan cerró el kiosco para llevarnos a almorzar a un bistró típico del barrio, de los que hoy en día son casi imposibles de encontrar. Pensamos que se dirigía hacia un enorme caracol dorado que colgaba a cinco metros sobre la entrada del restaurante L'Escargot D'Or, pero estábamos equivocados.

—No vamos a L'Escargot —aclaró Nathan—. Ya no es lo que era en los tiempos en que Marcel Proust y Sarah Bernhard se encontraban allí para cenar. Ahora es un sitio para turistas, a quienes puede impresionar la decoración opulenta de moda durante el reinado de Napoleón III. No quiero que ustedes se sientan como en la ópera. Prefiero mostrarles otro lado de París en un bistró auténtico para trabajadores, con una comida mucho mejor.

Lo seguimos hasta la otra esquina a un local más pequeño llamado Le Zinc por su mostrador de peltre de más de cien años. Tenía paredes simplemente pintadas color crema, techos abovedados y estantes repletos de botellas de vino añejo famoso, cubiertas de polvo y con algunas telarañas.

Luego de presentarnos, el orgulloso dueño y cantinero volvió con una garrafa de Chiroubles que, como nos informó, procedía de un barril recién llegado de la región del Beaujolais. El primer plato fue inolvidable: una preparación muy sutil de huevos hervidos en vino tinto, llamados oeufs en meurette, un plato de Borgoña. El resto del almuerzo fue amenizado por la historia de la vida de mi tío, quien nos deleitó con una serie interminable de anécdotas y experiencias. Había sido conductor de camiones en la Resistencia francesa durante la Segunda Guerra Mundial y, sacando una borrosa fotografía de su billetera, mostró cómo su camión había caído por un barranco cerca de Lyon, al escapar de un ataque alemán. Más tarde luchó con la Legión Extranjera en Indochina, hasta la última etapa de la guerra, cuando el Viet Minh atacó Dien Bien Phou, dejando a Nathan y a los pocos sobrevivientes franceses en el caos. Después participó en la guerra de Argelia, pero prefería no recordar esa época de su vida.

Exhaustos por las emociones de nuestro primer día en París, nos dirigimos hacia el hotel para pasar la noche. Por la mañana volvimos a buscar a Nathan, como habíamos planeado, en el popular café La Boule D'Or, cerca de la fuente de St. Michel.

Mi tío consideraba este sitio como su "cuartel general", y allí lo encontramos sentado magníficamente, escribiendo frente a una ventana. Él amaba este café proletario en el Barrio Latino, en donde se sentía como un rey. Además consideraba que allí servían el mejor café crème de la ciudad, a un precio muy razonable. Aunque trabajaba mucho en su kiosco, no hubiese podido pagar los precios abusivos en Deux Magots o el Café de Flore en Saint Germain, los que frecuentaban Sartre y Simone de Beauvoir. Nathan estaba redactando su primer borrador de una Historia de los cafés literarios en Francia y, cuando podía permitírselo, iba a investigar a otros sitios como la Closerie de Lilas en Montparnasse, la favorita de los poetas del siglo XIX, Baudelaire y Paul Verlaine, y más tarde de Hemingway y de Beckett.

Nunca supimos si terminó de escribir su libro. Cuando falleció, sus hijos se deshicieron de sus manuscritos y, para entonces, nosotros estábamos muy lejos, en los Estados Unidos, para rescatarlos.

Después de que todos tomáramos un cafecito y de que los hermanos fumaran sus cigarrillos, Nathan nos guio en un largo trayecto por las calles de París, en especial por la orilla izquierda del Sena, pero también por el Marais, su barrio favorito. Por cierto que causamos una gran impresión por sus calles, corriendo detrás de este hombre diminuto pero tan animado, con su delantal azul oscuro —el uniforme característico de la clase trabajadora en Francia— gesticulando para señalar cada punto de referencia histórico en el camino.

Así comenzó nuestra formación no convencional de París, sus rincones enigmáticos y vasta historia, contada por uno de los parisinos mejor informados. Conocía cada adoquín y la fachada de numerosos edificios. En un momento dado, se detuvo ante un colegio en una callecita simpática para mostrarnos una placa conmemorativa muy triste con los nombres de los niños judíos deportados por los alemanes durante la Guerra. Nathan los hizo revivir con sus descripciones tan elocuentes de esos eventos. En nuestro paseo por el Marais nos sentimos transportados a un París diferente, el que había existido no solo unas décadas antes, sino el de la Edad Media. Así descubrimos que la ciudad oculta enigmas innumerables y que íbamos entrando poco a poco en un universo diferente al que observan tantos turistas.

Cuando nos acercábamos al Sena por la calle del puente Louis Phillipe, de pronto nos pasó un joven muy enérgico vestido con una corta capa negra, marchando con un bastón muy raro —alto hasta el pecho y con una serie de círculos concéntricos de colores cerca del tope. Caminaba con determinación hacia un enorme edificio de piedra gris, justo al lado de una iglesia bastante antigua. Pensando que esa era mi oportunidad de emular al gran Cartier Bresson y de captar su foto en el "momento decisivo", corrí hacia el joven cuando entró en el edificio y desapareció. Al verme parado y perplejo, se acercó Nathan para explicarme que el joven era un compagnon, y pertenecía a una orden masónica conocida desde hace siglos.

—Su nombre viene del francés antiguo y significa: 'alguien con quien compartimos el pan'.

Y entonces mi tío nos sorprendió, invitándonos a entrar en la sede central de la orden para tomar un almuerzo simple, pero delicioso.

El enorme salón rectangular del inmueble recordaba al refectorio de algún monasterio de la Edad Media, con sus altas vigas de madera y una larga mesa comunitaria, en donde divisé al joven que nos había pasado afuera, comiendo con sus compañeros. Nos sentamos bien cerca de su grupo para compartir la comida, de modo que más tarde les ofrecimos una donación. Me arreglé para acercarme al muchacho y tratar de entablar conversación. Así pude enterarme de que el bastón con que marchaba era la insignia de los peregrinos del mundo entero. Arriba de los círculos coloridos que había observado, tenía un tope de marfil grabado con símbolos secretos —una escuadra, un compás y un hacha—, además de las letras U V G T, el emblema de la asociación de carpinteros, uno de los gremios de artesanos que la orden supervisaba e instruía desde hacía varios siglos. El joven compagnon había recibido el bastón ceremonial al completar sus estudios. De acuerdo con la tradición, ahora debía partir en peregrinaje por uno o dos años, en Francia o en un país extranjero. Aunque lo usual era ir a pie por las rutas, en este caso él decidió volar para un internado en Dinamarca con un maestro carpintero muy reputado. Otras ramas de la asociación enseñaban artes culinarias, como panadería o pastelería, de muy alto nivel. Joël Robuchon, quizá el mejor cocinero de Francia y uno de mis chefs más admirados, se había entrenado como compagnon.

Demostrando su enorme conocimiento de la historia de Francia, Nathan nos describió los orígenes muy antiguos de la orden y la leyenda de maître Jacques, un sabio de Provenza que llegó a Jerusalén cerca del año 970 a. C. y fue contratado por el rey Salomón como tallador de piedra para ayudar a construir el Primer Templo. Sus discípulos conservaron sus enseñanzas secretas hasta nuestros tiempos, y fueron masones, maestros albañiles de los grandes monumentos. Otra historia esotérica mostraba a maître Jacques en Orleans en 1401 como constructor de las torres de su famosa catedral.

Saliendo del edificio, Nathan nos mostró la puerta de la iglesia de St. Gervais. El cementerio vecino supuestamente conservaba las reliquias y huesos de otros compagnon famosos, los albañiles y carpinteros que habían construido la catedral de Nôtre Dame. Explicó que la orden poseía una larga historia de persecución por los papas, por varios gobiernos y hasta por los alemanes durante la Segunda Guerra, todos los que desconfiaban y odiaban a los masones por sus secretos. También ahora la orden tenía sus desafíos, al competir con los poderosos gremios de la Confederación General del Trabajo (CGT).

Finalmente llegó el domingo, el día fijado para el encuentro de la familia entera. Después de un ligero desayuno, nos vestimos para la fiesta, ya que íbamos a conocer a todos los hijos de Nathan y a sus familias.

Habíamos quedado a mediodía para un banquete en el Café Procope, un sitio histórico en la rue de L'Ancienne Comédie. Era un sitio formal con grandes candelabros de cristal y numerosos retratos de gente ilustre, aunque no tuvimos ocasión de investigarlos, ya que nos esperaba una muchedumbre alborozada a la entrada del salón principal. Nathan, rebosante de alegría, anunció nuestra llegada a la familia entera. Estas cincuenta personas, aun desconocidas para nosotros, se pusieron en fila en un orden prefijado para recibirnos con los acostumbrados dos besos en cada mejilla. La primera de la fila era la diminuta Sophie, la esposa rumana de Nathan, una dínamo de peso liviano que se nos pegó, charlando alegremente sin parar hasta el final de la fila familiar. Esta incluía a sus tres hijos, nietos, esposas y primos segundos, ninguno de cuyos nombres pudimos retener. Una prima lejana, jovencita entusiasta de unos catorce años, nos acompañó para practicar su rudimentario inglés.

Pronto nos vimos con las caras coloreadas por el maquillaje de tantas primas. Alborotados por el tamaño de nuestra nueva familia lejana, fuimos subiendo las escaleras para una foto de grupo en un balcón a la calle del segundo piso, tomada por un fotógrafo profesional desde la vereda opuesta. El balcón, bajo el peso de la familia Lindner completa, comenzó a vibrar de un modo amenazador y temí que fuese a desplomarse. Grité alarmado, pero Sophie contestó con su tan simpático acento franco-rumano:

—Tranquilo, si este edificio ha aguantado trescientos años, aguantará tres minutos más hasta que tomemos esta fotografía.

El almuerzo constó de muchos platos, un menú orquestado por Nathan en honor a mi padre, con innumerables discursos de los dos hermanos y algunos familiares. De postre, una tarta St. Honoré de un metro de alto, la pièce de résistance, puso fin a las celebraciones oficiales. Entonces pude explorar el extraordinario edificio y leer algunos de los afiches en las paredes y los folletos en las mesas. Nathan había elegido un lugar perfecto para esta reunión: el Café Procope había sido el primer café literario de Francia y solo se transformó en restaurante recientemente.

Un tema que siempre fue de gran interés para mí es la historia de cómo comenzó el café a ser una bebida en Europa. La inolvidable reunión de familia me inspiró a informarme mucho más al respecto. Así descubrí que en 1669 durante el reinado de Luis XIV, fue Soliman-Agha, el embajador de la Sublime Puerta, el gobierno del Imperio Otomano, quien introdujo la infusión en Francia. Poco después, un armenio llamado Pascal abrió un café en el mercado de St. Germain. Cuando este pequeño negocio quebró, un tal Procopio, un siciliano aventurero, imaginó abrir el establecimiento actual en la misma calle en que estaba originalmente la Comédie Française. Aquí los caballeros aprendieron la costumbre de beber café, que antes del Procope solo se tomaba en las tabernas. También allí ofrecían sorbetes en tacitas de porcelana, servidos por camareros vestidos como "armenios" en trajes exóticos. Pronto el Procope llegó a atraer a un ilustre grupo de filósofos, escritores y políticos. Setenta años más tarde, Bach eternizó la costumbre que ya había arraigado en toda Europa en su cómica Cantata del café.

Recorriendo el Procope descubrí unas mesitas con placas de bronce dedicadas a los clientes famosos: Rousseau, Voltaire, Napoleón III y el enciclopedista Diderot. Me senté a una de ellas, admirado y soñando despierto que tomaba un café turco con alguien como Voltaire, quien tenía fama de haber ingerido hasta cuarenta tacitas diarias, mezclado con chocolate. Fue en el Procope donde Voltaire había conocido a Benjamin Franklin y a Thomas Jefferson. Durante la Revolución francesa, el Gorro Frigio (de "la libertad") debutó en este café, en donde Robespierre, Dantón y Marat eran clientes regulares. Más tarde el Procope fue popular entre escritores como Alfred de Musset, George Sand y Anatole France, y también entre políticos y oradores como León Gambetta, quien allí aprendió el arte de hablar en público. Sentado frente a la supuesta mesita de Voltaire, me sentí invadido por su espíritu y medité sobre los efectos del café en la creatividad y en activar la mente.

Sabía que Nathan estaba escribiendo su libro en la Boule D'Or, pero nunca imaginé que un día iba a tratar de emular su conducta mientras estudiaba para mis exámenes en un café de la esquina cerca de la Facultad de Medicina en Buenos Aires. Y que hoy estoy registrando estos detalles en otro café, el Storyville del mercado de Pike Place, en Seattle.

Siento mucha gratitud hacia el granjero que descubrió en Etiopía cómo tostar ese pequeño grano rojo para extraer un néctar esclarecedor. Y que Dios bendiga a aquel yemenita que aprendió a cultivar los granos más delicados y deliciosos de esa variedad de café que llamamos "arábica". Él contribuyó a crear un hábito que se extendió a través de Arabia y de Turquía, para llegar un día a Europa y finalmente amerizar en América. No es casual que el lugar de donde partían los barcos con el milagroso grano hacia el resto del mundo fuera el yemení puerto de Moca, en el mar Rojo.

El interés por el café me ha acompañado durante muchos años, pero los cambios sufridos en el universo de esta bebida terminaron influyendo mi propio quantum de café. Por ejemplo, el mismo café Procope fue remodelado en 1988 en un estilo del siglo XVIII, con muros color rojo de Pompeya, un piano tintineante y camareros disfrazados con uniformes de un estilo supuestamente revolucionario. Al regresar una vez al Procope me desilusionaron estos cambios. ¡Robespierre hubiera opuesto de manera radical, poniendo en marcha otra vez la guillotina!

También supe que las damas que al principio acudían al Procope acompañadas pronto desaparecieron y, por mucho tiempo, nadie mencionó su ausencia en los salones de café. Me alegra saber que esta situación ha quedado para la historia, pero igualmente protesté porque la mujer sentada hoy a mi lado en Storyville cantaba en voz baja o tarareaba la misma canción mientras componía música para su clase.

Por todas estas razones, El Procope representa la localización concreta de un quantum crucial que contribuyó a mi fascinación por el café. Esto se hizo evidente al recibir un mensaje en

Facebook de una persona desconocida, usando el pseudónimo "Dominó-Dominó". ¡Aseguraba ser mi prima segunda! Pero lo que un principio creí que sería un fraude electrónico terminó siendo cierto, cuando me contó que era una de las nietas de Nathan y que había estado en el banquete para mi padre. ¡Se trataba de la jovencita de catorce años que había practicado inglés con nosotros!

Poco más tarde pudimos reencontrarnos en persona en el Café Costès en París, frente al Centro Pompidou, muy cerca del sitio en donde nos habíamos conocido. Así como a mi padre le llevó cuarenta años volver a Francia, a Dominique (su verdadero nombre) y a mí nos llevó el mismo tiempo encontrarnos nuevamente, gracias al Internet.

El café quántico
Quantum No. 3: Café Florián

Mi tercer quantum se materializó en Venecia, donde los mercaderes turcos introdujeron el café en el siglo XVI. Lo inesperado fue que la posición de los quanta, así como la de los electrones es indeterminada y no podemos predecir por dónde van a presentarse. Solo se vuelven "concretos" cuando interactúan con algo más. En este caso, la partícula me encontró cuando estaba con mi familia en el histórico Café Florián, fundado en 1720. En su ostentosa "sala del Senado" yo preparaba mi cámara fotográfica para documentar la escena, cuando vimos entrar a una pareja de mediana edad, aspecto severo y cara de pocos amigos. Ocuparon la mesa de un rincón menos iluminado que da a la Piazza San Marco, de modo que nuestra primera impresión fue cinematográfica, como en la película "Tercer hombre", con Orson Welles en la Viena del 1949. Curiosamente, el corte y estilo de sus ropas sugería un origen en Europa del Este, en Austria o más probablemente en Alemania Oriental.

Por respeto, cuando fotografío gente me gusta establecer contacto antes o pedir permiso para hacerlo. Ese día hubo algo que me impulsó a tomar esa foto descaradamente en contra de los deseos evidentes de la misteriosa pareja. La diapositiva que aún conservo, una agfachrome de colores muy barrocos, los muestra indignados y asombrados por mi atrevimiento, y una copia enorme cuelga todavía, muchos años más tarde, en un sitio prominente de nuestro comedor. Es un recuerdo imperecedero por la aventura en que participó nuestro hijo Serge a los doce años.

Monté mi cámara en un pequeño trípode de mesa y apunté. La mujer encendió un cigarrillo, y los dos volvieron la mirada hacia nosotros, entre incrédulos y ansiosos. Accioné el cable disparador mientras disimulaba hablando con mi familia. No dejaron de mirarme con odio durante el resto de la velada. Resultaba molesto, casi atemorizante, pero al mismo tiempo azuzó nuestra imaginación. ¿No serán espías o agentes del Stasi? Dicen que algunos andan muy activos en esta época, en muchos países de Europa.

Nos distrajo la llegada de un mozo en un elegante esmoquin negro con moñito. Era alto, delgado y serio, hubiera pasado desapercibido en una cena de cancillería en cualquier país europeo. Pedimos un negroni para Diana, expreso para mí, y un virgen Bellini (con duraznos frescos) para Serge. Desde nuestra mesa de mármol ornamentada, nuestro hijo estudiaba admirado el opulento salón, decorado con pinturas excesivamente elaboradas de un tal Giacomo Casa. Una de ellas, "La civilización educando a las naciones", mostraba incomprensibles signos masónicos, como un ángel tocando una roca con el número XIX. Desde nuestra perspectiva cultural moderna se veía muy presuntuosa. Cuando el mozo volvió con las bebidas, Serge aprovechó para interrogarlo:

—Perdone, señor. ¿Es cierto que Florián ha estado abierto sin interrupciones desde 1720?.

—Así es, joven—, respondió el mozo en un excelente inglés. —Solo nos obligaron a cerrar por unos días en 1918, durante la Primera Guerra Mundial cuando las tropas de Alemania y Austria nos cercaban desde el este, y hubo que evacuar la ciudad. Pero transportamos gratis a casi todos los habitantes, con gran eficiencia, a otras partes de Italia. Las bombas caían cerca, en el puente de los suspiros, pero por fortuna no destruyeron el café.

—¿Por qué se llama Florián?

—En la época de la Revolución Francesa, acá se reunían los Jacobinos, los republicanos opuestos a toda influencia extranjera. El nombre original del Café era 'Venecia triunfante' pero cuando las tropas francesas entraron en la ciudad, sonaba inapropiado. Por eso se lo cambiaron a 'Florián,' el nombre del dueño en ese momento".

—¡Cuánta historia!—, respondió Serge. —Me gusta este sitio. Seguro que acá venía mucha gente importante.

—Usted es muy jovencito. ¿Conoce a nuestro escritor Goldoni? También venían Goethe, Charles Dickens, y Marcel Proust. Seguro que no oyó hablar de Casanova, quien nos frecuentaba porque éramos el único café que permitía la entrada a mujeres en aquella época—, le contó con una sonrisita un poco conspiratoria.

Mientras tomábamos nuestras bebidas, los de la mesa cercana continuaban mirándome de un modo inquietante. Pero eso no me impidió deleitarme por la calidad del expreso, hecho con una mezcla de granos llamada Venezia 1720, de un aroma intenso pero balanceado. El mozo me explicó con palabras rimbombantes que este café tenía excelentes propiedades 'organolépticas'.

Terminada la visita a Florián caminamos un poco por las estrechas callejuelas y sus muchos puentes y tomamos el encantador y muy turístico vaporetto, (aunque los locales no aprecian la competencia por sus asientos con los extranjeros). Seguimos explorando después de la cena. Oscureció. Se encendieron las ventanas y las vidrieras y la ciudad tomó un aspecto teatral. Al rato se levantó una niebla espesa, y nos encontramos en un laberinto de pasajes oscuros, y angostas veredas bajo puentes sobre algún canal, por detrás de la Opera La Fenice. Al pasar por la calle del Caffetier, la bruma se hizo más intensa y la ciudad nos pareció desolada, en un mundo extrañamente vacío y tenebroso, a lo Chernóbil después de la explosión. Quisimos regresar al hotel, cuando vimos a lo lejos, adelante nuestro, a una pareja. Casi al unísono nos dijimos: —¿No son los espías del café?— Los seguimos en la bruma por unos cien metros, sin estar del todo seguros de su identidad. Sorpresivamente, desaparecieron por una puerta lateral frente al canaletto, la que resultó ser el muelle y entrada para barcos del Hotel Luna. Cuando miramos con cautela hacia adentro, solo se veía a los empleados de la recepción, y un elegante salón barroco, con tapicerías y muchas pinturas de marcos dorados. ¡Ni señal de nuestros presuntos espías!

De regreso al hotel, Serge nos sorprendió con una pregunta:

—¿No me dejarían salir solo mañana para dar una vuelta por la ciudad? No me voy a perder.

Lo pensamos bastante, la idea nos inquietaba. Siempre lo habíamos sobreprotegido, pero nos pareció apropiado dejarlo hacer su experiencia por esta vez. Armado de un mapa con la localización del hotel no tendría problemas en esta ciudad tan calma y amigable. No del todo tranquilos, al fin le dimos el permiso.

—¡Buenísimo! Aquí está el hotel, aquí los canales y las paradas del barquito— dijo señalando el mapa, —y en caso de dudas, seguro que los venecianos entienden algo de español.

Serge salió por la mañana después del desayuno. Le recomendamos mil veces que volviera para la cena y le dimos un poco de dinero para almorzar y comprar algún recuerdo.

Aún había mucho que explorar. Visitamos galerías, fábricas de cristales, rincones del medioevo. En el Café Segafreddo, el expreso era suave y la gente amable. Pronto sentimos como si hubiésemos nacido en esa callejuela tan angosta, y conociéramos a varios vecinos: La mujer alta, elegante en sus ropajes algo bohemios, paseando un perrito blanco y peludo; el viejito de barba gris leyendo fábulas de Ítalo Calvino; la dueña de casa cargada de provisiones y pescados del mercado detrás del Rialto; y los chicos corriendo con globos multicolores. Desde ese ángulo se veía la parada del vaporetto, y casi al atardecer vimos reaparecer a Serge, radiante y llevando con cuidado un paquetito marrón en su mano derecha.

—¡Hola Serge! ¿Cómo te fue? Parecés muy contento.

—Me fue bárbaro y solo me perdí una vez cerca de la Accademia, pero un mozo de café me indicó cómo encontrar el vaporetto. Me entienden mucho el español y en Venecia hasta dicen calle en vez de vía. ¡Pero miren lo que compré!

Allí mismo abrió el paquetito, y muy orgulloso puso sobre la mesa una colección de diez cisnes de cristal claro de tamaño creciente, en fila india detrás de su madre.

—¿Y que más hiciste?

—Primero crucé el Rialto y fui a ver el mercado de pescados. Nunca había visto tantos mariscos diferentes, de todas formas y colores..., pero lo que más me impresionó fueron los pescadores compitiendo a los gritos en dialecto. Entendí lo suficiente para darme una idea. Como los mariscos me dieron hambre, en una esquina me comí una porción de pizza—. Se puso colorado, algo culpable, porque en esa época era todavía gordito.

—Nuestro rabino y el cantor que me prepara para el Bar Mitzva me habían recomendado visitar el Guetto viejo, un barrio antiguo, y sin carteles ni señales. Pero un viejito vecino muy amable me acompañó hasta la entrada de la 'Gran Escuela Alemana,' la primera sinagoga askenazi de Venecia, fundada por los 1500s. Lástima no haber podido sacarme una foto para mostrarle al cantor. Me gustaron las decoraciones, la bimah, y la inscripción en letras doradas con los Diez Mandamientos. ¡Ah, y la galería de arriba era solo para las mujeres!

—¡Qué linda experiencia estar en un sitio tan histórico! Les va a encantar cuando les cuentes.

—¡Se van a reír de mí! Desde una esquina salía un delicioso perfume a pasta. Me encantó el nombre en la puerta: 'Osteria ai Quaranta Ladroni,' como los de Ali Baba. El menú era muy barato. Como dice papá, 'hay que guiarse por el olfato', y entré a comer. ¡Los ladrones no estaban, pero sí me dieron unos fabulosos linguini con salsa di pomidoro!— Entonces hizo una larga pausa, con una sonrisa picaresca, y se negó a contarnos nada más. —Les guardo lo más interesante para el final.

—¡Dale, no te hagas el misterioso!

—¡Cuando tomé el vaporetto para volver del Guetto, volví a encontrarme con los espías del Café Florián! Por suerte no me reconocieron. Desde el medio del barco los vi pasar y sentarse adelante, del lado opuesto, junto a un hombre que ya estaba allí. ¿Por qué eligieron ese asiento, si el vaporetto viajaba casi vacío? El hombre llevaba el Herald Tribune pero lo extraño fue que al bajar dos paradas más adelante ya no lo tenía. En cambio, su vecino de asiento se apresuró a bajar en la estación de la Accademia y ¡tenía en sus manos el mismo diario! Allí mismo decidí bajarme y seguirlo. Él parecía conocer bien la zona. Se metió por una callecita lateral, que zigzagueaba por partes cubiertas y más oscuras. Yo iba detrás a unos veinte metros. Había poca gente y me dio un poco de miedo. Pero pronto salió a una vereda junto a un canal que terminaba en otro muy grande, el Giudecca según el mapa. Había más gente, y como el tipo no me conocía, me animé a seguirlo de lejos. Total, ¿quién iba a sospechar de un pibe turista?.

—¡Serge, eso es una locura!, ¿cómo se te ocurrió tal cosa? ¿Hasta dónde fueron?

—Antes de llegar al Giudecca entró en un bar de esos donde venden cicchetti, las tapas venecianas. El tipo se paró junto al mostrador, se compró una, y pidió un vaso de vino blanco. Me animé a entrar y mirar alrededor. Los cicchetti tenían el precio escrito. Aunque ya no tenía hambre, solo para disimular pedí uno de polenta con langostinos. Salí a comerlos frente al bar sobre una baranda con otra gente. Del otro lado de ese canal estrecho unos obreros trabajaban en una antigua fábrica de góndolas, y me quedé un rato mirándolos.

—¿Y el tipo?

—Estaba adentro. No, no lo perdí de vista. Al rato entró un gordo, con una barbita de varios días y medio sucio, como el actor de 'Topkapi'. Parecía extranjero, pero no curioseaba a su alrededor como un turista. También comió algo sobre el mostrador, cerca del tipo del vaporetto. Cuando salieron, cada uno por su lado y un minuto aparte, no lo van a creer...el gordo llevaba la copia del Herald Tribune. ¡Me juego que era la misma! Debo ser el único que se dio cuenta de que se la fueron pasando de mano en mano.

Serge nos miró, esperando una reacción.

—Quizá no sean más que dos turistas cualquiera, y nos estamos haciendo una novela—, dijo Diana

—Pero mamá, ¿No te parece rarísimo eso de pasarse el mismo periódico? ¿No serán espías del Stasi? Lástima no conocer a nadie del gobierno o de la policía, aunque se reirían de nosotros.

Al rato se me ocurrió una idea:

—¿Se acuerdan de mi amigo George, el diplomático del State Department? Antes del viaje yo le había pedido algún buen contacto en Venecia en caso de tener problemas, o para consultarlo sobre eventos, o lugares interesantes. Tengo el número del consulado y podría llamarlo, su nombre es Phillips.

Nos citamos el día siguiente en el Florián con el agregado cultural de la embajada. Pedimos un aperitivo y lo esperamos en la Sala Orientale, que mostraba una pintura de Marco Polo, (uno de los héroes de Serge), entre otros venecianos notables. Al rato entró un hombre que solo podía ser americano: de unos 40 años, con un traje gris claro, camisa celeste sin corbata, y una expresión indefinida, con una sonrisa algo plástica y poco apropiada en este café. Alguien fácil de olvidar, que puede pasar desapercibido en cualquier parte. Nos reconoció de inmediato y se sentó a acompañarnos.

—¡Gusto de conocerlos! Hace rato que no tenía noticias de George, con quien hemos trabajado juntos en Europa. ¿Qué les parece Venecia? Yo vengo a Florián a menudo—. Conversamos un poco sobre la historia del lugar, y luego fue al grano, —¿En qué puedo ayudarlos...?

Le explicamos la razón de nuestra llamada, y le dimos la palabra a Serge para que le cuente en detalle sus aventuras. Phillips lo observaba con un poco de curiosidad, pero siempre inexpresivo, con cara de póker. Solo pude detectar un brillo nuevo en sus ojos cuando Serge dijo que el sujeto del bar de cicchetti se parecía a Peter Ustinov.

—¿Tenía una barbita oscura, y una verruga en la nariz? — preguntó, como por casualidad.

—¡Así es! — respondió Serge de inmediato, quien resultó ser aún mejor observador de lo que le conocíamos.

—Usted dice haber tomado una foto de la pareja en este café,— me preguntó, inesperadamente. —¿Hizo una copia?

—No, lo siento. Llevo todas las diapositivas para revelar en Seattle. Nos vamos pronto.

—¡Bien!—, dijo Phillips. —Muchas gracias por el relato. Es imposible saber si esto tiene alguna importancia, lo vamos a estudiar, pero les agradezco que se hayan molestado en contarnos lo que vieron. Les deseo una buena visita a Venecia.

Nunca tuvimos oportunidad de pedirle sugerencias turísticas. Nos quedamos pensando cuál sería su verdadera ocupación en el consulado. Sus comentarios y conducta no revelaron nada relacionado con la cultura.

Los próximos dos días visitamos el Lido y pasamos unas horas en la playa. No podíamos perdernos la famosa fábrica de las hermanas Sent en Murano, conocidas por sus joyas en cristal contemporáneas. Terminamos la visita con un almuerzo tradicional en Ai Frati, una pasta con scampi y el hígado a la veneciana. Allí comen muchos grandes artistas de vidrio de Murano. De a ratos nos volvía a la mente la imagen de la pareja del Florián.

La mañana antes de nuestra partida, encontramos sobre la mesa del desayuno una copia del 'Venice English News'. Un artículo en primera página nos llamó la atención:

Actividad policial nocturna en el Hotel Luna:

Anoche, cerca de las 23 horas, el personal del hotel confirmó que la policía federal se había presentado buscando a una pareja de extranjeros, registrada bajo el nombre de Morgenthaler. Estos no se encontraban en la habitación, pero un momento después, con gran ruido de motores marinos, partió a toda velocidad un barco desde la salida lateral hacia el gran canal, y se perdió pronto de vista. El barco no llevaba encendidas sus luces reglamentarias, y no se pudo determinar si era un barco-taxi o uno privado. Presumen que los huéspedes se habían registrado con un nombre falso, y que gracias a su exitoso escape fluvial la policía no pudo localizarlos. Se ignoran detalles sobre las actividades de estas dos personas y las razones por la presencia policial.

La foto de la misteriosa pareja que yo tomé indiscretamente en aquel viaje a Venecia sigue inmutable en su sitio de preferencia en nuestro comedor, bien iluminada por una fuerte luz LED. Muy cerca de ella, en un nicho designado sobre un estante, una exquisita familia de cisnes en cristal claro parece flotar sobre las aguas de la histórica laguna.

El café Florián continúa en funcionamiento, casi sin interrupciones desde 1720, en la absoluta ignorancia de que un quantum esencial de mi vida cafetera se concretizó en ese recinto con consecuencias imborrables.

372

El médico de Santa Claus

Supe que debía escribir este relato cuando una niña de ocho años me preguntó, con toda la inocencia, si era cierto que yo era el médico de Santa Claus. Durante una cena con amigos, ella escuchaba fascinada el relato de mi experiencia con un paciente. Su pregunta me sobresaltó porque los chicos suelen decir la verdad y eso me hizo confrontar dudas que llevaba guardadas, desde hacía tiempo, sobre los límites entre lo real y lo imaginario.

Conocí a Santa a principios de diciembre del 99, el mismo día en que comenzó a nevar copiosamente. Ya el campo inmenso imitaba a una sábana de dunas blancas, como una gran extensión de la cama de mi vivienda temporaria.

Había aceptado reemplazar a un médico local por un mes, durante sus vacaciones. Era la primera vez que estaba en Idaho y en una pequeña ciudad de provincia. Muy pronto me encontré rodeado por los hijos y los nietos de antiguos inmigrantes vascos, criadores de ovejas y productores de las famosas papas de la región. Algunos todavía jugaban al jai alai, una modalidad de pelota vasca, en un frontón. Entre los pacientes también descubrí a varios survivalistas, los cuales, obsesionados por sobrevivir a una hipotética catástrofe, ya estaban preparados para el fin del mundo. Algunos construían refugios subterráneos con comida para aguantar meses y armamento más potente que el de los talibanes. Un cartel en la sala de espera les recordaba la prohibición de entrar en la clínica con armas de fuego o con cuchillos de más de cuatro pulgadas. No sabría decir si Santa se había establecido en esa región por sentirse cómodo entre ellos o para asegurarles que al terminar el milenio el mundo seguiría adelante, como siempre.

Esa mañana la clínica estaba repleta de gente y la sala de espera parecía una estación de trenes en un feriado nacional. En la lista de pacientes leí que el próximo era un tal "Nicolás Claus". Para ganar tiempo, me asomé a llamarlo:

—¡Señor Claus, pase, por favor!

Esperé unos segundos y, como nadie se levantaba, insistí:

—¡Señor Nicolás Claus! —nuevamente, sin resultado.

Me pregunté si no me entendía por el acento o si quizá el mal tiempo le había impedido llegar, aunque en esa zona la gente estaba acostumbrada a la nieve. La enfermera me explicó que lo recordaba de alguna visita anterior, pero que había que llamarlo de otro modo; y salió para preguntar ella misma, en voz alta y perentoria:

—¿Está Santa en la sala?

Al instante se levantó un hombre grande, tanto en edad como en volumen, con una sonrisa deslumbrante en medio de una barba desmesurada, tan blanca como la nieve que se veía desde la ventana.

Caminó sin apuro hacia mi consultorio. Aunque algo excedido en peso, su cuerpo parecía macizo como el de un luchador profesional, pero su actitud era dulce y calma. Llevaba puestos unos vaqueros y una camisa roja de cuadros, ropa tradicional en esa zona. Lucía también un chaleco sin mangas, de suave lana marrón, de un animal que no supe reconocer, pero que no era oveja.

Cuando se sentó, lo noté algo preocupado y comencé por preguntarle la razón de su visita.

—Mucho gusto, doctor. Mire, no me siento bien. Tengo muy alta la presión, me duele la cabeza y he perdido el apetito. Se me hinchan un poco las piernas y cuando camino me fatigo y siento que me falta el aire. En realidad, hace rato que no me ve un médico y no estoy tomando nada. Estas molestias interfieren con mi actividad y ya falta menos de un mes para las Navidades. Voy muy atrasado con los preparativos, debo leer las cartas de la gente y conseguir las cosas que me piden.

Hablaba con una voz grave y enigmática, como de bajo, con el acento de los granjeros de la zona. Sus síntomas eran fáciles de interpretar, pero sus comentarios sobre "actividades y preparativos" para la Navidad me resultaban misteriosos. No se me ocurría cuál podría ser su ocupación, pero preferí no ahondar por el momento.

—Bueno, señor Klaus, quisiera examinarlo y hacerle unos análisis para ver cómo se encuentra.

Por favor, quítese la camisa, le voy a tomar la presión y voy a auscultarle.

—Doctor, llámeme Santa, como todo el mundo —me contestó con suavidad, sentándose frente a mí con la agilidad de un hombre más joven.

Considerando su aspecto de granjero o de marinero, me sorprendió que hablase con precisión y se moviera con una elegancia indefinible.

Cuando lo vi por primera vez me recordó a los pescadores de Alaska que había visto recientemente en un vídeo. Transmitían fuerza, decisión y gran coraje para navegar por esos mares tormentosos, y no sufrían mareos como yo, en ese bamboleo incesante. Le pregunté si era de Alaska y afirmó que sí y que había sido pescador en su juventud. Solo estaba de paso por Idaho y se había quedado aquí para descansar cuando su salud empeoró.

Le confesé que envidiaba su chaleco, que me gustó muchísimo. Entonces me aclaró que era de lana de reno de su rebaño. Imaginé qué lujo sería pasearme con uno así o entrar en un café del centro cuando regresara a mi casa en enero. Lo sorprendente es que, si bien en Idaho había ciervos, en ningún momento escuché a nadie mencionar renos, más típicos de Laponia. Seguramente lo había traído de Alaska.

Procedí a tomarle la presión. Mientras se quitaba el chaleco y levantaba la manga de la camisa, observé que en la muñeca izquierda llevaba un brazalete enorme de oro macizo, tal vez de 18 K. En el centro se leía la inscripción "Santa", en grandes letras de imprenta. No tuve más remedio que preguntarle por eso. Me explicó que un gran amigo, un minero en Alaska, había descubierto una veta de oro la Navidad anterior y que mandó fabricar este brazalete como regalo.

—Pero, Santa —yo había comenzado a llamarlo por ese nombre, después de comprobar que solo respondía de esa manera—, ¡eso debe costar una fortuna! ¿No tiene miedo de que puedan asaltarlo?

—No se preocupe, doctor, la gente me aprecia y nunca me ha pasado nada. En realidad, le confieso que siento una cierta debilidad por las joyas y, hasta el momento de entregarlas a sus nuevos dueños, me gusta tenerlas cerca para admirarlas. Déjeme mostrarle, a ver qué le parecen.

A pesar de que aun tenía puesto el manguito de la presión, estiró el brazo y tomó su mochila, de la que extrajo una bolsa de seda negra del tamaño de una pelota de fútbol. De allí comenzó a sacar joyas de todo tipo: aros con rubíes, anillos con piedras de aguamarina, sofisticados relojes suizos de oro blanco y collares de exóticas perlas negras. Otro de los collares, de oro pálido y piedras preciosas en varias filas paralelas, semejaba a uno que estaba en la exposición de Tutankamón que había visto en el Museo de Arte.

Todo esto me alarmó sobremanera, no sé si

por la sorpresa ante ese despliegue apabullante de alhajas o por la incongruencia de su gesto en esta pequeña clínica en las praderas de Idaho. Me pregunté si serían joyas robadas, pero no parecía en absoluto un ladrón. Tampoco tenía el aspecto de ser un rico ranchero o un ejecutivo de las grandes compañías electrónicas de los estados vecinos de la costa del Pacífico. En todo caso, le pedí con urgencia que las guardara, con el pretexto de continuar con el examen físico. Comencé a dudar si este hombre necesitaba tratamiento psicológico más que por la alta presión. Además, mi olfato detectó un levísimo efluvio de vodka, o ginebra, aunque quizá estos vapores estaban solo en mi imaginación. Pero las joyas eran reales y las había tocado con mis propias manos. Ni la locura ni el alcohol eran suficiente explicación sobre el origen de los tesoros que me había mostrado con tanto entusiasmo y con tanto candor.

Preferí proseguir el examen. Al rato lo mandé al laboratorio para hacerle unos análisis de urgencia y le pedí que esperara en la sala hasta tener los resultados. No protestó y se marchó tranquilo con su mochila al hombro.

Una hora más tarde, cuando aparecieron los resultados en la computadora, lo invité a entrar para comunicarle su diagnóstico y tratamiento.

—Bueno, Santa, me alegro de que haya pasado a vernos. Usted presenta varios problemas que deberíamos resolver. Su presión ha estado sin controlar durante bastante tiempo y eso ha tenido consecuencias en el corazón y en los riñones. Por eso le duele la cabeza y se le hinchan los pies. Su situación entraña un riesgo considerable y quisiera que nos pusiéramos de acuerdo para comenzar hoy mismo un tratamiento. Esto consiste en un régimen dietético, en reducir el consumo de cerveza y otras bebidas y la ingesta de varios medicamentos. Pero lo importante es que acepte la responsabilidad de ayudarse a sí mismo.

—Voy a hacer todo lo que usted me recomienda, aunque lo de la cervecita es bien difícil. Pero quisiera que me asegurara que voy a sentirme mejor en los próximos días. ¿Se imagina la desilusión de tanta gente si llega la Navidad y no encuentran nada en sus calcetines al despertarse? Tengo una caja enorme llena de cartas con pedidos, incluso varias que me han entregado en la clínica otros pacientes. Así, hinchado y sin energía, no estoy para bajar por las chimeneas, tiene que ayudarme. ¡Ni siquiera me siento con fuerzas para cuidar y alimentar a los renos!

Pensé que todo esto eran alucinaciones y que más adelante tendría que pedir consulta psiquiátrica. Algunos bebedores crónicos pueden llegar a un estado de demencia, como en el síndrome de Wernicke, en que pierden la memoria, pero fabulan sin parar. Por suerte, Santa tenía buena memoria por ahora.

Fuera cual fuera su problema, era necesario

bajarle la presión y ayudarlo a sentirse bien.

—Mire, Santa, quisiera que empezara una dieta a base de verduras y frutas frescas, con poca sal, nada de comidas congeladas ni de lata. Voy a darle un diurético para la hinchazón de piernas, otra medicina para la presión y para proteger su riñón al mismo tiempo. Pero quiero volver a verlo pronto para comprobar su estado y para hacer varios ajustes. Como nunca ha sido tratado, no puedo predecir cómo va a responder a estos cambios. Le voy a dar cita para la semana que viene, pero llame por teléfono si le surgen preguntas o si empeora. Por favor, pase por el laboratorio para que le repitan los análisis, unas dos horas antes de verme.

Al salir, noté que flirteaba con las recepcionistas y que la enfermera le entregaba con disimulo un sobrecito blanco. La llamé con cualquier excusa y, con desparpajo, me animé a preguntarle qué le había entregado, si era la próxima cita u otra cosa. Se sonrojó y me contó que, por si acaso este paciente fuera el verdadero Santa, no perdía nada al hacerle un pedido. Pero no era para ella, sino para su hija adolescente, que nunca había visto el mar y que soñaba con una playa de arena blanca y fina. Si bien la idea de la carta con el pedido me resultó humorística, ese sueño no era descabellado, considerando el clima de Idaho en invierno, apropiado solo para descendientes de vascos montañeses.

Cuando lo vi dirigirse hacia la salida se me ocurrió que este hombre era realmente raro y parecía inducir pensamientos mágicos o supersticiones en cierta gente, como en el caso de la enfermera. Por eso me disculpé como si necesitara pasar al baño y, como quien no quiere la cosa, me fui también en dirección a la salida. Entonces lo vi salir, mientras la puerta automática volvía a cerrarse sola. Cuando llegué a la puerta principal, miré hacia el estacionamiento, en donde ya los autos estaban casi cubiertos por la nieve, pero no pude ver a Santa, ni se observaba movimiento alguno. No identifiqué tampoco huellas de pisadas recientes en la nieve. Esperé afuera casi cinco minutos y solo distinguí a un par de personas yendo hacia los autos. Finalmente el frío me hizo tiritar y tuve que volver a mi consultorio sin comprender cómo había hecho este hombre para marcharse sin dejar rastro.

La semana siguiente transcurrió con rapidez, hubo bastante trabajo y no tuve ocasión de pensar en mi paciente hasta el día en que volví a ver su nombre en la lista. Lo encontré sentado en la sala con una compresa en la frente, sosteniendo su cabeza como si le doliera. Parecía más preocupado que en la primera visita. Lo hice entrar enseguida y me contó lo que había ocurrido.

—Hola, doctor. Recién vengo de la sala de emergencia. Me tuvieron que poner unos puntos en la frente porque esta mañana me caí del trineo y me hice un corte. Le he hecho caso en todas sus indicaciones, pero el tratamiento me ha bajado la presión demasiado. En general me siento mejor, no me fatigo y camino bien. Pero hoy estaba cargando el trineo y al levantar la cabeza me mareé, me giró todo alrededor y perdí el equilibrio. Cuando me levanté, me sangraba la frente y tuve que ir deprisa a la emergencia. Por suerte, no ha sido nada. Pero, mire, faltan dos semanas para la Navidad y sigo sin poder organizarme. ¡Me temo que esta será la primera vez que no esté listo para satisfacer a tanta gente que me espera con ilusión! ¿Cree que pronto estaré en forma?

—Seguro que sí. Por suerte su presión ha bajado con rapidez, pero lamento que se haya mareado y cortado la frente. Eso no debería haber ocurrido. Por otro lado, observo que ha perdido peso y que no tiene más las piernas hinchadas. Sus análisis también han mejorado y el riñón ha vuelto a funcionar bien. Creo que estará listo para hacer el trabajo que sea para la Navidad.

—Muchas gracias, doctor Moguilevski. Usted me inspira confianza. Pero, permítame una pregunta. Por su nombre, creo que usted debe ser judío y quizá no conozca nuestras tradiciones. ¿Ustedes celebran algo en Navidad o creen en los milagros?

—No se preocupe, que le entiendo y lo respeto. En cuanto a los milagros, creemos en algunos, pero son diferentes a los suyos. ¿Conoce el significado de Jánuca la Fiesta de las Luminarias? Nosotros celebramos la rebelión de los Macabeos, cuando un pequeño grupo de guerrilleros derrotó a las tropas romanas y pudo restablecer el segundo templo en Jerusalén. Y el segundo milagro fue que al entrar en el templo encontraron una lámpara con solo un poco de aceite y que, sin embargo, siguió encendida durante ocho días. Por eso en la actualidad lo recordamos encendiendo una vela nueva cada día. También respetamos los milagros que otros aceptan. En cuanto a su tratamiento, no necesito compartir sus creencias; igual haré todo lo posible para que mejore de modo que pueda cumplir con sus obligaciones justo para la Navidad. Desde hoy reduzca la dosis de sus medicinas a la mitad y vuelva dentro de una semana; si realmente está bien controlado, le daré el alta con mucho gusto.

Las noches siguientes tuve algunas pesadillas en las que Santa hacía correr con furia descontrolada, como borracho, su trineo y pegaba a los renos con un látigo para que saltasen cada vez más alto entre tejado y tejado de las casas nevadas. En un momento dado perdía totalmente el control y caía desde una gran altura, con lentitud, como flotando entre las nubes, para al fin llegar a tierra y cortarse la frente al chocar con su trineo. Me levantaba ansioso y molesto. Otra noche, en cambio, soñé que veía a muchos chicos gozando y saltando de alegría con sus juguetes nuevos, mientras las velas de Jánuca titilaban y se reflejaban en las ventanas de las casas vecinas. En los sueños se me mezclaban unas festividades con otras.

Tal y como como le había pedido, Santa volvió el 23 de diciembre. Parecía más joven y menos preocupado, como si hubiese recuperado la confianza. Caminaba a paso rápido y sin dificultad para respirar y la herida había curado bien, sin dejar cicatriz en su frente, que llevaba mucho más alta que en la primera visita. Esta vez no detecté alcohol en su aliento. Lo examiné y descubrí con satisfacción que su presión se había normalizado y que su corazón latía ahora con la fuerza de un corredor joven. Como le había prometido, le di el alta, convencido de que su mejoría demostraba una nueva actitud y le auguraba un futuro más saludable. Al escucharme, Santa lanzó un fuerte suspiro de alivio y recuperó una gran sonrisa de oreja a oreja. Entonces, pronunció unas palabras inesperadas:

—Doctor, le agradezco mucho lo que hizo por mí, aun sin creer demasiado lo que yo le contaba. Claro, usted es muy escéptico y racionalista, pero reconozco que es un experto en su trabajo y al ayudarme también va a hacer feliz a mucha otra gente. Por eso quisiera dejarle un regalo ahora, sin tener que entrar por su chimenea. ¡Me parece que esto le va a gustar!

Y así, sin más, se sacó su impresionante

chaleco de lana de reno y me lo ofreció con las dos manos juntas, en un gesto vagamente oriental, parecido al que haría un coreano al entregar una misiva. El gesto me emocionó, aunque no sabía si era correcto aceptar regalos de un paciente en esta sociedad tan preocupada por la apariencia de corrección. Al fin lo acepté, con algunas reservas, pero convencido de que, si este hombre ahora podía celebrar la Navidad cumpliendo con sus propósitos, reales o imaginarios, entonces yo merecía su agradecimiento.

—¡Le deseo unas felices fiestas! Y recuerde que nos conocimos. ¡Que la vida le depare muchas agradables sorpresas! —me dijo con amabilidad, se dio la vuelta y salió del consultorio con paso firme.

El día 25 amaneció claro y frío. Agradecí no tener que ir temprano a la clínica y que solo me quedaran unos pocos días de trabajo para volver a estar con mi familia en Portland y a mi rutina diaria. Me afeité sin apuro y comencé a calentar el desayuno con bastante apetito. Esa noche no había tenido pesadillas y me sentía de buen humor. Fui al dormitorio a vestirme y me puse mi flamante chaleco, lo que no hubiese adivinado jamás antes de venir a reemplazar a un médico en Idaho. Me miré con admiración frente al espejo y me quedaba perfecto. Una vez pasado por la tintorería quedaría como nuevo. Supe que daría mucho que hablar entre mis amigos de Portland. Pero al mismo tiempo me carcomía una gran curiosidad por saber quién era exactamente este paciente tan especial. ¿Sería realmente un psicótico o solo un ranchero rico, algo excéntrico pero bondadoso, repartiendo sus bienes entre gente necesitada? Nunca podría resolver mis dudas, ni pensé volver a verlo.

Al día siguiente fui a la clínica y, por suerte, había muchos menos pacientes. Llevaba puesto con orgullo mi impresionante chaleco de piel y la enfermera salió a darme un abrazo con una gran sonrisa.

—Doctor, ¡qué gusto verlo vestido como si fuera de este pueblo! El chaleco le queda divino. Pero déjeme que le cuente: mi hija recibió un regalo inesperado por Navidad. Encontró un certificado promocional para un vuelo con estadía gratis para dos personas en un modernísimo hotel en Cancún; la voy a acompañar muy pronto. ¡Por fin va a poder conocer el mar!

Pocos días después regresé a Portland luciendo mi chaleco nuevo.

Han pasado varios años desde aquel curioso reemplazo en Idaho. El milenio finalizó sin novedades o cataclismos (seguramente con gran desilusión para los survivalistas que conocí en ese viaje). Ahora agradezco a la niña que me hizo esa pregunta inocente y que me trajo a la memoria a este misterioso paciente. El chaleco sigue siendo mi atuendo favorito y es muy abrigado; y no me lo quito ni cuando arrecia el calor.

Acknowledgments

This book was possible thanks to the enthusiasm and long-term involvement of my friends, Rita and Elwin Wirkala. They stimulated me to write these stories in two languages, especially in my native Spanish, after more than half of my life in the United States. They discussed the original plots over a glass of wine, read and criticized every story, and finally offered their expertise in the formatting and layout of the book. Rita's help in the writing and completion of this work has been invaluable.

My wife of many years, Diana, always supported my work and contributed with her common sense and pointed observations. I'm also grateful to our friend Katherine Kita, for her insightful comments and for her literary good taste. The English version of the narratives was greatly improved by the expert advice of my editor, Stephanie Lawyer, who made sure the syntax, grammar, and the internal logic of the plot were respected. And Lupe Rodriguez Santizo, from her home in Madrid, kept me on my toes with her exacting editorial skills, respecting some of my Argentine expressions which often conflicted with the Castilian.

I'm greatly indebted to my patients, who taught me about fortitude and resilience, and who inspired me to develop these fictional characters. My Pilates teacher kept me sane and healthier during the Pandemia and led me to write about the circus and Russian oligarchs; while my friend Steve W., now in Porto, provided personal recollections for the maharajah story. Yuriko Courtney, who might have been a samurai on a previous incarnation, heavily influenced the character's depiction on the first story. Above all, I'm grateful to my parents who instilled in me the pleasures of French cuisine and aromatic coffee, the importance of democratic values and of heartfelt family ties.

Agradecimientos

Este libro ha sido posible gracias al entusiasmo y la participación de Rita y Elwin Wirkala. Mis amigos me estimularon a escribir estos cuentos también en español, mi lengua materna, luego de haber pasado la mitad de la vida en los Estados Unidos. Con un vasito de vino en mano, pudimos discutir la trama de muchas historias y me ofrecieron su crítica acertada y su experiencia hasta el momento de diseñar y dar forma al libro. La ayuda de Rita en completar este trabajo ha sido inestimable.

Diana, mi mujer, apoyó mis esfuerzos contribuyendo con su sentido común y sus agudas observaciones. También estoy agradecido a nuestra amiga Katherine Kita por sus acertados comentarios y su buen gusto literario. La versión en inglés de los relatos fue mejorada enormemente por los expertos consejos de mi editora, Stephanie Lawyer, quien aseguró que la sintaxis, la gramática y la lógica interna de los argumentos fueran respetados. Lupe Rodríguez Santizo, desde su casa en Madrid, me mantuvo alerta con su habilidad editorial y exactitud, respetando algunas de mis expresiones argentinas que conflictuaban con su castellano.

Estoy especialmente en deuda con mis pacientes, por darme tantos ejemplos de resistencia y de coraje, y por inspirar la ficción y el desarrollo de algunos personajes. Mi profesora de pilates ayudó a mantenerme cuerdo y en buena salud durante la pandemia y me impulsó a escribir sobre el circo y los oligarcas rusos; luego mi amigo Steve W., ahora radicado en Oporto, me regaló sus memorias personales para la historia del marajá de Kapurthala. Yuriko Courtney, que pudo haber sido un samurái en encarnaciones anteriores, tuvo gran influencia en la descripción del protagonista de Matsumoto-san.

Y sobre todo, debo agradecer a mis padres por inculcarme el gusto por la cocina francesa y el café aromático, y por enseñarme la importancia de los valores democráticos y los fuertes lazos familiares.